Borderline

Liza Marklund

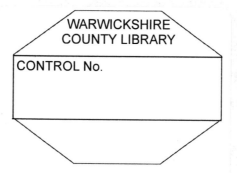

W F HOWES LTD

This large print edition published in 2016 by
W F Howes Ltd
Unit 5, St George's House, Rearsby Business Park,
Gaddesby Lane, Rearsby, Leicester LE7 4YH

1 3 5 7 9 10 8 6 4 2

First published in the United Kingdom in 2014
by Transworld Publishers Inc.

A CIP catalogue record for this book is available
from the British Library

ISBN 978 1 51001 808 2

Typeset by Palimpsest Book Production Limited,
Falkirk, Stirlingshire

Printed and bound in Great Britain
by TJ International Ltd, Padstow, Cornwall

DAY 0

TUESDAY, 22 NOVEMBER

I wasn't worried. The roadblock looked the same as the others we'd been through. Rusting oil-drums on either side of the track (you couldn't really call it a road), a tree-trunk, which had been stripped of most of its branches, and a few men with grimy automatic guns.

There was no real cause for concern. But still I felt Catherine push her leg closer to mine. The gesture transferred itself through muscles and nerves and ended up in my cock. It wasn't a conscious reaction and I did nothing about it, just glanced at her and gave her an encouraging smile.

She was interested, just waiting for me to make my move.

Ali, the driver, wound down his window and leaned out, holding our security clearance in his hand. He was sitting right in front of me; the car was right-hand drive, built for use in the Common-wealth. A hot wind full of dusty earth swirled into the car, dry and abrasive. I looked out over the countryside: low thorn bushes, jagged acacia trees, scorched earth and a sky without end. There was a covered truck up ahead on the right, a pile of empty bottles and old boxes, a body. The other Land Cruiser pulled up alongside us on the left, and the German clerk waved at us through the window. We both pretended not to see her.

Why send a clerk on a trip like this? The rest of us couldn't help wondering.

I looked at the time – 13:23. We were slightly late. The Romanian delegate had taken loads of pictures, and Catherine had already sent out some sort of briefing for the conference. I thought I knew why. She didn't want to have to sit there writing it this evening. She wanted to skip the official dinner and be alone with me. She hadn't asked me yet, but I could feel it.

She was leaning against me now, but I decided to make her work a bit harder.

'Thomas,' she said, in her cut-glass English accent, 'what's going on?'

Our driver had opened the door and stepped out on to the red soil. The men with automatic weapons were circling the car. One opened the front passenger door and said something to the interpreter in a loud, commanding voice, and the skinny young man raised his hands above his head and got out too, I heard one of our guards in the seat behind us take the safety-catch off his weapon. A sudden flash of metal met my eyes. I was starting to find the situation uncomfortable.

'Don't worry,' I said, trying to sound calm. 'Ali will sort it out.'

Now the rear passenger door on the left-hand

side of the car was opened. The French delegate, Magurie, who was sitting nearest, sighed and got out. The dry heat overcame the air-conditioning, and red dust swept over the leather seats, like a coating of lace.

'What's going on?' the Frenchman asked, in his nasal voice. He sounded genuinely indignant.

A tall man with a very long nose and high cheek-bones stopped outside the door on my side of the car and stared at me. His face came very close to mine. One of his eyes was criss-crossed with red, as if he'd just been hit. He raised his gun and tapped on the glass with the barrel. The air behind him was white and parched, vibrating in the heat.

Fear grabbed me in a stranglehold.

'What are we going to do?' Catherine whispered. 'What do these men want?'

An image of Annika flashed through my mind, her big eyes and hair like rain.

'They're just showing how powerful they are,' I said. 'Don't worry. Just do as they say and everything will be fine.'

The tall man opened the door on my side of the car.

DAY 1

WEDNESDAY, 23 NOVEMBER

CHAPTER 1

The woman was lying on the hillside, covered with snow, in the forest some twenty metres behind the nursery school. One brown boot was sticking up, like a windswept branch, or perhaps the roots of a fallen tree. A ski-track on the path seemed to hesitate at that point, marks in the snow showing where the poles had lost their rhythm. But apart from that the snow was undisturbed.

If not for the boot, the body could have been a rock, an anthill, or a sack full of last year's leaves. It bulged like a white seal among the low scrub, shimmering and soft. The snow crystals on the boot glittered intermittently in the fading light.

'You shouldn't be here.'

Annika Bengtzon pretended she hadn't heard the policeman as he came up behind her. She had trudged towards the body from a path behind Selmedalsvägen, via an abandoned football pitch, then up the hill and into the low-growing forest. Her boots were full of slowly melting snow, and her feet were so cold she was starting to lose the feeling in them.

9

'I can't see any cordon,' she said, without taking her eyes from the body.

'This is a crime scene,' the policeman informed her, sounding as if he were trying to make his voice deeper than normal. 'I'm going to have to ask you to leave, at once.'

Annika took two more pictures with the camera on her mobile, then looked up at him. He was so young he hardly needed to shave. 'Impressive,' she said. 'The body's still covered, but you already have a preliminary cause of death. What did she die of?'

The policeman's eyes narrowed. 'How do you know it's a she?'

Annika looked at the body again. 'Trannies might wear high heels, but usually not in size . . . What do you think? Thirty-six? Thirty-seven?'

She dropped her mobile into her bag, where it drowned in a sea of pens, children's gloves, passcards, USB memory sticks and notebooks. The policeman's colleague came panting up the hill with a roll of tape in his hand.

'Has she been reported missing?' Annika asked.

'Fucking liberty,' the policeman said.

'What?' Annika said.

'That the Regional Communication Centre call the evening papers before alerting a patrol car. Get lost.'

Annika hoisted her bag on to her shoulder, turned away from the body and walked back towards the football pitch.

In recent months RACEL, Radio Communications for Effective Leadership, had been introduced throughout Sweden: a digital radio system for the police, ambulances and fire brigade that couldn't be tapped into. At a stroke all the civilians who used to pass on tips about police were out of a job. The staff at the regional communication centres had enthusiastically taken on the task, as well as the extra income that came with letting the media know about outbreaks of violence and misery.

She reached the edge of the forest and stopped to gaze out across the suburb.

The grey-brown nine-storey blocks below her were wrapped in a veil of frost and fog. The black branches of the forest were reflected in blank windows. The flats must have been built at the start of the massive house-building boom that had begun in the mid-1960s: the façades seemed to hint at some attempt at quality, as if there had still been an ambition to make the place worthy of its inhabitants.

Her toes were numb now. It was late afternoon. She could feel the wind blowing between the blocks.

Axelsberg. A residential district with no obvious limits, a name on a windy underground platform.

'A dead body behind a pre-school in Axelsberg. It can't have been there long.'

She'd been on her way back from Ikea at Kungens Kurva when the newspaper's switchboard

11

called. She had cruised through the slush, crossing the four lanes of the motorway and pulling off at the Mälarhöjden junction. Sure enough, she had got to the scene thirty seconds before the first patrol car.

She sent two of the pictures from her mobile to the desk, an overview of the crime scene and a close-up of the boot.

A dead body didn't necessarily mean that a crime had been committed. All types of suspicious death were investigated by the police, but most turned out to have some natural explanation, or to have been accidents or suicides.

Something told Annika that this wasn't one of those cases. The woman hadn't been out jogging and then had a heart attack, not in those shoes. Anyway, she wouldn't have been jogging through the undergrowth alongside the footpath. And she couldn't have just tripped and fallen, not that far, and not right into the middle of a clump of bushes.

She had been covered with snow, but the caller had been correct: she couldn't have been lying there for very long.

It had started snowing late the previous evening, sharp ice crystals that lashed at windows and stung like needles on the face of anyone who had to go out and buy milk at half past ten at night, as Annika had had to. During the morning the snow had started to fall more heavily and the Meteorological Office had issued a class-two warning: 'Dangerous conditions for the public, damage to property and severe disruption of public services.'

An hour ago it had stopped.

The woman couldn't have been lying there all night: if she had, her foot would also have been buried in the snow. She had ended up there some time this morning, Annika thought. What's a woman doing, walking along a path behind a nursery school in high-heeled boots through a snowstorm at eight o'clock in the morning?

Annika headed right, down towards the street.

There were two nursery schools next to each other on Selmedalsvägen, one run by the council, the other private. Three patrol cars, the lights on their roofs flashing, were parked up, spreading a cloud of exhaust fumes in front of the entrances to the schools, which gradually dissipated among the climbing-frames and slides. As long as the lights were flashing, the engines had to run or the batteries would die. On more than one occasion a potential car-chase had never happened because the police vehicle wouldn't start.

A few parents, two mums and a dad, were arriving at the private nursery school, wide-eyed with anxiety. Had something happened? Surely not at their school. And not to their children because someone would have called, wouldn't they?

Annika stopped behind one of the patrol cars and watched them. The father took charge and

13

went up to the rookie cop who'd been left in the cold to fend off the press and any other curious onlookers.

A body had been found, presumably deceased, in the forest . . . No, not in the nursery-school garden, up on the hillside . . . No, it was unlikely that any of the children had seen it . . . No, the cause of death wasn't known at present, and there was nothing to suggest that the death had any connection to the nursery school . . .

The parents breathed a sigh of relief and hurried in to their offspring, clearly relieved that, once again, death was someone else's concern.

She went over to the rookie cop. 'Bengtzon,' she said. '*Evening Post.* Which one of the nursery schools were her children at?'

The rookie glanced over at the council-run school. 'Child,' he said. 'She only had one, as far I know. A boy.'

Annika followed his gaze. A red cardboard star was hanging in the window next to the door. White snowflakes had been cut out and stuck to the glass. 'And it was her workplace that sounded the alarm, wasn't it? When she didn't turn up this morning?'

He shook his head. 'A neighbour,' he said, taking a step back. 'But you'll have to talk to the regional communication centre about that, or a senior officer. I don't really know anything.'

She felt a rumble of anxiety in her midriff, and thought it funny that she never got used to hearing news like this. A young mother with small feet and

14

high heels drops her child off at nursery school and dies on a path as she's heading home through a snowstorm.

Annika was so cold now that she was shaking. The cardboard star was moving gently in the window. A man went past down Selmedalsvägen on a bike.

She ransacked her bag for her mobile, then took a picture of the nursery school, nodded to the rookie and went back to the newspaper's car.

The temperature had dropped significantly since it had stopped snowing. Her breath turned to ice on the windscreen and she had to sit there with the defroster on full blast for several minutes before she could drive off. She undid her boots and wiggled the toes of her left foot frantically in an attempt to get some feeling back into them.

Ellen and Kalle made their own way home from their afterschool club, these days. It was on the other side of Hantverkargatan, and was one of the reasons why Annika had never tried to find anywhere else to live, even though the three-room flat she rented was far too cramped.

The traffic eased slightly so she took her foot off the clutch and the car moved a few metres forward. Not even the Essinge motorway had seen a snowplough. She wasn't sure if the drifts on the road were the result of climate change or the consequence of a policy decision by the city's new right-wing council.

She sighed and pulled out her private mobile, pressed to redial the last number and listened to the crackle as the signal made its way through storms and satellites. There was a click on the line, no ringtone. 'Hello, you've reached Thomas Samuelsson at the Department of Justice . . .'

Annoyed and slightly embarrassed, she clicked to end the call. Her husband hadn't been answering his mobile since the evening before last. Every time she tried to get hold of him she heard that pompous message, which he insisted on keeping in English, even though they had been back from Washington for almost four months now. And the way he emphasized 'Department of Justice', Christ . . .

Her other mobile, the newspaper's, rang somewhere deep in her bag. She dug it out without hurrying since the traffic wasn't moving.

'What the fuck are these pictures you've sent through?' Patrik Nilsson, head of news on the printed edition, had evidently received the photos she'd taken with her mobile.

'Dead mother. She'd just dropped her son off at nursery school and died on the way home, unknown how. I'd put a tenner on her being in the middle of a divorce and the kid's father beating her to death.'

'Looks like the root of a fallen tree. How did you get on with Ingvar?'

Ingvar?

'*I*ngvar *K*amprad, from *E*lmtaryd *A*gunnaryd?'

16

She had to search her memory to remember the job she'd initially been sent out to cover. 'No good,' she said.

'Sure?'

Patrik had got it into his head that the roof of the Ikea branch at Kungens Kurva, the biggest in the world, was about to collapse because of the amount of snow on it. Which would undeniably have been a great story if it had been true. The staff at the information desk had looked totally blank when Annika had asked if they were having problems with the roof. She'd told them they'd had a tip-off from a member of the public, and that it clearly wasn't true. In fact the 'tip-off' had arisen during the eleven o'clock editorial meeting that morning, presumably somewhere inside Patrik Nilsson's head. In other words, she'd been sent out to see if reality could somehow be adapted to fit the *Evening Post*'s requirements, which, in this particular instance, had turned out to be a fairly difficult task. The staff on the information desk had phoned someone in Maintenance at a head office somewhere, and he had guaranteed that the roof could cope with at least twenty-two metres of snow.

'No broken roof,' she said sardonically.

'Yeah, but, what the hell, did you see it for yourself?'

'Yep,' she lied.

'Not even any cracks?'

'Nope.'

The traffic around her started to move. She put the car into first gear, slid on the snowy slush and was able to get up to almost twenty kilometres an hour. 'What are we doing with the dead mother?' she asked.

'The tree root?'

'The police seem pretty certain who she is – a neighbour called to report her missing during the day – but they probably won't be releasing her name this evening.'

'And she was found behind a nursery school?' Patrik asked, with new interest in his voice. 'By one of the kids?'

'No,' Annika said, moving up to second gear. 'It was someone out skiing.'

'You're sure? Maybe one of the kids ran into her on a sledge. Maybe an arm got caught in the runners.'

'The traffic's moving now,' Annika said. 'I'll be with you in a quarter of an hour.'

She left the car in the newspaper's garage, then headed down the steps to the underground tunnels. There used to be four ways up to the office, but bomb threats and box-tickers had made sure that all but one were now blocked. The only way to avoid the caretakers was to go from the garage into the basement, then use the lift situated beyond the reception desk. She'd also have several run-ins with a former employee . . . admittedly, Tore Brandt had been fired after he was found to be selling black-market booze to the night editors, but the discomfort of having to walk past that long desk was still in her blood and she almost always used the basement entrance.

She had to wait several minutes for the lift. On the way up her stomach clenched, as it always did when she was on her way to the newsroom, a sort of expectant tension at what she might find when she got there.

She took a deep breath, then stepped out on to the stained carpet.

The open-plan office had been redesigned a couple more times during the three years she had spent as the paper's Washington correspondent, to suit the new age's demands for collaboration and flexibility. In the centre of the room the newsdesk floated like a luminous spaceship. It had reproduced: there was no longer just one but three. Like two half-moons, Print and Online sat with their backs to each other, staring at their screens. Berit Hamrin, Annika's favourite colleague, called them the 'Cheesy Wotsits'. The webcast unit was situated alongside, where the reception desk used to be. A dozen huge television screens above their heads showed flickering feeds from a mixture of online sites, text-TV and docusoaps. Marketing and Advertising were now part of Editorial, physically as well as in organizational terms. The screens around the dayshift reporters' desk had been removed altogether.

In fact, everything was much the same, just

closer together. The hundreds of fluorescent lights spread their indirect glow in the same flickering blue tone. Desks were covered with drifts of paper, heads lowered in concentration.

Her years in Washington felt like a story someone had told her or the remnants of a dream. Life was back to square one. This was precisely where she had started as a summer temp thirteen years ago, in charge of the tip-off phone-line, running errands, a dogsbody in the service of the news.

She was seized by weariness. She was still hearing about the same murders of women as she had that first summer, just despatched to cover them by different heads of news. She was back, even living in the same block, albeit in a different flat.

'Have you eaten?' she asked Berit, who was typing furiously on her laptop.

'I got a sandwich,' Berit replied, without looking away from the screen or slowing down.

Annika got out her own computer. Even her mechanical gestures were the same: plug in the socket, lift the screen, switch it on, log into the network. Berit's hair was greyer now, and she'd got different glasses, but otherwise the world around Annika was the same as it had been the year she turned twenty-four. Then it had been the height of summer, and a young woman had been found dead behind a headstone in a cemetery. Now it was freezing winter and bodies were found in the forest behind a nursery school, in car parks or residential streets or . . . She frowned. 'Berit,' she said, 'don't you think rather a lot of women have been murdered in Stockholm this autumn? Outdoors, I mean.'

'No more than usual,' Berit said.

Annika logged into mediearkivet.se where much of the Swedish media stored their published articles and columns. She searched for 'woman murdered stockholm' since the beginning of August that year and got a number of hits. The texts weren't full articles, just notes, most of them from the prestigious morning paper.

Towards the end of August a fifty-four-year-old woman had been found dead in a car park in Fisksätra outside Stockholm. She had been stabbed in the back. Her husband had once served a prison sentence for beating and threatening her. He had evidently been held for her murder, but released through lack of evidence. Because he had been picked up at once, the story had never made it beyond the 'news in brief' column of the paper's Stockholm section. It was labelled a domestic tragedy and written off.

The next report came from the same section, published about a week later. A nineteen-year-old immigrant woman had been found murdered at a popular beach by a lake north of the city, Ullnäsjön. She had died from multiple stab wounds. Her fiancé, who also happened to be her cousin, was in custody charged with her murder. He denied any involvement.

21

And in the middle of October a thirty-seven-year-old mother of three had been found stabbed to death on a street in Hässelby. The woman's ex-husband had been questioned on suspicion of murder, but it wasn't clear from the report whether he had been taken into custody and charged or released.

There had been a number of murders in the home in other parts of the country, but the reports were even shorter.

'Hey, Annika,' Patrik said, looming above her. 'Can you go and check out a fire in Sollentuna? Probably the start of the Christmas fire season, old dears getting a bit carried away with their Advent candles. Do an overview of how crap Swedes are at using fire-extinguishers and changing the batteries in their smoke alarms – could be a good consumer piece, "How to Stop Your Candles Killing You" . . .'

'I've already got the dead mum outside the nursery school,' Annika said.

Patrik blinked uncomprehendingly. 'But that's nothing,' he said.

'The fourth murder since I got back,' she said, turning the laptop towards him. 'All women, all from Stockholm, all stabbed. What if there's a serial killer on the loose?'

The head of news looked suddenly uncertain. 'Do you think so? How did this one die? Where was it again? Bredäng?'

'Axelsberg. You saw the picture, what do you think?'

Patrik stared across the newsroom, clearly digging out the picture from somewhere in his brain. Then he snorted. 'Serial killer? Wishful thinking!' He turned on his heel and went off to talk to another reporter about his killer candles.

'So you got that one,' Berit said. 'Mum with a young kid. Divorce? Reports of threatening behaviour that no one took seriously?'

'Probably,' Annika said. 'The police haven't released her name yet.'

Without her name, it was impossible to track down her address, and thereby her neighbour, which meant no background and no story, if she really had been murdered.

'Something good?' Annika asked, nodding towards what Berit was writing as she fished an orange out of her bag.

'Do you remember Alain Thery? There was quite a bit written about him last autumn.'

Last autumn Annika had been immersed in the Tea Party movement and the American congressional elections. She shook her head.

'French businessman, blown up on his yacht off Puerto Banús?' Berit said, peering at her over her glasses.

Annika thought hard. Puerto Banús. White boats and blue sea . . . That was where she and Thomas had got back together, in the Hotel Pyr, a room overlooking the motorway. She had been covering the story of the Söderström family, killed in a gas-attack at their home, and Thomas had been living

23

with Sophia Grenborg at the time, but was in Málaga for a conference, at which he'd been unfaithful to her with his wife.

'A film's been posted on YouTube,' Berit said, 'claiming that Alain Thery was Europe's biggest slave trafficker. His whole business empire was a front for smuggling young people from Africa to Europe and exploiting them, in some cases until they died.'

'Sounds like slander of the deceased,' Annika said, throwing her orange peel into the paper recycling bin and eating a segment. It tasted bitter.

'According to the film, there are more slaves in the world today than ever before, and they've never been cheaper.'

'That's the sort of thing Thomas is busy with,' Annika said, and ate another segment.

'Frontex,' Berit said.

Annika threw the rest of the orange into the bin. 'Exactly. Frontex.'

Thomas and his fancy job.

'I think it's appalling,' Berit said. 'The whole Frontex project is an incredibly cynical experiment, a new Iron Curtain.'

Annika logged into Facebook and scrolled through her colleagues' status updates.

'The point,' Berit went on, 'is to exclude the world's poor from the riches of Europe. And with a central organization in charge, individual governments can shrug off a whole load of criticism. When they chuck people out, they can just refer to Frontex and keep their own hands clean, like Pontius Pilate.'

Annika smiled at her. 'And when you were young you were in the FNL and protested against the Vietnam War.' Eva-Britt Qvist was looking forward to going to the theatre that evening; Patrik had eaten a thin-bread wrap forty-three minutes ago, and Picture-Pelle had posted a link to an *Evening Post* documentary that had been made in the summer of 1975.

'Frontex's latest idea is to get developing countries to close their borders themselves. All very practical. And in the developed world we, with our long-established freedoms, don't have to deal with the issue. Gaddafi in Libya was given half a billion kronor by our very own EU commissioner to keep refugees from Somalia, Eritrea and Sudan in enormous concentration camps.'

'True,' Annika said. 'That's why Thomas is in Nairobi. They're trying to get the Kenyans to close the border with Somalia.' She got her mobile out and dialled his number again.

'Didn't you get a new phone?' Berit wondered.

'Yep,' Annika said.

'Hello, you've reached Thomas Samuelsson at the . . .'

She clicked to end the call, trying to work out what she felt. The main question was who he was sleeping with that night. She no longer felt any anger at the thought, just resignation.

That summer, when the family had returned to

Sweden, Thomas had got a job as fact-finding secretary at the Agency for Guidance in Migration Issues. It wasn't a particularly glamorous appointment and he had been pretty grumpy about it. He'd been expecting something better after his years in Washington. Maybe he'd consoled himself with the thought of all the conferences he'd be able to go to.

Annika thrust the thought aside and called the public prosecutors' office that had responsibility for crimes committed in the area covered by Nacka Council – they answered calls round the clock.

But the operator was unable to help her find out which prosecutor was in charge of the investigation into a murder that had taken place in a car park in Fisksätra in August. 'I can only go by what I've got on the screen,' the woman said apologetically. 'I'd have to transfer you to the office, but they close at three p.m.'

Oh, well, it had been worth a try.

She called the prosecutors' offices in the Northern and Western Districts as well, but they couldn't tell her who was in charge of the investigations into the murders at the beach in Arninge or the residential street in Hässelby. (But, in marked contrast, everyone always knew who was responsible for the sexy investigations, like security vans held up by a helicopter, or sports stars taking drugs.)

'And now Frontex have started chartering planes,' Berit said. 'They gather up immigrants with no official papers from all over Europe and dump them in Lagos or Ulan Bator. Sweden's got rid of people like that several times.'

'I think I'm going to pack it in for the day,' Annika said.

She closed down her laptop, folding it away with practised movements and putting it into her bag, then pulled her jacket on and headed towards the door.

'Hey, Bengtzon!' came a cry from the caretakers' desk, as she was on her way out through the revolving doors.

Shit, she thought. The car keys.

She followed the door round and emerged back in the entrance hall with a strained smile. 'I'm really sorry,' she said, putting the keys to TKG 297 on the reception desk.

But the caretaker, who was new, just took the keys without shouting at her or asking if she'd filled the car up again or made a note in the logbook (she hadn't done either).

'Schyman's looking for you,' the new caretaker said. 'He's in the Frog conference room. He wants you to go and see him at once.'

Annika stopped mid-stride. 'What for?'

He shrugged his shoulders. 'Even worse working hours?' he suggested.

Maybe there was hope for the caretakers after all.

She set off for the conference room. Why on earth was it called 'Frog'?

27

The editor-in-chief opened the door for her. 'Hello, Annika, come in and sit down.'

'Are you relocating me?' she asked.

Three serious-looking men in dark overcoats stood up as she walked through the door. They had spread out around the small birch-wood table. The reflection of a halogen spotlight off the whiteboard on the far wall dazzled her. 'What's going on?' she asked, raising a hand to shield her eyes.

'We've met before,' the man closest to her said, holding out his right hand.

It was Jimmy Halenius, Thomas's boss, under-secretary of state at the Department of Justice. She shook it, unable to think of anything to say.

'Hans-Erik Svensson and Hans Wilkinsson,' he said, gesturing towards the other two men. They didn't move.

She felt her back stiffen with wariness.

'Annika,' Anders Schyman said, 'sit down.'

Fear appeared out of nowhere and dug its claws into her with a force that left her breathless. 'What?' she managed to say, and remained standing. 'Is it something to do with Thomas? What's happened to him?'

Jimmy Halenius took a step closer to her. 'As far as we know, Thomas isn't in any danger,' he said, looking her in the eye.

His eyes were quite blue. She remembered being struck by the intensity of the colour before. I wonder if he wears contact lenses, she thought.

'You know that Thomas is attending the Frontex conference in Nairobi about increased co-operation concerning European borders?' the under-secretary of state said.

Our new Iron Curtain, Annika thought. Land of the free, and all that.

'Thomas attended the first four days of the conference at the Kenyatta International Conference Centre. Yesterday morning he left the conference to act as Swedish delegate on a reconnaissance trip to Liboi, close to the Somali border.'

For some reason an image of the snow-covered body behind the nursery school in Axelsberg came into her mind. 'Is he dead?'

The dark-clad men behind Halenius exchanged a glance.

'There's nothing to suggest that he is,' Jimmy Halenius went on, pulling out a chair and waving her into it. She sank down and noted the look that passed between the two men called Hans.

'Who are they?' she asked, gesturing at them.

'Annika,' Halenius said, 'I want you to listen carefully to what I'm going to say.'

She looked around the room: no windows, just a whiteboard, an antiquated overhead projector in one corner and some sort of ventilation shaft in the ceiling. The walls were pale green, a shade that had been popular in the 1990s. Lime green.

'The delegation consisted of representatives from seven EU member states who were going to find out more about border security between

Kenya and Somalia, then report back to the conference. The problem is that the delegation has disappeared.'

Her heartbeat was pounding in her ears. The brown boot with its pointed heel was sticking straight up to the sky.

'They were travelling in two vehicles, both Toyota Land Cruiser 100s, and there's been no word of either vehicles or delegates since yesterday afternoon . . .' The under-secretary of state fell silent.

Annika stared at him. 'What do you mean?' she said. 'What does "disappeared" mean?'

He started to speak but she interrupted him. 'How . . . I mean, what does "there's been no word" mean?' She stood up. The chair toppled over behind her.

Jimmy Halenius got to his feet too. His blue eyes were crackling. 'The tracking equipment from one of the vehicles has been found just outside Liboi,' he said, 'with the delegation's interpreter and one of the guards. They were both dead.'

The room lurched and she grabbed the table for support. 'This can't be true,' she said.

'We haven't had any information to suggest that anyone else in the group has been injured.'

'It must be a mistake,' she said. 'Maybe they took the wrong turning. Are you sure they haven't just got lost?'

'It's been over twenty-four hours now. We can dismiss the idea that they got lost.'

'How did they die? The guard and the inter-preter?'

Halenius studied her for a few seconds. 'They were shot in the head at close range.'

She grabbed her bag, threw it on to the table and hunted through it for her mobiles, but couldn't find one. She turned the bag out on the table. An orange rolled off and landed beneath the overhead projector. She picked up her private mobile with trembling fingers and dialled Thomas's number, but pressed the wrong button and had to start again. The call went through, with a good deal of crackling and hissing, buzzing and clicking:

'Hello, you've reached . . .'

She dropped the phone on to the floor, where it landed next to her gloves and a notebook. Jimmy Halenius bent down and picked it up.

'It isn't true,' she said, unsure if she'd spoken aloud. The under-secretary of state said some-thing but she couldn't make any sense of it: his lips were moving and he took hold of one of her arms. She pushed his hand away. They had met a few times but he knew nothing about her; he had no idea about the state of her relationship with Thomas.

Anders Schyman leaned forward and said some-thing as well; his eyelids looked swollen.

'Leave me alone,' she said, slightly too loudly, because everyone was staring at her. She gathered all her things back into her bag, apart from the notebook, which she really didn't need – it was just her notes from the idiotic job at Ikea – then headed towards the door, the way out, escape.

'Annika . . .' Jimmy Halenius said, trying to stand in her way.

She slapped him across the face. 'This is your fault,' she said.

And then she left the Frog conference room.

CHAPTER 2

The truck was lurching along slowly. There were no roads where we were going. The wheels bounced over lumps of rock and caught in holes. Plants scraped the chassis, branches brushed the truck's covered sides, the engine roared and the gears shrieked. My tongue was swollen, and stuck to the roof of my mouth. We hadn't had anything to drink since that morning. Hunger had subsided to a rumbling ache, and dizziness had taken over. I hoped that the others' sense of smell had stopped working at the same time as mine – or, at least, that Catherine's had.

Sébastien Magurie, the Frenchman, had finally shut up. His nasal whining had made me wish they'd get rid of him as well. (No, no – what am I saying? I didn't mean that. Definitely not. But I'd found him hard to deal with before this had happened. But enough about that.)

On the other hand, I admired the Spaniard, Alvaro. He had kept his cool throughout, and hadn't said anything unless he was spoken to. He was lying at the back of the truck, where the shaking and bouncing were worst, but hadn't uttered a word of complaint.

To begin with I tried to keep track of which direction they were taking us. The sun was at its zenith when we were stopped, possibly slightly to the west, and at the start we were driven south (I think, which was good, because it meant we were still in Kenya, and Kenya is a functioning state, with maps and infrastructure and mobile phones), but after a few hours I think we turned east (which was nowhere near as good: it meant we were somewhere in southern Somalia, part of the country that had been in a state of total collapse and anarchy for the past twenty years since civil war had broken out). But today I was pretty sure we were heading north, then west, which ought to mean that we were back more or less where we had started. I realized this wasn't very likely, but I had no way of knowing.

The first thing they did was remove our watches and mobile phones, but it had now been dark for a while, which meant it was something like thirty hours since we'd been abducted. Someone must have sounded the alarm. After all, we were an official delegation, so help should be on the way.

I worked out that it must be about six o'clock in the evening in Stockholm – Kenya is two hours ahead of Sweden. Annika must have been told by now, and was probably at home with the children.

Catherine was lying against me. She had stopped

sobbing, and her cheek was pressed against my chest. I knew she wasn't asleep. My hands were tied behind my back – they'd been numb for several hours. The men had used those narrow strips of plastic with a ridged underside that could be tightened but never undone – cable ties, I think they're called. They cut into your skin. How important was blood circulation to your hands and feet? How long could you manage without it? Were we going to be left with lasting damage?

Then the truck hit a particularly vicious hole and my head collided with Catherine's. The truck stopped at a severe angle and I found myself pressed up against the German clerk's generous frame, as Catherine slipped down towards my lap. I could feel a bump growing on my forehead. Doors opened, and the angle of the vehicle's lean intensfied. The men were yelling – it sounded as if they were arguing. After a while (five minutes? A quarter of an hour?) they fell silent.

The temperature was dropping.

Catherine started to cry again.

'Can anyone reach anything sharp?' Alvaro said quietly, from the back of the truck.

Of course. The cable ties.

'This is totally unacceptable,' the Frenchman, Magurie, said.

'Feel around you for a protruding part of the truck,' the Spaniard said.

I tried to feel along the floor of the truck with my fingers, but Catherine was lying on top of me, the German was pressed up against me, and my fingers had lost their agility. A moment later we heard a diesel engine approaching.

It stopped next to the truck and some men got out. I heard a clatter of metal and angry voices. The canvas roof of the truck was pulled open.

Anders Schyman was sitting in his glass box looking out over the newsroom. He preferred to think of the open-plan office as the newsroom, even if, these days, it also contained Marketing, sales analysts and the IT department.

It had been a thin day for news. No major disturbances in the Arab world, no earthquakes, no politicians or reality-TV stars making fools of themselves. They could hardly lead again tomorrow with the chaos caused by the weather. Yesterday they had warned of chaos, today they had reported on the chaos, and Anders Schyman knew his readers (or, rather, he trusted the sales analysts). They'd have to lead with something other than the snowstorm, and for the time being they were considering an emergency solution. Patrik, still annoyed that his story about Ikea's collapsing roof hadn't worked, had found something on an American website about a woman with something called 'alien hand syndrome'. After an operation, the two halves of sixty-year-old Harriet's brain had refused to co-operate, each side refusing to allow the other to dominate. One consequence was that some of her limbs no longer obeyed orders from her brain. Among other things, poor Harriet was regularly attacked by her right hand, as if it were controlled by some extra-terrestrial force (hence the name of the condition). It could hit or scratch her, give her money away or undress her, and she was unable to stop it.

Anders Schyman sighed. Here he sat, aware of a global exclusive, while his staff out in the newsroom were putting together a front page about alien hand syndrome.

He had certainly considered ignoring the Justice Ministry's plea for secrecy and publishing the story about the missing EU delegation anyway, but a residual measure of inherited ethics from his time at Sweden's national broadcaster had stopped him. And, to a certain extent, consideration of Annika. The blogosphere's conspiracy theories about how the media protected their own were wildly exaggerated, and the reverse was usually the case (everyone had an unhealthy obsession with their peers and consequently went overboard on what other journalists said and did), but he could still have a modicum of common human decency. And, besides, the story was hardly going to run away from them. So far, only those most closely concerned had been informed of events, and there were no journalists among them – he had been given assurances about that.

His main concern was what this would do to Annika – and what he would do with her. He got up and went to stand by the door, where his breath fogged the glass.

It was a new age out there. There was no longer any room for reporters who did in-depth investigative stories. What was needed were multimedia producers who could come up with filmed items for television, write short online updates and maybe put together an article some time in the evening. Annika belonged to a dying breed, at least on the *Evening Post*. There were no resources to cover complex legal cases or investigate complicated criminal networks, the sort of things Annika was predisposed towards. He knew she regarded having to work on Patrik's wacky ideas as a form of punishment, but Schyman couldn't carry on making a distinction between her and the others for ever. He couldn't afford to keep her in Washington or slap Patrik down every time he came up with one of his daft ideas. The *Evening Post* was still the second largest newspaper in Sweden, and if they were ever going to beat their main rival they needed to think more broadly, more imaginatively.

He needed Patrik far more than he needed Annika.

He turned away from the glass door and walked restlessly around his little office.

It wasn't as if she'd done a bad job as a foreign correspondent – far from it. For instance, she'd covered the murder of the Swedish ambassador to the USA a year or so ago in an exemplary fashion. And getting back together with her husband seemed to have done her good. She'd never been a bundle of happiness and contentment, but the year she had spent separated from Thomas hadn't been much fun for anyone around her.

Schyman didn't want to think of how she might react if anything happened to Thomas. He was aware that he was thinking very coldly, almost callously, but the *Evening Post* was no care home. If Thomas didn't come back, the only option would probably be to lay her off with a hefty redundancy payment, then hope that the mental-health services and her own social network could handle the fallout.

He sighed again.

Alien hand syndrome.

For Heaven's sake.

'When's Daddy coming home?'

They've got a sixth sense, Annika thought, stroking her daughter's hair. 'He's working in Africa, you know that,' she said, tucking Ellen into her bed.

'I know, but when's he coming home?'

'On Monday,' Kalle said irritably, from his bed. 'You never remember anything.'

When Annika had lived on her own with the children in the flat, Ellen and Kalle had had their own rooms. Annika had slept in the living room. That hadn't worked when Thomas moved back in. Kalle had had to share Ellen's room, which he had taken as a personal insult.

She looked over to her son's bed.

Should she tell them? What could she say? The truth? With a bit of a positive spin?

Daddy's gone missing in Africa and probably won't be home on Monday. In fact, he may never come home so you'll be able to move back into your own room, Kalle. That'll be nice, won't it?

Or lie, to be kind?

Daddy thought it was so exciting working in Africa that he decided to stay on a bit longer. Maybe we could all go and visit him some time. How about that?

Ellen hugged Poppy (new Poppy: as the original had gone up in flames when the house had burned down), curled up into a ball and closed her eyes. 'Sleep tight,' Annika said, switching off her daughter's bedside lamp.

The living room was in semi-darkness. The lamps left by the last tenant glowed warm and yellow in the window alcoves. The television was on with the volume turned down. It looked like Leif G. W. Persson was talking on *Crimewatch*, a programme she usually tried to see. The blonde woman he was working with said something, then a recording started to play. The two presenters were walking among kilometres of files and recorded interviews. It must be the Palme archive, she thought, picking up her old mobile. No missed calls or texts.

She sat down on the sofa with the phone in her hand, and stared at the wall behind Persson. Schyman and a mobile number she didn't recognize, presumably Halenius, had been calling her non-stop on her work mobile since she'd left the Frog conference room. In the end she had switched it off. Almost no one knew the number to her personal mobile, just Thomas and the school, her friend Anne Snapphane and a few others, and it lay in her hand like a dead fish.

In spite of the gloom, all the colours seemed clearer than usual. She could feel her pulse beating.

What should she do? Should she tell? Could she tell? Was there anyone she *had* to tell? Her mum? Thomas's mum? Should she go to Africa to search for him? But who would look after the children if she did? No, she couldn't call her mum. Could she?

She rubbed her face with her palms.

Barbro would be upset. She'd feel sorry for herself. Everything would be so *difficult*. The conversation would end with Annika trying to comfort her and apologizing for burdening her with all this worry. Always assuming she wasn't drunk. If she was, she wouldn't get any sense out of her at all. Either way, it wouldn't be a good conversation, and that wasn't because of Thomas or Africa.

Barbro had never forgiven Annika for not coming home for her sister Birgitta's wedding. Birgitta had married Steven (who was as Swedish as you could get, in spite of his name) towards the end of the American presidential campaign, and Annika had neither wanted nor been able to abandon her new job as correspondent to go to a party in Hälleforsnäs village hall. 'This is the most important day in

41

your sister's life,' her mum had snapped, from her flat in Tattarbacken.

'Neither you nor Birgitta came to my wedding,' Annika had countered.

'Yes, but you got married in Korea!' Uncomprehending indignation.

'So? How come distances are always so much shorter for me than you?'

She hadn't spoken to Birgitta since the wedding. And not much before it, if she was honest. Not since she'd left home at eighteen.

And she didn't feel like calling Berit either. Admittedly, she'd keep the news quiet, but it didn't feel right to burden a colleague with knowledge of the missing EU delegation.

Obviously she ought to tell Thomas's mother, Doris. But what could she say? Your son hasn't answered his mobile for several days, but I wasn't bothered at first because I thought he was off fucking some other woman?

She got up from the sofa, still clutching her old mobile, and went out into the kitchen. A new electric Advent candelabrum, from Åhléns at Fridhemsplan, was shining weakly in the kitchen window. Kalle had chosen it. Ellen was in the middle of an angels phase and had been allowed to get three fridge magnets of little cupids instead. The plates with the remnants of that evening's Indian takeaway were on the draining board; she switched on the light and began to load the dishwasher mechanically.

There was comfort in those methodical gestures, turning on the tap, holding the brush, rinsing off the food with a circular motion, putting the brush back into the drainer, stacking the plates in the right part of the dishwasher.

Without any warning she started to cry. She dropped the cutlery into the sink and sat on the kitchen floor as the hot water ran.

She stayed like that for a long time.

She was pathetic. Her husband was missing, and there was no one she could call or talk to. What was wrong with her?

She got up, turned off the tap, blew her nose on a sheet of kitchen roll, and went into the living room with her mobile.

No missed calls or texts.

Annika sat down on the sofa. Why had she never managed to build up the sort of network Thomas had? Old football friends and schoolmates, some people he knew in Uppsala, a bunch from work and the other guys in his hockey team. Who did she have, apart from Anne Snapphane?

They had worked together during Annika's first summer at the *Evening Post*, but then Anne had moved into broadcasting. Over the years, their friendship had had its ups and downs. Annika's time as Washington correspondent meant they hadn't had much contact over the three years she was there, but they'd seen each other a bit more in recent months. They would meet for coffee on Saturday afternoons, maybe go to a museum on a Sunday.

Annika found it relaxing and undemanding to hear about her friend's escapades and high-flown plans. Anne was always on the point of *a breakthrough*. She was meant for big things, all of which would eventually culminate in her becoming a celebrated television presenter. She came up with new television formats every week, quizzes and chat shows; she was constantly checking out new possibilities for documentaries, and accumulated masses of research in the hope of finding problems to uncover in some investigative programme. Usually her ideas got no further than a blog entry or a cheery Facebook update (Anne wrote a popular blog that she called 'The Wonderful Adventures of a TV Mum', and had 4,357 friends on Facebook). As far as Annika was aware, she had never written more than half a page on any of her television pitches, and she never had time to meet any commissioning editors. She earned her living as a researcher for a production company that made reality shows.

'Annika! God, it's so weird that you've phoned. I was just thinking about you.'

Annika shut her eyes. Someone cared after all.

'Those brown Tecnica boots, do you need them this weekend?'

'Thomas has disappeared,' Annika managed, then started to sob helplessly. Tears ran down her mobile and she tried to wipe them away so it wouldn't get waterlogged.

'Fucking bastard,' Anne said. 'Why can't he ever manage to keep his trousers zipped up? Who's he after this time?'

Annika blinked, and stopped crying. 'No,' she said, 'no, no, not like that . . .'

'Annika,' Anne said, 'you don't have to make excuses for him. You mustn't take the blame for this. It isn't your fault.'

Annika took a deep breath. 'You mustn't say anything because the whole thing's confidential for the time being. His delegation has gone missing, on the Somali border.'

She had forgotten the name of the town.

Stunned silence flowed down the line to her. Then Anne said, 'A whole delegation? What the hell were they travelling in? A jumbo jet?'

Annika blew her nose on the kitchen roll. 'There were seven of them, in two cars. They disappeared yesterday. Their guard and interpreter have been found dead, shot in the head.'

'Oh, Annika! Have they shot Thomas as well?'

A little wailing sob rose from her stomach. 'I don't know!'

'Christ, what are you going to do if he dies? And how are the children going to cope?'

Annika rocked to and fro on the sofa, her arms wrapped tightly round herself.

'Poor, poor Annika! Why does everything seem to happen to you? God, I feel so sorry for you. You poor thing . . .'

It was nice that someone cared.

'And poor Kalle – imagine him having to grow up without a father. Has Thomas got life insurance?'

Annika stopped crying again. She was speechless now.

'And Ellen's still so little,' Anne went on. 'How old is she? Seven? Eight? She'll hardly be able to remember him. Annika, what are you going to do?'

'Life insurance?'

'I don't want to sound cynical, but you have to be practical at times like this. Go through all your papers and see where you stand. Do you want me to come over and help you?'

Annika put her hand over her eyes. 'Thanks, maybe tomorrow. I think I'm going to bed now. It's been a tough day.'

'God, of course, you poor thing, I do understand. Call as soon as you hear anything, okay?'

Annika sat for a while on the sofa with the mobile in her hand. Leif G. W. Persson had gone home and the beautiful woman on the late news had replaced him. They were showing pictures of the chaos caused by the snow all over Sweden – stranded lorries, overworked tow companies, the roof of an indoor tennis court that had collapsed . . . She reached for the remote and turned up the volume. So much snow falling in November was unusual, but hardly unique, the woman was explaining. There had been similar events in Sweden in the 1960s and 1980s.

She switched off the television, then went to the

bathroom to brush her teeth and splash cold water over her face so her eyes wouldn't be too swollen tomorrow.

Then she lay down on Thomas's side of the bed, her limbs aching.

Once they cut the cable ties round our wrists we fell over less often.

That was a huge relief.

The moon had risen. We were being marched along. The landscape around us was like a dark blue photograph with silver edges: thorny bushes, big termite mounds, sharp rocks and distant mountains. I didn't know how to describe it, savannah or semi-desert, but it was uneven and difficult to walk across.

Magurie was at the front. He had appointed himself leader, regardless of anyone else. After him came the Romanian, then Catherine and I, the Dane, Alvaro, and last the stumbling German. She was snorting and sobbing.

Catherine was having trouble walking. She'd put her foot down awkwardly soon after we left the truck and twisted her left ankle. I supported her as best I could, but I was dizzy and so thirsty I thought I would faint so I'm afraid I wasn't much help. My trousers kept catching on the thorns of the bushes, and I had a deep tear below my right knee, through cloth and skin.

During the day I had seen hardly any animals while we were driving, just the occasional antelope and something I'd thought might be a wild boar, but the night was full of their black shadows and luminous eyes.

'I demand to know where you're taking us!'

I couldn't help admiring Sébastien Magurie's persistence.

'I am a French citizen and I demand to be allowed to talk to my embassy!'

He spoke English with an almost comical French accent. No more than five minutes passed between his outbursts. What he lost in vocal weakness, he made up for in raw indignation.

'This is a crime against international law! *Jus cogens!* We are members of an international organization, and you, gentlemen, are committing a crime against *jus cogens*!'

I didn't have the faintest idea where we were. Kenya? Somalia? Surely we hadn't gone far enough north to be in Ethiopia. The night was dense in every direction, no sign of any town glowing on the horizon with its halo of electricity.

The men with guns were walking in front of and behind us. There were four of them, two young boys and two grown men. They weren't Kenyan, according to Catherine. She could speak Arabic, Swahili and Maa (the local language of the Masai), as well as English, obviously, and she couldn't understand what they were saying when they spoke among themselves. It might have been another of the sixty local Kenyan languages, but it wasn't Bantu, or any of the Nilotic tongues. She guessed

48

it was Somali, from the Afro-Asiatic, or East Cushitic, group of languages. One of the men, the tall one who had opened my car door, spoke to us occasionally in poor Swahili. Among other things, he told us that we were faithless dogs who deserved to die a slow and painful death, and that the Great Leader, or the Great General, would decide our fate. He called the man Kiongozi Ujumla, unless that was the word for 'leader' in one of his languages. Who or where the great leader was was unclear.

The two men ahead of us stopped. The tall one said something to the boys behind us, sounding tired and irritable. He was waving his hands and gun about.

One of the boys scampered off into the darkness.

The tall man pointed his gun towards us.

'*Kaa! Chini! Kaa chini* . . .'

'He's telling us to sit down,' Catherine said, and slumped to the ground.

I sat beside her. I could feel insects on my hands, but made no effort to brush them off. I lay down, and ants crawled into my ears. I got a hard kick in the back.

'*Kaa!*'

I struggled up to a sitting position. Evidently the women were allowed to lie down, but not us men.

I don't know how long I sat there. Cold was creeping into my sweaty, damp clothes, turning them ice-cold, and soon my teeth were chattering. Maybe I managed to sleep for a while, because suddenly the boy with the gun was back and the tall man shouted at us to get up (we didn't need a translation of the Swahili: his gesture with his gun was perfectly clear).

We started to walk back the way we had come, or perhaps we didn't, I don't know, but Catherine couldn't take any more. She collapsed into my arms and I fell to the ground, with her on top of me.

The tall man kicked her bad ankle and pulled her hair until she was on her feet again.

'*Tembea!*'

The Romanian – I hadn't caught his name at the reception and had forgotten to look in the notes to find out what it was – appeared at Catherine's other side. I thought it was a bit forward of him to grab her as he did but I was hardly in a position to protest.

I don't know if it's possible to walk upright when you're unconscious, but I know that I kept drifting in and out of consciousness for the rest of the night.

Faint signs of dawn started to show and suddenly we were standing in front of a wall of branches and dry bushes.

'A *manyatta*,' Catherine whispered.

'This is completely unacceptable!' the Frenchman cried. 'I demand that we be given water and food!'

I saw the tall man walk up to Sébastien Magurie and raise the butt of his rifle.

DAY 2

THURSDAY, 24 NOVEMBER

CHAPTER 3

Kalle always wanted chocolate milkshake in the morning. Annika wasn't very keen on this – his blood-sugar rocketed, making him first hyperactive, then lethargic and irritable. They had reached a compromise: he could have it as long as he ate his bacon and scrambled eggs – fat and protein with a low glycaemic index. Ellen loved thick Greek yoghurt with raspberries and walnuts so Annika didn't need to make a breakfast deal with her.

'Can we go to the ice-hockey on Sunday?' Kalle asked. 'It's the local derby, Djurgården against AIK.'

'I'm not sure that's a good idea,' Annika said. 'They're usually quite violent, those derbies. The Black Army throw firecrackers on to the ice and the Stoves retaliate. No, thank you very much.'

Ellen, wide-eyed, had a spoonful of yoghurt poised halfway to her mouth. 'Why do they do that?'

'They're fans,' Kalle said. 'They love their team.'

Annika shot Kalle a surprised look. 'Love?' she said. 'Is that how you show that you love a team? By throwing fireworks at the players?'

Kalle shrugged.

'I feel sorry for the fans,' Annika said. 'What dull lives they must have. They haven't found anything to be interested in, not school, not work, not other people, not politics. Instead they devote themselves to a hockey team. Tragic.'

Kalle shovelled in the last of the egg and emptied his mug. 'Well, I like Djurgården, anyway.'

'And I like Hälleforsnäs,' Annika said.

'Me too,' Ellen said.

They hadn't asked about their dad. Annika didn't mention him now, because what could she say?

The children brushed their teeth and got dressed without her having to nag.

For once they actually left home on time.

It was milder today. The sky was thick and colourless. There was a smell of damp and exhaust fumes. The snow on the streets already looked like brown coal.

The children's school, the American International Primary School of Stockholm, was on the way to the newspaper, just behind Kungsholmen High School. She took them to the wrought-iron gate facing the street, gave Ellen a quick hug and watched them disappear behind the heavy oak door. She remained where she was, children and parents flooding past her through the gateway, boys and girls, mums and dads, a steady and powerful stream. There were a few hard hands and irritated voices, but mostly there was love, tolerance, patience and boundless pride.

She stayed until the torrent had subsided and her toes were frozen.

It was a good school, even if most of the teaching was in English. It certainly hadn't been her idea for them to come here. Thomas had insisted that the children should carry on studying in English after they got home, but she was sceptical about the benefit to them. They were Swedish, and were going to live in Sweden: why make things more complicated?

She could hear his voice now: 'Who's making things more complicated? They'll do Swedish in their language lessons anyway. Think of the advantage to them of being completely bilingual. Let them build on what they already know.'

And she had given in, but it wasn't the children's ability to communicate internationally that she cared about (to be honest, it didn't bother her at all), but rather her own experience of the traditional, council-run Swedish school system. Kalle had had a rough time at the hands of the spoiled little monsters in his class who felt they had to assert themselves at someone's expense, and preferably someone who didn't make much of a fuss, like Kalle.

The thought hit her like a brick: what would she do if Thomas didn't come back?

She had to lean against a wall, and concentrate on breathing steadily.

Would she go on sending the children there, as Thomas had wanted, or would she take them away? Would she honour the memory of her children's father and allow his initiative to shape their upbringing? That would be her responsibility. She would be their sole custodian. This was her and the children's lives she was dealing with . . .

As she stepped through the door at the paper she had no idea how she'd got there. The reception desk was swaying like an out-of-focus boat. By some miracle she managed to pull out her passcard and sail past it as if she was riding on a big wave.

Berit wasn't in yet.

The newsdesk was still there, which steadied her. There was a smell of paper, extension leads and scorched coffee. She unpacked her laptop, logged into the network, went on to Facebook and immediately stumbled over Eva-Britt Qvist's paean of praise to *Waiting for Godot*. She could hear her colleagues talking on the phone, news jingles, the rumble of the ventilation system. She pushed her laptop away and grabbed a copy of that day's paper from the next table.

HARRIET ATTACKED – BY HER OWN HAND!

The front page was dominated by a picture of a fat woman in a hospital bed, scratching her face and apparently howling in pain. Evidently she was suffering from 'alien hand syndrome'.

It was almost comforting. Her husband might have gone missing in north-eastern Kenya, but at least Annika wasn't being attacked by her own right hand. Mothers with young children might be getting murdered, but at least she had a job to go to.

She leafed quickly through the news section, with hands that did exactly what she wanted them to.

Not one word about the mother murdered outside the nursery school in Axelsberg.

She tossed the paper into the recycling bin, went over to the sales analysts' desk and borrowed (okay, stole) a copy of the prestigious morning paper. In the Stockholm section, under 'news in brief', there was a report about the dead body that had been found in a patch of woodland in Hägersten. No indication that a crime had been committed, no mention of the nursery school or of a human being. A dead body. Found. In a patch of woodland.

She despatched the morning paper the same way as its evening colleague, pulled her laptop closer and began to search the blogs.

On the internet there wasn't a trace of the caution, ethical restraint or possible disinterest that the established media had shown towards the murdered mother. Speculation about what had happened to the dead woman behind the nursery school covered several pages. Most of the theories were presented as incontrovertible fact, and four names had been attributed to the victim. Either Karin, Linnea, Simone or Hannelore had lost her life: take your pick. Most had supplied her with too many children or no children at all, but one blog, 'The Good Life in Mälarhöjden', expressed concern, in a hideously misspelled post, over how poor little Wilhelm would manage, in much the same terms as Anne Snapphane had worried about Annika's own children's impending fatherless state.

'And Linnea Sendman was allways so nice, even tho you could tell the divorse had been reelly awful . . .'

That might be something, if her name really was Sendman, but the name might have been misspelled too.

She searched for 'linnea sendman', and found pages on Facebook and LinkedIn, results from the Järfalla national swimming competition, that autumn's new high-school students, and bingo!

She leaned closer to the screen. A post from a Viveca Hernandez, blogging at one of the *Evening Post*'s own servers.

When Linnea reported Evert to the police they took her seriously. The list of offences was so extensive and had been going on for so long that they said they were going to charge him with aggravated harassment. But they never did. Evert carried on as usual, calling at all hours of day and night, kicking the door and yelling so loudly it echoed up the stairwell. A week later Linnea called the prosecutor's office and asked why they hadn't picked him up, seeing as she'd filed an official complaint. The prosecutor told her that the crime had passed the statute of limitation. Abuse, unlawful threats and sexual assault of the sort she had described in her report had a time limit of two years. But aggravated harassment, Linnea said, had a limitation period of ten years, because she'd checked. Then the prosecutor told her the law didn't work like that. Aggravated harassment wasn't regarded as a continuous crime, apparently. Each offence had to be considered separately, and would have its own limitation period. He said that the ten-year period was purely hypothetical . . .

Annika was astonished. Could that really be true? She herself had written plenty of articles and interviewed loads of experts and lawyers about aggravated harassment, and she'd thought she had a fairly good idea of what the law meant.

For a woman living in a violent relationship it could be difficult to remember if she got her black eye on Thursday and the cracked rib on Friday, or the other way round. That was why the law concerning aggravated harassment had been passed, so that the abuse would be considered as a whole, not as various separate incidents. And the statute of limitations had been raised to ten years to underline the seriousness of this type of crime.

Had she misunderstood? It was possible, but wouldn't that mean all the other journalists and lawyers had as well?

The phone on her desk rang. An internal call, judging by the screen. She picked up the receiver.

'You can't just switch your mobile off and unplug your landline when something like this is going on,' Anders Schyman said. 'Halenius has been trying to get hold of you all night. What if something had happened, if there was something to tell you?'

It sounded as if he was outside: there was a lot of wind and interference on the line.

'So what?'

'What?'

'What's happened?'

'Nothing, as far as I know.'

'So it didn't make any difference that I unplugged the phone, did it?'

'You're behaving irrationally and irresponsibly,' Schyman said angrily. 'What if Thomas had tried to reach you?'

'I have another mobile that Thomas calls me on. That one was switched on.'

In the background, she heard a large vehicle, a bus or lorry, thunder past, then heard Schyman yell, 'Watch where you're going, you fucking moron!'

When he came back he sounded more focused. 'Halenius wants to inform you of the current situation, and tell you how the government is going

60

to handle things. He can come round to yours or meet you somewhere in the city, but he can't come here to the office again. They want to keep this under the radar for a bit longer.'

'I don't want him in my home.'

'You can go to the department if you'd rather.'

'Did you know that aggravated harassment doesn't actually have a limitation period of ten years?'

A siren went past.

'What did you say?'

She shut her eyes. 'Nothing. Where are you?'

'My wife's just dropped me at Fridhemsplan. I'll be in the newsroom shortly.'

They hung up. Annika pulled her laptop closer and logged on to one of Sweden's biggest online databases. It wasn't a comprehensive list of everyone in the country, but almost all of the phone numbers that weren't ex-directory were listed there, usually with the address of the subscriber, maps and directions.

There was no Linnea Sendman in the database. Either she had no phone in her own name or she was ex-directory. But Annika found the blogger, Viveca Hernandez: she was listed at Klubbacken 48 in Hägersten. According to the instructive little map that accompanied the listing, she lived behind the two nursery schools on Selmedalsvägen. Presumably the blocks up the hill that Annika had seen from the path.

She went back to the blog. The text suggested

that Viveca Hernandez was well aware of Linnea Sendman's situation: '. . . yelling so loudly it echoed up the stairwell . . .'

I'd be willing to bet that Linnea Sendman lived at Klubbacken 48, too, Annika thought. And that Viveca Hernandez was the neighbour who had sounded the alarm that she had gone missing.

She picked up the phone to call Viveca Hernandez and saw the editor-in-chief standing in front of her, a woolly hat on his head and ice in his moustache.

'We're going to Rosenbad,' he said. 'Right now. That's an order.'

CHAPTER 4

The main government building, originally built as the headquarters of the Nordic Credit Bank at the turn of the last century, stood majestically beside the waters of Norrström, like some late-Gothic palace. Nordic Credit had gone bankrupt during the First World War, but its emblem was still engraved above one of the side entrances, Anders Schyman had forgotten which.

He paid for the taxi with the newspaper's credit card, then glanced at the reporter beside him. She looked like an unmade bed.

At the time of the Crown Princess's wedding a year or so ago, he had introduced a new dress-code at the paper. Torn jeans, micro-skirts, washed-out college shirts and tops cut down to the navel were banned, and a certain degree of style expected. Annika hadn't had to change much of her wardrobe. She usually wore fairly good labels, but still managed to look as if she'd fallen into them by accident. He often got the impression she'd put on one of her husband's shirts without noticing. Today was worse than usual.

She was wearing a shirt with a tanktop, a style that had been fashionable when he was still at junior school.

Most people put on weight in the USA, but not her. She was, if possible, even more angular and sharp-boned now. If it weren't for her generously proportioned bust she could easily have been mistaken for a long-haired teenage boy.

'That woman who was found dead outside the nursery school in Hägersten,' she said. 'She'd reported her husband for aggravated harassment, but the investigation was dropped because the offences had passed the statute of limitations.'

'Don't forget your gloves,' Schyman said, pointing at a number of things that had fallen out of her bag on to the floor of the taxi. He stepped out, walked up to the brushed brass panel embossed with three crowns to the left of the entrance, pressed it and the door swung open. Annika trailed three steps behind him up the white marble stairs, through the white marble foyer, with its pillars and vaulted ceiling, to the security desk at the far left-hand side. From the corner of his eye Schyman saw her stop and stare at one of the statues by the wall.

With a sudden pang of loss he remembered his time as a political reporter, how a gust of wariness would sweep through these government buildings whenever he appeared (walking, striding, even forging forward) with his television crew. Politicians, businessmen and press secretaries had treated him respectfully, occasionally even fearfully. What was he doing today?

He glanced back at Annika. 'ID,' he said.

She went to the security desk and tossed over her driving licence.

A human-resources manager, that was what he was. And a profit machine for the family that owned the paper. An exploiter of modern life, an explorer in the boggy outer reaches of journalism.

Alien hand syndrome.

The guard was a young woman who was doing her best to exude authority. Her hair was pulled into a tight bun and she was wearing a tie. She asked him rather pompously for his own ID and carefully read his press card. She evidently didn't recognize him. She probably didn't follow current affairs. Then she tapped at a computer, picked up a phone to check that they had authorization to proceed, and instructed them to head up the stairs towards the lifts.

Thank you very much. He knew perfectly well where to go.

'We'll take the one on the right,' Schyman said. 'The one on the left is a goods lift that stops at every floor.'

Annika didn't seem remotely impressed by his local knowledge.

So this was where he worked.

Thomas's really, really, really important job.

Annika avoided looking at her reflection in the lift. She had never been here before. She'd never come to pick him up from work, had never been for coffee in the staff cafeteria, had never surprised him with tickets to the theatre or cinema, then gone out for a pizza afterwards.

Thomas had allied himself with the state, and it was her job to hold it to account.

They got out on the sixth floor, one below the Cabinet Office. Thomas was based on the fourth. Every time he had to come up to the sixth floor he would talk about it over dinner with a note of respect in his voice. This was where the real power lay: the minister, the under-secretary of state, the directors-general for legal affairs, the office manager, head of administration and political advisers. White walls, thick, pale grey carpets, doors ajar. The smell of influence and furniture polish hung in the air.

'Welcome,' Jimmy Halenius said, coming over and shaking their hands. 'We're sitting through here . . .'

He didn't look as if he belonged there. He was too crumpled and unkempt. She wondered how he had managed to get the job. Sycophancy and contacts, probably. 'Have you heard from Thomas?' she asked.

'No,' Halenius said. 'But we do have some other information.'

All sounds were muffled, as if the carpets devoured voices. The doors concealed invisible eyes: they could see and hear everything.

They walked down a corridor to a conference room with a view of Tegelbacken and the little island of Strömsborg. It was fitted out with pale wooden furniture and bottles of Swedish mineral water. She shivered, but that had nothing to do with the temperature in the room. The two men from the previous day, who were both called Hans, were already there, but without their coats this time.

She didn't want to be there. She was obliged to be there. It was an order.

She sat down on the chair closest to the door, ignoring the men called Hans.

Halenius pulled up a chair and sat directly in front of her. Annika leaned back instinctively.

'I appreciate that this is very difficult for you. Just say if there's anything you'd like,' Jimmy Halenius said, looking at her with those bright blue eyes.

She hunched her shoulders and stared at the table.

I'd like my husband back, please.

'We've been in touch with Nairobi this morning, and we've got more details of what happened. Feel free to interrupt me if there's anything you're wondering.'

Wondering?

He looked straight at her as he spoke, leaning forward with his elbows on his knees, in an attempt to get closer to her. To get through. She turned to the window. The tower of the City Hall reached up to the sky, with its three crowns at the top. She couldn't see the water.

'The delegation that Thomas was part of took off in a private plane for Liboi early in the morning of the day before yesterday. The group consisted of seven representatives, three guards, one interpreter and two drivers. The interpreter and one of the guards have been found dead, of course, but one of the drivers was discovered alive by a shepherd outside Liboi. He had received a blow to the head, but was able to take part in a short telephone interview this morning. Would you like some water?'

Would she?

She shook her head.

Halenius reached for a sheet of paper on the conference table, put on a pair of reading glasses and read it in silence. How old was he? He had once told her: three years older than her, about forty. He looked more.

'The delegates are, apart from Thomas, a fifty-four-year-old Frenchman called Sébastien Magurie. He's a Member of the European Parliament, and fairly new to this. It was his first conference on the subject.' He waved the document. 'You'll get a copy of this a bit later, when we've had everything formally confirmed.'

Wasn't there an awful lot of dust in here? Sticky grey dust that caught in your throat?

'Maybe I will have that water,' Annika said.

One of the men called Hans stood up and

fetched a bottle of Loka from a side-table. Wild raspberry flavour. Awful. Tasted like paraffin.

'Catherine Wilson, thirty-two years old, the British delegate. She speaks Arabic and Swahili. She spent part of her childhood in Kenya and was acting as the group's secretary. She managed to send one report back to the conference before the group disappeared. Alvaro Ribeiro, thirty-three, is the Spanish delegate. A lawyer, he works for the Spanish government. Helga Wolff, German, aged sixty. It doesn't say so here, but someone said she was a clerk in Brussels. The Danish delegate's name is Per Spang, and he's sixty-five, a member of the Danish parliament, not in good health. Sorin Enache, the Romanian delegate, is forty-eight. An official from their Ministry of Justice, in a similar post to Thomas. Also a marathon runner.'

Helga Wolff, what a cliché. You couldn't get more German than that. Sixty years old, so it wasn't her. Unless she was a government minister, skinny and had had a facelift. But not a clerk. Thomas would aim higher than that.

'Did he volunteer to go?' Annika asked.

Halenius lowered the document. 'How do you mean?'

She was prepared to bet that the thirty-two-year-old Englishwoman was petite and blonde. 'Was there any prestige to be gained in going?' she asked.

Halenius looked tired. 'No,' he said. 'This sort of assignment isn't particularly prestigious. None of the other delegates was especially senior. I don't know if he volunteered or was asked to go, but I can check.' He reached for another sheet of paper.

Annika looked round the small conference room. This wasn't a powerful room: it wasn't the Blue Room where the department's cabinet meetings were held, just some shitty little room where you took the wives of men who'd gone missing, maybe somewhere you prepared minor changes in the law about women who go missing and are found murdered behind nursery schools and in car parks.

'The delegation secretary's first report is a short description of the town of Liboi and a summary of the conversation the delegates had with the chief of police there,' Halenius said. 'Apparently the border crossing to Somalia isn't manned. The police station acts as the border post, even though it's several kilometres from the border . . .'

Annika leaned forward. 'Why are you claiming that aggravated harassment has a statute of limitations of ten years?'

Anders Schyman put his hand over his eyes and groaned. 'Annika . . .'

Halenius regarded her silently.

'Because it isn't true, is it?' she went on. 'That law was just playing to the gallery, wasn't it? The Ministry of Justice wanted the applause of the women's movement and human-rights activists, but you passed a law that's completely toothless.'

The two men called Hans were staring at her as

if she'd suddenly started to speak an entirely different language. Jimmy Halenius studied her face as though he were looking for something.

'So, the surviving driver has been able to give a short description of what happened,' he said slowly. 'The delegation was stopped at a roadblock by a group of armed men, seven or eight of them. The driver isn't sure of the number. He claims the men were Somalis, but obviously that can't be verified.'

The chill in the room was creeping into her spine and she wrapped her arms round her body. Didn't Anne Snapphane know a man from Somalia? A rapper, seriously handsome?

'The cars were on an unofficial road a few kilometres south of the A3 highway, close to the Somali border. At least one of the guards was working with the men at the roadblock. He disconnected the tracking devices on both Toyotas.'

One of the men called Hans suddenly spoke. 'The Toyota Land Cruiser 100 is extremely popular in Africa,' he said. 'They can get through most terrain, and the US Army used them during the invasion of Iraq. In Kenya they're known as "Toyota Takeaways" because of the demand for stolen vehicles.'

Annika turned towards him. 'And what does that have to do with anything?' she asked.

The man called Hans blushed.

'It tells us quite a lot about the men at the roadblock,' the under-secretary of state said. 'They

71

knew what they were doing. The attack wasn't just a coincidence. They were waiting for the EU delegation. They knew the cars were equipped with trackers, and they knew where they were. And they had sufficient financial awareness to know that the vehicles themselves were of considerable value.'

They'd known what they were doing.

Did anyone really know what they were doing, how they were doing it, and why? She could feel herself getting confused.

'An inside job?' Anders Schyman asked.

'It looks like it. The group had chosen the location for the attack carefully. They got themselves there in another vehicle, a covered truck. The driver recognized the make, an old Mercedes.'

She was fighting an urge to stand up and walk over to the window. She clutched the chair's armrests instead. 'So where are they now?' she asked.

'We don't know,' Jimmy Halenius said. 'The truck was gone by the time the police and the military got there so it was probably used to move the members of the delegation.'

Don't know. Looks like it. Probably.

'You don't really know anything, do you?'

She saw Anders Schyman exchange a look with the two men called Hans. The editor-in-chief reached for a bottle of water and asked something about the tracking devices the cars were fitted with, and they started talking about them, as if they were remotely important, as if they mattered.

They were a German model, small but reasonably powerful, combining two established methods of positioning, part GSM, part traditional radio . . .

She felt the words flow through her head without settling. The trackers didn't need either an external aerial or satellite coverage, and the smallest model, which was evidently the one used in this instance, was smaller than a mobile phone and weighed just 135 grams; they had been hidden in the engine compartment, behind the antifreeze container.

She looked out over Riddarfjärden again. It was about to start snowing. The clouds were hanging just above the rooftops.

'You're right. We know very little with any certainty. But we can make a number of assumptions. We could be dealing with a hostage situation – the people in the group have been kidnapped. It isn't unusual in that part of the world. You might have heard of the Somali pirates who hijack ships at sea. This could be a land-based version of that.'

'Like the Danish family on that yacht?' Anders Schyman asked.

'Kidnapped?' Annika said.

'If we're dealing with kidnap, we'll find out about it within the next few days, probably today or tomorrow.'

Annika couldn't sit still any longer. She got up and went to the window. Ducks were swimming about in the water: how come their feet didn't freeze?

73

'There are routines in most things,' Jimmy Halenius said. 'If we're lucky the kidnappers will just demand money. If we're unlucky this could be a political kidnapping, and some fundamentalist group will assume responsibility and start demanding the release of terrorists held captive around the world, or that the US withdraws from Afghanistan, or that global capitalism be dismantled. That's much more difficult.'

Annika could feel her hands starting to tremble: alien hand syndrome.

'There's no chance that they'll just turn up?' the editor-in-chief asked. 'Shaken but unharmed?'

'Of course it's a possibility,' Halenius said. 'We don't know anything about the men at the roadblock or their motives so the scenario is completely open.' He stood up and came over to stand beside her at the window. 'From the government's side,' he went on, 'we'll keep you informed of everything that reaches us from Brussels, Nairobi, and the authorities in all the other countries concerned. In other words, Britain, Romania, France, Germany, Spain and Denmark. What information we receive will determine how we proceed. You can count on our support, no matter what happens. I've got your email address, so I'll send you the delegation secretary's report and details of the other delegates as soon as it's been checked and cleared. Is there a number I can reach you on?'

She hesitated, then put her hand into her bag

74

and pulled out the newspaper's mobile. 'This one,' she said quietly, switching it on and tapping in her PIN.

Behind her Schyman stood up, and the two men called Hans followed suit.

'We've looked into the limitation period for aggravated harassment,' the under-secretary of state said quietly. 'It was done here in the department back in 2007, precisely because of the issue you raised. The inquiry concluded that aggravated harassment was not a continuous crime but consisted of separate offences. That means they each have a separate statute of limitation. Anything else would be out of the question. There'd be a risk of miscarriages of justice.'

She turned and looked up at him. He had been listening to what she had said. 'There are still prosecutors calling this a political law,' she said. 'Did you know that?'

Halenius nodded.

'So what are all other laws?' she said. 'God-given?' She walked out of the little room.

Behind her she heard Anders Schyman and the under-secretary of state mumbling. She knew exactly what they were talking about. How long could this be kept from the public? Until some group claimed responsibility, probably, but no longer than that. There were too many countries involved, too many organizations. When could Schyman go to press? Who was going to make a statement?

She took the lift down without waiting for Schyman.

The hut consisted of a single windowless room. The inside was pitch black with soot. In the centre of the floor there was a hearth that presumably acted both as a stove and a source of heat and light, but at the moment just took up space. A hole in the roof to let the smoke out was spreading a gloomy light, making our bodies look dark and indistinct. Our hands had been tied behind our backs again. They had removed our shoes.

It was very cramped.

I was lying with my face towards the crotch of Alvaro the Spaniard. He had had to relieve himself in his trousers, like the rest of us. The stench was heavy and acrid.

The Dane, Per, was having difficulty breathing. He didn't complain, but his wheezing filled the gloom. The German woman was snoring.

We were in a camp for people and livestock behind a wall of branches and thorny bushes, known as a *manyatta*. I'd managed to count eight huts in the moonlight before we were shut inside this one. But I hadn't seen anyone apart from our guards. No cows or goats either. I think I must have slept for a while during the morning.

The air was perfectly still. It was incredibly hot. The square of light in the roof showed that the sun was approaching its zenith. Sweat was running into my eyes. The salt made them sting, not that it mattered.

We'd been given food. *Ugali*, boiled maize flour, the staple in East Africa. I ate too quickly and got stomach cramps.

But I was feeling confident. This would soon be over. The tall man had assured us of this in his rough Swahili. We were just waiting for Kiongozi Ujumla, the great leader. The tall man clearly didn't have the authority to sanction our release on his own. It had to be Kiongozi Ujumla who took that sort of decision, and we must understand that if you didn't have authority, then you didn't have authority. Everyone knew that.

Even Sébastien seemed satisfied. He had stopped demanding medical treatment for the wound to his head, from when he was struck with the butt of the rifle.

Annika was smiling at me in the semi-darkness. I could smell her shampoo.

These people didn't mean us any harm. They were using us as pawns in an unpleasant game, but they were still people, just like us. They knew perfectly well that we were important people in our respective homelands, and that we had children and families. They were doing this to draw attention to their cause, and then they'd release us. The tall man had assured us of that several times.

And if they didn't keep their word, it would cost them dear. The entire police forces of Kenya and

Somalia would be after them, not to mention the whole of the EU.

I tried to turn my head to get away from the stench of excrement.

Soon I would be at home with Annika and the children again.

The façade of the building on Agnegatan had been scrubbed and repainted during their time in Washington. The nondescript dirty-brown façade was now sparkling white, with a hint of green. In spite of the cloud Annika had to squint when she looked at it.

Anders Schyman had sent her home after the meeting at Rosenbad. It had been a reasonable decision.

She tapped in the door code and took the stairs up. She dropped her outdoor clothes in a heap inside the door, walked into the living room with her bag, put her laptop on the coffee-table, went into the kitchen to switch the kettle on, then to the toilet. As she was washing her hands she found herself staring at Thomas's towel, hanging next to the basin; he was the only member of the family who insisted on having his own.

She dried her hands on it.

She fetched a fresh roll of toilet paper from the top cupboard in the children's room, plugged in the landline, made some instant coffee in a mug with the words 'The White House', then checked her email.

Halenius hadn't sent her the report from the British woman who was guaranteed to be pretty and blonde.

She stared at her inbox with her hands tightly clenched in her lap. For some reason the picture of the fat woman on the front page of the *Evening Post* had stuck in her head.

Perhaps it was all just a terrible misunderstanding.

Perhaps the men at the roadblock had thought the EU delegation were Americans, maybe CIA agents, and as soon as they realized their mistake they'd drive Thomas and the others straight back to the airport in that town, Liboi. Thomas would have a beer in the bar and take the opportunity to do some duty-free shopping, perfume for her and maybe some half-kilo bags of sweets for the children. He'd get home tired and dirty, complain about the facilities at the airport in Liboi and moan about the food on the plane . . .

She checked her email again.

Nothing. No British woman.

She wondered if he'd slept with her yet.

She got up from the computer and went into the children's room. Kalle had made his bed, but Ellen hadn't.

Living with the children made it worthwhile. She'd tried the alternative, and it had driven her to the brink of madness. The year when Thomas had lived with Sophia Grenborg and she had had the children every other week had been a nightmare.

Plenty of other people managed it, most of them, even, but not her.

She slumped down on Ellen's pillows.

She really had made an effort.

When they'd got back together and moved to the USA, she had done her best, with sex and cooking and sensible working hours. She had masturbated when she was alone in an effort to build up some sort of sex-drive, bought cookbooks with Mexican and Asian recipes, and blamed the time difference when she wriggled out of the newsroom's demanding schedule to bake chocolate-chip cookies for the school fête.

But she had always known there were other women. No one in particular, just women he could get into bed without too much effort. She assumed he must have done pretty well. He looked like a Viking, with his blond hair, grey eyes and broad shoulders. He laughed easily and was a good listener; he was competent at most sports, from bowling to hockey, and he was reasonably domesticated.

Conferences, like the one in Nairobi, were his prime hunting ground. The fact that he worked for the government did nothing to harm his chances. His involvement in Frontex wasn't, of course, particularly sexy, so he usually said he worked in international security analysis. Which was probably true, at least in part.

She resisted the urge to make Ellen's bed, went back to her laptop and Googled Frontex.

She was completely uninterested in Thomas's new job. The knowledge that he would be going off to international conferences several times a year had been enough. She knew very little about the actual organization.

One of the first hits came from her own paper. The question of EU border security had been the responsibility of the Swedish EU commissioner for the past couple of years, which meant that a number of inquiries into the subject were being organized from Sweden.

And, yes, they occasionally landed on Thomas's desk.

On the organization's official website she read that its latest initiative had been introduced early: the waters off the Italian island of Lampedusa were being patrolled by air and sea to stop refugees from the turbulence in North Africa making their way to Europe. According to the Swedish EU commissioner, Frontex was there 'to save lives', which might be true. Refugees coming ashore on the beaches of Spain and Italy were so common that no one cared. They didn't even merit a mention in the media now, not in the Mediterranean countries and certainly not in Sweden. If they ever came up, it was because some Swedish tourist had tripped over a body and not been granted compensation by their tour operator.

There was a ping from her inbox, and there, attached to an email from Halenius, was the report from the pretty little British woman. It was in

English, fairly short, and described the situation in the border town.

The crossing between Kenya and Somalia was mostly unmanned. A sign next to the police station in Liboi, saying, 'Republic of Kenya, Department of Immigration, Liboi Border Control', was the only indication that it existed. There were neither staff nor a permanent presence at the border.

At present there were more than four hundred thousand people, most of them Somali, in refugee camps in the neighbouring town of Dadaab.

Annika looked up from her computer. Where had she heard of Dadaab? Something about drought in the Horn of Africa?

She went into Google Maps and typed 'liboi, kenya' in the search box. She was rewarded with a yellowish-brown satellite image of parched earth. Liboi was shown as lying in the middle of a great expanse of nothing, and was no bigger than the head of a pin. A yellow road, identified as Garissa Road A3, ran across the image. She clicked to zoom out, and Dadaab appeared in the south-west, then Garissa, the sea and Nairobi. Kenya lay right on the equator, circled by Somalia, Sudan, Uganda and Tanzania. Christ – what a bunch! She stared at the satellite image with a deafening sense of unreality. All those people, living and going about their business in those countries, and she knew absolutely nothing about them.

A phone rang somewhere in the flat. She pushed the laptop away and stood up, at first unable to work out where the sound was coming from. Then she realized it was the landline. No one called her on it except her mother, and that hardly ever happened. She ran towards the door to the children's room and grabbed the receiver.

It was Jimmy Halenius. 'Annika,' he said. 'We've received two messages from the group holding Thomas and the other members of the delegation.'

She collapsed on to the living-room floor, her mouth as dry as tinder. 'What do they say?'

'I'd rather not go into it over the phone . . .'

'Tell me what they said!'

The under-secretary of state seemed to pause for breath. 'Okay,' he said. 'It's not really a good idea to hear this kind of information over the phone, but okay . . . The first message was picked up by the Brits. A man in a shaky video saying in Kinyarwanda that Fiqh Jihad have taken seven EU delegates hostage. The rest of the message consists of political and religious slogans.'

'What did he say? In Kinyar-what . . .?'

'A Bantu language spoken in East Africa, mainly Rwanda. The message really doesn't tell us anything that we didn't already suspect, that they've been kidnapped by an organized group.'

She looked round the room, at the little lamps in the windows, the throw that Thomas's mother had given him for Christmas, the disks from Kalle's video game. 'So it's political,' she said. 'A political kidnapping. You said those were worse.'

'It's political,' Halenius said, 'but there may be another opening. The second message came to Alvaro Ribeiro's home phone number. His boyfriend took the call and received a short, concise message, in East African English, that Alvaro had been kidnapped and that he would be released in exchange for forty million dollars.'

Annika gasped. 'Forty million dollars? That's . . . what? In kronor? Quarter of a billion?'

'Something like that.'

Her hands started to shake again – alien hand syndrome the whole damn time. 'Oh, fuck . . .'

'Annika,' Halenius said. 'Calm down.'

'Quarter of a *billion*?'

'It looks like there might be a number of different motives behind this kidnapping,' Halenius went on. 'There's the political aspect, as indicated by the video, and then there's the demand for money, which suggests a standard kidnap for ransom. You're right about the second being preferable.'

'But a quarter of a billion? Who's got that sort of money? I certainly haven't.'

Kidnap for ransom?

The words triggered something inside her, but what? She pressed her shaking hand to her forehead and searched her memory. An article she had written, an insurance company she had visited during her first year as a correspondent, in upstate New York: they were specialists, K&R Insurance – Kidnap and Ransom Insurance . . .

She jumped to her feet. 'Insurance,' she yelled

down the line. 'The department must have insurance! Insurance that will pay out the money and everything's sorted!' She was practically laughing with relief.

'No,' Halenius said. 'The Swedish government has nothing like that. On a point of principle.'

She stopped laughing.

'Insurance of that sort offers a short-term and dangerous solution. It increases the risks and drives up ransom demands. Besides, the Swedish government doesn't negotiate with terrorists.'

She could feel the ground opening beneath her and struggled to cling to the doorframe.

'But,' she said, 'what about me? What do I do now? What happens next? Are they going to call me as well, on this number?'

'That would be an excellent starting point.'

She could feel panic rising and her field of vision shrank. She heard the under-secretary of state's voice from a long way away.

'Annika, we need to talk about your situation. I know you don't want me in your home, but right now I think that would be the most straightforward solution for you.'

She gave him the code to the front door.

The Frenchman was protesting again. He was shouting relentlessly to our captors, and ordering Catherine to translate his words into Swahili, which she did in a subdued voice with her head lowered. Now he wasn't just raging about the wound to his head, but also our sanitary predicament. None of us had been allowed to go to the toilet since we were captured two days ago. Urine and excrement were stinging our skin and making our clothes stiff.

The German woman was crying.

I could see irritation and anxiety rising among the guards. They were nervous each time they opened the wooden door of the hut, and would explain quickly and angrily that they didn't have the authority to let us out. We had to wait for Kiongozi Ujumla, the leader and general, but we had no idea if this was one person or two, but only he/they had the right to make decisions about prisoners, they said. (The prisoners were us, *wafungwa*.)

When I heard a diesel vehicle pull up outside I actually felt relieved. The Frenchman fell silent and listened, along with the rest of us. We could hear muttering.

The sun was going down. It was almost completely dark inside the hut.

It seemed an extremely long time before the door was opened again.

'This is completely unacceptable!' the Frenchman cried. 'You're treating us like animals! Have you no decency?'

The black silhouette of a short, thick-set man filled the doorway. He was wearing a turban on his head, a short-sleeved shirt, loose trousers and heavy shoes.

His voice was high, like a young boy's. 'You no like?' he said.

The Frenchman (I had stopped using his name: I was trying to dehumanize him, distance myself) replied, *c'est vrai*, he didn't like our situation.

The short man shouted something we didn't understand at the guards. When he turned round I saw a large knife, curved like a scimitar, hanging from a strap across his back: a machete.

Fear, which had settled like a lump in my stomach, exploded with a force I had never experienced before. All the guards were armed, so it wasn't the half-metre blade itself that had provoked my reaction, but something else about the short man, something in the way he moved, or his ice-cold voice. He must be Kiongozi Ujumla.

Two of the guards came into the hut. It was dark and cramped and they trod on us. They went over to the Frenchman, picked him up by the feet and shoulders and carried him to the door. The German woman screamed when the tall one put his foot on her stomach and almost lost his balance on her soft bulk. They carried him out through the doorway and, for the first time, the view through the opening was clear. Fresh air swirled through the hole, and I breathed deeply, blinking up at the light. The sky was red and yellow and ochre, incredibly beautiful.

They stood the Frenchman on the ground immediately in front of the doorway, and his feet were quickly covered with the billowing dust. The opening was so low that we could only see up to his shoulders, even though we were lying on the ground. The short man went and stood in front of the Frenchman in the twilight.

'No like?' he asked again.

The Frenchman started to tremble, either from fear or the effort of having to stand upright after lying down for so long. His feet and hands were still bound with cable ties, and he was visibly swaying. 'This is a crime against international law,' he began once more, in a shaky voice. 'What you're doing is a breach of international rules and regulations.'

The leader and general stood with his legs apart and folded his arms over his chest. 'You say?'

Catherine, who was lying to my left, pressed closer to me.

'I am a French member of the European Parliament, the EU,' the Frenchman said, 'and I demand that you release me at once from this situation.'

'EU? Work for EU?' The short man smiled a broad but stiff smile. 'You hear?' he said, turning towards us. 'Work for EU!'

With an agility that was surprising, considering his bulk, the short man reached back with his arms and, with a sweeping gesture, swung the machete down in a wide arc to the left side of the Frenchman's groin.

Catherine screamed and hid her face in my armpit. I wished I'd had the sense to hide my face in an armpit, but I looked on wide-eyed as the Frenchman collapsed, like a sawn-off pine-tree, letting out a wheezing sound as the air went out of him.

It was rapidly getting dark outside.

CHAPTER 5

Annika was standing by the window in the living room, staring up at the concrete sky. She was empty inside, just a shell, fumbling for some sort of reality. Part of her still thought the whole thing was a terrible misunderstanding, a communications breakdown in Africa. Soon Thomas would call her mobile, annoyed that his flight hadn't taken off on time. Another part of her was worrying about little things, such as the fact that she would be alone with Jimmy Halenius again. And what would she say to Thomas's mother? Who would write about the dead mother in Axelsberg?

Jimmy Halenius was on his way. Perhaps her anxiety could be traced back to the photograph that had been taken outside the Järnet restaurant a few years ago. She had gone for dinner with the under-secretary of state to pump him for information, and as they were leaving the restaurant a paparazzo had snapped a picture as Halenius was demonstrating to Annika the Spanish way of air-kissing. When Bosse from the rival evening paper had confronted her with it, she had been scared.

She knew what could happen once the media had got its claws into you.

When the bell rang she hurried into the hall and opened the door. Jimmy Halenius walked in and stumbled over her boots. Annika turned on the ceiling light, kicked her boots towards the bathroom and snatched up her jacket from the floor.

'So what have you done with Hansel and Hansel?' she asked. 'Have you left them at home?'

'Yep, busy making gingerbread,' Halenius said, putting down his briefcase. 'Have you had any calls?'

She hung her jacket on a coat hook and shook her head.

'Are the children at home?'

'They'll be back at five. That's when I normally leave work. They don't know I'm at home.'

'You haven't told them anything?'

She turned to him. He took his own coat off and reached for a hanger, surprising her. She wouldn't have thought him the sort of man who used hangers for his outdoor clothes.

She shook her head again.

He stood in front of her, and she was struck by how short he was. Only a few centimetres taller than her, and Thomas called her a pygmy. 'It's good that you haven't said anything so far, but you're going to have to tell them now. The story will be in the media this evening, tomorrow morning at the latest, and the children have to hear it from you.'

She put her palms over her eyes. They smelt of salt. When she spoke her voice sounded flat. 'What can I say?'

Her hands dropped to her sides. Halenius was still standing there.

'Be as vague as possible. Don't mention any details about where they went missing, how long they've been gone, who the others are. You can say that a group of men are holding him captive. That's what the man in the video says, and that's what the media will spread.'

'What was it he said again?'

'That Fiqh Jihad have taken seven EU delegates hostage as punishment for the decadence of the Western world, more or less.'

'Fiqh Jihad?'

'A group nobody knows anything about. We haven't had any intelligence about them before now. "Fiqh" means the expansion of Islamic law, the interpretation of the Koran and so on, and you probably know what "Jihad" means.'

'Holy war.'

'Yes, or just "struggle" or "striving", but in this case we don't believe the words themselves have any literal meaning. They've been chosen for their symbolic value. There are a couple of things I'd like to go through with you. Can we go in and sit down?'

She felt her cheeks turn red – she really was a hopeless host. 'Of course,' she said, gesturing towards the living room. 'Would you like coffee?'

'No, thanks.' He glanced at his watch. 'The call to the Spaniard's home number came precisely one hour and nine minutes ago. Just before I left the office I heard that the Frenchman's family had also received a call, on his wife's mobile.'

He'd said 'the office' rather than 'the department'.

'We don't have a lot of time,' he added. 'You could get a call at any moment.'

The room lurched. She glanced at her mobile and gulped. 'What did they say to the Frenchman's wife?'

'She was so shaken she couldn't remember the amount of the ransom they wanted. Unfortunately she made several fundamental mistakes during the call. Among other things, she promised to pay the ransom at once, no matter how much they wanted.'

'Isn't that good?' Annika said. 'Being co-operative?' She sank into the sofa.

He sat beside her and looked into her eyes. 'We don't have kidnap insurance,' he said, 'but we've spent time with the FBI, learning how to handle a hostage situation. Hans and Hans-Erik have more experience of this sort of situation, but we didn't feel that you and they had made much of a connection. So I was asked to come and talk to you.'

She suddenly felt freezing, pulled her knees up under her chin and wrapped her arms round her shins.

'We still aren't entirely sure what sort of kidnapping this is,' Halenius went on, 'but if it's about

93

business rather than politics, then things usually follow a particular pattern. If the ransom is the key demand, you might be looking at a fairly protracted period of negotiations. Do you speak English?'

She cleared her throat. 'Yes.'

'What sort? Where have you done most of your talking? Were you an exchange student some-where, have you worked abroad, have you picked up a particular accent?'

'Washington correspondent,' she said.

'Of course,' Halenius said.

After all, he had arranged for Thomas to have a research post at the Swedish Embassy while she was there.

'Speaking the language is incredibly important for anyone negotiating in a kidnapping case,' he continued. 'Even minor misunderstandings can have serious consequences. Do you have any recording equipment here?'

She put her feet on the floor. 'What for? The telephone?'

'I was in too much of a hurry to find anything in the department.'

'So I'm supposed to sit here, at home in my living room, and talk over the phone with the kidnappers? Is that the plan?'

'Have you got a better suggestion?'

She wasn't the one who'd sent Thomas to Nairobi, or made him get on the flight to Liboi, but she was having to deal with the consequences.

She stood up. 'I've got a recorder for interviews

but I don't use it much. It takes too long to listen to the files afterwards so I prefer to take notes.' She went into the bedroom, poked about on the top shelf of the linen cupboard, and eventually found the antiquated digital recording device, which could be plugged into the phone and directly into a computer through one of the USB ports.

Halenius whistled and stood up. 'I haven't seen one of those for a while. Where did you get it? The Historical Museum?'

'Funny,' Annika said, pulling her laptop closer and plugging it in. 'Now you just have to attach the phone or mobile and it's ready to go.'

'Do you want to take the call when it comes?'

She held on to the back of the sofa. 'You're sure there's going to be one?'

'If there isn't we're stuffed. Our only option is to negotiate, and someone has to do it.'

She brushed her hair away from her face. 'What do I need to do?'

'Record the conversation, take notes, write down any specific demands, all instructions and comments. Show you're taking the situation seriously. Try to establish a code that you can use the next time, so you know you're talking to the same person. That's very important. And try to get a specific time for the next call. But you mustn't promise anything. You mustn't talk about money. You mustn't be threatening or confrontational, suspicious or nervous, and you mustn't start crying.'

She sat down. 'What are they going to say?'

'The person who calls will be nervous and intense. He – it's usually a man – will demand a ridiculous amount of money, which has to be delivered within a very tight timescale. The intention is to throw you off balance and make you agree to demands that you can't back out of later.'

'Like the Frenchman's wife,' Annika said. 'What's the alternative? That you take the call? Have you done this sort of thing before? You said you did that course with the FBI.'

'I could take it, or Hans or Hans-Erik . . .'

At that moment the front door flew open and Kalle and Ellen tumbled into the hall.

Halenius nodded to her. 'Do it.'

She caught them both in her arms, kissing and hugging them. Their cheeks were cold and red, like frozen apples. She pulled off their coats and scarves, asked Ellen where her gloves were, and was told, 'Gone.' She rubbed and blew on the little girl's hands.

'We'll be eating after children's television tonight,' she said. 'But first there's something I want to talk to you both about.'

Out of the corner of her eye she could see that Jimmy Halenius had connected the landline to the recording device. He was standing in the living room, balancing the phone, the gadget and Annika's laptop in his arms, and smiled at the children. The top button of his green shirt was undone and his hair was a mess. 'Hello,' he said. 'My name's Jimmy, and I work with your dad.'

Kalle stiffened and frowned at him suspiciously.

'Jimmy's here to help us,' Annika said, crouching down. 'You see—'

'Sorry to interrupt, Annika, but is there anywhere you could take a call without being disturbed?'

She pointed towards her and Thomas's bedroom. 'There's a phone socket under the desk,' she said, then turned back to the children. Ellen was twirling a lock of hair and cuddling up to her, but Kalle was still stiff and unapproachable.

'What's happened to Daddy?' he asked.

Annika tried to smile. 'He's been taken prisoner in Africa.'

Ellen twisted in her arms and stared up at her. 'In a castle?' she asked.

Kalle's eyes were wide with confusion.

'I don't know, darling,' Annika said. 'We only found out this afternoon. Some men in Africa have taken Daddy and some other people prisoner.'

'Will he be coming home on Monday?' Ellen asked.

'We don't know,' Annika said, kissing her daughter's hair. 'We don't know anything, darling. But Jimmy from Daddy's work is here to help us.'

'What about the others?' Ellen said. 'Aren't they going to be set free?'

'Oh, yes, them too. Kalle, come here.'

She reached out to the boy, but he ran past her into his and Ellen's room. He slammed the door.

The phone rang.

'I'll answer!' Ellen cried, trying to wriggle out of her arms.

'No!' Annika shouted, loud and desperate, grabbing the top of her daughter's arm hard. Tears sprang to the child's eyes.

The phone sounded again. She heard the bedroom door close.

'No,' she said, trying to sound normal again, and letting go of Ellen's arm. 'It might be the kidnappers. You and Kalle mustn't answer the phone for a while.'

Ellen was rubbing her arm. 'You hurt me.'

The phone rang a third time and the receiver was picked up.

Annika swallowed and stroked the child's hair. 'I'm sorry, I didn't mean to. But it's very important that you don't answer the phone. Do you understand?'

'But I could talk to the kidnappers,' Ellen said. 'I could tell them that they're silly, and that Daddy has to come home.'

'No,' Annika said firmly. 'Only grown-ups are allowed to talk to them. Do you understand?'

Ellen's lower lip started to tremble. Annika sighed. She wasn't making a very good job of this.

Halenius came back into the living room.

Annika stood up and the world spun. 'What did they say?' she managed to gasp.

'It was a woman called Anne Snapphane. She

wanted to know if you'd heard anything from Thomas.'

Relief.

'Sorry,' she said. 'I had to talk to someone.'

'Have you told anyone else?'

She shook her head.

'What sort of mobile phone have you got?'

She pointed at the coffee-table, where both mobiles were lined up beside each other.

Halenius picked up her personal phone. 'This makes your recording equipment look almost modern. Impressive.'

'Don't make fun of my Ericsson,' she said, taking it from him.

When she'd got home from Washington she had been given a magnificent new mobile, which, to judge by her colleagues' enthusiasm, could tap-dance, do the ironing and win the Olympic long jump. And maybe it was brilliant if you wanted to create dance music or film forest fires, but as a phone it was hopeless. She hardly ever managed to answer it when it rang because she managed to nudge the wrong part of the screen and the call was cut off; sending a text was so fiddly it took half the day. She'd kept hold of her Ericsson, which was so ancient that it was still called Ericsson rather than Sony, but it was a nuisance having to charge two mobiles, and she kept hoping iPhone was about to go bankrupt, which was unlikely, if you consid-ered the amount of free advertising her own paper alone produced in its delight at every new product.

Halenius picked up the shiny new mobile. 'Which one does Thomas usually call?'

'My private one.'

'Not your work phone?'

'I don't think he's got the number.'

Halenius nodded. 'Excellent. So we know we won't be getting the call on that phone.'

He went back into the bedroom and closed the door behind him.

The BBC put the news on its website just after six p.m., local time. Reuters issued a short, general report a few minutes later. The identities and nationalities of the kidnapped delegates weren't released, just that they had been taking part in a security conference in Nairobi. The editorial management team of the *Evening Post* was sitting in a handover meeting, which might explain why the news seemed to pass them by at first, but Schyman knew better.

No one ever cared about news from Africa. The continent was a black hole on the news map, except when it came to famine, misery, piracy, Aids, civil war and mad dictators, which weren't among the issues the *Evening Post* covered.

Assuming no Swedes were caught up in anything, of course. Or other Scandinavians, possibly, like those Norwegians who were sentenced to death in Congo or the Danish family whose yacht was seized by pirates.

Anders Schyman found the report because he

100

had set out to look for it. He had held back from mentioning Thomas's disappearance at the meeting, and was planning to wait and see what happened internationally first. Reuters were reporting that a group calling itself Fiqh Jihad had taken seven European delegates hostage, and had issued a non-specific political statement in connection with the kidnapping. The message had been conveyed in Kinyarwanda, and was hosted by a server in the Somali capital, Mogadishu. Readers were referred to the BBC, which had a link to the shaky video from the kidnappers.

Anders Schyman clicked the link and held his breath.

A man in basic military uniform with a scarf wrapped round his head appeared on the screen. The background was out of focus, dark red. He looked about thirty and was staring at a point just to the left of the camera, presumably reading his message. The BBC had subtitled his words in English, which Schyman appreciated (his Kinyarwanda wasn't what it should have been).

The man spoke slowly, his voice strangely high and clear.

'Fiqh Jihad has taken seven EU delegates hostage as punishment for the evil and ignorance of the Western world. In spite of all the weapons and resources surrounding the EU, the Lion of Islam managed to seize these infidel dogs. Our demands are simple: open the borders to Europe. Share the world's resources. Abolish punitive import tariffs.

Freedom for Africa! Death to the European capitalists! Allah is great!'

The video ended. Thirty-eight seconds, including a shaky introduction and a black final frame.

This isn't going to be a picnic, Schyman thought, and headed out to the newsdesk.

The phone didn't ring.

It didn't ring and didn't ring and didn't ring.

Annika was walking round the living room, biting her nails until her teeth hurt.

Schyman had emailed to tell her that Reuters and the BBC had released the news of the kidnapping, without mentioning any identities or nationalities. The *Evening Post* would be the only paper the next day with the news that the Swedish delegate was one of the hostages.

Patrik had texted to ask if she wanted to do a sob-story in the print edition. Ideally he'd like a picture of her and the kids surrounded by stuffed toys, with tears in their eyes, and the suggested headlines 'DADDY'S BEEN KIDNAPPED BY TERRORISTS' or 'DADDY, COME HOME!' She had replied, 'Thanks, but no thanks.'

Berit had emailed to ask if there was anything, anything at all, she could do to help.

She pursed her lips and glanced towards the bedroom. Jimmy Halenius had disappeared in there with his briefcase while she and the children had eaten meatballs and macaroni bake with ketchup. They had sat on either side of the wall, him solving international kidnappings and her feeding the kids.

Could he really sort this out?

She wandered into the kitchen, and heard Halenius talking in the bedroom.

Dinner had been cleared away, the table wiped, the floor swept. The dishwasher was rumbling quietly. The children had changed into their pyjamas and brushed their teeth.

Annika sucked at a bleeding cuticle and went into their room. 'Shall we play a game?'

Kalle brightened. 'Monopoly!'

'That would take a bit too long. Dominoes? Ellen, do you want to play?'

Kalle dug out the box, sat on the floor and methodically laid out the pieces, one by one, upside down. 'We take five each, don't we?'

'Five each,' Annika confirmed.

She looked at the children as they selected their dominoes and lined them up. They'd be able to manage without Thomas. Somehow they would cope.

'Come on, Mummy,' Kalle said.

She sank on to the floor and picked five dominoes.

'I've got double five,' Kalle said.

'You're probably highest then,' Annika said.

Kalle put down his double five and Ellen had her go.

Annika felt as if she was about to start crying.

'It's your turn, Mummy.'

She put a domino down and the children groaned. 'You're doing it wrong, Mummy . . .'

The game took for ever.

And the phone didn't ring and didn't ring and didn't ring.

Jimmy Halenius came out into the living room and stood in front of the television. 'Can I watch the news?'

'Of course,' Annika said.

'How long is he going to be here?' Kalle whispered, glaring at the under-secretary of state.

'I don't really know,' Annika said. 'That depends on what the kidnappers say, if they ever actually call.'

'Why can't you talk to them?' he asked.

Annika pulled him closer to her – he actually let her. He curled up into a ball in her arms and put his hand in her hair. 'I daren't,' she whispered. 'I'm scared of them. Jimmy's spoken to lots of bad guys before. He'll be much better at it than me.'

Kalle's eyes showed a new awareness: grown-ups could feel small and scared.

'Well, it's time for the two of you to go to bed, and tomorrow it's Friday. Would you like to go and see one of your grandmothers this weekend?'

Kalle hid his face against her shoulder. 'Boring,' he muttered.

'I like Scruff,' Ellen said.

Scruff was Doris's fat cocker spaniel.

My darling sunbeam, Annika thought. For you the glass is always half full.

'I'm going to talk to Grandma Doris and Grandma Barbro this evening,' Annika said, 'so I'll ask if we can go and see them.'

'Are you going to talk about Daddy?' Kalle asked.

'The news about him will be in the paper tomorrow,' Annika said, 'so it's probably best if I tell them tonight.'

'Otherwise they might keel over,' Kalle said, and Annika actually laughed. She pulled her son even closer, breathing in his smell.

'Yep,' she said, 'you could well be right. Right! Into bed now!'

And, remarkably, the children crept into bed and were asleep in moments.

Annika turned off the lamp in their window, then went back to the living room, shutting the door quietly behind her.

'They feel safe with you,' Jimmy Halenius said.

'I've known them quite a while,' Annika said, sinking down on the sofa next to him. 'Has there been anything on the news?'

'Nope,' Halenius said. 'Do you reckon they even read the report from Reuters?'

Annika shrugged. 'They get thousands of messages from the news agencies each day. Most of them are of no interest to the wider world, but they're always important to someone.' She looked at him. 'How common is this really, kidnapping and so on?'

He stretched and rubbed his eyes. 'There aren't any reliable statistics. It mainly occurs in countries with weak policing, a non-existent justice system and plenty of corruption. In Africa it's most common in Nigeria and Somalia – they're in the global top ten. Don't suppose you've got a sandwich or something?'

She blushed and stood up. 'Of course, sorry. I forgot you hadn't eaten. Would you like macaroni and meatballs warmed up in the microwave?' She felt she had to ask. Thomas didn't eat that sort of thing, unless the meatballs were hand-rolled from elk mince and the macaroni scented with truffle.

She went out into the kitchen, opened the fridge, scraped the food out of the Tupperware box on to a plate and put it into the microwave. She clicked the display, three minutes ought to do, then pressed start. The machine began to hum.

She went to the sink and rinsed the box – it was the one she took to work most days.

The closure of most of the entrances to the paper's offices meant that no one had lunch at the Seven Rats any more: it was too far to walk round so lunchboxes had taken over. She missed the salad bar, the coffee machine in the corner and the dusty little biscuits next to the packets of sugar. The problem with lunchboxes was that people kept forgetting about them: they were sent out on jobs or went to the pub instead, and the boxes were left sitting in the fridge until the contents were unrecognizable. She leaned against the cupboard door and made a promise to herself. When this is over and Thomas is back home, I'm going to start going to the Seven Rats again. No more lunchboxes.

The microwave bleeped three times. She sliced a tomato for decoration.

And the phone didn't ring and didn't ring and didn't ring.

'Not exactly Operakällaren,' she said, putting the plate, cutlery and a glass of tap-water in front of him on the coffee-table.

'Thomas's mother is still alive, isn't she?' Halenius said, shovelling a forkful of macaroni into his mouth – he was evidently hungry.

'Doris,' Annika said. 'Yes, she is.'

'You ought to call her.'

'Yes,' Annika said. 'Or maybe you should.'

He took a sip of water. 'Why?'

'She doesn't like me. Do you want a napkin?'

'No, I'm fine. Why not?'

She raised an eyebrow. 'Thomas was married before, to a bank director. She thought her son ought to have found someone better than me. Holger, his brother, is married to a doctor.'

Halenius put a meatball into his mouth, chewed and swallowed. 'What about the grandchildren?'

'Holger and his husband, Sverker, have a little girl called Victoria. They had her with some friends, a lesbian couple. Doris loves Victoria. How are the meatballs?'

'A bit cold in the middle. Your father's dead, isn't he?'

She stiffened. Ingvar, her father, had been a union boss at the works in Hälleforsnäs, something he had been very proud of, but that hadn't helped when the business had started to make a loss at the end of the 1980s. He was surplus to requirements, and was fired along with hundreds more. His already fairly heavy drinking had toppled into addiction. He had frozen to death in a snowdrift beside the road to Granhed when Annika was eighteen.

'How did you know that?' she asked.

'Roly,' he said, and pushed the plate away. 'Have you got her number? Doris Samuelsson?'

'It's in my contacts, under "Dinosaur",' Annika said, handing over her work mobile and taking the plate out into the kitchen. From the living room she heard him sigh.

'Mrs Doris Samuelsson? Good evening, my name is Jimmy Halenius. I'm under-secretary of state at the Department of Justice . . . Yes, that's right, Thomas's boss . . . I'm sorry to call so late, but I'm afraid I've got some bad news . . .'

She stood beside the microwave, squeezing the dishcloth between her fingers as she waited for Halenius to finish the call. Afterwards her hands smelt disgusting, and she had to scrub them with lemon-scented washing-up liquid.

'She didn't take it terribly well, then?' Annika

said, putting a plate of sticky chocolate cake on
the table.

'No. Have you been baking?'

Why did he sound so surprised?

'Raspberries and cream?'

'Definitely.'

She whipped some cream and thawed some
frozen raspberries in the microwave, then put
them on the coffee-table and sat on the sofa,
straight-backed.

'I should call Mum as well, shouldn't I?'

'It would be pretty odd if she found out from
the media.'

She took a deep breath, picked up her work
mobile and dialled her childhood telephone
number. It had never changed.

She could hear her heartbeat above the ringing.

'Mum? It's Annika. How are you?'

Her mother's reply was indistinct. She picked
up something about lumbago and overdue social-
security payments.

'Mum,' she interrupted, 'I'm afraid something
awful's happened. Thomas has gone missing in
Africa.'

There was silence at the other end of the line.

'What do you mean, missing?' her mother said.
'Has he gone off with some woman?'

Now she could hear that her mother wasn't
entirely sober. 'No, Mum, he's been kidnapped.
We don't know how serious it is yet, but I thought
you ought to know.'

'Kidnapped? Like that millionaire? Whatever for? You haven't got any money!'

Annika closed her eyes and put a hand to her forehead. She had no idea what millionaire her mother was referring to. 'Mum,' she said, 'could the children come and stay with you for the weekend? I don't know how long this is going to take, but I'll be pretty busy over the next few days.'

Her mother muttered something.

'It would be a huge help.'

'Kidnapped?'

'With six other delegates at a security conference in Nairobi. As far as we know, he hasn't been hurt. Is there any chance you could look after Kalle and Ellen? Even for just one day?'

'I can't,' her mother said. 'I've got Destiny.'

Annika blinked. 'What?'

'Birgitta's working an extra shift at Right Price this weekend. I have to look after De-hestiny.'

Barbro had started to hiccup. Birgitta's one-year-old daughter was called Destiny, poor little thing.

'But,' Annika said, 'isn't Birgitta married? Can't Steven look after his own child?'

Her mother dropped something, and Annika heard swearing in the background. Perhaps she had a new boyfriend.

'Listen,' her mother said, 'I've g-got to go. And you need to apologize to Birgitta.'

'Sure, Mum,' she said. ''Bye.'

She pressed to end the call and lowered the mobile. Tears burned behind her eyelids. 'Is there anything more shameful than not being loved by your own mother?' she said shakily.

'Yes,' Halenius said. 'Not being loved by your own children.'

She laughed. 'Isn't that a scene from a film?'

Halenius smiled. 'Yep,' he said. 'One starring Sven-Bertil Taube.'

The phone rang.

They carried us out, one by one, and they started with me.

It had got completely dark. No moonlight. No fire anywhere. They carried me by my feet and shoulders, just as they had the Frenchman, and I was surrounded by black nothingness on my way towards a swaying nothingness. I was on the point of losing consciousness, and my bowels and bladder emptied in fear. I thought I could see sabre-like knives glinting in the darkness, and they probably were – the plastic tie around my feet came off. Someone pulled down my trousers and threw a bucket of water over my crotch. Cold, but it stung my inflamed skin. I didn't cry out, because that wasn't permitted, 'No allowed,' Kiongozi Ujumla had said, and no talking either. We had lain tightly packed together until the noises died away outside and only the Dane's wheezing breaths were audible in the darkness.

The temperature fell rapidly at night. My teeth were chattering.

One of the guards, I couldn't see which, wrapped

a length of checked cloth round me in place of my trousers. I was allowed to keep my shirt, the one I had selected with such care the morning we took off for Liboi, the pale pink one with the slight shimmer. It's Annika's favourite – she calls it my 'gay shirt': 'Can't you wear your gay shirt today?' she often says, grinning with that big mouth of hers . . . Then I had to walk to the other end of the *manyatta* and they shut me inside a different hut. It was smaller and smelt different. There had never been any fires in this one. The sounds as I moved were harsh and metallic. There was no hole in the roof.

They bound my feet again. I must have lost consciousness because when I came round the Dane, Per, was lying next to me, with the Romanian whose name I didn't know, and Spanish Alvaro. They had split us up, men and women.

Per's breathing was rasping and uneven.

There were four of us men left now.

CHAPTER 6

'Forty million dollars, to be paid in Nairobi first thing tomorrow morning,' Jimmy Halenius said, sitting down in the armchair in front of her.

She covered her face with her hands.

'It isn't a disaster,' he added. 'We wanted contact, and now it's been established.'

He sounded reassuring.

Annika let her hands fall and concentrated on breathing. 'That's the same amount they told the Spanish guy.'

'I explained that the family doesn't have access to that sort of money, and not so quickly. The man spoke perfect East African English. Well educated, I'd say. His demands were unreasonable, and he knew it. I asked how Thomas was, but he didn't answer.'

'Who did you say you were?'

'A colleague, and a friend of the family.'

'Not his employer?'

'In purely formal terms, the Swedish government isn't involved in this.'

She looked out through the window. The sky

was so strangely red at night, a dusty, greyish red from the pollution and the city's lights on the clouds. 'What else did he say?'

He hesitated. 'Thomas will die if we don't deliver the money before ten tomorrow morning, local time. Do you want to listen to the recording?'

She shook her head.

He took one of her hands between both of his. 'This is likely to go on for a while,' he said. 'Most kidnaps for ransom last anywhere between six and sixty days. It's possible that you'll have to pay up to get him released.'

She pulled her hand away. 'Can't the police do anything?'

'Interpol in Brussels have set up a JIT, Joint Investigation Team. They'll collect and collate the information from all the cases and circulate it to everyone involved. National Crime are sending two men to act as contacts in Nairobi. They'll be working through the Swedish Embassy. And Hans and Hans-Erik have been assigned to deal with it within the department.'

She nodded, aware that the Swedish police couldn't act in any official capacity abroad. 'What about the Kenyan police?'

He didn't reply for a few moments. Then he said, 'They're renowned for their violence and corruption. I was there over Christmas one year when the police announced they were going to be mounting raids to seize hidden weapons in north-western Kenya. That corner of the country emptied

114

of women and children because the police usually rape anyone they come across during that sort of raid. It causes massive problems, because many of the police have got HIV, so when a woman is raped her husband rejects her. If we get in touch and involve the Kenyan police, there's a serious risk that they'll demand part of the ransom. It would make it more dangerous and more expensive.'

Annika held her hand up. 'No Kenyan police. What about the Somalis?'

'Somalia has been without a government or any national authorities since 1991. There is something called the Somali police force, but I don't know if they actually do anything.'

She clenched her hands in her lap.

'We're going to talk to a couple of other organizations,' Halenius said, 'but you should take a look at your finances. We could reach a point where you need to pay a ransom. Have you got any money?'

The insurance money from the villa in Djursholm, she thought.

It had finally been paid out almost two years after the fire, almost six million kronor in an account with Handelsbanken, something like a million dollars. She had two hundred thousand or so in another account, which she had saved while they were in the USA.

'They won't get in touch again until tomorrow evening at the earliest. But, if it's okay, I'll come

115

over as soon as I wake up. There's a lot of preparatory work to get done.'

'Haven't you got a job to do?' she asked.

'Yep,' he said. 'And that's exactly what I'm doing.'

The hanger rattled as he pulled his coat off it. She got up from the sofa on legs of lead and stood in the hall doorway. He looked tired. His hair was thinner than she remembered.

'What sort of preparatory work?'

He scratched his head, making his brown hair stand on end. 'That depends on what you want to do, whether you do the rest yourself or need help from us.'

A flash of panic ran through her. 'Not myself,' she said.

He nodded. 'We need to set up a command centre, where we can keep our equipment and notes.'

'Would the bedroom work?'

'We need to start a log covering everything that happens. Agree on our respective roles. I'd suggest that I handle the negotiations and you deal with the logistics. Your job will be to make sure that the equipment works, that we've got food and coffee, that our mobiles are charged. Is that okay?'

So, she was moving from kidnap negotiator to coffee maker in 0.2 seconds.

'If your landline rings while I'm not here, make sure to start recording before you answer,' he said. 'If it's them, don't say you're Thomas's wife. Tell them you're the child-minder and that everyone

116

else is out. Then call me at once. You've got all my numbers in that email I sent you.'

'Do you remember what I said to you the very first time we met?' she asked. 'The very first sentence?'

Jimmy Halenius zipped up his coat and tucked his briefcase under his arm. He was concentrating on putting his gloves on as he answered. '"I thought only small-time gangsters had names ending in Y,"' he said. 'That's what you said. And "How come there are never any escaped prisoners called Stig-Björn?"'

He flashed her a quick smile, then opened the front door and disappeared.

DAY 3

FRIDAY, 25 NOVEMBER

CHAPTER 7

**Swedish
Father of Two
THOMAS
HOSTAGE
IN KENYA**

Anders Schyman polished his glasses with his shirtsleeve and examined the front page with a stern and reasonably neutral gaze.

This was one of their best covers all year. Not just because they were the only paper who had the Swedish angle but because Thomas Samuelsson was very photogenic. Blond, handsome, sporty, dignified and smiling, the sort of man all Swedish men wanted to be and all women wanted to have.

Admittedly, the headline was a slightly modified version of the truth. That Thomas had children probably wasn't his defining characteristic, and nobody was sure what country he was actually in, but the headline writers always preferred even lines, and Somalia would have made the bottom line too long. But those were just details, hardly the sort of thing the press ombudsman would penalize them for.

The articles inside the paper had been written largely by Sjölander, the veteran reporter who had previously been head of crime and editorial, US correspondent and online editor. He was one of the rare members of staff who had adapted to the new age without a huge fuss; he produced short film sequences on his mobile with the same enthusiasm as he covered world exclusives. The fillers around the main story (fact boxes, summaries, background information and other things that could be dressed up to look like news) had been written by the evening shift at the newsdesk, mainly Elin Michnik, a talented girl who was apparently related to Adam Michnik, editor-in-chief of *Gazeta Wyborcza*, the biggest paper in Poland.

If you were to believe the articles, Thomas Samuelsson was the most vital employee in the entire Swedish Cabinet Office, an international security analyst with responsibility for all of Europe's external borders. The main question was whether anyone in Sweden could actually dare to go to sleep while Thomas Samuelsson wasn't watching over them from Rosenbad.

Schyman let out a small sigh.

The articles were thin on facts, but correct, albeit occasionally so tangential that they were practically irrelevant, but it was all neatly put together, and didn't contain any actual errors, as far as he could tell, and the main article about the kidnapping was very well constructed, without being over the top.

He put the paper down and rubbed his eyes. They'd sell plenty of copies today, maybe not quite as many as they used to back in the good old days of print alone, but not far from it.

He leaned over to his computer to dig out the latest quarterly sales figures from Newspaper Statistics Ltd, the so-called NS numbers, and glanced at the tables. The *Evening Post* had a way to go to match the sales figures of *Gazeta Wyborcza*, but the gap between the two biggest-selling papers in Sweden had never been narrower. No matter how the other evening paper tried to cover up its print sales, flooding the market with free copies and complaining about the way the figures were collated, the fact remained: the gap between the two behemoths had been shrinking for years, and was now down to 6,700 copies per day. If he could just hold out a bit longer, the *Evening Post* would move ahead and become the biggest-selling newspaper in Scandinavia, and he would go down in history.

He tugged at his moustache. He might have been the first person to receive the Journalist of the Year Award twice, but that wasn't what he would be remembered for. His legacy would be as the editor who broke new ground, and shifted the ethics of the Swedish media to a new low. There was every chance he would reach that goal with Thomas Samuelsson's help. Print sales were the only thing that mattered.

He looked out across the newsroom. Patrik Nilsson was already there. He couldn't have had much sleep. Schyman had banned the editors from sleeping in the rest room, and demanded they at least go home and shower, but he doubted that Patrik obeyed him. He probably went out and dozed for a while on the back seat of his company car.

Berit Hamrin was arriving. With her raincoat and briefcase, she looked like his old English teacher at high school. She had only just survived the transition to film and audio reporting: her speaking voice sounded unengaged and her audio- and video-editing skills left a lot to be desired, but she was a walking, talking encyclopedia when it came to facts and background. Besides, she had been working at the paper since the year dot, and would be far too expensive to pay off.

Sjölander wouldn't be there for several hours yet: he was a man who guarded his beauty sleep jealously. Elin Michnik had stayed behind to update the later editions for the big cities; he had bumped into her when he arrived that morning.

He had been there thirty years now, first as head of the newsroom, later as editor-in-chief and legally accountable publisher. People could say what they liked about his contribution, but one thing was clear: he really had tried. He had done what had been expected of him without too much reflection or prevarication along the way, and on a number of levels he had succeeded.

The organization functioned like a strongly beating heart; distribution channels and sales outlets were assured, the numbers firmly in the black. He had even cultivated a group of potential heirs. The sense of emptiness that gnawed at him would probably have arisen anyway – at least, that was what he tried to tell himself. His body had got heavier, and his lack of interest in sex had coincided with his diminishing engagement in press ethics, but he couldn't be bothered to speculate as to whether there was any connection between them.

He looked at his watch. Three hours until the eleven o'clock meeting.

He had time to go round to Annika's and see how his legacy was progressing.

Annika was lying in bed, staring up at the ceiling. Her body felt heavy. She had always been blessed with the ability to sleep anywhere, at any time, but this morning she had been lying awake since 04:18. Her work mobile had rung – the morning editor at Swedish Television wondering if she fancied going to sit on the breakfast television sofa and have a bit of a cry about her kidnapped husband. (Okay, so he hadn't exactly said 'have a bit of a cry' but that was what he'd meant.) Fifteen minutes later TV4 called, and after that she'd switched off the phone.

She stretched in bed and gazed out of the window.

The sky was grey, and looked undecided.

All the media in Sweden would be calling her today, trying to get an interview, and preferably exclusive rights to her story in their particular sphere. The thought of appearing on television to cry her guts out, or turn herself inside out for a fellow journalist with a notebook and a miniature recorder, filled her with unease, which was both illogical and hypocritical. After training at the College of Journalism, three years on the local paper in Katrineholm, and thirteen years on a tabloid in Stockholm, it was actually a dereliction of duty not to agree. How many reluctant interviewees had she herself persuaded (or, to be more honest, threatened or tricked)? She saw them drift past in her memory: victims of muggings, men who'd killed their partners, politicians who'd Skyped with the wrong Russian women, doped sports stars, lazy policemen, tax-fiddling builders, a steady stream of watchful, even scared, eyes. Too many to count.

She didn't want to sit there with the children in her arms, missing their daddy. Didn't want to talk about the day before he'd left (she had been angry and uptight), didn't want to be the poor wife everyone felt sorry for. The children were still asleep. They would have to stay at home today, or some overambitious freelance photographer would find them at school and try to get them to cry on camera.

I don't have to participate in this media circus, she thought. She could already hear the whispering behind her back: 'Look, it's her, the woman whose husband has been kidnapped in Somalia, and that must be their children, poor little things – don't they look pale?' And then the whisperers would move on, feeling a bit happier because whatever happened to them that day wouldn't be as bad as that.

Then she felt ashamed of herself – so self-centred. To atone, she screwed her eyes shut and tried to think of Africa and Liboi, to conjure up an image of Thomas at that moment, where he was, what state he was in, but she couldn't. In her memory she roamed across the yellow satellite picture from Google Maps, but she had no frame of reference, nothing to relate to. She had no idea.

A moment later the doorbell rang and she jerked bolt upright. Confused, she stumbled out with her dressing-gown more or less fastened round her, made her way into the hall and put her ear to the door. It might be some zealous editor who'd come up with the idea of paying her a visit. That was what she would have done.

It was Halenius. He stepped inside, rather bleary-eyed and unkempt. She pulled the dressing-gown tighter, feeling naked and embarrassed. She also needed to go to the toilet. The under-secretary of state glanced at her, shrugged off his coat, said, 'Nice pyjamas', then disappeared into the unaired bedroom with his briefcase. She heard him cough as he poked about in there. The whole situation felt bizarre.

She went for a pee and put some water on to boil, then took two mugs of instant coffee in to Halenius, one for each of them. He had set up his computer and was staring intently at the screen.

'Where are the children?' he asked, pushing it aside.

'Asleep.'

He reached for his notes. 'The man who called last night used your landline. Did Thomas give him the number, or could he have got hold of it in some other way?'

She gave him his coffee, then felt unsure as to what to do. There were two chairs in the room. The under-secretary of state was sitting on one, and the other was hidden under yesterday's clothes. Instead of moving them, she went to the bed and got back in, spilling some coffee on the duvet.

'His business card,' she said, trying to rub away the stain. 'He has a load in his wallet, with his mobile number and the landline. We argued about it, because our home number is unlisted and I didn't think he should put it on his cards. I thought people who wanted to get hold of him about work could call him on his office number or mobile.'

'Your mobile number wasn't on the card?'

'On his business card? Why on earth would it be?'

'So we can assume that the kidnappers will go on using your landline. We can also be fairly confident that we're negotiating with the right people.' He reached for his computer again.

'The right people?'

He turned to her, and she pulled the duvet up to her chin.

'It's not unusual for people who aren't involved to pretend to be kidnappers. Some fairly big ransom payments have even been paid to the wrong people. But we've got witnesses saying that Thomas was taken hostage, we've got the official video confirming the fact, and they've got his unlisted home phone number.' He went back to his computer and tapped at it.

Annika drank her coffee, strong and bitter. 'What happens today?' she asked.

'Quite a lot,' he said, without taking his eyes from the screen. 'I spoke to Superintendent Q at National Crime on the way here. The Joint Investigation Team at Interpol is up and running, and the two officers from National Crime will be joining them today. Hans and Hans-Erik are co-ordinating things in the department, and soon there'll be so many cooks involved in this particular soup that they'll be tripping over each other.'

He turned to her again. 'You ought to see how much money you can get hold of. How much can you borrow? Does either Doris or your mother have any savings?'

She put her mug on the bedside table.

'Now that the story's out in the media, there's no reason to keep quiet about the kidnapping,'

Halenius went on. 'You'll have to decide if you want to join in with the mass media. If you do agree to be interviewed, we'll have to go through what you can and can't say. You mustn't breathe a word about me being here, for instance. Or let on that we're in touch with the kidnappers.'

She raised a hand. 'I don't think that's going to happen. What else?'

'There's a chance that we might get another call this evening, but it's far from certain. You need to think about what to do with the children, particularly in the short term.'

'How do you mean?'

'Are they going to school? Is there anyone who could look after them if we have to go anywhere?'

She stiffened. 'Like where?'

'We need to plan for the eventuality that the ransom will have to be paid, and the perpetrators are hardly likely to fly up to Stockholm to collect it.'

In her mind's eye she saw the brownish-yellow satellite image of Liboi. The whole situation felt ridiculous. 'So, you're assuming that we just give these bastards a load of money?' she said. 'Isn't there any other solution?'

'The video's already online, so the Brits and Americans are probably working on other solutions.'

Annika blinked.

'The American Army has a massive base not all that far from Liboi,' Halenius said. 'Obviously it isn't on any maps, but they've got more than five thousand men on the border with southern Somalia. The British are there as well. I'm trying to find their contact details, but I can't for the life of me remember where I put them.'

She couldn't help smiling.

He knew where the Americans had their secret military bases, but he couldn't find their phone number in his own computer.

She reached for the mug of coffee and got out of bed. Her dressing-gown slid open, revealing her thighs, but Halenius didn't notice. 'Nice pyjamas,' he had said. Yes, they were nice: thick, cream-coloured silk, she'd bought them as a birthday present to herself in the Pentagon City shopping centre. Thomas had got her a chrome, fifties-style toaster. It needed a 110-volt power supply, so she'd had to leave it behind when they moved back to Europe.

What stupid things we remember, she thought, as she headed towards the bathroom for a shower. She stopped in the living room and turned back towards the bedroom or, rather, Kidnap Control.

'What about your children?' she said. He had twins, didn't he? A boy and a girl, the same age as Ellen.

He didn't look up from the screen. 'My partner will look after them,' he said.

The words scorched her face. His partner. He had a partner. Of course he had a partner. 'I thought you were divorced?' she heard herself say.

'New girlfriend,' he said. 'Here it is. I'll give them a call straight away.'

She drifted towards the bathroom, her feet barely touching the floor.

The children woke up while she was in the shower. Kalle was standing in the hallway looking thunderous when she came out with a towel wrapped round her head. 'Why is he still here?' he said quietly.

Through the wall she could hear Halenius talking loudly and quickly in English. Annika crouched beside Kalle and gave him a hug. 'Jimmy's talking to some people who might be able to help us free Daddy,' she said. 'What do you want for breakfast?'

'Not scrambled eggs,' Kalle said.

'Okay,' Annika said, standing up. 'You can have them boiled. Or Greek yoghurt with walnuts.'

'Have we got any raspberries?'

She'd given the last of them to Halenius with his cake the previous evening. 'You can have jam,' she said.

Ellen was sitting in bed, playing with her stuffed toys. She had eighteen, and they all lived on her bed, although only Poppy was allowed to lie on the pillow with her. Annika got into bed beside her, tickled her tummy, and they agreed it was time for breakfast. She went into the kitchen to get it ready.

The phone rang in the bedroom: the landline, their home number.

Annika froze mid-stride. They had been expecting the kidnappers to call that evening, if at all. She strained her ears to hear what Halenius was saying, and thought she could hear him muttering in Swedish. Then he hung up.

'You'll have to tell Anne Snapphane to stop calling the landline,' Halenius said, then went into the bathroom. She could hear him peeing behind the thin wooden door as she got out the yoghurt.

'Put the dishes in the sink when you've finished,' she told the children, then went into the living room with her work mobile.

She had had it switched off since TV4 had called, and once the phone picked up a signal thirty-seven new text messages flooded in. She clicked to mark all as read, then called Anne.

'Bloody hell, Annika!' Anne said. 'This is terrible. Absolutely ghastly! And who was that man who answered your phone?'

Halenius came out of the bathroom and passed her on his way to the bedroom.

'Someone from Telia, here to fix the phone,' she said, watching him as he passed. 'Have you seen the papers?'

'The papers? So old-fashioned!' Anne said. 'You're out of touch.'

Their ongoing argument about the internet revolution and social media was almost as old as the papers themselves. Annika smiled. 'What are the soothsayers on the blogs saying?'

'Well, do you know what they usually do to people they kidnap down there? It's outrageous!'

Annika got up from the sofa and went over to the window. The thermometer outside said it was minus fifteen. 'I'm not sure I really want to know. I only care about my own husband right now. Do any of the bloggers know where he is?'

'Very funny. The Kenyan government's Facebook page has got more than fifty-one thousand likes. We're everywhere.'

'I feel much safer knowing that,' Annika said, and realized she sounded like an advert for nappies.

'Okay, I've been thinking,' Anne said. 'It's in your name, isn't it?'

Kalle came into the living room with yoghurt on his top lip. 'I've finished,' he said.

'What?' Annika said. 'What's in my name? Go and wash, Kalle, brush your teeth, then put some clothes on.'

'The flat, because you're not actually married, are you? The divorce went through, but you never remarried, did you?'

'Aren't we going to school today?' Kalle said.

'Housing associations are completely unscrupulous,' Anne said. 'If they get a chance to chuck you out, they'll do it, then sell the contract to the highest bidder. Everyone knows that's how it works.'

Anne had just bought a contract on the black

market, so she probably knew what she was talking about.

'You can have the day off,' Annika told Kalle. 'And maybe you could go and stay with someone this weekend, one of your grandmothers.'

Ellen, who had yoghurt on her fingers, grasped one of Annika's legs. 'I want to stay with you, Mummy.'

'Annika! Do you know what else occurred to me? You're not married so everything will go to his brother and mother. Have you thought about that? It could end up like Stieg Larsson all over again if he hasn't got a will. Has he got one?'

'Ellen, you've got yoghurt all over my dressing-gown. Go and wash, do your teeth, then get dressed. Quick march!' She shepherded her out into the hall.

'Do you know if he's got a solicitor? Or a safe-deposit box in a bank? You'll have to go through his computer and personal papers.'

The doorbell rang.

Halenius came out into the living room and pointed towards the hall. 'Anders Schyman,' he said. 'I'll get it.'

'The children would inherit everything,' Annika said into her mobile. 'I've got to go – there's someone at the door.'

'Ah, of course. Yes, Stieg didn't have any children.'

'And, Anne,' Annika said, 'could you call me

on my work mobile from now on? There's something wrong with the landline. Got to run.'

Schyman wasn't alone: Berit Hamrin had come with him.

Annika hurried into the bedroom, shut the door and threw on the previous day's clothes. Oddly, it seemed far more reasonable for the under-secretary of state at the Ministry of Justice to see her half naked than her boss.

The editor-in-chief had brought a bundle of newspapers with him: their own, the main competition, the two morning papers and a couple of the free-sheets. He dropped them all on to the coffee-table; they landed with a dusty thud. The *Evening Post* was on top, with Thomas smiling at her from the front page, a tie knotted tightly round his neck.

It was his official photograph from the department. He always said he thought it made him look pushy.

'There's something I want to talk to you about,' Schyman said to Annika. 'There's no hurry. You don't have to give me an answer until tomorrow.'

Annika picked up the paper. Swedish father of two, Thomas, hostage in Kenya.

The floor started to sway and she let go of the paper as if it were burning her.

Berit came over and gave her a hug. She'd never done that before. She knew Annika wasn't much of a hugger. 'It'll be all right,' she whispered. 'You just need to get through it.'

Annika nodded. 'Do you want coffee?' she asked.

'Please,' Schyman said.

'Not for me,' Berit said. 'I was thinking of asking if Ellen and Kalle would like to go to Kronoberg Park with me.'

The children roared with delight, and hurried to get dressed.

Annika went into the kitchen and filled the kettle with trembling hands. She could hear the men talking but not what they were saying. Berit was helping Ellen with her shoes. 'Would you like to come?' Berit asked.

Annika stood in the kitchen doorway. 'I don't dare leave them alone here,' she said, trying to smile in the direction of the living room. 'I want to keep an eye on what they're doing.'

'We'll be back in an hour or so,' Berit said. 'Are those your sledges out in the stairwell?'

'The blue one's mine!' Ellen yelled.

They disappeared in a cacophony of heavy shoes and bright voices.

Over the noise of the kettle she could hear Schyman and Halenius talking in relaxed but clear voices, the sort powerful men use when they want to show that they're at ease but still focused.

'. . . obviously a great deal of interest from the rest of the media,' Schyman was saying, in a tone of cheery acceptance.

She opened the fridge and stared into its cool interior without seeing anything.

'. . . and in Nigeria the heads of the foreign oil

companies are called "white gold", or just "ATMs", cash machines,' Halenius said, sounding confident and well-informed.

She got out cream, milk and liver pâté, then put back the pâté and the milk.

'. . . of course we want to know what we can expect, which scenarios are most likely,' Schyman said eagerly.

She plugged in the electric whisk and whipped the cream, even though there was still some left from the previous evening. She closed her eyes and kept them tightly shut for so long that the cream almost turned into butter. There were no raspberries left, but she heated some jam and put it into a bowl. She made instant coffee in three mugs, then got out a tray and loaded it with the mugs, three side-plates, coffee spoons, milk, sugar, jam, cream, a cake-slice, three forks, and the rapidly drying-out sticky chocolate cake. There was only just room for the cake on the tray: it balanced dangerously close to the edge. She stopped for a moment in the hall.

'What are the odds?' Schyman said, through the wall.

'The prognosis is good. Nine out of every ten kidnap victims survive, although there's some evidence that the number of dead is rising.'

So one in ten doesn't make it, Annika thought.

'And they get home in reasonable condition?'

Reasonable condition?

'Another twenty per cent of victims suffer severe

physical injury . . .' Halenius fell silent as she walked in. 'Ah,' he said. 'That cake is lethal.'

She put the tray on the coffee-table, then sat at the far end of the sofa without unloading it. 'Help yourselves,' she said.

Halenius and Schyman did just that. The thought of eating anything sweet made her feel sick, but she picked up the dark blue coffee mug with the words 'The White House' embossed in gold. It wasn't from the White House but a souvenir stand outside, about as genuine as a Chinese Volvo.

'We were talking about what usually happens in kidnap situations,' Halenius said, filling his mouth with cream and jam. 'Do you want to hear?'

As if words could make any difference. As if the situation could be made any worse by the dangers being spelled out. She huddled in the corner of the sofa.

'Abuse is fairly usual,' Halenius said, without looking at Annika. 'Although, of course, we have no idea what will happen in this specific case.'

'What scenarios are you working on?' Schyman asked.

The doorbell rang again. She got quickly to her feet. 'That could be our colleagues from the rest of the media,' she said.

At first she didn't recognize the men in the stairwell. They were standing silent and grey in their raincoats, staring at her.

She closed the door without saying anything, went back into the living room and felt her brain steaming. 'What is this?' she said. 'Have I become some sort of outpost of Rosenbad?'

Halenius got to his feet, gazing at her quizzically.

'Hasse and Hasse are standing outside,' Annika said, gesturing towards the front door. 'But enough's enough. Tell them to leave.'

'They might want—'

'Tell them to send an email,' she said, and went into the bathroom.

She heard Halenius go out into the stairwell and have a short conversation with the two men called Hans. Then he came back in, alone, shut the door and returned to the living room. 'Colleagues from the department,' he said apologetically to Schyman.

The legs of an armchair scraped the wooden floor.

'Do you think you could give an overview of an incident like this?' the editor-in-chief said.

'That depends on what sort of crime it is. Commercial kidnappings are often easier to resolve. Politically motivated ones are considerably more complicated, and often more violent.'

'Daniel Pearl,' Schyman said.

Annika locked the bathroom door.

She had written an article about the Pearl case during her time in the USA. Daniel Pearl had been a journalist, head of the *Wall Street Journal*'s office in South East Asia when he was kidnapped by al-Qaeda in January 2002. Nine days later he was beheaded. The video had still been on the internet several years later – maybe even now –

three minutes and thirty-six seconds of utterly revolting propaganda. She had forced herself to watch it. Daniel Pearl addressed the camera, naked from the waist up, with images of dead Muslims surrounding his face. After one minute and fifty-five seconds a man came into shot and cut Pearl's throat. The last minute of the video consisted of a list of political demands scrolling across the screen over the image of the journalist's severed head. Someone was holding it up by the hair.

'Female kidnap victims are often raped,' she heard Halenius say quietly, in the living room. 'Men too, for that matter. In Mexico ears or fingers are amputated and sent to the victim's family. In the former Soviet Union it's teeth.'

'And in East Africa?' Schyman asked, almost in a whisper.

She straightened and pricked her ears.

Halenius cleared his throat. 'I don't have any exact statistics, but mortality rates are high. The kidnappers have plenty of weapons. It's striking how many hostages end up getting shot. And Somalia is a country where amputations form part of the legal system. It's traditional that all the external parts of young girls' genitals are cut off . . .'

She turned on the cold tap in the basin and let the water run over her wrists. She felt like crying, but was too angry. There had to be limits. She didn't want to hear about mutilated little girls. She needed help, but not at any cost. The government might

141

want to keep its hands clean, but she refused to accept responsibility for all the violence in the world. She wasn't going to surrender her home and her bedroom to a load of strange men.

She turned the tap off, dried her hands, unlocked the door and went out.

'There seem to be several different motivations behind this kidnap, financial as well as political,' Schyman said, as she wandered over to her corner of the sofa.

Halenius pulled his legs out of the way to let her pass. 'Unless there's a combination of motives that aren't necessarily contradictory. When you consider the political situation in East Africa . . .'

Annika sank into the cushions. She hoped the children weren't too cold up in Kronoberg Park. She had got frostbite in her left foot one winter's day at her grandmother's cottage at Lyckebo, on the Harpsund estate, which the old woman had been allowed to rent because of the years she had spent as housekeeper at the prime minister's country residence. To this day Annika had problems with the toes of her left foot, which stiffened and turned bluish-white when there was frost. The first time Thomas had seen them he had been horrified and wanted to call for an ambulance. He'd never been very good at dealing with bodily matters. But no doubt he wasn't freezing at the moment. It was probably very hot in Somalia, she thought, recalling the parched yellow soil in the satellite picture of Liboi.

'. . . geographic and cultural circumstances,' Halenius was saying.

'And the kidnappers?' Schyman said. 'What sort of people might they be?'

'These groups are strikingly similar all over the world,' the under-secretary of state said. 'Often it's a group of eight to ten people under the leadership of one strong commander. Commercial kidnappers regard themselves as employees. Just like everyone else, they go to work and take holidays and spend their free time with their families. Often they're childhood friends, or studied together, or belong to the same political or religious groups. They usually start as small-time criminals, raiding shops and banks, things like that.'

She looked at Halenius, sitting on her sofa, so relaxed and comfortable, with the top button of his shirt undone, his hair sticking out, his sleeves rolled up. For Jimmy Halenius this was just another working day, perhaps a bit more exciting than usual because he had the chance to use what he knew – and, my goodness, how much he knew!

'It's a bit different with religious or political kidnappings,' he was saying. 'Their leader is often a fairly well-educated man who saw the political light while he was at university. He may have embarked on this in a noble attempt to change the world, but once he gets a taste for the ransom money, the ideological fervour tends to diminish.'

'Is that what we're dealing with here?' Schyman asked.

Halenius finished his coffee. 'I think so,' he said. 'The kidnapper who called spoke clear East African English, the sort you hear at the universities in Nairobi.'

'How do you know that?' Annika said, aware that her eyes had narrowed to slits.

'My ex-wife studied there,' he said. 'The universities in South Africa weren't open to people like her during apartheid.'

An African wife. She'd had no idea. She said something about 'How?' and 'Why?'

'The Swedish Social Democratic Youth Movement helped arrange an ANC Youth League congress in Nairobi in 1989,' he said. 'The president of Kenya at the time, Daniel arap Moi, had just released all political prisoners and was in the middle of some sort of charm offensive. That was where we met. She was born and raised in Soweto.'

He turned to the editor-in-chief. 'That's one of the reasons I was asked to handle this case. I'm not a native, of course, but of everyone who could have done it, I'm most familiar with the language and dialect.'

'So you know Nairobi?' Schyman asked.

'We got married there. She moved to Södermalm once she'd graduated.'

'But you're divorced now?'

'She works for the South African government,' Halenius said. 'She actually has much the same job as me, but in the Ministry of Trade.'

'What's her name?' Annika asked.

'Angela Sisulu.'

Angela Sisulu. It sounded like a song.

'Any relation to Walter Sisulu?' Schyman asked.

'Distant.'

Annika was breathing through her mouth. They knew everything, were aware of everything, and she knew nothing. 'Who's Walter Sisulu?' she asked.

'ANC activist,' Halenius said. 'Nelson Mandela's right-hand man, you could say. He was convicted along with Mandela in the Rivonia trial in 1964, and was with him throughout his time on Robben Island. He was elected deputy president of the ANC at their first legal congress in 1991. He died in 2003.'

Schyman nodded, striking right at the heart of her insecurity. She didn't know the names of all the old ANC leaders off by heart. She hadn't graduated in Nairobi or grown up in Soweto. She had only just made it through journalism college, and had grown up in Tattarbacken in Hälleforsnäs. They were sitting in her living room, talking hypothetically and in general terms about hostage-taking and kidnapping, but this was happening for real, it *had* happened, and her family had been hit by it, and there was nothing she could do.

'What was it you wanted to talk to me about?' she asked Schyman.

'I've informed the chairman of the board about your situation and have been given the go-ahead to help you. I understand that it's difficult to avoid the question of a ransom, so the newspaper would like to propose an agreement that would give you the chance to pay the ransom and bring Thomas home.'

She opened her mouth, but couldn't find any words. Stunned, she shut it again. The newspaper was offering to pay? 'How much?' she managed to say.

'As much as it takes,' Schyman replied simply.

'They want forty million dollars,' Annika said, and was rewarded with a glare from Halenius. She bit her lip. She wasn't supposed to reveal any details of the negotiations.

Schyman went rather pale.

'If we agree on a figure for the ransom, it will be considerably lower than that,' the under-secretary of state said. 'But I must ask you not to divulge that information anywhere else.'

Schyman nodded again.

'And what do I have to do in return?' Annika asked.

'The *Evening Post* gets exclusive rights to the story,' Schyman said. 'Either you write about it and do the filming yourself, or you pick a reporter to follow you the whole way through. Behind the scenes, through all the negotiations, possibly to Africa if that turns out to be necessary. If anything happens that may threaten the lives or wellbeing of other people, obviously we can edit that out, but otherwise the job would be a documentary account of the entire sequence of events. Tears, loss, pain, relief and joy.'

She leaned back in the sofa. Of course! She should have realized at once. Maybe it was because she hadn't eaten anything, but she suddenly noticed how nauseous she was feeling. 'Do you want me to blog as well?' she asked. 'I could be "The Hostage's Wife". A photographic blog, perhaps?' She stood up, spilling coffee over the table. 'I could take pictures of the children every day, show how they're wasting away because they miss their dad so much. I could describe how much I miss getting fucked at night, because sex sells, doesn't it? How about a fashion blog with the latest trends in widow's weeds? Fashion blogs are the most popular ones, aren't they?'

She went out into the hall, tripping over Kalle's video game on the way, blinded by tears.

'Annika!'

She aimed for the bathroom door, managed to get it open, stumbled over the threshold and locked herself in. She stood still in the pitch black- ness, her heartbeat seeming to fill the whole room.

'Annika?' Schyman said, knocking on the door.

'Get out of here,' she said.

'Think about it,' the editor-in-chief said. 'It's an offer, that's all. You don't have to accept it.'

She didn't answer.

CHAPTER 8

The Dane was wheezing and rattling, whistling and gurgling with every breath. His chest was rising and falling with fluttering jerks. Even though he was lying right next to me, I couldn't make out his features. It was darker there than in the last hut. There were no windows or other openings: the only light came from cracks and gaps between the panels that made up the walls. The door looked like a blinding rectangle against the light outside, if it could be called a door: a sheet of tin held in place by some sort of bar and a few bricks.

I had managed to find a position where I wasn't lying on my hands, without having my face pressed into the bare floor. My head was resting on a stone I had found. My weight was resting on my right shoulder and left knee, in a sort of flattened recovery position, just with my wrists and ankles tied.

I hadn't had to relieve myself again, which was some comfort, but it probably wasn't a good thing: seeing as the main reason was that I hadn't been given anything to eat or drink. My head felt light and I think I was drifting in and out of consciousness.

The Spaniard and Romanian weren't moving. Perhaps they were asleep.

The heat inside the tin shack was stifling. My mouth tasted of sand.

None of us had mentioned the Frenchman.

I thought about Catherine, who was in the other hut with the German woman. She had no one to comfort her now. She was completely alone – but perhaps she always had been. What sort of support was I?

Tears stung my eyes, not only because of the sand and dust.

An image of Annika was hovering in front of me in the darkness, smiling at me like she does when she's really looking at me, so close and vulnerable, that hesitant smile of hers, as if she's unsure she has the right to be happy, or even to exist. You wouldn't think it, but she's so fragile, and I've been so heartless. I've seen the way I've hurt her and it's made me cross and irritable. She makes me feel as if I've been found out. Unmasked. I can be standing right in front of her, and she can see into eternity through me. She has a remarkable ability to see through people, to understand their weaknesses, and she refuses to adapt. That can be a nuisance, embarrassing, even. I'm not saying that was why I went with other women – that would be shifting the blame on to her, and that's not what I mean . . . but those women (there weren't very many, not that that's any excuse), what did they give me? Validation, I suppose. A diversion. Adrenalin, the joy of the chase, and a bitter aftertaste. They may have seen me for a short while, but they never really *saw* me.

What's wrong with me?

Why do I keep hurting the person I love most?

Berit and the children came back with a clatter of noise and snow-caked boots. Annika had made baked cod with prawns, cream, dill and white wine, and had boiled some rice. It wasn't Kalle's favourite, but he'd eat it if he was allowed to pick out the prawns.

Halenius ate in the bedroom (Kidnap Control), but Berit sat down with them at the kitchen table. The children chattered about the snow and their sledges and how funny it was not being at school on a normal Friday. At the end of the meal, when they were waiting for Ellen to finish, Kalle fell silent and withdrew into himself, the way he sometimes did.

'What's up, sweetheart?' Annika asked.

'I'm thinking about Daddy,' he said.

She wrapped her arms round him, her big boy, and rocked him until Ellen had put her plate on the draining board and he wriggled free to go into their room and watch a film, an unbelievable luxury for a Friday afternoon.

'Have you had a chance to look at the papers?'

Berit asked, rinsing the gratin dish with hot water.

'Don't know if I want to,' Annika said.

'I wrote a piece about the mother who was found outside the nursery school in Axelsberg – I got hold of a talkative detective last night.'

'Have they picked up the father yet?'

'Looks like he's got an alibi. He works for a haulage company that uses time stamps. He was on a job up to Upplands-Väsby all morning.'

'Or so he says,' Annika said.

'His mobile supports his version of events.'

Annika threw her arms out, and water from the dishcloth sprayed across the kitchen window. 'Yeah, but how difficult is it to hide your mobile in someone else's car? Or make sure it doesn't send signals to a base station while you go off and kill your ex?'

Berit filled the kettle. 'Now we're talking conspiracy theories.'

'Not at all,' Annika said. 'Thieves and murderers are usually fairly fucked up, but if you were going to go off and kill someone, wouldn't you switch your mobile off while you were doing it?'

Berit stopped, holding a spoonful of instant coffee in mid-air. 'You've got a point there,' she said.

Annika put *Finding Nemo* on the children's television (she had an almost new, but bulky and old-fashioned set that Thomas hated; he'd bought a flatscreen model as soon as they'd got back from

151

the US, and the old one had ended up in the children's room), then went back out into the kitchen.

'Schyman had a proposal for me,' she said,
sinking down at the kitchen table and reaching for
her coffee. 'The paper will pay the ransom if I
agree to give them exclusive rights to the whole
story.'

Berit nodded. 'I know. He asked me to try to
persuade you to agree to it. Do you want to?'

Annika looked around the kitchen, her domain
during the kidnap crisis. She was in charge of
logistics, tasked with making sure they had food
and water, and keeping the mobiles charged. 'He
said it as if it was to my advantage. As if I ought
to want to, as if I should somehow enjoy exploiting
my own tragedy.'

'Maybe he's trying to help you.'

'I'm not going to do it. No way.'

'If you want, I could do the writing.'

She smiled at Berit. 'That would be one reason
to agree to it. Thanks, but no thanks.'

Halenius's mobile was ringing on the other side
of the wall. He answered. It sounded as if he was
speaking English, but she couldn't make out the
words. Annika got up and put her almost untouched
mug on the draining board. 'Let's go and sit in
the living room – these chairs make my arse go
numb.'

Berit stood up on slightly stiff legs. 'I see what
you mean. You've never thought of replacing
them?'

'They came from Thomas's parents.'

'Ah.'

Halenius's voice was fainter in the living room, but Annika could still hear English.

She curled up on the sofa and reached for the *Evening Post* from the pile of newspapers. She leafed quickly through the articles about Thomas, six pages plus the centrefold, including pictures of her and the children. Thank you very much. 'Nice work,' she said tartly, 'considering there was hardly a single fact to go on.'

There were articles about the conference in Nairobi, about Nairobi as a city, about the Kenyatta conference centre, about Frontex, about Thomas, about Thomas's really, really, *really* important job, about the Swedish EU commissioner who was responsible for Frontex, about the video that had been posted online from a server in Mogadishu, about Mogadishu as a city, about Somalia, about the civil war in Somalia, and an overview of other kidnap videos. The one featuring Daniel Pearl wasn't mentioned.

'Elin Michnik is a real star,' Berit said. 'All the boys in the newsroom have got it into their heads that she's related to Adam Michnik of the *Gazeta Wyborcza*, but she isn't.'

Annika had no idea what the *Gazeta Wyborcza* was and had no intention of finding out. 'She seems to have forgotten about Daniel Pearl,' she said, turning the page.

The article about the murdered mother behind the nursery school was covered in detail on page fifteen, and on page sixteen Berit had written an overview of the three other women who had been murdered outdoors in Stockholm during the autumn.

'Do you believe the theory about a serial killer?' Annika asked, holding up the page with the headline 'THREE DEAD WOMEN, THREE STABS IN THE BACK'.

Berit had taken her coffee with her into the living room and sipped it. 'Not remotely,' she said. 'And the headline isn't accurate. One of the women, the young girl found at the beach in Arninge, was stabbed forty-five times. From the back, the front, the sides, even from below. She had knife-wounds to her genitals.'

Halenius had stopped talking inside Kidnap Control (the bedroom). In the children's room Nemo had been caught in the dentist's aquarium in Sydney.

Annika scanned the article about the young immigrant woman.

'Her fiancé is still in custody,' Berit said. 'If he's convicted, he'll be deported. He arrived here as a refugee when he was fifteen, but was never granted residency. When he was due to be deported he ran away from the camp and went into hiding. He stayed under the radar for four years, until his engagement to his cousin was announced about a year ago.'

The landline rang, and Annika stiffened from her toes to the roots of her hair. Her hearing intensified until she could hear the echo of the kitchen tap dripping, Halenius tapping at his computer and switching on all the recording equipment. Then he answered: 'Hello?' Annika couldn't make out what he was saying, not even what language he was speaking; she didn't hear him hang up. She just saw him come out into the living room with his hair all over the place.

'Sophia Grenborg wants to talk to you,' he said. 'I told her you'd call her back.' He put a note with a phone number on her lap and went back to Kidnap Control (would she ever be able to sleep in there again?).

Her pulse slowed, but not by much. After the kidnappers, Sophia Grenborg was the last person on the planet she wanted to talk to.

She pulled out her work mobile, fourteen missed calls, and dialled the number before she had time to change her mind.

'Annika?' Thomas's former mistress said, in a cracked voice.

'What do you want?' Annika said, adrenalin surging through her head.

Sophia Grenborg sobbed down the line. 'I'm so sorry,' she managed to splutter.

Bitch! How dare she?

'Sorry to disturb you, but I had to call and find out what's happening, or what has happened. Is it true? Has he been kidnapped? Is he being held hostage? Do you know where he is?'

'Yes, it's true. No, we don't know where he is.' She got up from the sofa, too restless to remain seated. 'Did you want anything else?'

Sophia Grenborg blew her nose and took a deep breath. 'I know you're angry with me, but you won.'

Annika lost her train of thought. An insult was poised on the tip of her tongue, but she swallowed it in surprise.

'He chose you,' Sophia said. 'You and the children. I think about him every day, but I don't imagine he ever thinks about me. I don't even have the right to feel sad.' And then she cried some more.

Annika screwed up her eyes. Berit was watching her thoughtfully. She sat down again. 'Of course you've the right to feel sad,' she said.

'Is anyone helping you? What are they saying at Thomas's work? Have they heard anything? Have you heard anything?'

Annika glanced towards the bedroom. 'We haven't heard anything,' she lied, feeling strangely guilty.

There was silence on the line. Sophia Grenborg had stopped crying. 'Sorry I called,' she said. 'I didn't mean to intrude.'

'That's okay,' Annika said, and meant it.

'How are the children? Are they coping? Are they horribly upset?'

'They're watching a film,' Annika said. '*Finding Nemo.*'

'Okay,' Sophia Grenborg said.

More silence. Annika waited. Sophia cleared her throat. 'If there's anything I can do,' she said, 'if there's anything at all I can help with, something practical . . .'

How about mortgaging your massive house in Östermalm to pay the ransom? Annika thought.

'Don't call the landline again,' Annika said. 'I want to keep it clear in case Thomas rings.'

'Of course,' Sophia Grenborg whispered. 'Sorry. Say hello to the children.'

Like hell.

Annika clicked to end the call.

'I wouldn't like to fall out with you,' Berit said.

'As long as you don't take my husband away from me, I'm gentle as a lamb,' Annika responded.

'Hmm,' Berit said. 'Maybe I could help you with the kids. Take them out to the country over the weekend, so you get a bit of space to deal with this.'

Berit lived at a stables outside Norrtälje, although she had no horses apart from the neighbour's, just a Labrador bitch called Soraya. Kalle and Ellen had been out there plenty of times. Annika and the children had even lived in the guest cottage when their villa in Djursholm had burned down.

Annika felt her shoulders relax.

And in the children's room Nemo had just been reunited with his father in the sea off Sydney.

The mosquitoes on Gällnö were large and noisy. They sounded like nasty little jets when they flew around my bedroom on summer nights while I was a boy. *Biiisszzz, biiisszzz, biiisszzz,* they used to go, but that wasn't the problem. It was when they went quiet that you had to turn the light on and go on a bug hunt, and I was good at bug hunts, smashing insects with blood-filled stomachs, making centimetre-wide stains on the pink wallpaper. Mum used to moan that I was spoiling the wall, and of course she was right. Over time the wallpaper around my bed took on more and more of a rust colour.

There were many more mosquitoes in the tin shack than in the last hut; they were much smaller than the ones out on Gällnö, and completely silent. They swirled like specks of dust in the darkness and only made a noise if they happened to fly right into my ear, which had happened several times. When they bit I didn't feel it. Not until afterwards, when the bites would swell up to the size of half a tennis ball. They itched terribly, and I tried to rub them on the bare floor where I could get at them, but it didn't help.

I was extremely hot and sweaty, the sort of heat that comes from within and filters out through your pores as steam.

'Is there malaria here?' the Romanian asked. 'Is this a malarial region?'

I still didn't know his name, but I couldn't ask it now: then he'd know I'd never learned it or, worse, forgotten it.

'Yes,' the Spaniard said, 'but the ones in here aren't malaria mosquitoes. They're not active in daylight, only at dusk, at night and around dawn. But there is malaria here. Not much, perhaps, it's a bit too dry, but it's hot enough. There's definitely malaria.'

We were feeling brighter. We had been given some food, *ugali*, and water, and some sort of vegetable, a bit like spinach, boiled and salty. It was good, although the water wasn't clean. The Dane was the only one who didn't want any food. He drank a bit of water, then lay still, breathing very shallowly. He wasn't rattling as much, which was a relief.

One by one we had been helped up and allowed to empty our bowels and bladders in a bucket in the corner, it stung as I pissed and smelt strong. None of the others looked towards the bucket when anyone else was there: it was a sort of tacit understanding.

'It's a parasite, isn't it?' the Romanian said. 'Malaria's a blood parasite?'

'Plasmodium,' the Spaniard confirmed. 'The illness is an advanced form of interaction between mosquitoes and human beings, spread by the mosquitoes' saliva, and is found throughout almost all of sub-Saharan Africa.'

'How long does it take before you get ill?' I asked, thinking of the steam inside my body.

'Half an hour after you get bitten the parasite has established itself in your liver. But it takes at least six days before the symptoms start to show, and sometimes considerably longer, even up to a couple of years . . .'

'*Hakuna majadiliano,*' a guard outside shouted. I thought it sounded like the tall one.

None of us knew what he meant and Catherine wasn't there to translate. It sounded almost like *hakuna matata* – wasn't that a Disney song? The children had the film on DVD. *The Lion King*, maybe?

Silence fell inside the shack. Even the Dane's breathing was inaudible. Everyone lay still in the darkness.

Then there was a clatter behind the door and the sheet of tin was removed. Light shone in like a square metre of laser beam. It blinded me, but I could hear several guards come into the shack. '*Moja ni hapa,*' they said. '*Nyakua naye kwa miguu.*' I felt the draught as they grabbed the Romanian. They picked him up by his legs and shoulders and dragged him towards the doorway. He was whimpering, maybe because it hurt as they hauled him out but possibly from fear.

We hadn't spoken about the Frenchman. Not at all. Not a single word.

It was as if it had never happened.

And now the Romanian was gone, and I still didn't know his name.

They put the tin door back in place. The darkness returned, deeper and heavier than before.

A shiver ran through me.

Anders Schyman scratched his beard. They mustn't lose the initiative now. They had two really big stories on the go, and they had to keep hold of both – the kidnapping and the potential serial killer in the suburbs of Stockholm. Patrik had called a few of his old contacts and found a police inspector who had said that there were similarities between the three murdered women: they were women, they had been stabbed to death outside, and they'd lived in the greater Stockholm region. The conversation with the inspector had been recorded and saved on the newspaper's secure server. Schyman had listened to it and couldn't work out if the policeman was being sarcastic, or if he was so screwed up that he was actually serious. Either way, it gave them a mandate to run the serial-killer angle with more weight in tomorrow's paper, and if nothing spectacular happened with the kidnap story, the hypothetical serial killer was a potential alternative lead.

The editor-in-chief slurped his coffee. He usually drank it until four o'clock in the afternoon, then had to stop or switch to decaffeinated: otherwise he couldn't sleep.

The follow-up articles on the kidnapping were

proving to be a problem. The fact was that they had blown all their ammunition on that day's paper. There really wasn't much else they could do but rehash the same things once more in a slightly different guise, which was neither unusual nor especially difficult, but they needed some sort of basis for it, some sort of news.

Obviously he couldn't refer to his long conversation with Halenius: that was strictly off the record. It was common for journalists to know far more than they wrote or broadcast: politicians' wives who had been found guilty of fraud, celebrities taking drugs, police investigations that dragged on and on and on . . .

One of his first jobs as a summer temp in the newsroom of the *Norrland Social Democrat* up in Älvsbyn had been to cover the police investigation into the theft of some bank boxes in the forested hinterland. Shortly after the first theft, notes with a distinctive colour and unpleasant smell had begun to appear in shops and restaurants all around Norrbotten. They weren't the result of any dye cartridges in the bank boxes, but something else entirely. The police were at a loss, but that had been only the start. Over the following months large quantities of stinking brown Swedish banknotes appeared all over Europe, as far away as Greece. It took the police almost a year to investigate the whole thing, but in the end they had a reasonable idea of the sequence of events: the thieves, a group that the police were already aware of, had stored and smuggled the money inside animal carcasses. The foul-smelling brown substance was blood. As a young reporter, Anders Schyman had been fed information throughout the course of the investigation, on the understanding that he wouldn't write anything until the time was right, but it never was. The story never came out, either through him or anyone else. Why had he been so loyal? And why hadn't the police wanted him to write about it? Were they trying to cover up the fact that they'd messed up? Had they? If so, how? Because they'd never caught the thieves?

Why on earth was he thinking about this now?

He went back to the outline of the first edition, the editor's vision for the following day's paper (or wishful thinking, if you prefer).

Of course there were the stories of the other kidnap victims, the rest of the EU delegation, but kidnapped foreigners were about as interesting to the *Evening Post*'s readers as reheated porridge. Another front page would be justified if one of them died, and only then in the context of the threat to Sweden's Thomas Samuelsson, the man on whose shoulders the security of all Europe rested.

He skimmed what the rest of the European media were doing with the story. They might be able to make something out of the Romanian's wife. She'd agreed to be photographed, and now the pictures were on sale via an agency in Paris.

163

They could always publish it and pretend it was Annika and the children until people read the caption: they could lead with an enticing headline, drawing readers to one of the inside pages.

He looked at his watch. Still a few hours before the deadline, but Schyman wasn't expecting any miracles. They'd have to get things moving.

He finished his coffee, stood up and went out to the newsdesk.

Annika gasped as she stepped on to the pavement. It was bitterly cold. The sky was deep blue and clear, and the sun was about to disappear behind the headquarters of Stockholm County Council. It was already dusk between the buildings.

The snow crunched under the soles of her shoes. Her woolly hat was itchy. The streets still hadn't been swept.

Handelsbanken was two blocks away, on Fleminggatan, close to the children's old nursery school. Her account was only a couple of years old, and she hadn't been into the bank since she had opened it. Now she had an appointment for a personal finance advice session at three fifteen. At first the woman on the phone had been rather patronizing, and explained that it wasn't possible to get an appointment at such short notice. 'Oh, well,' Annika had said, 'I'll just have to move my money to a bank that has time to see me,' and all of a sudden a cancellation had miraculously made way for her that afternoon.

She clenched her jaw. She as a person didn't matter a damn, but her bloated online savings account meant she got to jump the queue for financial advice.

Stop whining, she thought. Who had brought up the subject of that account? Who had used it as a stick to beat up the poor financial advice woman?

The path round the back of the Central Courthouse had been scraped smooth, and she slipped, straining her right thigh. She stopped to catch her breath as the pain flared, then subsided, her breath billowing in clouds around her face.

Where did all this anger come from? Why was she so unreasonable? Why had she taken Schyman's generous offer as an insult? Why did she want to murder a woman at Handelsbanken who was tired because it was Friday afternoon and she couldn't be bothered to have yet another idiot banging on about their personal finances?

She pulled off her glove and put her hand over her eyes. She had to get a grip or she'd fall to pieces.

They hadn't heard any more.

Halenius was in constant communication with the relatives and employers of the other victims, but none had been contacted again.

She pulled on her glove and carefully set off.

She stopped abruptly, certain that she was being watched. She spun round and looked: the entrance to the underground, the fronts of buildings, a multi-storey car park, a few builders' skips, parked cars, an elderly couple coming out of the café on the corner. No one looking at her. No one there. No one who cared about her.

She swallowed and headed towards Fleminggatan.

The bank was situated at the busy junction of Fleminggatan and Scheelegatan, a dull, brown brick building with orange awnings. It would have been a fairly safe bet to win 'ugliest building in Stockholm'.

The personal finance adviser was a man. The woman who had answered the phone was probably a receptionist.

They sat down in a booth in a corner of the open-plan office. Annika said no to coffee, but accepted a glass of water, which the man went off to get from a machine.

There didn't seem to be many customers in the bank, but plenty of employees. All around her people, in neatly ironed clothes, were talking into headsets in quiet voices, typing discreetly at their computers, occasionally getting up with a sheet of paper and moving among the tightly packed desks on high heels, or with gently swaying ties.

'I understand that you wanted to discuss a loan,' the man said, putting a plastic cup of water in front of her. He sat down on the other side of the desk and looked at her with rather weary eyes.

'Erm,' Annika said. 'Yes. Possibly.'

'You have a fairly sizeable amount in your online savings account.'

She looked at the expression on his face. Did he recognize her as the wife whose husband had been kidnapped by outlaws in Liboi on the border between Kenya and Somalia? Did he realize she was after ransom money?

Not a chance.

'Yes,' Annika said. 'I know what I've got in that account. This would be a loan on top of that.'

The man cleared his throat and tapped at his computer. 'Apart from your online savings account, you also have an ordinary account which has an overdraft facility,' he said. 'That would give you some room for manoeuvre if you have any unexpected expenses – if your dishwasher breaks down or you get tired of your sofa . . . You don't think that would be enough?'

'This would be a more substantial loan,' she said.

He nodded understandingly. 'We offer personal loans for slightly larger things, house renovation, new boilers, an extension, perhaps . . .'

'How much could I borrow?' she asked.

'That depends on what sort of security you're able to offer against the loan, perhaps a mortgage on a property or lease, or someone to guarantee the loan.'

She shook her head. 'No guarantor,' she said, 'and no property. Not any more, anyway. How much would I be able to borrow like that?'

The man peered at his screen. His face was completely neutral. He was reading intently. The other staff were drifting around them, like fish, and she glanced at them from the corner of her eye. They lived their whole lives here. They came in every day, moved their documents about and typed at their computers, and then when the sun had gone down behind the courthouse they went into the underground and travelled home to a flat in a suburb, watched the news and maybe a quiz show, put their feet up on the coffee-table because they ached after all that tiptoeing around on the hard floor at the bank. They didn't need to be kidnapped: they were already locked up for life, tangled in conventions and expectations and hopeless longings . . .

'In that case we've got our Leisure Loan,' the bank man said. 'Up to three hundred thousand kronor, with credit available at twenty-four hours' notice. That might be more suitable for you – you could buy a car, or perhaps a boat. Then you could use whatever you buy as security, and the interest is determined individually by us here in your branch. You fill in the application, you and the seller sign the agreement concerning the car or boat or whatever it might be, then the seller receives the money once he's sent the signed contract to the bank.'

Annika could feel the walls tumbling over her, shutting her in. She reached for the water and drank some. It tasted of money and mildew and didn't help. She was falling and falling.

'And then there's our Direct Loan, up to a hundred and fifty thousand without any security, available within—'

'Sorry,' she said, standing up and scraping the chair on the floor. 'Sorry. I'm going to have to think about this, thank you, sorry . . .'

The man started to get to his feet behind the desk, and was saying something, but she stumbled out of the bank and found herself on the wide pavement with cars rushing past, from Barnhusbron and towards Kungsholmstorg, or from Fridhemsplan and towards the central station and the city centre. They hid her from the world with their roaring engines and shrieking brakes, and she breathed their ice-cold exhaust fumes into her lungs and felt the ground solidify.

It was almost dark now.

CHAPTER 9

When the Co-op on the corner of Kungsholmsgatan and Scheelegatan had first opened, back in the mists of time, Annika had been impressed by the service, the quality, the range. Her mother had worked behind the till (well, she'd helped out when she was needed) in the Co-op in Hälleforsnäs, and Annika thought she knew a fair bit about grocery stores, but this Co-op was a monster. Hadn't it been awarded 'Supermarket of the Year'?

Since then things had gone steadily downhill.

The automatic doors slid open with a groan and she stepped into the slush-spattered entrance. She turned right, took a trolley and found herself confronted by a large sign above the vegetables, saying, 'Cucumber, Swedish, great for aioli! 19.90/kilo'.

That seemed fairly indicative. Maybe they couldn't spell tzatziki.

She let her gaze roam over the fruit and vegetables, and tried to conjure an image of the inside of her fridge. She could see liver pâté, yoghurt and eggs, but the milk rack was alarmingly empty, there was no cream and no raspberries.

What were they going to have tonight? The children had gone off with Berit, but presumably she and Halenius would have to eat. She was in charge of logistics, after all, responsible for food and charging mobile phones.

She knew the layout of the shop like the back of her hand, and glided off with her squeaking trolley, past nappies and dog food and Christmas cards and all the freezers. She got some pork chops, broccoli, rocket salad, cherry tomatoes, French goat's cheese and raspberry balsamic vinegar. Carrots and batteries of various sizes, instant coffee and marker pens.

At the checkout she noticed that the carrots were mouldy and asked if she could change them.

'They're organic,' the boy behind the till said, as if that were a justification.

She checked the cherry tomatoes, then changed them as well.

'I hope things work out with your husband,' the boy said.

She pulled her hat down over her ears.

The bags were heavy even though she'd tried not to buy too much. She had to walk very slowly on the icy pavements. The load felt reassuring, as if the weight of the bags was keeping her on the ground.

Her back was sweaty by the time she reached the door of the flat on Agnegatan.

'The ICA shop on Kungsholmstorg is actually closer,' she panted, when Halenius met her in the hall, 'but I refuse to shop there. The Co-op by the courthouse is fairly shit, but at least it doesn't pretend to be a delicatessen for the upper classes.'

She stopped when she saw the look on his face and let go of the bags. 'What?' she said.

'It's not about Thomas,' Halenius said, 'but I've got bad news about one of the other hostages.'

Annika grabbed the doorframe. 'Who?'

'The Frenchman. Come in and close the door. Give me those bags. Do you want coffee?'

She shook her head.

'Go and sit down in the living room,' he said.

She took off her coat and did as she'd been told.

He had lit the lamps in the windows and turned the television on with the sound down. The news in sign language was on. A tank rolled across the screen – maybe it was an item about Afghanistan.

She sat on the sofa. Halenius came into the room with a mug of coffee in his hand, and sat beside her. 'Sébastien Magurie has been found dead,' he said.

The Frenchman, the MEP, hadn't Thomas mentioned him at some point? He used to tell her about the other delegates at his conferences when he called home (but never about the women, or not the young, beautiful ones), which used to annoy Annika: what did she care if a Belgian was being arrogant or some Estonian was brilliant?

'Thomas didn't like him,' Annika said.

'He was lying in a street in Mogadishu. The Djibouti embassy had a phone call telling them where the body was.'

'Djibouti?'

'The country to the north of Somalia – I think it's the only country in the world that has an embassy in Mogadishu, these days. The embassies of all the Western countries have been abandoned. Sweden's ambassador to Somalia is based in Nairobi.'

'How did he die?'

Halenius hesitated, and she got up without waiting for the answer. 'Annika . . .'

'You always do that,' she said, backing away from him. 'You always go quiet when you have something really dreadful to say. I'm not made of china, you know.'

'The body was found in a bin-bag in a street next to the building that used to house the French embassy. Close to the harbour in the old part of Mogadishu, an area that's supposed to be completely abandoned. It's only a kilometre or so from Djibouti's—'

'You haven't answered my question. How did he die?'

He took a deep breath, then let the air out in a sigh. 'Machete, probably. His body was dismembered. It's still not one hundred per cent certain that it is the Frenchman they've found, but everything suggests that it is.'

'Because?' she said.

'The remains of the clothes found in the bag match the description of the clothing he was wearing when he disappeared. His wedding ring was still on his hand. An appendix scar on the torso matches his medical records.'

'But?'

'His head is missing.'

She sank on to the sofa.

'This means we're in a worse position,' Halenius said. 'It suggests that the kidnappings are political, after all. The Frenchman's wife was busy trying to put together forty million dollars, but the kidnappers weren't willing to wait. And presumably the rest of the captives are in Somalia as well, not Kenya, which also makes things more difficult for us. Kenya is a functioning society, but Somalia is a nightmare.'

Annika looked out into the semi-darkness of the living room, at the warmth of the ornamental lighting, the DVDs on the bookcase next to the television, the books piled up by the radiator. 'Dismembered how?' she asked. 'And why?'

Halenius studied her face. 'Arms, legs, trunk,' he said.

'Bodies are usually dismembered to make it easier for the killer to move them without anyone noticing,' Annika said. 'That could hardly apply here.'

Halenius frowned. 'What do you mean?'

'I mean, why was he chopped up? Doesn't that suggest excessive brutality, extreme aggression?'

'Who knows what these madmen are driven by?'

'If they're ordinary madmen,' Annika said, 'the sort of madmen who kill people here in Sweden, then excessive brutality usually suggests that the killer is motivated by extremely personal reasons. Had the Frenchman been in Kenya before?'

Halenius shook his head. 'Before he became a politician he was a civil servant at the nuclear power station in Agen. He'd hardly ever been abroad.'

Maybe the killer didn't like nuclear energy, Annika thought, but said nothing. 'The idea that the wife of a civil servant could get her hands on forty million dollars isn't particularly realistic,' she said instead. 'The kidnappers might have realized that, and decided not to bother negotiating with her.'

'They would have killed him before now, if that was the case,' he said.

Annika sat up. 'The kidnappers had seven hostages, didn't they? Maybe they're sacrificing one to put pressure on the rest of us. Maybe they saw it as a smart investment. Kill one in an attention-grabbing way, then the rest of the negotiations would go faster, better?'

Halenius was looking at her warily.

'Otherwise they wouldn't have called the Djibouti embassy and told them where to find the body,' Annika went on. 'They wanted it to be found, and there was a reason behind the dismemberment.

175

And that phone call – they're trying to tell us something. And they dumped the bag outside the former French—' She stood up. 'What did the man in the turban say in his video? That Frontex should be scrapped, the borders opened, and trade tariffs abolished? Is France particularly active in Frontex?'

'They've got a president who talks openly about clearing the rubbish from the streets, in other words throwing out the immigrants, and they've got Le Pen who fights elections with racism as an ideology, but all the Mediterranean countries have been more or less equally involved.'

'And the headquarters are in Poland, so that can't be the reason,' Annika mused, pacing back and forth in front of the television. She sat down again. 'This can't just be political. Do we know who the turban is?'

'He isn't in any registers held by the Yanks, the Brits or the French.'

'Was it him you spoke to on the phone?'

Halenius ran his fingers through his fringe. 'I don't know,' he said. 'It's possible. In the video he's talking Kinyarwanda, but the man who phoned spoke faultless Nairobi English. Mind you, both voices were quite high, a bit whiny, so it could have been the same person.'

'What are the French saying?'

'Their government isn't involved and I haven't spoken to anyone there – the French are always a bit stand-offish. I don't know if their officials have any insurance, but members of the European Parliament certainly don't.'

'What about the others?'

'The Spaniard has someone negotiating for him, the German woman too. I don't know about the Romanian or the Dane. The British have told Sky News that they never negotiate with terrorists, which isn't a smart move considering the situation the hostages are in. What did the bank say?'

She put her feet up on the coffee-table. 'Borrowing forty million dollars with no security might be a bit tricky,' she said. 'But a hundred and fifty thousand kronor would be okay, if God and the bank management can have receipts and contracts covering exactly what I want to buy, or if I can give them some form of security in the form of property or a car, or a guarantor . . .'

'Isn't there anyone who could guarantee a loan? Thomas's mother?'

Annika shook her head. 'We asked if she'd be a guarantor when the lease on the flat was up for sale, because then we would have paid a lower rate of interest. It was a policy decision, she said, always to say no to being a guarantor. Alvar, her father-in-law, apparently agreed to act as guarantor for his reckless brother and it all ended disastrously. The family lost everything.'

'Shame. Your mother?'

'She asks me once a year if I can guarantee a loan for her, usually because she's found an unmissable investment opportunity online . . .'

He raised one hand. 'I get it. So how much money have you got?'

'Barely six and a half million,' she said. 'Kronor, that is.'

Halenius opened his eyes wide. 'Really? Do you mind me asking . . .?'

'Insurance. Our house out in Djursholm burned down – well, of course you know that. You came out there once.'

'The Kitten,' he said.

The contract killer who had eventually been linked to the fire at Annika's home had been part of a highly dubious prisoner exchange (well, Annika thought it was dubious), and as a result the insurance company had finally, at long, long last, agreed to pay up. By that time Annika and Thomas had been on their way to the USA, so the money had been deposited in the new savings account with Handelsbanken.

'Exactly,' she said. 'The Kitten.'

'Does Thomas know how much money is in that account?'

'No. Nor do I. Not down to the last krona, anyway. Why?'

'But he has a rough idea? That there's about a million dollars there?'

'Yeah, I'd say so.'

Halenius wrote something in a notebook. 'Have

you got anything valuable that you could sell? Anything of Thomas's?'

'He did have a yacht, but his ex-wife got that. And then he bought a motorboat with Sophia Grenborg, but she got that when he left her. As a consolation . . . Why do you ask?'

'Why Handelsbanken?' Halenius asked.

'Because they don't pay bonuses to their directors,' Annika said.

The under-secretary of state let out a short, genuine laugh. 'I've switched my accounts too,' he said, 'for exactly the same reason. The bankers took it for granted that they had a right to their millions in bonuses, even though the financial crisis was their fault.'

'Mind you, to start with they need several million as an annual salary just to turn up at work. And then they demand the same again as a bonus to do anything,' Annika said.

'For bankers, money is purely hypothetical,' Halenius said. 'They don't understand that someone always has to pay, and it's usually the poor fellow at the bottom of the food chain.'

'Or girl,' Annika said.

They smiled at each other.

'So, one million dollars,' Halenius said. 'That's what we've got to play with.'

'One million dollars,' Annika confirmed.

It was radiant white, like an angel's wing, the Andreas Church in Vaxholm, the church of the missionary parish (although in those days it was called the Swedish Missionary Society): I was one of Paul Petter Waldenström's young lambs, small and innocent (at least to start with).

Sunday school was great. It was always sunny in the parish hall, no matter what the weather was like outside. First we would sing and pray together, then the bigger children would go off into the back room for Bible study, and not just any Bible study: the Bible in cartoon form! Every Sunday we got a new sheet, folded in half to make four pages. The paper was of such poor quality that there were splinters in it. If you tried to rub out a pencil mark, it disintegrated. If you were really lucky, there were cartoons on all four pages, but that didn't often happen. On the fourth and final page, and sometimes even on the third, there were questions to be answered, crosswords made up of Christian words, articles of faith to discuss, and that was all very boring, but I still went, every Sunday, because the cartoon was like a serial that seemed to have no end.

But of course it did. Everything comes to an end.

Even this will come to an end.

They've been to collect the Spaniard now, Alvaro Ribeiro. I remembered his name because my grandfather was called Alvar and there was once a promising tennis player called Francis Ribeiro. He trained in Finland for a while. I wonder what happened to him.

They collected him after it had got dark. He didn't say anything when they came for him. No goodbye, nothing.

The Romanian hadn't come back.

I listened to the sounds inside me, to the darkness.

The lambs who were thirteen and above and were good at Bible study became shepherds for the younger ones – actually, everyone did except me. I don't know why I wasn't allowed to be a shepherd. I haven't thought about it for ages but I used to wonder about it. Perhaps I wasn't pious enough. Perhaps I played too much ice-hockey. Perhaps the older shepherds knew that Linus and I smoked behind the boat refuelling station, or that we'd drunk the beer Linus's dad kept hidden in the boot of his car.

There were far more mosquitoes now. They were biting me the whole time, on my fingers, arms, ears, cheeks, eyelids.

Annika's laughter was echoing around me. She doesn't believe in God. She usually says He's a patriarchal construct invented by men to hold the masses and women in their place. I know it isn't rational, but every time she says something like that, I get a bit scared. I find it so unnecessary, because *if* He exists I doubt He'd appreciate being described as a patriarchal construct. Who would? I said that to her once, and she stared at me with a really odd look in those big eyes of hers. She said: 'If God does exist, then He knows what I'm thinking, doesn't He? Otherwise He's not really up to much, is He? Maybe He appreciates the fact that I'm not a hypocrite.'

Now there were only me and the Dane left. He was lying completely still beside me. It was a relief that he wasn't rattling and groaning any more. His chest seemed nice and quiet. It was completely dark. The guards had lit a fire outside the shack – I could see the light from the flames through the gaps around the tin door.

We hadn't been given anything else to eat. I had emptied my bladder on the floor once.

I wondered if God could see me now.

The landline rang at 23:44.

Annika had almost dozed off on the sofa and jumped as if she'd been kicked.

'Do you want to listen in?' Halenius asked. His eyes were red and his skin chapped; his shirt had come untucked from his trousers.

Annika shook her head.

But perhaps she should. She could be some sort of support in the bedroom, pointing at notes on the walls to remind him of different aspects and keywords they'd agreed on, make sure that the recording equipment was working and that everything was being saved to the hard-drive the way it should be.

'I'd rather not,' she said.

The telephone rang a second time.

Halenius stood up rather heavily and went into

the bedroom, shutting the door behind him. Now he was starting the recording. Now he was checking that it was working. Now he was waiting for the next ring, and then he would answer.

The third ring and, sure enough, it was cut off halfway, and Annika could hear Halenius speaking, forming sentences, but couldn't make out the words.

The clock on the DVD-player clicked to 23:45, the exact angle of the tilt of the Earth.

She had spent the evening answering all the text messages, voicemail and emails she had received from journalists wanting to interview her. 'Thanks for your enquiry about interviewing me on my husband's situation. But I won't be making any comment for the time being. If I change my mind I'll get in touch. Please respect my decision.'

Bosse, from the other evening paper, was the only one to get in touch after that, with a long, antagonistic text in which he demanded at least to know what was going on, even if he didn't use it in an article the following day. He thought they could discuss the matter, if nothing else, maybe come to some agreement. Annika answered, 'Do I look like a carpet-seller?'

Possibly a little too abrupt, she thought, as she stared at the time on the DVD-player. The truth was that she found Bosse difficult to deal with. He was the one who had tried to stir up a scandal around her Spanish air-kiss with Halenius outside the Järnet restaurant. It had been his revenge for

183

her breaking off the beginnings of a flirtation between them about a century and a half ago.

Halenius was talking and talking and talking in there.

Anders Schyman was the only person she hadn't replied to. She realized she had reacted irrationally to his proposal. It wasn't that bad an offer. The real question was what it actually meant. They would hardly stretch to forty million dollars, but on the other hand it was unlikely that the ransom would end up being that large, not if Halenius's theory was correct.

23:51. He had now been talking to the kidnapper for six minutes. That was roughly how long the first conversation had lasted. Halenius had listened to the recording several times during the evening, and had made a transcript, which he had asked her if she wanted to read. 'Maybe later,' she had said. She didn't want to hear what the kidnapper sounded like, but maybe she could read what he had said, absorb his message without needing to deal with the individual. But not now, not tonight.

Right now it was quiet in Kidnap Control, but the phone hadn't clicked, so the call hadn't ended. What was he doing in there? Had something gone wrong?

'Yes?' she heard him say, and felt herself letting go of the air in her lungs.

She would have talk to Schyman again and find out what his offer actually meant. How much money was the paper prepared to pay? How much would she be forced to reveal about her relationship with Thomas? Sex, cooking, their favourite television programmes? Would the children have to be involved?

She went out into the kitchen with Halenius's muffled voice surrounding her like fog. They had eaten grilled goat's cheese on rocket salad with pine nuts, cherry tomatoes, honey and raspberry balsamic vinegar as a starter (an old classic), then pork chops with potato wedges and chanterelle sauce (she had picked her own, then parboiled and frozen them). Halenius had had the last of the sticky chocolate cake as dessert.

'I'm going to end up rolling out of here,' he had said, as he pushed the chocolate-smeared plate away from him.

Annika had loaded the dishwasher without replying.

Between six and sixty days: that was the usual length of a commercial kidnapping. And a politically motivated kidnapping could last much longer. Terry Anderson, head of the Associated Press bureau in Beirut, had been held for almost seven years by Hezbollah. Ingrid Betancourt had spent the same amount of time with the FARC guerrillas in Colombia.

She could still hear Halenius murmuring on the other side of the wall; they seemed to have a lot to talk about. She wiped the draining board again. The stainless steel sparkled. She opened the fridge, took out a cherry tomato and bit into it. It exploded with a little pop inside her mouth.

Why was he talking for so long?

She went back into the living room and sat down on the sofa.

23:58. Almost a quarter of an hour now.

The television was still on, with the sound turned down. She switched it off.

All the news programmes that evening had included short items on Thomas Samuelsson, the Swede kidnapped in Kenya. The rest of the hostages hadn't been named. News that the Frenchman's body had been found hadn't yet leaked out, but it was only a matter of time. Tonight, or tomorrow morning at the latest, it would crash-land in the mass media. Then all the colleagues she had replied to that evening would get in touch again and ask if she had any comment on the fact that the hostages had begun to be executed.

She shut her eyes.

What would she do if Thomas died – if they killed him? How would she react? Would she go to pieces? Go mad? Feel relieved? Would she agree to cry in public? Maybe Letterman would call. Or Oprah. Did she still have her own programme, or had she stopped doing it? Who would she ask to the funeral? Would it be a small, intimate affair for close family, or should she invite all the news crews, the papers, everyone he had studied with in Uppsala, Sophia Grenborg and his first wife, Eleonor, the stuck-up bank director?

She opened her eyes.

He wasn't dead.

He was still living and breathing: she could feel his breath right beside her.

Or was she just imagining things? Like when old people lose their husband or wife and suddenly start seeing ghosts, conjuring up the image of their deceased soulmate and communicating with them in words and thoughts.

00:07.

It was taking a very long time. Twenty-three minutes now. What were they talking about?

The telephone gave a little ring. 00:11. They had talked for twenty-seven minutes.

The whole flat was filled with thunderous silence. She was breathing softly, shallowly.

Now he was checking that the recording had worked, saving it on the server, switching it off . . .

Her legs felt heavy. Halenius came out of the bedroom door and Annika watched him float across the room.

'He's alive, and contactable,' the under-secretary of state said, sinking on to the armchair.

'Did you talk to him?' Annika asked, her mouth dry. She could feel a pip from the cherry tomato between two of her teeth.

Halenius shook his head and ran his fingers through his hair; he seemed utterly exhausted. 'They seldom call from where they're holding the hostages. They've watched too many cop shows on television and think the police and authorities

187

just have to press a button to trace where the call is being made from.'

'Do they have cop shows in Somalia?' Annika asked.

'The man who phoned is clearly in touch with the guards somehow, probably by mobile phone. I asked the control question we agreed on, "Where was Annika living when you first met?", and a couple of minutes later I got the answer. "Across the yard from Hantverkargatan thirty-two."'

Across the courtyard from Hantverkargatan 32.

She had a flash of memory, of her demolition-threatened flat at the top of the building in the yard, with no hot water or bathroom, the light from the sky and the draught from the badly fitting window in the kitchen. The sofa in the living room was where they had first had sex, her on top of him.

'Can the call be traced? Can we find out where they're calling from?'

'The British are working on it. The calls seem to be routed through either Liboi or a mast on the other side of the border, inside Somalia. But the areas covered by each of those masts are enormous.'

'So where's Thomas? Do they know which country he's in?'

He shook his head. 'Not from these conversations, anyway.'

'The Frenchman was found in Mogadishu,' Annika said.

'But it's not certain he was killed there. Bodies

start to decay very quickly in those areas because of the heat, but a doctor at the Djibouti embassy thought he'd been dead for at least twenty-four hours before he was found. And we know that the kidnappers have access to a vehicle. Or vehicles. At least three.'

'The truck and the two Toyotas,' Annika said.

A fleeting smile crossed Halenius's face. 'So you were listening, then.'

'Toyota Takeaways,' Annika said. 'What were you talking about for so long?'

He rubbed his eyes. 'Building trust,' he said. 'We were discussing politics. I basically agreed with everything he said, and I didn't actually have to lie. I think Frontex is a disgrace, but at least I'm not involved with it at the department. We could rid the developing world of poverty tomorrow, if we set our minds to it, but we don't want to. We profit too much from it.'

Annika didn't answer.

'I said you weren't in a position to pay a ransom of forty million dollars. I explained that you live in a rented flat and have two young children, and an ordinary job, but I mentioned that you have some savings from the insurance pay-out after a house fire, and that you'd be seeing your bank on Monday to find out how much you can get hold of.'

Annika straightened on the sofa. 'What the hell did you tell him that for? Now he knows we've got money!'

'They'll ask Thomas all about your assets, and he'll tell them.'

'Do you think so?'

Halenius looked up at her. 'Guaranteed.'

Annika stood up and went out into the kitchen. Halenius followed her.

'They must never think we're lying to them. If they do, we have to start the negotiations again. Not just from zero, but somewhere way below that.'

She leaned back against the draining board and folded her arms over her chest. 'So you and the kidnapper are best friends now?'

Halenius stopped right in front of her. His eyes were bloodshot. 'I'd stand on my head and sing "The Marseillaise" backwards if it would help get Thomas home to you and the children,' he said, then went into the hall and put on his coat and shoes. 'I'll leave the computer here,' he said. 'I'll be back first thing tomorrow morning.'

And before she had time to say anything else or apologize or thank him, he was gone.

DAY 4

SATURDAY, 26 NOVEMBER

CHAPTER 10

The smell woke me up. It was like nothing I'd ever smelt before. Not fermented herring, not rotting prawns, not rubbish: something thick and heavy and acrid, with a hint of ammonia.

'Hey,' I whispered to the Dane. 'Can you smell that? Do you know what it is?'

He didn't answer.

It was light outside the shack: the rectangle around the door was dazzlingly bright and clear. I wondered what time it was. It got light early on the equator, maybe six or seven o'clock. Sweden was two hours behind, so it would be four or five there. Annika was probably asleep. The children might be with her, in our big bed. We had supposedly agreed that beds were personal space, and that everyone should stick to their own, but I knew Annika relaxed the rules when I wasn't there, especially with Kalle. Sometimes he had really bad nightmares, and she used to let him come into our bed so she could rock him back to sleep.

The lack of water was making my head pound. My mouth was full of dust. Both my hands had gone numb, and I rolled on to my stomach to try to get some feeling back into them. They had tied them with rope this time, perhaps because they'd run out of cable ties.

In the middle of the night the tall man had come into the shack, shone a torch in my face, dragged me up into a sitting position and yelled, '*Soma, soma!*' Then he had given me a piece of paper with the words 'Where did Annika live when you met her?' 'What?' I said, my heart hammering. The torch was dazzling me and all I could see were spots of light. How could he know about Annika? Was this some sort of trick? What did he want?

I turned towards the Dane, but I couldn't see him through all the spots of light dancing in my eyes.

'*Andika,*' the tall man shouted. '*Andika jibu.*'

He leaned forward with a large knife in his hand, and my vision went dark. He didn't stab me, just cut the cable tie binding my wrists, then tossed a pencil into my lap.

'*Andika jibu,*' he repeated, holding out the piece of paper.

Did he want me to write the answer?

My hands wouldn't do as I wanted, I tried to grasp the pencil but kept dropping it. The tall man was barking above my head, '*Haraka, haraka!*' and I managed to write the answer shakily. Then the guard tied my hands again, turned off the torch and vanished into a darkness that was denser than ever.

194

'What was that about?' I whispered to the Dane, but he didn't answer.

I was exhausted, and fell asleep almost instantly.

Now, in the morning light, the mystery remained.

How could they know about Annika? I hadn't mentioned her to anyone, not the guards or any of the other hostages. How could they know? My mobile had been switched off when they took it from me, and I hadn't given them my PIN so they couldn't have got anything from there. My wallet?

I heard the air go out of my lungs. Of course. I had pictures of her and the children, with names and dates on the back.

But why did they want to know where she was living when we first met? What a ridiculous question to ask. What could they do with that information? It was utterly irrelevant, something hardly anyone knew . . .

I gasped. *They'd spoken to her.* Oh, God, they'd spoken to her and she wanted to check I was still alive, that they really were holding me captive. That had to be it! A wave of relief washed over me and I laughed out loud.

But how had they got hold of her phone number? All our numbers were ex-directory, apart from my mobile, and obviously they couldn't have reached her on that.

I peered out at the light filtering through a gap under one of the sheets of tin that formed the walls. My field of vision was at the same level as a small spider. We stared at each other for a minute or so in the gloom, the spider and I, before it scuttled to my face and climbed up it, as if it were a small rock. I shut my eyes and felt its tiny feet scrambling over my eyelids. Once it had passed my ear and vanished into my hair I could no longer feel it. I didn't think it was poisonous, but just to be on the safe side I shook my head fairly vigorously to make it fall off.

Then I lay still and listened towards the light. I could hear the guards moving around out there, one saying something to the other. The smell in there really was terrible.

'Hey,' I whispered to the Dane, shuffling into a sitting position. 'Where's that stink coming from?'

From my new position I could see the Dane properly, Per. He was lying on his back and staring up at the roof with eyes that had a greyish look to them. His face was grey, his whole body was grey. His grey lips were wide open, as if he were shouting up at the roof. Something was crawling inside his mouth, something was moving in there, and a cry rose up to the roof and out through the cracks round the door and right across the *manyatta* and off towards the horizon, but it wasn't the Dane shouting, it wasn't Per, it was me, screaming. I screamed and screamed until the tin door was removed and the light fell in on the body, like an explosion, and I saw all the ants.

Annika was looking at her face in the bathroom mirror, running her fingers along the dark rings under her eyes. That was where loneliness settled, the absence of the children, her inability to work, her unfaithful husband . . .

She listened to the sounds of the building: Lindström, her neighbour, running a tap on the other side of the wall, the hiss of the bathroom extractor fan, the rattle of the lift. The sounds weren't hers any more: her home had been occupied by kidnappers and civil servants.

Mind you, it wasn't much of a home – at least, not according to Thomas. He thought the flat was too small and difficult to furnish nicely, which was true after he had moved in and demanded furniture that didn't come from Ikea. He hated the bathroom most of all, the plastic floor, the shower curtain, the cheap little basin. In Vaxholm he and Eleonor had had a spa complete with sauna and Jacuzzi. She ran her hand down the bathroom mirror, as if she were apologizing.

It wasn't the apartment's fault, and it wasn't hers.

It was Thomas who had put himself on that plane, in that Toyota. It had been his decision, but she had been dragged into paying part of the cost.

She had an ice-cold shower.

She got dressed, made the bed and had breakfast.

By the time Halenius rang the doorbell she had cleared up in the kitchen. His hair was wet, as if he'd just got out of the shower as well, and he was wearing the same jeans as yesterday, but with a pale blue shirt, freshly ironed.

I wonder if he does his own ironing, or if his girlfriend does it, she thought, as he hung up his coat.

'Sorry,' she said. 'I won't question your methods or your judgement again. I'd be completely lost without you. Thank you for everything you're doing. I can't tell you how much I appreciate it. Honestly. If you want Hans and Hans here as well, that's fine. It really is.'

She fell silent. When she'd practised it in her head, she'd thought her speech sounded humble and poetic and vulnerable, but everything had tumbled out in a rush and in the wrong order.

She bit her lower lip, but he was smiling.

'It's okay,' he said. 'I'm easily bribed with coffee and cake.'

She smiled back, surprised by how relieved she was. 'I've been feeling like a right arsehole since you left,' she said, hurrying into the kitchen to fill the kettle. He took it without milk, didn't he?

'The families of the Romanian and the Spaniard have received proof of life,' he said. 'They have received video films, emailed directly to them.'

He said it in a neutral voice, but Annika felt her muscles tense. 'I haven't checked my email today,' she said.

'I've checked for you,' Halenius said. 'You haven't received anything.'

She didn't bother asking how he had managed to do that.

'And a French passenger plane crashed in the Atlantic this morning,' Halenius said. 'No Swedes on board.'

'A terrorist attack?' Annika asked.

'Bad weather,' Halenius said, disappearing into the bedroom. She heard him switch on the computer and fiddle with the mobile phone.

She leaned back against the draining board for a minute to let the information sink in.

Proof of Life. Wasn't there a film with that title, starring Meg Ryan and Russell Crowe? Hadn't Meg and Russell got together while they were making it? And then she'd divorced Dennis Quaid?

She turned the oven on, 175 degrees, melted a large lump of butter in the microwave, took out a bowl and cracked some eggs, then added sugar, vanilla sugar, a pinch of salt, syrup, cocoa, the melted butter and a large scoop of flour.

So the Spaniard and the Romanian were alive. I wonder what the Frenchman did wrong.

She greased the tin, the one with the loose base, then poured in the mixture and put it into the oven. She waited fifteen minutes for it to bake, then got some vanilla ice-cream out of the freezer, heated some blackberries, and went into the bedroom (Kidnap Control), with coffee, cake, ice-cream and blackberries. 'I took you at your word and made a sticky toffee cake.'

Halenius gave her a look of total bemusement.

He was obviously immersed in something far removed from her baking exploits.

All of a sudden she felt ridiculous. There was nowhere to put the tray – the desk was covered with recording equipment, computer accessories and notes, and there was still a great heap of clothes on the other chair (why did she never tidy up after herself?). She felt herself starting to blush.

'Let's have it out there,' Halenius said, standing up.

She turned away gratefully, went into the living room and put the tray on the coffee-table, then curled up in the corner of the sofa with the fake White House mug and let her hair fall in front of her face.

'What sort of films were they?' she asked.

'I haven't seen them,' Halenius said. 'The families don't want to go public with them, but I'll see if I can get hold of them off the record. They're evidently fairly poor quality, the hostages sitting in a dark room with a lamp shining in their faces, saying that they're being treated well and that their families should pay the ransom as soon as possible. The usual, really.'

Annika's heart was pounding: *proof – of – life*, it throbbed, *proof – of – life* . . . 'How did they look?' she asked.

'Pretty much as expected, apparently, unshaven and dirty, but otherwise okay. No signs of maltreatment, or nothing visible.'

She took a deep breath. 'Do you think we'll be getting one as well?'

'Probably.'

'When?'

'Today, maybe tomorrow. The kidnappers seem to be doing everything in a strict sequence. You were the last person to get the initial call. Maybe Thomas is number seven on their list.'

She nodded and bit the inside of her cheek. 'What else is likely to happen?'

'If I were to hazard a guess,' Halenius said, 'I don't expect them to be very communicative today. They know you can't get to the bank before Monday morning, and they want us to sweat.'

She blew on her coffee. 'Because sitting and waiting for a call is much worse than getting one?'

He nodded. 'Kidnappers have two weapons: violence and time. They've already demonstrated that they're prepared to use the first, so they probably won't object to using the second.'

Violence and time. How long would Halenius be able to spend all his waking hours in her bedroom? How long would the media maintain any sort of interest?

'I have to go and see Schyman today,' she said.

'That's probably a good idea,' Halenius said.

'Has the news about the Frenchman got out yet?'

'Not as far as I've seen, but it'll probably happen today.'

201

'I was wondering,' she said, 'what the Frenchman might have done wrong.'

'To get himself killed? Nothing at all, probably. It might have depended on the negotiator, or the relatives, or both. Unless he tried to escape. Or there may not be a reason. Maybe the kidnappers just wanted to make an example of someone.'

She pushed the cake to him. 'Help yourself,' she said.

He leaned back in the armchair, her armchair, and laughed. He had such a big laugh that his whole face seemed to crack open, and his eyes narrowed until they were almost closed. 'You're really nothing like I imagined,' he said.

She stood up. 'Is that good or bad?'

He smiled and swallowed his coffee. She picked up his mug, went into the kitchen and made some more, grabbed a handful of napkins and went back to the living room. 'What will it mean for us, when news of the Frenchman gets out?' she asked, putting the fresh mug and the napkins in front of him.

'The whole story gets hotter,' he said. 'The hunt for the kidnappers will intensify, although the Yanks and Brits are already pretty hot.'

He cut himself a decent slice of the steaming cake. The inside was still almost liquid.

'All the eager editors who got in touch with me yesterday will be wanting a new comment today,' she said.

He nodded, his mouth full. 'This is seriously good with ice-cream,' he said.

She looked at the ice-cream, wondering if she should put it back in the freezer, or if she could leave it out a bit longer . . . Here she was, worrying about a tub of ice-cream, trying to guess whether or not the man on the other side of the table had had enough, instead of just asking him. Her husband was missing somewhere in East Africa, and she was fretting over whether her baking was up to scratch. She started to tremble and covered her face with her hands. 'Sorry,' she managed. 'Sorry, it's just . . .'

'You don't have to respond, if you don't want to,' he said.

She blinked at him.

'All those eager editors,' he said.

She tried to smile, reached for a napkin and blew her nose. 'This whole thing is so sick,' she said.

He carried on eating his cake. She looked at the time on her mobile. 'I'm meeting Anne. She's got yoga at twelve o'clock.'

'Make sure you talk through Schyman's offer with him properly,' he said. 'I'm going to go through last night's conversation and make a transcript of it. I'm planning to call Q later. Do you want to talk to him?'

She got to her feet, with the tub of ice-cream in one hand. 'Why would I?'

Halenius shrugged. She stuck the ice-cream into the freezer, then put on her coat in the hall. 'Your children,' she said, pulling on her gloves. 'What do they say when you're away so much? Doesn't it make them wonder?'

'Yes,' Halenius said. 'But they're flying down to see Angie tonight – the schools there are having their summer holidays now. It's her turn to do Christmas.'

'They go all that way on their own?'

He smiled and stood up, holding his mug and plate. 'My girlfriend's going with them,' he said, then went into the kitchen and put the china into the dishwasher.

She unlocked the front door and left the flat.

Anne Snapphane was waiting in the Kafferepet café on Klarabergsgatan with juice and a whole-wheat open sandwich in front of her. It looked as though she'd bought a copy of every newspaper she could find on her way there: the pile on the wobbly café table was even bigger than the one Schyman had brought with him the day before.

'It's terrible, this serial-killer business,' Anne said, holding the *Evening Post* towards Annika. 'And did you hear about that plane that crashed into the Atlantic? Terrorists everywhere, these days . . .'

Annika put her coffee on the last free patch of table, dropped her bag on to the floor and peeled off her padded jacket. 'Wasn't it bad weather?' she said, taking the newspaper.

Photographs of three women smiled out at her from the front page. Above them floated 'Police Suspect:' and below, in screaming capital letters:

'Beautifully even lines,' Annika said, leafing through to pages six and seven.

Elin Michnik, the talented temp, had written the article. An anonymous police source was said to support the theory suggested in the previous day's *Evening Post* that the murders in the sub-urbs of Stockholm showed 'similarities', and that they were 'keeping an open mind' about the investigations.

That meant, Elin Michnik had written, that the police might well consider combining the investi-gations into the three murders and look for the common denominator.

'Dear God,' Annika muttered. 'The epitome of noncommittal statements.'

'What do you mean?' Anne shovelled a forkful of prawns into her mouth.

'It's pretty obvious that there are similarities between the murders. They're all women, they were all stabbed, and they're all from Stockholm. And name one police investigation where they *haven't* kept an open mind. Well, apart from the Palme murder, obviously. And of course the police "might well consider" combining the investiga-tions. Christ . . .'

Anne frowned. 'What's this got to do with Olof Palme?'

Annika sighed and turned the page. 'The Palme

investigation collapsed because the chief of police in Stockholm sat in his office and decided that the prime minister was murdered by Kurds. Which turned out to be utterly wrong, but by then a year had passed and it was too late.'

She carried on through the paper.

Pages eight and nine focused on the dead women's relatives. 'Mummy's Gone' was the headline running across the spread. Thomas had been demoted to page ten. A different photograph, one from his days playing ice-hockey, probably from the paper's archive, accompanied by a flabby article about 'the feverish hunt' continuing. Opposite was a full-page advert.

But the next two pages were more interesting.

A pretty blonde woman sitting on a flowery sofa looking into the camera with tears in her eyes, two little children in her arms, beneath the headline 'Come Home, Daddy!' The caption read, 'Held hostage with Swedish Thomas in East Africa'.

Annika sighed to herself. The Romanian's wife. She closed the paper and put it down. 'How's Miranda getting on?'

Anne's daughter was a year or so older than Ellen.

'I'm not one to make a fuss,' Anne said curtly. 'As long as she's happy, that's great. She really does seem to like Mehmet's new kids . . .'

'Her half-siblings, you mean?'

'. . . so I'm not going to be the one to upset the

applecart. It's easier if she stays there during the week, but we get on well, Mehmet and I, and his new partner, of course. We all muck in and help each other out. Always.'

Annika blinked. 'Wow,' she said.

'What?' Anne said.

Annika cleared her throat. 'You had something exciting you wanted to talk about?'

Anne leaned forward, and one of her breasts fell into the mayonnaise on the sandwich. She'd had them enlarged to a D-cup six months ago, and hadn't got used to judging distances with them. 'I've got a brilliant idea for a programme that I'm going to pitch to the bosses at Media Time on Monday.'

Annika hadn't got much of a grip on all the new digital channels that had sprung up while she had been away.

'It's a serious channel,' Anne said. 'They run an online news agency as well, mediatime.se. My idea is for an in-depth interview programme, not entertainment, serious, and all the more entertaining because of that, if you get what I mean?'

'Like *Oprah* and *Skavlan*, you mean?' Annika asked.

'Exactly!' Anne said, wiping the mayonnaise off her lambswool jumper. 'Do you think you could help me put something together?'

Annika pushed back her hair. 'Anne,' she said, 'you know what's happened to Thomas . . .'

Her friend raised both hands in a defensive

gesture. 'Absolutely,' she said. 'And it's really terrible, and you need to prepare yourself for the worst. I mean, the kidnappers hardly shot the guards and translators in the head so they could take all the others off to Starbucks, did they?'

Annika shrugged and shook her head more or less simultaneously. What could she say to that?

'Just say you'll help me,' Anne said. 'That you'll be there to support me.'

'Of course I will.'

Anne reached for her mobile phone. 'How can you be so sure it was bad weather?' she asked, as she posted a status update on Facebook.

Annika looked around the crowded café. The tables were close together, the air smelt of damp wool and the windows facing the street were streaked with dirt. No one was watching her. No one was feeling sorry for her. She was fifty-four kilos of human being in a room full of DNA and nerve cells, no more, no less, and she was hidden behind dirty windows.

'Maybe it was a terrorist, blowing the plane up with lip-gloss,' Anne went on, putting her mobile down. 'Or another of those lethal substances you have to put in a little transparent plastic bag before you get on a plane.'

'Air France have had problems with planes crashing before,' Annika said. 'Some problem with the air-speed meters, or maybe the altimeters, I don't remember.'

'You always think everyone means well,' Anne

said. 'Maybe al-Qaeda just want to make the world a better place.'

She picked up the papers from the table and offered them to Annika. 'Do you want these?'

Annika shook her head. Anne put the bundle into her gym bag.

'Wouldn't you like to come along? Ashtanga yoga, breathing techniques, body control and concentration. You could do with a bit of that.'

Annika looked at the time. 'I'm going up to the paper to talk to Anders Schyman.'

Anne stiffened. 'What about?'

Annika nodded towards the gym bag. 'The "serial killer",' she lied, pulling on her coat.

The smell lingered in the walls and the floor even after they had taken the Dane away. I thought there was a darker patch where he had been lying. Maybe it was traces of bodily fluids, unless the shadows were just deeper there.

I moved further over, towards the opposite corner, snaking along on my side with my hip rubbing on the ground. My insect bites were itching, one of my eyelids had swollen, and the grit was soothing as it scratched the scabs on my arms.

A breeze was forcing its way through the gaps in the tin panels.

I had talked to the Dane a bit before we'd set off on our reconnaissance trip: he had sat down next to me in the hotel bar and started telling me about his children and grandchildren. His son had just had a little girl and he showed me pictures of them. I'd done my best to get rid of him, because Catherine was sitting on the other side of me, and we'd had other things to discuss . . .

I hadn't heard anything from Catherine or the German woman since they'd moved us into the tin shack, no talking, no screams, nothing. I stared into the darkness, trying to ignore the stain on the ground, trying to picture her face in my mind, but I couldn't find it. I couldn't remember what she looked like. Instead I saw Ellen, my little girl, who was so like me, and my throat suddenly felt tight and I hardly noticed when the sheet of tin covering the entrance was removed.

The tall man yanked me off the ground and dragged me over towards the stain left by the Dane. I resisted instinctively, not there, not the damp patch, but the tall man hit my ear and I stopped struggling. He put me down with my back against the tin wall. The stench enveloped me and I felt the damp seeping through the blanket they had wrapped me in.

'*Subiri hapa*,' the tall man said, then went out again without blocking the entrance. The blinding rectangle filled the whole space, and sent flashes of lightning through my brain. Everything went white. I shut my eyes and lifted my head towards the roof.

Then the gap was filled and the skies vanished. A broad, squat figure leaned into the gloom and wrinkled its nose. 'You stink,' he said.

It was the man with the machete, Kiongozi Ujumla. He was so short he could stand upright in the shack. His face vanished in the dust under the roof, but I could see his eyes flash.

'Who Yimmie?' he said.

I felt my breathing get faster. He was asking me a question – what did he mean? Yimmie? What was Yimmie? A person? I didn't know a Yimmie.

'Who?' I said.

He kicked me in the chest. I heard a rib crack and twisted away.

'Yimmie Allenius,' the man with the machete said.

Yimmie Allenius? Did he mean Jimmy Halenius?

'The under-secretary?' I asked. 'The under-secretary of state? Where I work?'

A row of teeth flashed above me. 'Very good! Colleague at work. You secretary, research secretary.' He bent over and pressed on the place where he had kicked me. I heard myself groan.

'You rich man?' he whispered to the wall behind me.

'No,' I muttered in reply, 'not at all.'

He pushed his fingers deeper into my ribcage. 'You rich man?' he screamed in my ear, and the whole world roared in answer.

'Yes,' I said, 'yes, yes. I'm rich man.'

He stood up and turned towards the doorway. '*Picha vifaa*,' he said, and the tall man crept into the shack with a big lamp and a video camera. I remembered the journalist Annika had written

211

about in the USA, the American whose head had been cut off in a video on the internet, and the air filled with blood-red panic.

That day's print edition wasn't much to shout about, he had to admit. The potential serial killer they had come up with for the front page was more tenuous than was strictly acceptable, but what was an editor with ambitious sales targets to do?

Apart from that, the Nightmare Scenario, with capital letters, had occurred in the early hours of the morning. The newsflash about the French passenger-plane crash had come in precisely two minutes after printing had reached the point where it was no longer possible to add any extra pages to the paper. They could have produced a new edition for the big cities, and there was a risk that the other evening paper would do that, but in Schyman's opinion a serial killer in the suburbs of Stockholm, no matter how theoretical he might be, was at least as commercially appealing as a plane crash in which no Swedes were involved. Obviously the online edition was leading with the plane, and in the blogosphere the self-appointed experts were already broadcasting their evaluations: Islamic fundamentalists had blown the plane up, or rather down, into the sea. They clearly hadn't learned anything from events in Norway.

The online edition had taken the speculation a step further and was running summaries of famous terrorist attacks in a fact box next to the article about the air disaster. To distance themselves from the mob mentality of the net, they had included boxes about Osama bin Laden and Anders Behring Breivik.

Personally Schyman had serious doubts about the terrorism theory. He had done his military service in the air force, at base F21 up in Luleå (admittedly only on fatigue duty), and had some very basic knowledge of the subject. If nothing else, his military service had given him an interest in the aeronautics industry and plane crashes. It was the second time this century that Air France had suffered an incident of this sort. A few years ago an Airbus A330 with 228 people on board had crashed on a flight from Rio de Janeiro to Paris, falling into the Atlantic. Only last summer had they finally managed to recover the black box from the seabed. They still didn't know the exact cause of the accident: it might have been pilot error or bad weather – turbulence, lightning, strong storm winds. He found it highly improbable that the cause of the latest crash was some confused Muslim, explosives hidden in the heels of his shoes, or, for that matter, a Norwegian Christian.

From the corner of his eye he saw a familiar face fill the television screen on the far wall. It was everyone's favourite Swedish EU commissioner, the talented young liberal politician who spoke five languages fluently and had responsibility for immigration into Europe and internal security.

She was being interviewed in the Sky News studio. He reached for the remote and turned up the volume.

'Absolutely,' she said, in reply to a question he hadn't heard. 'The conference in Nairobi was a great success. The agreements haven't been signed yet, but our collaboration with the African Union has been expanded, and each side has a greater understanding of the other's respective policies and wishes.'

'So there's no chance that the kidnappers' demand for Europe to open its borders will be considered?'

The EU commissioner's head jerked slightly. 'In light of the recent turbulence in North Africa and the Middle East, Frontex is more necessary than ever,' she said. 'Not only to protect the population of Europe, but to help and support refugees in the countries affected. Frontex is working to save lives. Without Frontex the torrent of refugees would—'

'To save lives? But in this case the kidnappers are threatening to kill the hostages.'

'The border crossings with Somalia need to be strengthened. That's one of our key demands.'

His intercom buzzed, a little grating sound that always made him jump.

'You have a visitor on the way up to see you,' the caretaker said, the new one who actually seemed to have a brain.

'Thanks,' the editor-in-chief said, and pressed the

button he thought he was supposed to press. Then he got the remote control and switched off the EU commissioner.

He looked out across the newsroom and saw Annika Bengtzon materialize in the office with her usual evasive body language, as if she were floating a centimetre or so above the floor. Maybe she did it to make herself less visible, but it had the opposite effect. Whenever she walked in, a silence would form around her, like a sort of vacuum. The light seemed to get more intense and everyone would look up: a quick glance to see what was disturbing the status quo.

She knocked on the glass door of his office as if he hadn't seen her until then.

He waved her in.

'Have the councils given up clearing snow all over Sweden, or just in Stockholm?' she asked, as she pulled off her padded jacket and let it fall in a heap on to the floor.

'Living in a democracy means that you only get what you want half the time,' Schyman said. 'And it was the public, in its boundless wisdom, who voted in this administration.'

She slumped on to his visitor's chair with her hair pulled into a bird's nest on top of her head. 'I've been thinking,' she said. 'I might have been a bit hasty when I rejected your proposal yesterday.'

She had dark rings under her eyes, but seemed together. And she'd changed her clothes: a red sweater and black jeans.

'I said you could think about it,' he reminded her.

She squirmed on the chair. 'The idea of talking about this in public feels so sleazy,' she said. 'Like standing in the square naked so that people have something to be shocked about.'

He nodded and waited. If it had been someone else sitting in front of him, pretty much anyone at all, he would have seen that remark as the beginning of lengthy negotiations about amounts and conditions. But Annika rarely had a hidden agenda. She had no talent for guile or manipulation. Her way of working was more like a tank's: straightforward, as hard as possible, until all resistance had been crushed.

'I don't know yet if I need the money,' she said. 'How long have I got to make up my mind?'

'The board needs a decision on Monday morning,' he replied.

That wasn't true. He could do what he liked with the money. It was in his budget (for 'additional external costs') and the board had no idea. But he didn't have forty million dollars at his disposal. The upper limit was set at three million kronor.

Annika's gaze had settled on that day's paper, which was lying front-page up on his desk. 'Do you believe that?' she asked.

He felt his mood drop like a stone. 'Annika . . .'

She pointed at the picture of Linnea Sendman. 'She'd reported her husband four times for abusing her. Did you know that? She tried to get a restraining order twice, but failed both times. Have you checked that?'

'Maybe there was a reason why the complaints weren't acted upon,' Schyman said, and heard how contrary he sounded. Bengtzon always managed to provoke him. Now she was sitting on the edge of her seat and leaning over his desk. She'd really got the bit between her teeth.

'The prosecutor thought she was a silly, hysterical woman who ought to try being reasonable instead of getting stressed over little things. The same old routine, in other words.'

'So what do you think we should have done? We can't accuse her husband of something for which we've got no evidence against him,' Schyman said, aware that he was on thin ice. And, sure enough, Bengtzon shut her eyes the way she always did when she couldn't quite believe how incredibly stupid he was being.

'But the plane that crashed was blown up by terrorists?' she said.

He stood up, irritated. What did this have to do with his proposal to pay the ransom for her kidnapped husband? 'We don't point the finger at individuals, you know that,' he said.

She leaned back in her chair. 'Did you read the Europol report about terrorism in Europe a few years ago?'

Schyman tried to gather his strength.

'Four hundred and ninety-eight acts of terrorism were committed in Europe within the space of a year,' she went on. 'Hundreds of people were arrested, under suspicion of various types of terrorist activity. The majority were Muslim. But do you know how many of those four hundred and ninety-eight acts of terrorism were committed by Islamic terrorists?'

'Annika . . .'

'One.'

He looked at her. 'One?'

'One. Most of the other four hundred and ninety-seven were carried out by various separatist groups, ETA and the Corsican nutters, neo-Nazis and animal rights activists, the odd Communist and a few complete lunatics. But every time we wrote about terrorists, we implied that they were Muslims.'

'That's because—'

'Just look at what happened after the bombing in Oslo and the shootings on Utøya. Even the most stuck-up morning papers let their correspondents write analytical pieces about how international terrorism had arrived in Norway, and how they shouldn't really be surprised, because if you got involved in Afghanistan that sort of thing was bound to happen.'

Schyman didn't respond. What was he supposed to say?

'We spread myths and fear that, to a very large extent, are utterly unfounded,' she went on, 'but when we've got a mother with a young child who gets murdered, suddenly the demands for proof are so high that we can't even write a simple report without a guilty verdict from the Court of Appeal. Assuming we haven't managed to invent a fictitious serial killer, of course. Because then we can really go to town.'

Schyman sat down again, completely drained. 'The last contact with the plane was an automated fault report about an electrical short-circuit,' he said. 'There's nothing to suggest an explosion, or any form of terrorist attack.'

She looked at him in silence for a long time. He let her stew – he didn't have the energy to try to work out what was going on inside that stubborn head of hers. Once, several years ago, he had actually considered her as one of his potential successors. He must have been mad.

'The Frenchman's dead,' she said. 'Chopped up into little pieces. The body was found near the Djibouti embassy in Mogadishu. The head's still missing.'

He felt the hair on the back of his neck stand up. 'Executed?'

She didn't answer.

'I haven't heard anything about that,' he said.

'I don't know why they're taking their time breaking the news,' she said. 'Presumably there's a good reason, some close relative they haven't managed to get hold of. Well, now you've got a head-start. I've got one question.'

'A question?'

'How much money does your proposal run to?'

Unable to stop himself, he answered in the same

way as her, unthinking, straight, and without any negotiating tactics. 'Three million.'

'Kronor?' She sounded incredulous and disappointed.

'At most,' he replied.

She chewed the inside of her cheek for a few moments. 'Could I have it as a loan?'

'And pay it back by acting as my press-ethics conscience, free of charge until I retire?'

He saw her shrink in her chair, and wondered what he was playing at. Why did he feel the need to belittle a reporter whose husband had been kidnapped and who was negotiating the price of selling her dignity?

'Sorry,' he said. 'I didn't mean—'

'When would the articles and online posts be published? Straight away? Or could they wait until the whole thing's over?'

'They could wait,' he heard himself say, even though he'd decided the exact opposite.

'Do the children have to be included?'

'Yes,' he said. 'That's part of the deal.'

'Only if there's a happy ending,' she said. 'If he dies, you just get me.'

That seemed reasonable.

'I'll write the articles myself,' she said, 'as a diary starting from when I found out that Thomas was missing. I haven't got a video camera, so I'll need to borrow one. I'll write and film without any preconceived ideas. We can edit the material together once it's over. And as far as my regular work is concerned, I'm on leave until further notice.'

He could only nod.

'I'll refer Picture-Pelle back to you when I get the camera,' she said, picking up her coat. She stood up. 'I'll email you my account details. How quickly can you transfer the money?'

The negotiations about the size of the payment had evidently come and gone without him noticing. 'It'll take up to a couple of working days,' he said.

She left his glass box without looking back, and Schyman couldn't decide if he felt pleased or deceived.

CHAPTER 11

She bought a takeaway from the Indian curry house and got back to the flat with red cheeks and steaming bags. Halenius took care of the food while she shook off her outdoor clothes.

'Any video?' she asked.

'Nothing. How did you get on?' he asked, from the kitchen.

'Schyman can't work me out,' she said, hanging up her jacket. 'He thinks I'm a bit stupid, all impulsive and emotional, a hysterical woman. I got exactly what I wanted.'

'Congratulations. How much money was he offering?'

'More than I expected,' Annika said. 'Three million.'

Halenius let out a whistle.

'Are you hungry? Probably best to eat while it's still hot,' Annika said, pushing past him into the kitchen. The top of her arm nudged his chest.

It felt so odd to have him in her home, walking about in her kitchen and bathroom while she was out meeting people for coffee, sitting in her bedroom while she was away at the newsroom. He radiated warmth, like a paraffin heater.

'I don't know what Schyman paid the King's mistress when she spilled the beans in the paper the other year,' she said, getting two plates out of the top cupboard without looking at him, 'but it must have been something like the same amount.'

Halenius was leaning against the doorframe, and she could feel his eyes following her as she laid the table. 'Do you think so?' he said. 'That the paper paid for the interview?'

She stopped and looked at him. 'I don't know for sure,' she said. 'I was in Washington at the time. But why else would she have agreed to do it?'

'For the attention?' Halenius suggested.

'If she was after a bit of time in the limelight she could have done the rounds of the chat shows and gossip magazines, rather than just the *Evening Post*. She's a smart woman. Tandoori chicken or lamb korma?'

He leaned over the aluminium trays. 'Which is which?'

She wasn't sure she'd be able to eat, but she sat down anyway and spooned some of the chicken on to her plate. He sat opposite her and their knees collided under the table.

'You were right,' he said. 'Thomas volunteered to go on the reconnaissance trip up to Liboi. How did you know?'

She chewed for a few moments. The chicken seemed to be swelling in her mouth. 'Thomas

223

doesn't really like roughing it. He likes vintage wine and restaurants that serve complicated food. There are three reasons why he'd go on a trip like that: prestige, compulsion, or a woman.'

Halenius had already dismissed the idea of it being prestigious when they'd met at the department, and now compulsion was ticked off as well. For some reason the realization seemed to embarrass him.

'What?' she said, taking a bite of naan bread.

He shook his head without replying.

She put the bread down. 'It's not your fault,' she said. 'Thomas isn't monogamous. I think he tries, but it doesn't work.'

'Does it have to be anyone's fault?' he said, with a faint smile.

Suddenly she felt very tired. She popped the last piece of chicken into her mouth, then stood up. 'I think I'll go and have a lie-down,' she said.

She slept for half an hour on Kalle's bed. When she woke it was dark outside, a grey, moonless darkness with no stars. Her head felt leaden. Halenius was talking quietly on his mobile in the bedroom. She crept into the bathroom in just her T-shirt and pants, and swallowed two headache pills, peed, brushed her teeth, then sat on the toilet for a while letting herself wake up properly. When she went out into the hall again Halenius was standing there with his hair on end and a mug of coffee.

'Come with me,' he said simply, and went into the bedroom. 'The kidnappers have posted a new video online.'

'Is it Thomas?'

'No. The man in the turban.'

She dashed into the children's room, pulled on her jeans and cardigan, then followed him on bare feet. He was sitting at his computer with a frozen film clip on the screen.

'News of the Frenchman is out,' Halenius said. 'They seem to have been waiting for the announcement because this video was posted just a couple of minutes after the AFP newsflash.'

Annika leaned over his shoulder. The picture showed the man in the turban and military outfit from the previous film. Even the dark red background and the rest of the setting seemed to be the same. 'Have they used the same server as well?' Annika asked.

The under-secretary of state scratched his head. 'You're not really asking the right person, seeing as I have trouble logging into my own computer . . . Apparently there are two or three internet providers in Somalia. The largest is called Telcom, but it's not their servers that are being used, it's one of the smaller companies. Do you want to see it?'

'Can you understand what he's saying?'

'This is the BBC's link and they've subtitled it. Pull up a chair.'

She stretched, and realized that her hair had fallen

across his shoulder. She quickly grabbed the clothes from the chair by the window and threw them on to the bed, then moved the chair to the desk, where she positioned it at a decent distance from Halenius. He clicked the screen and the image shook into action. Annika had to crane her neck to see, and Halenius moved back so she could get a bit closer. The man in the turban was staring straight into the camera. His eyes were very small. He presented his message in the same language as last time, with the same slow, deliberate pronunciation. The content was much the same, although his demands had escalated.

'The evil and ignorance of the West will not go unpunished. The hour of vengeance is at hand. Fiqh Jihad has killed the French dog on account of his sins. But there is still a chance for absolution. Our demands are simple. Open the borders to Europe. Abolish Frontex. Distribute the Earth's resources fairly. Remove protective customs tariffs.

'More will meet the same fate as the Frenchman if the world doesn't listen. Freedom for Africa! Allah is great!'

The image trembled slightly, as if someone had had to press hard to switch off the video-camera. The screen faded to black. Halenius clicked to close the Explorer window. 'This one's thirty-eight seconds long as well,' he said.

'Does that matter?' Annika said.

'I don't know,' Halenius said.

They sat in silence, staring at the dark monitor.

'So, what does this mean?' Annika said.

'We can draw a few conclusions from it,' the under-secretary of state said. 'The group's claiming responsibility for the Frenchman's death, that goes without saying, but the justification, that he had sinned, is harder to understand.'

'Had he been pushing hard for Frontex in the EU?'

Halenius shook his head. 'Since he was a newcomer to the issue. The Nairobi conference was the first time he'd been involved. And he doesn't seem to have demonstrated any racist or extreme nationalist views privately either. His wife was born in Algeria.'

Annika leaned closer to the computer. 'Play it again,' she said.

Halenius clicked the wrong thing a few times, but eventually the video was running again. Annika looked at the man's eyes while he was talking. He glanced to the left a few times, as if to check a written script.

'He's educated,' Annika said. 'I mean, he can read.'

The image shuddered and faded out.

'And there are at least two of them. Turban Man and someone standing behind or next to the camera, who switches it off. Is it possible to check with the internet provider who's been using that server?'

'The legal position is unclear,' Halenius said. 'Internet providers aren't allowed to give out

227

information about their users to anyone. Certainly a series of crimes has been committed in this instance, but the demand to reveal information has to come from some official body, and there aren't any in Somalia.'

'But surely the British and Americans don't let that sort of thing bother them,' Annika said.

'True. The Yanks got it into their heads that bin Laden was using Somali servers for financial transactions around the year 2000, so they simply shut off all internet traffic in the entire country. It was down for months.'

Annika bit her lip. 'He talks about "dogs" and "absolution". That's fairly high-flown stuff, isn't it? Symbolic, maybe. Maybe the Frenchman's sins symbolize something else. The sins of France, or the whole of Europe?'

'There's another aspect of the message, which is more important,' Halenius said.

Annika looked out of the window. Yes, she'd realized that. 'He's threatening to kill the rest of the hostages if their demands aren't met.'

Halenius nodded.

Annika stood up. 'I'll go and put my mobiles on silent.'

The first call to her work mobile appeared four minutes later. She let it go to voicemail. It was from the main Swedish news agency, TT: they wanted her reaction to the latest developments in the East African hostage crisis.

Instead of waiting for the rest of the media onslaught, she put the phones in the hall and shut herself into the children's room with her laptop. She had the best-paid freelance article of her life to write: 'How it felt when my husband was kidnapped'. She had no ambition to be politically correct. Truthful, certainly. Detailed and thorough, too, but only to the extent that she saw fit. She decided to write in the present tense, a device that was forbidden in tabloid journalism but, in this context, might work. If nothing else, it would break the usual structure. She wrote without holding back, letting the words pour out without stopping because there was no way of knowing if it would ever be read. There was no point in focusing on any particular aspect of the story for the time being so she recorded everything she'd been bottling up since Thursday, dividing it into days, hours, even minutes.

She wrote for several hours, until she started to feel hungry.

Then she set up the video camera on a tripod, aimed it at Ellen's bed, pressed record, crept in among the stuffed toys and did a test, one, two, one, two. She went back to the camera and checked the result: the camera was aimed too low, pointing at her stomach. She tilted it up slightly, but overdid it. After a couple more attempts she was in the middle of the picture, just like the man in the turban, and spoke into the camera.

'It's Saturday, the twenty-sixth of November,'

she said to the black lens. It stared back at her, like the eye of a Cyclops, an extra-terrestrial or some ancient beast, ice-cold and watchful.

'My name is Annika Bengtzon. My husband has been kidnapped. His name is Thomas. We have two children. He disappeared outside Liboi, in north-eastern Kenya, four days ago . . .' She realized she was crying. She shut her eyes to the blank lens and let the tears fall. 'I've just found out that the hostages are going to be executed unless the kidnappers' demands are met,' she whispered.

She sat there for a while, letting the camera run, then wiped her tears with the back of her hand. Her mascara was stinging her eyes.

'Opening Europe up to the developing world,' she went on, 'relinquishing our privileges and doing something about injustice: these are unreasonable demands. Everyone can understand that. The governments of Europe aren't going to change their bunker mentality just because a few low-ranking civil servants are threatened with execution.'

Her nose was blocked now, and she was breathing through her mouth.

'Maybe it's our turn to pay,' she said, turning to the window. 'Those of us in the old, free world, those of us on the right side of the wall. Why should we get everything for free?'

She looked at the lens, slightly bewildered. This was hardly what Schyman wanted. But on the other hand she hadn't been given any instructions.

In which case it was up to her to work things out for herself, wasn't it?

She got up from the bed and switched off the camera, probably causing the same sort of shaking as she'd noticed in Turban Man's film.

In the hall the doorbell rang.

She looked at her watch. It was hardly surprising that she was hungry.

Halenius cracked open the door to the children's room. 'Are you expecting anyone?'

Annika brushed the hair from her face. 'At half-past eight on a Saturday evening? Maybe they're here for my private disco. Have we had a video yet?'

'Negative. I'll go and hide,' Halenius said, then vanished into the bedroom.

Annika took a deep breath. A process of elimination was telling her that someone from the rival evening paper was in the stairwell. They'd had several hours to put together an article based on the fact that hostages in East Africa were being executed. Now all they needed was a picture of the kidnapped Swede's distraught wife. The moment she opened the door a flashbulb would go off in her face. No matter how much she argued about the right to privacy and press ethics, she would find herself quoted alongside a big portrait of herself in the following day's paper. Assuming it was actually their rivals. And assuming she opened the door.

Why hadn't she got round to fitting a peephole?

She went out into the hall and put her ear to the wooden door. She could hear nothing.

The doorbell rang again.

'Annika?' she heard Bosse say.

He knocked on the door, right where her ear was, and she took a step back.

'Annika? I saw your lights on. We only want a brief comment. Can't you open the door?'

How could he know which windows belonged to her flat? Bosse's desire to talk to her seemed to have got out of hand.

'Annika? I know you're in there.'

He pressed the doorbell, and kept it pressed for a long, long time. The sound shredded the air and filled the whole flat. Annika stayed where she was, and forced herself to remain calm. They wanted her to yank the door open and tell them to stop. They wanted her upset and wide-eyed and, in photographic terms, inconsolable.

Halenius put his head into the hall. 'Aren't you going to open it?' he mimed.

Annika merely shook her head.

'What are you playing at?' a bass voice shouted from the stairwell.

It was Lindström, her next-door neighbour. He was a retired police superintendent, and not to be trifled with.

The ringing stopped at once.

Annika put her ear to the door again.

'We're from the media,' Bosse said quietly.

'What you're doing counts as disorderly conduct

under chapter sixteen, section sixteen of the Penal Code. Get out of here before I have you arrested.'

She heard shoes scraping on a gritty floor, the lift door opening and closing, then the whining of cables. Lindström's door closed.

She breathed out and looked up at Halenius. 'Dinner?' she asked, heading into the kitchen.

Anders Schyman had been standing in the doorway, on his way home, when the news about the dead Frenchman was confirmed and the new video from the kidnappers was made public. The temperature in the newsroom immediately hit the roof and he took off his jacket again. It didn't matter. His wife was away on a spa break for the weekend with her girlfriends, and all that was waiting for him at home was a frozen fish pie and Henrik Berggren's biography of Palme, *A Wonderful Time Ahead*. It was a brilliant depiction of twentieth-century Sweden as seen through the story of the Palme family, and Olof in particular, but it would still be there tomorrow.

He had sat at his computer, going through international reaction to the kidnappers' second message, while he waited for Sjölander to get back from a sudden death on Kungsholmen: an elderly woman had been found dead in a laundry-room. It didn't sound as if it could be linked to their serial killer, but you didn't win a circulation war by leaving anything to chance.

When he saw the reporter appear at the far side

of the newsroom, over by the sports desk, he stood up and slid the glass door open. 'Sjölander? Come here a minute.'

The reporter left his coat and the bag containing his laptop on a chair by the newsdesk and walked across to Schyman. 'It's going to be tricky to make anything out of that,' he said, shutting the door behind him. 'A seventy-five-year-old woman, no sign of violence, two previous heart attacks. They'd already moved the body when we arrived, but we've got pictures of the drying room with a concerned neighbour in the foreground . . .'

Schyman raised his hand. 'You've heard that the Somali kidnappers have started killing the hostages?'

Sjölander nodded and sat down.

'There've been demonstrations in Sudan and Nigeria this evening in support of the kidnappers' demands for more open borders and lower or non-existent import duties,' Schyman went on, gesturing towards his computer. 'They want the concentration camps in Libya emptied and Frontex closed down.'

'Oh, fuck,' Sjölander said. Schyman turned the screen so the other man could read the report.

'So far it's just a few demonstrations, but God knows what this could lead to,' Schyman added.

Sjölander read some of the newsflashes in silence. 'The rebel movements have lacked a figurehead since bin Laden was killed,' he said, sinking back into his chair. 'Maybe this fellow could take up the mantle.'

Schyman looked sceptical. 'Do you think? No one seems to know anything about him, not even the boys in Langley. Holy warriors don't usually appear out of nowhere. Bin Laden was an apprentice to Abdullah Azzam, and commanded battles during the Soviet occupation of Afghanistan before he founded al-Qaeda.'

Sjölander tucked a pouch of chewing tobacco under his lip. 'This man could have been a fighter too,' he said. 'The fact that we've never heard of him doesn't mean anything – there's a hell of a lot of armed conflicts in Africa that no one gives a damn about. And he must have learned the rhetoric from somewhere.'

'I saw our esteemed commissioner on TV earlier,' Schyman said. 'She didn't seem especially keen to abolish Frontex.'

Sjölander chuckled and adjusted the tobacco. 'Are you kidding? That's what her entire policy is based on, with some justification. Imagine the chaos in the Mediterranean during the rebellions in North Africa without Frontex's patrol boats. Christ, you'd be able to walk all the way to Libya over the torrent of refugees without getting your feet wet. We're bloody lucky she's prepared to take firm action.'

A shout from the newsroom made Schyman and Sjölander look up.

Patrik was rushing to Schyman's office with a printout fluttering above his head like a battle standard. He thrust the glass door open. 'We've got a murdered young mum on a footpath out in Sätra, stabbed in the neck.'

My first memory of the sea. I was rocking in it, with it, lying in it, as if it were a cradle. Above me white tufts of cloud floated past. I was on my back in a basket staring up at them. I knew I was on the sea. I don't know how old I was, but I knew I was in the boat, don't ask me how. Maybe it was the smell of salt water, the sound of waves breaking against the hull, the light reflecting off the surface of the sea.

It reached all the way in here, into the darkness inside the tin shack. The surf roared and algae stuck to my legs.

I'd forgotten how much I loved the sea.

For some reason that thought made me cry.

I had frittered away so much love and happiness. There were so many people I'd let down, not just myself but all of my nearest and dearest.

And I told them about the money, Annika. I know you were planning to buy a flat with it, but I was so scared, and my right side where he kicked me hurt so much. I know you wanted to use that insurance pay-out to make a future for us together, but you have to help me, Annika. I can't handle this any more . . .

And suddenly I was back at sea, in the boat on the way out to Gällnö, in the old sloop my dad had inherited from Uncle Knut, the sail that smelt like laundry and flapped in the wind. Behind me

236

were the jetty and the gravel path up to the village, the unpainted barn, the rusty boathouse. The low, red-grey buildings leaning against each other, as if for support against the wind. The grey rocks, the skinny pines, the shriek of the seagulls on the wind. Söderby farm, the fields and meadows, cows grazing . . . I was rocking towards the horizon, soft and endless, and felt my tears drying on my jaw.

Outside the guards' fire was dying. I could hear one of them snoring. It was very cold, and I was so cold I was shaking. Was I getting a fever? Had the malaria mosquito, *Anopheles gambiae*, installed its parasite in my liver? Was this the start of the symptoms?

I started to cry again.

I was so hungry.

They had given me some *ugali* that evening, with a little scrap of meat, but the meat was crawling with white maggots and I couldn't make myself eat it, and the tall man yelled at me and forced the meat into my mouth, but I clenched my teeth and then he held my nose closed until I fainted. When I came round he had vanished, taking the *ugali* with him.

I breathed hard in the darkness and tasted salt water.

Annika was sitting on the sofa next to Jimmy Halenius watching the television screen without really registering what was going on. The under-secretary of state, on the other hand, seemed to be following it pretty well, laughing, then tilting his head when things got sad and the violins started up.

The kidnappers hadn't been in touch. No video, no phone call.

But all the media in Sweden and quite a few from abroad had been calling her mobile non-stop since the news of the Frenchman had broken. It had been on the unit in the hall, vibrating silently, but after an hour or so it had vibrated its way on to the floor and was probably somewhere among her shoes by now.

She glanced at Halenius. He was leaning towards the television: something exciting must be happening. It was incredible that he was supporting her and Thomas like this, quite remarkable. Would any of her bosses have done the same? Schyman, or Patrik Nilsson? She snorted.

She wondered what sort of father he was. She'd never heard him talking to his children on the phone. He probably did that when he was shut in the bedroom. She knew the plane to Cape Town had taken off earlier that evening, but he hadn't mentioned it and she didn't want to seem nosy. She wondered who his girlfriend was. Probably one of the lawyers in the department. Where else would a single father of two with a top job meet anyone if not at work?

I wonder if she's beautiful or intelligent, Annika thought. A combination of the two was rare.

The film was evidently over, because Halenius

stood up and said something. She raised her eyebrows.

'Coffee?'

She shook her head.

'Is it okay if I have a cup?'

She flew up. 'Sit down. I'm in charge of supplies.' She got out a plate of buns from the previous day's raid on the Co-op, then sat in silence and watched him eat them. The television was on with the volume turned down. It was showing a repeat of some British detective series.

'Aren't you rather young to be an under-secretary of state?' she asked.

He swallowed a piece of bun. 'You're wondering who I had to sleep with to get this job.' He grinned. 'There's only one likely candidate, the minister himself. He selects his under-secretary of state personally. It's not a party appointment.'

She smiled back. 'So what do you actually do? When your staff aren't getting kidnapped.'

'The minister's work is focused outside the department, and the under-secretary of state deals with what goes on inside it. You have to get on very well together. There've been some real horror stories where it hasn't worked at all.'

'You must end up practically merging. You sound just like him now. But what do you actually *do*?'

He laughed gently and took another bite of the bun. 'Sometimes I have to answer to the media, but only when we're trying to play down something really difficult, really bloody awful.' He was chuckling now.

'And the minister chose you specifically because?'

He washed down the bun with a gulp of coffee. 'I didn't know him particularly well. We'd met at a party and played football a few times, but he must have needed someone with my particular abilities.'

'Which are?'

'I got my Ph.D. in administrative law when I was twenty-eight, and was working at the Supreme Court when his secretary called and asked me to go for an interview.'

She looked at him, trying to see him as a legal bureaucrat at the Supreme Court. It wasn't easy. She had the impression that everyone there was dusty and had threadbare suits and dandruff, not spiked hair and faded jeans. 'So if you lose the election next year, you'll have to resign?'

'Yep.'

'And then you'll end up in charge of some obscure authority?'

Halenius stiffened. 'Did the lift just stop up here?' he said quietly.

Annika got to her feet. She went towards the door in her stockinged feet without breathing. It certainly sounded as if someone was out there – she could hear scraping sounds and muttering. The lift went back down. The bell rang. She stood beside the door, trying to hear through it to the stairwell.

240

'Anki?'

She took a step back out of sheer astonishment.

'Who is it?' Halenius whispered.

Annika stared at the door. 'My sister,' she said. 'Birgitta.'

The bell rang again. Someone tried the handle.

'I'll pull back to Kidnap Control,' Halenius said.

Annika waited until he had gone, then opened the door.

Her little sister was swaying in the darkness of the stairwell beside a large man in a denim waistcoat.

'Hello, Anki,' Birgitta said. 'Long time no see. Can we come in?'

Annika's sister and her husband, presumably the Steven Annika had never met, had clearly had a bit to drink. She hesitated.

'Or am I going to have to piss out here?' Birgitta said.

Annika took a step back and pointed to the bathroom. Birgitta hurried in and closed the door. The large man filled the hall. Annika went round him and stood in the kitchen doorway, folding her arms over her chest, a gesture that clearly signalled defence and mistrust, but she couldn't help herself. They stood in silence until Birgitta emerged. In spite of the gloom in the hall, she could see that her sister hadn't managed to lose the weight she'd gained while she was pregnant. Her hair was longer than ever, reaching to below her waist.

'This is something of a surprise,' Annika said. 'To what do I owe the honour?'

241

'We've been to a concert,' Birgitta said. 'Rammstein. In the Globe. Brilliant.'

She's got exactly the same voice as me, Annika found herself thinking. We sound exactly the same. She's blonde and I'm brunette, but we're so similar. I'm her dark shadow.

'I thought you were working this weekend?' Annika said. 'Mum said she was going to be looking after . . . your daughter.'

She wasn't sure she could remember the name. Destiny? Crystal? Chastity?

'I don't work evenings, do I? When Steven got hold of a couple of cheap tickets online, we decided to go for it.'

Steven went into the living room. Annika started and hurried after him. Before she knew it he'd blunder into the bedroom and find Halenius sitting there with his computer and recording equipment and loads of Post-it notes on the wall with reminders for when the kidnappers called: suggested code-words, different negotiating tactics, facts that Halenius had dug out, transcripts of the conversations with the kidnappers . . .

'What exactly do you want?' Annika asked. Steven was a head taller than her, with thinning hair and liver spots on his forehead. So far he hadn't said a word.

'We were wondering if we could spend the night here,' Birgitta said. 'The last train to Flen has already left, and we can't afford a hotel.'

Annika looked at her sister and tried to work

out her own reaction. They hadn't seen each other in how long? Three years? Four? Now Birgitta had turned up in the middle of a hostage crisis because she'd *missed the train*?

'I don't know if you've heard,' Annika said, her voice thickening, 'but my husband's been kidnapped. He's being held captive somewhere in East Africa. They're threatening to execute him.'

Birgitta looked round the living room. 'Mum said. That's so awful. Poor you.'

The husband sat on the sofa with a thud. His upper body immediately began to lean alarmingly. He was on the point of falling asleep, and Annika felt her brain short-circuit. 'You can't stay here,' she said loudly. 'Not tonight.'

The man was making himself comfortable on the sofa, putting his feet up, shoes and all, on the armrest, and stuffing one of the scatter cushions under his head. Birgitta sat down beside him. 'What difference does it make if we . . .?'

Annika put her hands over her ears, hard, for several seconds. 'You have to go,' she said, grabbing the man's arm. 'Get out, both of you!'

'Calm down,' Birgitta said, sounding small and frightened. 'Don't pull him like that. He might get angry.'

'Haven't you a shred of decency in you?' she said. 'Forcing your way into my home in the middle of the night because you're too drunk to catch the train home? Get out!'

'Don't talk to Steven like that!' Birgitta squeaked.

243

The man opened his eyes and fixed his gaze on Annika. 'You, you fucking . . .'

Annika felt the draught as the bedroom door opened. Then Jimmy Halenius was standing right behind her – she could feel his chest against her back.

'You've got a man in your bedroom?' Birgitta said.

'Andersson, from the crime squad,' Halenius said, holding up his pass card from Rosenbad. 'This flat is a crime scene. We're in the process of investigating a serious crime. I'm going to have to ask you to leave immediately.'

The effect on the thickset man was striking. He sobered instantly and stood up with surprising agility.

'Steven, come on,' Birgitta said, pulling at his arm.

This isn't the first time, Annika thought. He's been spoken to by the police like that before, and it's left its mark on him, the sort of mark that cuts through a lot of drink.

'This way,' Halenius said, taking the man's other arm.

Annika saw them disappear into the hall, heard the front door open and close, then the clatter of the lift. She stood in the light of the television, heart pounding.

Birgitta, the darling daughter, the favourite child, the fair, pretty one. Mummy's little angel, the girl of distinctly average talents who always got picked to be the star of the annual Lucia festivities in December.

Annika had been Daddy's girl, dark and edgy even as a child, with her precocious breasts, big eyes and top marks in every subject without having to try.

Halenius came back into the living room.

'Andersson, from the crime squad?' Annika said.

He sighed and sat down in an armchair. 'Impersonating a public official,' he said. 'I confess. Could be fined ten days' wages if I'm found guilty. So that was your sister and brother-in-law?'

She felt her knees give way and sank on to the sofa.

'Thanks for your help,' she said.

'I remember her from school photographs,' he said. 'She was the year below you, wasn't she? Roly had a bit of a crush on her as well, but you were the one for him.'

'Everyone had a crush on Birgitta,' Annika said, leaning her head back. 'I think she actually went out with Roly for a while, in high school.'

'True,' Halenius said. 'But only because he couldn't have you.'

'That's her real hair colour,' Annika said. 'Different shades of blonde. People pay a fortune to look like her.'

'How old is she? Thirty-seven? She seems older.'

Annika raised her head and looked at Halenius. 'How the hell did you remember that she went out with Roly? I'd be surprised if she herself remembered that.'

He smiled and shook his head.

She leaned towards him. 'How well did you know Roly?' she asked. 'How much time did you really spend together?'

'A lot.'

'And he talked about me and Birgitta?'

'Mostly you. All the time, in fact.'

Annika looked at Halenius. He didn't look away.

'I grew up with you,' he said. 'You were Utopia, a mirage, the dream girl no one could ever have. Why do you think I came to dinner at yours that time out in Djursholm?'

Her mouth had dried.

'I wanted to see who you were,' he said quietly. 'See what sort of adult you'd become.'

'And shatter the dream?' she said hoarsely.

He looked at her for a few seconds, then stood up. 'See you tomorrow,' he said, then put on his outdoor clothes and left.

DAY 5

SUNDAY, 27 NOVEMBER

CHAPTER 12

I woke up when the tall man walked into the shack. His smell washed over me, like the waves around Gällnö. I experienced a few seconds of utter panic before I realized what he wanted.

He had brought tea, water, *ugali* and a fresh tomato. He was doing an unusual amount of smiling and talking, '*Kula ili kupata nguvu, siku kubwa mbele yenu.*' He leaned over me and untied the thick rope binding my hands behind me. It was a blessing to be able to massage my wrists and try to get a bit of circulation back into my fingers. When I reached cautiously for the tomato, he nodded encouragingly. '*Kula vizuri,*' he said, then walked out. He had left my hands untied, but they usually did when I was eating.

The tea was strong and sweet and tasted of mint. This was the nicest meal I'd had since I got there. The water was cool and tasted fresh, and the *ugali* was still warm.

Perhaps I was doing something right. Perhaps they'd understood that I didn't want to be a problem, that I really would co-operate, and this

249

was the reward. Maybe from now on I would be better treated.

The thought filled me with confidence.

Perhaps Annika had had something to do with this. I'd worked out that they had been in touch with her. I knew she'd do anything to get me released. Perhaps the ransom had already been paid. Soon they'd drive up in that big Toyota and take me back to the plane on the runway in Liboi.

I have to admit, I was crying with relief.

When I thought about it, the guards hadn't treated me too badly. Kiongozi Ujumla, the thickset man in the turban, had kicked me pretty viciously, but that was because I was lying. Of course I was a rich man in their eyes: to say anything different was ridiculous. The right side of my chest hurt, making me wince every time I took a deep breath, but that was just one of those things. The Dane wasn't their fault: he'd been asthmatic and, well, what could I say about the Frenchman? There had been moments when I'd felt like chopping his head off.

I hadn't seen or heard anything of the Spaniard or the Romanian since they'd been taken from the shack. Perhaps they'd be coming back with me to the landing strip in the Toyota. Maybe our governments had got together and negotiated our release in return for some sort of political gesture.

I'd gobbled the tomato first. Now I was eating the last of the *ugali*, finishing the water, and licking the inside of the tea mug to get the last of the sugar. My stomach felt completely full. If it hadn't been for the itching of the insect bites and the throbbing pain in my right side, I was actually doing pretty well.

I sat down in the corner and leaned against the tin wall, diagonally across from the dark stain where the Dane had died. I'd made that corner of the shack the toilet, not as a sign of disrespect, purely for sanitary reasons.

The tin was still cool against my back. It would get much hotter during the day.

Then I heard voices out in the *manyatta*, male and female. One was Catherine's, she was talking loudly in English, pleading.

I sat bolt upright and sharpened my senses. Weren't there other voices too? The Spaniard's? And the Romanian's?

Maybe Catherine would be coming back to the plane with us in the Toyota.

'*Please, please,*' I heard her say. I thought she was crying.

I stood up as best I could in the low shack. At the top of the wall, just under the roof, there was a fairly large gap. I closed one eye and put the other to it, cupping my hands over my forehead to see better. The wind blew sand into my eye. I blinked and tried again. I could see three huts, all made of cracked clay rather than tin, and there was a smell of fire and mould. The sun was still low, the shadows long and deep. I couldn't see the people whose voices I'd heard, but they had to be outside somewhere. Their words were being carried by the wind – they had to be behind one of the other huts. I looked all round, but couldn't see anyone. So I sat down and listened again, trying to hear what Catherine was saying, what she wanted. Wasn't a man talking as well? Answering her? And then she cried, '*No, no, no,*' and the screaming started.

The woman had been killed by four stab wounds to the neck. She was lying at the edge of the forest, close to a footpath, behind the buildings on Kungsätravägen to the south of Stockholm. There was a playground not far away. She had been found at about six o'clock in the evening by a man walking his dog. There were striking similarities to the murder of Linnea Sendman, according to the *Evening Post*, which, to be on the safe side, had presented them in list form, accompanied by big pictures:

- The murder weapon: a knife (didactic picture of a hunting knife, although the caption made clear that this was not the actual murder weapon).
- The stab wounds: from behind, in the neck (illustrated by an anonymous woman's neck, probably that of the reporter, Elin Michnik).
- The scene of the crime: next to a playground (photograph of abandoned swing).

- The suburbs: there were just five kilometres between the sites of the two
  murders (map with arrows).

The murdered woman's name was Lena
Andersson, she was forty-two, single, and had two
teenage daughters. Her laughing face looked out
at Annika from the newspaper, her red hair swirling
in the wind.

And now the theory about a serial murder in
the Stockholm suburbs seemed to have taken root
among the police. Two named detectives confirmed
that the investigations into Lena and Linnea were
being combined (the paper was already on first-
name terms with both murdered women).

'Where do you get all these photographs of
murder victims?' Halenius asked, eating a rye-
bread sandwich. 'I thought we'd blocked access
to those archives.'

Annika closed the paper and pushed it away
from her. She couldn't bear to think of the two
teenage girls left alone. Had they sat up waiting
for their mother on Saturday night, listening for
her footsteps? Or were they out with their friends,
not thinking about her at all, maybe not knowing
she was missing until the police appeared at the
door, 'We're very sorry . . .'?

'In some ways it's got harder since you blocked
the archives,' Annika said, 'but in the new digital
world there are countless new sources to dig
about in.'

'Such as?'

'Blogs, Twitter, online papers, discussion forums, the PR pages of various companies and public bodies, and Facebook, of course. Even the suicide bomber who blew himself up on Drottninggatan was on Facebook.'

'What about copyright?' Halenius said. 'I thought you were all very concerned about that.'

'It's a grey area,' Annika said.

The image of the red-haired woman was floating in front of her above the breakfast table. She had been living alone with her daughters for three years, according to Elin Michnik's article, and worked as a chiropractor at a clinic in the centre of Skärholmen. She had been on her way home from a yoga class when she'd met her fate in the winter darkness.

Annika drank some apple juice and took a bite of her sandwich.

Halenius wasn't quite so neat today, which supported her suspicion that his girlfriend did his ironing for him. 'Have your children got there yet?' she asked.

He glanced at his watch. 'They landed an hour ago. Can I have the newspaper?'

She pushed it across the table and stood up: if he didn't want to talk about his children, she wasn't going to force him. 'Well, I'm going to call mine,' she said, taking her mobile and going into the children's room, shutting the door quietly behind her.

She didn't bother turning any lights on. There

was a kind of grey, cloudy half-light outside, the sort that was incapable of penetrating the shadows. She curled up in a foetal position on top of Kalle's duvet, hugging his pillow to her. She needed to change the sheets – it had been a fortnight since she'd last done it. At least. And she needed to go through the children's wardrobes – she hadn't done that properly since they'd got back from the USA, had just chucked everything from their cases into the cupboard, along with all the things they'd grown out of. She sat up.

She'd have to see if they'd grown out of their Lucia clothes – they must have done by now. And on the day before 13 December the whole of Sweden had always been sucked dry of Lucia dresses and boys' robes. She must remember to buy new ones as soon as possible. Perhaps Kalle wouldn't want to join in any longer. And maybe their new American school didn't celebrate Lucia in the same way as Swedish schools.

She picked up her mobile and dialled Berit's home number. Thord, her husband, answered. 'Don't come and get them too early,' he said. 'We're about to go out fishing.'

Kalle came on the line.

'Do you know if there's going to be a Lucia procession at school this year?' Annika asked.

'Mum,' Kalle said, 'Daddy's promised to take us to Norway and go fishing for trout in Randsfjorden loads of times. If he doesn't come home can I go with Thord instead?'

She took a deep breath. 'Sure.'

'Yay!' the boy exclaimed, and passed the phone to Ellen.

'Mummy, can I have a dog? A yellow one, called Soraya?'

'Are you having a nice time with Berit and Thord?' Annika asked.

'*Pleeease?* Just a little dog?'

'I'll be coming to get you soon so make the most of Soraya while you can. And we can see her lots more times.'

'We're going fishing now,' Ellen said, putting the phone down with a thud.

She heard footsteps approaching, then crackling as the phone was picked up. 'It's full-on here,' Berit said.

'How can I ever thank you?' Annika said.

'How are you getting on?'

'Don't know,' Annika said. 'We haven't heard any more. I've agreed with Schyman to write and film everything, and we'll see what can be published when it's all over.'

'Sounds like a good deal,' Berit said. 'Just say if you need help with anything.'

She noticed that someone had scribbled on the wallpaper in felt-tip. 'Where are they going fishing? Isn't the lake frozen?'

'Thord's got a hole in the ice out by the perch fishing ground. He keeps it open all winter.'

They hung up, and Annika sat there for a while with the phone in her hand. Then she stood up and went over to the wardrobes, opened the first and looked at the mess inside. All the clothes they'd had when they were little had gone up in the fire, but Kalle and Ellen had grown a fair bit since then. At the front was a little Batman costume. She pulled it out and held it up. She'd had no idea it was still there. She put it on Kalle's bed, as the start of the pile of things to keep. Next came a jumper with a train on it that Birgitta had knitted for his third birthday. She was so practical. It had been at their grandmother's in Vaxholm and had therefore escaped the fire. That ended up in the 'keep' pile as well. A princess dress that Sophia Grenborg had bought: get rid of. Old pyjamas, odd socks and washed out T-shirts all ended up on the scrapheap. Just a few went back on to hangers and into the drawers.

She'd got halfway through the first wardrobe when Halenius knocked on the door.

'It's arrived,' he said.

He sat her on the office chair in the bedroom, with the computer on the desk in front of her. The screen was black. In the middle a little triangle inside a circle indicated that a video had loaded but was paused.

'It's nothing awful,' Halenius said. 'I've watched it. It's pretty standard, short and concise. Nothing weird, nothing shocking. It was recorded yesterday, as you'll see.'

Annika clutched the edge of the desk.

'This is exactly what we've been expecting,' he went on, crouching beside her. 'Our kidnappers have clearly done the whole kidnapping course. They've done this before. Thomas has been sleeping outdoors or in very basic conditions for almost a week, and it shows. Don't be alarmed by how unkempt he looks. The actual message is completely irrelevant. What matters is that he's alive and seems reasonably okay. Do you want me to play it?'

She nodded.

The image flickered, a beam of light moved across it, and then a terrified face appeared on the screen.

Annika gasped. 'God, what have they done to him?' she said, pointing at his left eye. It was swollen shut, and his eyelid looked like a bright red cocktail sausage.

Halenius froze the image. 'Looks like an insect bite,' he said. 'Could be a mosquito or some other flying pest. His face shows no sign of having been hit. You see he hasn't been able to shave?'

Annika nodded again. She reached out her hand and touched the screen, stroking his cheek. 'He's wearing his gay shirt,' she said. 'He really did want to impress her.'

'Shall I go on?'

'Wait,' Annika said.

She pushed the chair back and ran into the children's room, grabbed the newspaper's video-camera and hurried back into the bedroom.

'Film me while I watch the video,' she said to Halenius, passing him the camera. 'Can you do that?'

He nodded. 'Why?'

'Three million reasons. Or shall I get the tripod?'

'Give it here.'

She sat in front of the computer again, adjusted her hair, then stared into Thomas's frightened eyes. His hair was dark with sweat, his face shiny, his eyes bloodshot and staring. In the background there was a dark brown wall, something stripy. Wallpaper? Damp?

'He's thinking about Daniel Pearl,' Annika said. 'He thinks they're going to behead him. Have you switched the camera on?'

'Er, I don't really know how to . . .'

Annika took the camera and pressed play.

'Just point and shoot,' she said, then turned back to the computer.

She looked Thomas in the eye.

She thought, I'm doing this for us.

'Sunday morning,' she said, into thin air. 'We've just received a video from the kidnappers, so-called *proof of life*, to show that my husband is still alive. I haven't watched the film yet. I'm about to start it running.'

She clicked on the computer.

The picture shook slightly. Thomas was blinking against the harsh light shining into his face. He was glancing up to the right – perhaps someone was standing there, pointing a gun at him.

He was holding a piece of paper. His wrists looked red and swollen.

'Today is the twenty-seventh of November,' he said in English. She turned the volume up to maximum: the sound was poor and she could hardly hear what he was saying. There was a lot of hissing and crackling, as if it were windy. She could hear the video-camera whirring beside her.

'A French plane crashed into the Atlantic this morning,' Thomas went on.

Halenius froze the picture. 'The kidnappers don't have access to any newspapers,' he said. 'That's the commonest way to show that a hostage is alive at a particular moment. Instead they've got him to say something he couldn't otherwise have known.'

'Are you filming?' Annika asked.

'Course I am,' Halenius said.

The video continued.

'I'm well,' Thomas said hoarsely. 'I'm being treated well.'

Annika pointed to a mark on his forehead. 'There's something crawling there. I think it's a spider.'

He moved the note and read in silence for a moment, while the spider made its way up to his hair.

'I want to encourage all the governments of Europe to act on the demands of . . .' he moved the note closer to his face and squinted against the bright light '. . . Fick . . . Fiqh Jihad, to act on

260

their demands for openness and the distribution of resources. It is time for a new age.'

'That's the political message,' Halenius muttered.

'And I want to emphasize the importance of paying the ransom promptly. If Europe's leaders don't listen, I will die. If you don't pay, I will die. Allah is great.'

He lowered the note and looked up from his squatting position to the right. The picture faded to black.

'Someone's standing there,' Annika said, pointing to Thomas's right side.

'Can I stop filming now?'

'Just a bit more,' Annika said, and turned towards Halenius. She felt oddly strengthened by the camera lens, as if she'd been sucked through the black hole and found herself in a parallel reality where the outcome wasn't in the hands of crazy Somali kidnappers but in hers. Her own capacity to focus and concentrate made all the difference.

'He says he's being treated well,' she said quietly, 'but I don't believe him. They forced him to say that. I think he's having a terrible time.' She looked at Halenius. 'Now you can stop.'

He lowered the camera. Annika switched it off.

'The British are going to analyse the film,' Halenius said. 'They try to uncover things you can't see or hear at first, background noises, details in the image, that sort of thing.'

'When did it arrive?' Annika asked.

'Eleven twenty-seven. Twenty minutes ago. I watched it, forwarded it to the Brits, then came to get you.'

She put the camera down. 'I'm going to pick up the children,' she said.

The eleven o'clock meeting was drawing to a close. The atmosphere had been a bit too euphoric for Schyman's taste, too much backslapping, too many bad jokes, but that was what happened when people thought they'd done something big, and by that he didn't mean in-depth analysis of global events or natural disasters, but the type of thing that was invented within the newsroom by the editors or during meetings like this. Of course the cause of the excitement was the increasingly real serial killer. Not because women were being murdered but because the paper had taken a guess and struck lucky. So far the other evening paper hadn't caught on, but it was only a matter of time. On the other side of the city they would be tearing their hair out, trying desperately to find a way into the story without letting on that they'd been left standing at the starting gate.

'Okay,' he said, trying to sound stern. 'Quick run-through. What are we leading with?'

In front of him sat Entertainment and Sport, Online and Net-TV, Op-ed and Features, the head of news and his deputy. He pointed at Entertainment.

'The rumour that Benny Andersson is going to

be the new boss of the Eurovision Song Contest,' said the slight young woman, whose name he couldn't for the life of him remember.

Schyman sighed inwardly. Why the hell would Benny from Abba want that job? Particularly when it had once been held by the *Evening Post*'s old sports editor.

He looked encouragingly at Hasse, from Sport.

'Milan are against Juventus tonight, and Zlatan Ibrahimovic is playing, so something's bound to happen.'

Vague, but okay.

'News?'

Patrik straightened. 'Apart from the serial killer, we've got an old boy who lay dead in his flat for three years without anyone noticing or missing him. And a tip-off that the minister of finance has just had his apartment renovated using black-market labour.'

He exchanged a high-five with his temporary deputy, a young star called Brutus, and Schyman knocked on the table. 'We need to follow developments in the kidnapping in East Africa as well,' he said.

Patrik groaned. 'There's nothing going on with that,' he said. 'They're not letting anything slip, no pictures, no info. It's completely dead.'

Schyman stood up and walked out of the meeting room, heading for his glass office.

The story of the murdered women was troubling him.

As soon as he'd got to work that morning, before he'd even managed to take his coat off, his phone had rung: it was the mother of one of the victims, Lena. She was angry, shocked, upset. She was crying but wasn't hysterical, and spoke in a shaky voice, but she was clear and coherent.

'This was no serial killer,' she said. 'It was Gustaf, the lazy bastard she was with. He's been stalking her ever since she finished with him, and that was several months ago, July, the end of July . . .'

'So you're saying it was the girls' father who—'

'No, no, not Oscar. Lena always got on well with Oscar. This man came to see her at the clinic. He was on incapacity benefit, problems with his back. He wouldn't take no for an answer. He refused to accept that their relationship was over. What would she have seen in him? Just another expense, that's all he was . . .'

'Did he hit her?' Schyman asked, because he had read up about women's helplines.

'He wouldn't have dared,' Lena's mother said. 'Lena would have had him locked up instantly. You didn't mess with her.'

'Did she report him to the police?'

'What for?'

'You said he'd been stalking her?'

The mother sniffed. 'She shrugged it off, said he'd get tired, that it was nothing to worry about. And now look what's happened!'

She was crying inconsolably. Schyman listened.

Distraught people didn't affect him much. Maybe empathy eroded over time: an occupational injury caused by too many years' chasing and holding people to account, exploiting and exposing them.

'We're only reporting the suspicions of the police,' he said. 'Obviously their investigations will look into all the possibilities. If this man is guilty—'

'His name's Gustaf.'

'—then it's likely he'll be arrested and charged, and if it's someone else, they'll be convicted instead.'

The mother blew her nose. 'Do you believe that?'

'Almost all murder cases get solved,' Schyman said, in a confident tone, hoping he was right.

And with that they had hung up, but the sense of unease still hadn't left him.

What if all these murdered women were just ordinary, humdrum stories? The statistics certainly pointed in that direction. The victim, the weapon, modus operandi, motive: husband no longer in control of his wife kills her with a breadknife, inside or in the immediate vicinity of her home. He didn't need Annika Bengtzon there, banging on about press ethics, to feel his own doubts growing.

For some reason he had in his head a quote from one of Sweden's best-known and most controversial political scientists, Stig-Björn Ljunggren: 'One of the most common complaints in politics is that the media distort reality. It's a litany that assumes that the role of the media should be to function as some sort of mirror to society. This is a false assumption. The media are part of an experience industry whose purpose is to entertain rather than inform us . . . Their role is not to reflect reality, but to dramatize it.'

He looked at the time. If he left now, he would get home just as his wife returned from her break.

CHAPTER 13

The drive had been cleared and the yard sanded. Annika parked next to the farm-house, turned the engine off and sat in the car for a minute or so. Out on the frozen lake, far off to the south, she could see three dots: one large and two smaller. She hoped they'd managed to catch some perch. They could fry them in butter, and eat them with crispbread. Delicious, but a nightmare to fillet.

She went up to the porch and knocked. There was no bell.

She turned to look out over the lake again.

Berit and Thord had sold their house in Täby and bought the farm after their children had left home. Annika knew there had been another reason for the move: Berit had had an affair with Superintendent Q, and it had been a last-ditch attempt to save the marriage. It had evidently worked.

Berit opened the door. 'What are you standing out here for? Why didn't you just come in?'

Annika smiled wanly. 'Too urban?'

'They're still out fishing. You'll be eating perch for the next week. Coffee?'

'Yes, please,' Annika said, stepping inside the large farmhouse kitchen. It looked like something out of *Country Living* or *Homes and Gardens*: stripped pine tiles on the floor, a wood-burning stove, wood panelling, a drop-leaf table, grandfather clock, an Ilve gas hob and a fridge with an ice-maker.

She sat at the table and watched Berit as she dealt with the coffee percolator. She was wearing the same sort of clothes she wore at work, black trousers, a blouse and a cardigan. Her movements were calm and precise, economical, not calculated to impress.

'You never pretend to be anything but yourself,' Annika said. 'You're always . . . complete.'

Berit stopped what she was doing with the coffee scoop in mid-air. 'I do, you know,' she said. 'Sometimes I pretend to be different. But not usually at work, these days. I've grown out of that.'

She tipped the coffee into the percolator, switched it on and sat down at the table with two clean mugs.

On the table lay that day's papers, the *Evening Post* and its rival, and the two big morning papers with their huge Sunday supplements. Annika ran her fingers over them but couldn't bring herself to open one.

'We've received a video,' she said quietly. '*Proof of life*. He looked like shit.' She closed her eyes and saw his face before her, his swollen eye, terrified expression, hair dark with sweat. Her hands shook and she felt herself starting to panic – *If Europe's leaders don't listen, I will die, if you don't pay, I will die*, he's dying, he's dying, he's dying, and there's nothing I can do.

'Oh, God,' she said, 'oh, God . . .'

Berit came round the table, pulled up a chair beside her and took her in her arms, holding her tight. 'This will pass,' she said. 'One day this will all be over. You're going to cope.'

Annika forced herself to breathe normally. 'It's so awful,' she whispered. 'I'm so impotent.'

Berit handed her a piece of kitchen roll, and she blew her nose loudly.

'I can just about imagine it,' Berit said, 'but I can't say I really understand what it feels like.'

Annika pressed her knuckles against her eyes. 'I'm falling apart,' she said. 'I'm never going to be the same again. Even if I do manage to patch myself up, I'm never going to be the same person again.'

Berit stood up and went back to the percolator. 'Do you know,' she said, 'in the National Museum in Cardiff, in Wales, there's a Japanese dish that was broken deliberately and then repaired. The old Japanese masters often broke valuable porcelain because they thought it was much more beautiful after it had been repaired.'

She filled the mugs with coffee, then sat down opposite Annika. 'I really wish you didn't have to go through this, but it's not going to kill you.'

Annika warmed her hands on the mug. 'It might kill Thomas.'

'It might,' Berit said.

'He didn't have to be there,' Annika said. 'He volunteered to go on that trip to Liboi.' She looked out of the window. She couldn't see the lake from there. 'The reason's name is Catherine. She's British.' She had seen pictures of her online. Blonde, pretty, neatly proportioned, like Eleonor and Sophia Fucking Bitch Grenborg. Just his type, and as far from herself as you could get.

She turned to Berit again. 'I know it's possible to go on, I know . . .'

Berit smiled slightly.

Annika stirred her coffee. 'We were thinking of moving, but we're going to lose the insurance money now. Maybe it's just as well. It wasn't really mine in the first place. It was Ragnwald's.'

Annika had found a sack of euro notes in a junction box outside Luleå when she had uncovered a story several years ago. The ten per cent reward for finding it had given her the chance to buy the villa in Djursholm, and a flat for Anne Snapphane, both of which were now gone (burned down and sold, respectively).

'Do you want to carry on?' Berit asked. 'If he comes back?'

Annika put her hand over her mouth and felt tears falling once more. Berit tore off another sheet of kitchen roll and dried her cheeks. 'There, there,' she said. 'Don't meet trouble halfway. You can grieve for a divorce if you have a reason to do so in the future. Would you like some lunch? I was going to make rissoles with onion.'

Annika managed to smile. 'That sounds great.'

Berit went to the fridge and got out some potatoes and a bowl of rissole mixture. She peeled the potatoes and put them into a saucepan, lit the gas hob and set them to boil. She lit another ring and got out a frying pan.

Annika sat where she was, incapable of moving. Outside, the wind was tugging at a naked birch, and a great tit pecked at some seed on a bird-table. Soon it would be dark again. The butter began to sizzle in the pan on the stove. Annika pulled the *Evening Post* to her. 'Did you see about that latest murder? She had two teenage daughters.'

'It's starting to get really nasty,' Berit said. 'I still don't believe there's a serial killer, but the latest one clearly wasn't an ordinary domestic killing. The ex-husband is on a business trip in Germany – Düsseldorf, I think it was. He's cut it short to come home and look after the girls. No history of threatening behaviour or violence.'

Annika read the article again. 'It doesn't make sense,' she said. 'She wasn't chosen at random. Early evening, right outside where she lived, stabbed hard in the neck. It's too intimate, too personal.'

Berit rinsed her hands under the tap, then started to make the rissoles.

'The Haga Man, who raped women up in Umeå

over several years, picked his victims at random, and that was both intimate and very personal. And sometimes close to where they lived as well.' She turned on the extractor fan and put the first rissoles in the pan.

'Unless this is a copycat,' Annika said. 'Someone who's been inspired by Patrik Nilsson's idea and has gone out and put it into practice.'

'Unless I'm misremembering, it was actually your idea,' Berit said, smiling over her shoulder.

'I was pulling his leg,' she said. 'Do you have to signpost your jokes, these days?'

'I think we've got a gang of fishermen outside,' Berit said, nodding towards the porch.

The children's cheeks were rosy as Christmas apples, their eyes glistening. They had caught fourteen perch and a pike, carefully strung up on a length of birch. They were talking at the same time, waving the bundle of fish about, until one of the fins caught Annika in the eye. They agreed to share the catch, seven perch for Kalle and Ellen, and seven for Thord, who got to keep the pike as well because he had provided the rods and bait.

The rissoles were delicious.

As dusk fell the weather turned, becoming mild and damp. There was rain in the air.

The children were watching a film in the living room with Thord and Soraya. Berit was doing a crossword, and Annika fell asleep on the guest bed in the little maid's room.

When she woke up it was pouring with rain.

'It's going to be really slippery all the way back into the city,' Thord warned, as Annika waved goodbye through the open car window.

Good job I've got a killer car, she thought. Thomas had bought a secondhand Jeep Grand Cherokee when they'd got back from the USA, a big American SUV that was lethal to all other road-users but safe for anyone inside it.

'Mummy, can I have a dog?'

She ignored the question and concentrated on keeping the car on the road.

They stopped at McDonald's in Hägernäs and bought two Happy Meals and two Big Macs, then carried on into Stockholm. She reached Norrtull without mishap and even managed to find a parking space on Bergsgatan, just outside their building, probably because it was a street-cleaning night and she'd end up getting a hefty fine if she didn't move it before midnight.

Halenius was talking on his mobile when they got inside the flat. She mimed, 'Has anyone called?' and he shook his head. She left one of the Big Macs on top of his computer and went to have hers in the kitchen with the children. They were both exhausted and could hardly keep their eyes open long enough to finish their fries.

Kalle started to cry before he fell asleep. 'Is Daddy ever going to come home?'

'We're doing all we can to make sure he does,' Annika said, stroking his hair. 'As soon as I know, you'll be the first person I tell.'

'Is he going to die in Africa?'

She kissed his forehead. 'I don't know,' she said. 'I don't think so. The people who are holding him want us to pay them to let him go, and we've got a bit of money in the bank, so I'm going to pay them as soon as I can.'

He turned away from her.

'Would you like me to leave the light on?'

He nodded.

'That was one seriously revolting hamburger,' Halenius said, coming out with the remnants screwed up in the paper bag.

'Wasn't it just?' Annika said. 'Has anything happened?'

'Quite a bit,' the under-secretary of state said.

'Don't talk so loud,' Kalle called.

They went into the bedroom and shut the door behind them. Halenius sat on his usual seat (the office chair), and Annika opened the window to let some air in, then sat cross-legged on the bed. Outside it was raining gently, a steady winter drizzle that made the city greyer and the darkness thicker. Halenius looked tired. His hair was a mess and his shirt was unbuttoned halfway to his navel.

'The man in the turban has been identified,' he said. 'Grégoire Makuza, a Tutsi, born in Kigali in Rwanda. You were right – he's well educated, studied biochemistry in Nairobi. That's how he was identified.'

'And?'

'The British came up with this, and it's not much to go on, but it's still possible to draw a number of conclusions from even such scant information, and it does raise a number of other questions . . .'

'The genocide in Rwanda,' Annika said. 'Was he there? What was his name? Gregorius?'

'Grégoire Makuza,' Halenius said, with a nod. 'Exactly. A teenage Tutsi in Kigali in 1994 . . .'

'If he was actually there then,' Annika said, 'maybe he was already living in Kenya.'

'True.'

Annika shivered, got up from the bed and went to close the window. 'A biochemist,' she said. 'What made him turn to kidnapping?' She sat down on the other chair.

'He never graduated,' Halenius said. 'For some reason he broke off his studies when he had only one term left. He was no genius, but he was getting good marks. He seemed to be heading for a career as a researcher in the pharmaceutical industry.'

Annika got to her feet again and went to stand by Halenius's computer. 'Bring up a picture of him,' she said.

Halenius did a bit of clicking, searching emails and folders. Annika was standing behind his back, looking down at his head. He had some grey hairs, and a few white ones. His shoulders were enormous, broad and strong. She wondered if he lifted weights. She clenched her hands to fight an impulse to touch them, to feel if they were as hard as they looked under his shirt.

'Here,' he said, clicking to play the video. Annika pulled the chair over and sat down beside him.

It was the first of the two clips that had been posted online. The man's face appeared on the screen, in low resolution and fairly shaky. Halenius froze the image. 'Born in the early 1980s,' he said.

'So around thirty now,' Annika said.

'He could be older,' Halenius said, tilting his head as he studied the screen.

'Or younger,' Annika said.

They stared at the man's rough features in silence.

'Tutsis,' Annika said. 'The other group was the Hutus, wasn't it? What's the difference between them?'

'No one knows any more. The definitions have kept changing over the years. It's pretty much a class difference now.'

'And the Tutsis were the privileged ones?'

'The Belgians, who were given a mandate to rule Rwanda in 1916, reinforced the differences by introducing passports that included the term "racial identity", and gave the Tutsis better jobs and higher status.'

He started the film again. The thin voice crackled out of the computer.

'Fiqh Jihad has taken seven EU delegates hostage

as punishment for the evil and ignorance of the Western world.'

Annika closed her eyes. Without the English subtitles the words meant nothing. It was a song in a Bantu language she would probably never hear again in her life, an ode to a crime that would follow her for ever. '*Allahu Akbar*,' the song ended, and silence took over.

'That last bit is Arabic rather than Kinyarwanda,' Halenius said.

'Allah is great,' Annika said.

'Actually "the greater" or "the greatest". It's the opening phrase of all Islamic prayers, as instructed by the Prophet Muhammad himself.'

Annika squinted towards the black screen. 'But Rwandans aren't Muslims, are they?'

Halenius rolled his chair back. 'There weren't many before the genocide, but the Christian leaders managed to change all that. Loads of priests, monks and nuns took part in the massacre of Tutsis but the Muslims sheltered them.'

'But they were convicted afterwards?' Annika said.

'Some, but that wasn't enough to restore faith in Christianity. There've been a lot of conversions to Islam, and today something like fifteen per cent of the population of Rwanda is Muslim.'

'Rewind the clip a bit,' Annika said.

'Er,' Halenius said, 'I'm not sure how to do that . . .'

As Annika took the mouse from him, he snatched

away his hand. She clicked to bring up an image a couple of seconds before the end, where the man was staring straight into the camera with his small, expressionless eyes. Was that evil she could see? Pure, unadulterated evil? A weapon to be used for power and oppression, used by wife-beaters and dictators and terrorists with the same insane delusions of grandeur about their right to control: *you do as I say, and if you don't I'll kill you.* Or was she looking at something else, an indifference to life? Like Osama bin Laden, the son of a wealthy man who had finally felt validation when he had won a battle against the Soviet Union in the Afghan mountains just before the end of the war, a man who became a war hero and felt obliged to find himself a new war. He had certainly managed that, starting a self-proclaimed war against an enemy he knew little about, an enemy he called the Great Satan, and other young men without a cause suddenly found they had something to do, something to care about: they were going to fight for a God they had invented.

'Was this film posted on a server in Mogadishu as well?'

'No,' Halenius said. 'It's from Kismayo, a Somali city on the shore of the Indian Ocean. It's two hundred, two hundred and fifty kilometres from Liboi.'

'What does that mean, in practical terms? Were the kidnappers in different places when they posted the recordings? Or can they control that from a distance? What sort of communications are they using? Satellite phones, mobiles, some sort of wireless internet?'

Halenius fingered his chin. 'I've had this explained to me, but I'm not sure I can repeat it . . .'

She couldn't help smiling. 'Just the analysis, then.'

'It isn't possible to locate the kidnappers through the different servers they've been using. And the calls haven't been traced either, or not according to the information I've received. To be honest, I don't think the Yanks are telling us all they know – they usually keep things to themselves—'

He was interrupted by a persistent ringing on the doorbell.

'Show time,' Annika said.

Halenius gave her a quizzical look.

She went out into the hall, the bell still ringing. There were only two types of people who would behave so intrusively at eleven o'clock on a Sunday evening: a reporter from an investigative social affairs programme on television, or a journalist from an evening paper, and she doubted the former would be trying to get hold of her tonight. The bell kept ringing. She glanced towards the children's room: it was only a matter of time before he woke them both. She took a deep breath, unlocked the door and stepped on to the landing. A flash went off, dazzling her.

'Annika Bengtzon,' Bosse said, 'we just want to

give you the chance to comment on an article in tomorrow's paper about—'

'Shut up, Bosse,' she said. 'You don't have to pretend. This has nothing to do with you giving me a chance to comment. You want a picture of me looking distraught.'

She turned towards the photographer, who was loitering somewhere behind the flash. 'Did I look sufficiently upset?' she asked.

'Erm,' the photographer said, 'can I try again?'

She looked at Bosse, and felt strangely cold inside. 'I don't want to comment on anything at all,' she said. 'I want you and your paper to leave me alone. Freedom of speech means that I have the right to say what I think, but also the right not to. Okay?'

She turned to go into the flat, and the flash went off behind her back.

'Journalists have a duty to investigate,' Bosse snapped.

She stopped, looked over her shoulder, and was rewarded with another flash. 'Journalists are the only people who can get away with stalking and harassing others. Aren't you going film me with a hidden camera as well? It's against the law for the police and everyone else, but it's okay if you do it.'

He blinked in surprise. I've just given him an idea, she thought. Why can't I ever keep my mouth shut? She went in and shut the door behind her.

Halenius came out into the hall. His face was white.

'What?' Annika said, leaning against the wall. '*What?*'

'The British woman,' he said. 'Catherine Wilson. She's been found dead, outside a refugee camp in Dadaab.'

Her heart was pounding. Was this what Bosse had wanted her to comment on?

'How?'

Halenius hid his face in his hands, then let them fall to his sides.

'She'd been split open. From the inside.'

There were far more noises at night than during the day. They echoed inside the tin walls, rattling and scratching, howling and gnawing. The guards' fire crackled like a waterfall, the folds in their clothes squeaked, their footsteps shook the earth. I tried desperately to find a corner to hide, where the noises couldn't reach me. They'd tied my hands and feet again, but I could shuffle round, snaking and crawling. The noises hunted me, stalked me, and I couldn't get away from them. In the end I found myself lying exhausted on the dark patch where the Dane had died. The stench swept around me, but there was slightly less noise there – it was further from the door, from the huts in the *manyatta*, and from the blood that was instantly sucked up by the earth and turned brown and hard.

The ground was so dry that it felt like stone, but it wasn't stone, because it was alive: it devoured everything that fell on it, blood and piss and vomit, storing it and turning it to poison and bile. They tried to force me to eat but I threw the food on to the ground. They won't force me to do anything else. I gave the food and water back to the earth. I'm never going to touch their shit again. Her eyes stalked me, glassy with pain, but still scornful and judging. They could see me in every corner.

And the noises were so loud, I couldn't escape.

DAY 6

MONDAY, 28 NOVEMBER

CHAPTER 14

Annika was standing in the hall when the landline rang. She froze mid-step and listened in the direction of the bedroom.

'Aren't we going, Mummy?'

She could feel the children's restlessness at the delay. They were starting to get sweaty in their outdoor clothes. Why was he waiting so long before answering?

The second ring.

'Yes, of course, in a moment . . .'

Was this a carefully worked-out strategy among kidnap negotiators: wait for the third ring before answering? Did that make the ransom smaller, the process faster?

'We've got swimming today, Mummy.'

Shit. Swimming.

There it was, the third ring.

'Of course you do,' she said, rushing back to the children's room and pulling the clothes out of Ellen's wardrobe. She found her swimsuit among the socks.

The fourth ring. Halenius answered.

She had slept badly, an experience she wasn't

used to. She'd woken up several times and gone in to see the children, had sat in the darkness listening to them breathing, then by the window in the living room, looking for stars. There weren't any. Tiredness made her feel all at sea, off balance.

'Can I use this bag, Mummy?'

Her daughter had found a carrier from the Co-op. She was standing in front of her, all eager, a little clock-watcher who hated being late. Kalle was kicking at the lift door out in the stairwell.

'Of course,' Annika said, pushing the swimsuit and a towel from the bathroom into the bag.

Halenius was talking quietly in English on the phone. She shut the door on his words and turned her face towards the light.

The weather was as heavy and grey as stone. The snow on the pavements had compacted to ice, but some of the shopkeepers along Hantverkargatan had taken it upon themselves to cut away the ice, and some had even sanded the pavement, which made the walk slightly less dangerous.

'We've got geography today,' Kalle said. 'Did you know that Stockholm is fifty-nine degrees north and eighteen degrees east?'

'That's right,' Annika said. 'The same latitude as Alaska. So why's the climate better here?'

'The Gulf Stream!' the boy said, jumping with both feet into a patch of slush.

Liboi was at zero degrees latitude. And it was going to be thirty-eight degrees centigrade there today – Annika had looked it up online during her sleepless night.

She held tight to the children's hands as they crossed the road. They were heading uphill, into the wind. When they reached the school gate she crouched and pulled the children to her. Kalle resisted, embarrassed, but she held him tight.

'If anyone asks about Daddy, you don't have to answer,' she said. 'If you want to say anything, then of course you can, but you don't have to. Okay?'

Kalle wriggled free but Ellen gave her a hug. She craned her neck to keep them in sight as they squeezed into the school building with all the other children, then vanished into a forest of woolly hats and rucksacks.

She jogged back to Agnegatan. The lift was busy so she took the stairs and arrived breathless at the flat. Halenius was sitting at the desk in the bedroom with an earpiece in, and a distant look on his face. When she came into the room he clicked the screen, pulled out the earpiece and turned towards her. Panting, she sank on to the bed and studied his face.

'They've agreed to lower the ransom demand,' Halenius said. 'That's definitely a breakthrough.'

She closed her eyes. 'Is he still alive?'

'They didn't give any proof of it.'

She let herself fall back on to the pillows and duvet. The ceiling was swaying above her, grey from the daylight outside. It was so nice just to lie down, with her legs dangling off the edge of the mattress, listening to the building breathe.

When had they last made love? It had been in that bed – their adventures in the shower, on the sofa and the kitchen table were a thing of the past now.

'You ought to explore how to transfer a large sum of money to a bank in Nairobi,' Halenius said. 'And I think you should do it today.'

She raised her head slightly and gave him a questioning look.

'The people negotiating on behalf of the German, Romanian and Spaniard all say they're close to agreement. It's going quickly, but not impossibly fast.'

Annika sat up again. 'It usually takes between six and sixty days,' she said.

'The amounts in the other cases are all around a million dollars,' he said. 'We probably won't get away with less.'

'Do you think it's the man in the video? The one who calls and does the negotiating?'

'The Yanks have analysed the voices digitally. They say it's the same man.'

'What technique do they use to do that?'

Halenius raised his eyebrow. 'You're asking me?'

'Why doesn't he speak English in the videos?'

Halenius stood up and went over to the window recess, where he had set up a small laser printer. 'The conversation was fairly short,' he said. 'Nine and a half minutes. I've translated it and printed it out. Do you want to read it?'

He offered her a printout, just two pages of A4. She shook her head. He put the sheets on the desk and sat down again.

Annika looked out across the treetops. 'The British woman is dead,' she said. 'The Frenchman is dead. The Romanian, Spaniard and German are all negotiating, and we're negotiating. Wasn't there another, a Dane?'

'The Danes are negotiating, but they haven't got as far as us.'

He seemed stressed today, more tired than usual. He hadn't spent many hours at home last night, and he was having to sleep alone now that his girlfriend was in South Africa. Maybe he had trouble sleeping when she wasn't there. Maybe he rolled over to her side of the bed, immersing himself in her duvet, her pillows, her scent, the strands of her hair. Maybe they made love every night, or perhaps in the mornings.

'How are you feeling?' she asked.

He looked up at her, surprised. 'Fine,' he said. 'I'm fine. How about you?'

'The banks are open,' she said, and jumped off the bed. She went into the living room and packed the video-camera with the tripod.

She hadn't made an appointment for personal financial advice, which caused the woman on Handelsbanken's customer service desk to frown.

Annika had to wait for a while as the woman went round to see if anyone would take pity on her, which shouldn't have been that difficult as she was the only customer in the building. She ran her fingers over the video-camera and noted once again how carefully all the employees moved, the way their discreet gold jewellery shimmered, and how obvious any shortcomings seemed: creases on the back of a shirt, a ladder in a pair of tights. The man with the tired eyes, the one who had seen her last time, was nowhere in sight. Maybe her questions had been the straw that broke the camel's back. Maybe he'd succumbed to a severe bout of nervous exhaustion as a result of her lack of enthusiasm.

Her legs were aching, and she stamped her feet to make them feel better.

The woman appeared again and waved her over, then cruised between the desks towards one corner where another tired-looking man in steel-rimmed glasses sat behind a fairly messy desk. He was slightly younger than his colleague from last Friday.

'Pay no attention to this,' Annika said, setting up the tripod next to the visitor's chair and attaching the camera to the top of it, then pointing it at the astonished young banker and pressing 'record'.

'Er,' the man said, 'what's this about?'

Annika sat down opposite him. 'I want to make sure I don't miss anything,' she said. 'You don't mind, do you?'

'No video or audio recording is permitted in here under any circumstances. Put it away. Okay?'

She sighed, took the camera off the tripod, then put it back in its bag.

'I might need to send money to Nairobi,' Annika said. 'I'd like to find out how that would work.'

'Nairobi? In Kenya?'

'Is there another Nairobi?'

'And what's the reason for the transfer?'

Annika lowered her voice. 'Either I close all my accounts here at Handelsbanken, or you answer my questions. Okay?'

The man took a deep breath, then tapped at his computer, his glasses flaring. 'I'm obliged to ask,' he said. 'Depending on the amount, the Swedish tax office will have to be informed of the transfer. They need a code to explain what sort of payment you want to make – for instance, if you're importing something. If no code is provided, the payment won't go through. But with a code, the information is automatically sent to the tax office when the payment is processed.'

Suddenly she felt exhausted. 'Just tell me how it works,' she said.

'You need the IBAN number and Swift address of the bank the money is being transferred to, as well as the account details, of course.'

'The account? In a bank in Nairobi?'

'Obviously you can choose to send the money to anyone you want, providing the codes are filled in properly. The money is sent as a foreign payment.

291

That usually takes three days, and costs between a hundred and fifty and two hundred kronor. Express payments take a day, but cost more.'

'How much can I send?'

He gave her a sarcastic smile. 'That depends on the assets you have access to.'

She leaned across the desk and put her driving licence under the man's nose. 'I want to send the money in my online savings account to Nairobi, but I don't have an account in a bank there. And in Nairobi I want access to the money at once, in American dollars, small denominations.'

The man tapped her ID number into his computer and blinked several times, presumably unprepared for that amount. Schyman's money had been paid in during the early hours of the morning, meaning that the account now contained almost nine and a half million kronor. 'And you want to send this to Kenya? The whole amount?'

'How much would that be in dollars?' she asked.

'US dollars?' He tapped at the keyboard.

'One million, four hundred and ninety-four thousand, three hundred and fourteen dollars and eighty cents. At today's exchange rate, six kronor and thirty-three öre to the dollar.'

Almost one and a half million dollars. Her head was spinning.

'So, if I don't have a bank account in Kenya, how do I get the money out there? Can you send it somewhere else, to one of those Western Union offices?'

The banker's cheeks had turned red. 'It isn't possible to send money from Handelsbanken to Western Union in Kenya. If you're going to send money to them, you'd have to use their system, but for amounts of this size that isn't particularly efficient. You can send seventy-five thousand kronor at a time, a maximum of twice in one day.'

She was holding tight to the desk to stop herself falling. 'So I need an account,' she said. 'With a bank in Nairobi.'

He looked at her blankly.

'Could I take the money with me?' she asked. 'In a bag?'

'Each dollar bill weighs one gram, regardless of denomination. So a million dollars in twenty-dollar notes would weigh fifty kilos.'

He'd worked that out in his head: impressive.

'And you can't take that much money out of the EU without informing Customs,' the banker said. 'You have to fill in a special EU form, giving the purpose of the transfer, whose money it is, who's taking the money out of the EU, where the money comes from, what currency it is . . .'

'Fifty kilos,' Annika said. 'That would be tricky to take as hand-luggage.'

The last time she'd flown anywhere the check-in desk had been unwavering: a maximum six kilos in her cabin bag. Hers had weighed seven. According to the airline's crystal-clear logic, she was allowed to take a Jonathan Franzen novel out of the bag and put it into her coat pocket – apparently that was fine.

'I wouldn't recommend checking them in,' he said. 'All cases get X-rayed. But there is another way.'

Annika leaned forward.

'Cash cards,' he said loudly, almost derisively. 'The same as top-up cards for mobile phones, but for money.'

She thought the woman sitting closest to them glanced in their direction.

'Like a debit card,' he said, 'with a number but no account holder. You pay the money into the card's account and you can withdraw it anywhere in the world from an ordinary cashpoint.'

'A cashpoint?'

'Yes,' he said, 'although it would take a fair number of withdrawals. The shadier individuals who normally use this particular service usually employ a gang of people who go round and with- draw a couple of hundred at a time, but if you don't want to be filmed and registered by security cameras that's an option.'

Shadier individuals? Was that what she'd become? Someone who lived on the edge of life, trying to imitate real people and the lives they led? Ordinary people, like those who worked in this bank, for instance, who looked after their clothes and jewel- lery and presumably had their friends round for dinner-parties.

She got up on unsteady legs, holding the tripod

for support, then folded it and put her bag over her shoulder. 'Well, thanks very much,' she said. 'Most informative.'

She could feel the banker's glassy stare on her back as she stumbled towards the door. Some-where along the way the tripod knocked over a mug of coffee, but she pretended she hadn't noticed.

Schyman closed the last of the morning papers and leaned back in his office chair. It creaked alarmingly, but it had always done that.

He looked at the hefty pile of newspapers in front of him, all the publications that he read every day of the year, summer and winter, weekdays and weekends, when he was at work, when he was on holiday. In recent years he'd been speeding up and reading less thoroughly. In fact he skimmed them now, particularly the morning papers.

Today he had every reason to feel pleased after his read-through.

Their serial killer had been picked up by all the national media, even if the murderer was being presented as more or less hypothetical, depending on the affiliation of the paper in question. The fact that the police were merging the two investi-gations was at least indisputable, and he felt he could be happy with that. He wasn't guilty of deceiving his readers today.

The kidnap story had started to go cold. That the kidnapper had appeared in public again and said something else incomprehensible in Kinyar-wanda was obviously news, but not the sort that was going to sell many copies. The other evening paper had accompanied the story about the video with a terrible picture of Annika Bengtzon staring into the camera outside her flat, mouth half open, hair in a state. 'No comment,' she was reported as having said.

Informative, without a doubt. A triumph of investigative journalism.

He sighed.

But not quite everything in that day's media offering was superficial speculation. There was one story in the papers that had made a definite impact on him, the one about the old man who had been lying dead in his flat for years without anyone missing him. He had been found when they were installing broadband in the building where he lived. The front door had been unlocked, and the technician had clambered over the mountain of post and found him on the bathroom floor.

The food in the fridge, the postmarks on the letters in the hall and the body's advanced state of decay had led the police to estimate that he had been dead for at least three years. His pension had been paid directly into his bank account, the bills paid out by direct debit. No one had missed him, not his neighbours, not his son, none of his former workmates. The police didn't regard the case as suspicious.

An unlocked door for three years, Schyman thought. He hadn't even been worth burgling.

There was a knock on the glass door.

Berit Hamrin and Patrik Nilsson were standing outside, their hands full of printouts, files and notes, looking anything but cheerful. That didn't bode well. He waved them in.

'We need some advice,' Berit said.

'Everything has to be so complicated these days,' Patrik said.

Schyman gestured towards the chairs.

'The minister of finance's luxury renovation of his luxury apartment, carried out by black-market labour,' Berit said. 'It's a good story if it holds up, but there are a few problems with the facts.'

Patrik folded his arms. Schyman nodded for her to go on.

'First,' Berit said, 'it wasn't the minister himself who was renovating a luxury apartment, but a consultancy firm he has shares in.'

'That doesn't make any difference,' Patrik said.

Berit ignored him.

'Second, it wasn't a luxury apartment, but an office for the five employees of the consultancy firm.'

'So?' Patrik said.

'Third, it wasn't a luxury renovation, but an upgrade of the entire building. The plumbing in a total of thirty-six offices was being replaced.'

'These are just details,' Patrik said.

'Fourth, the consultancy firm had a contract

with an entrepreneur who was paid above board. The entrepreneur in turn farmed out a small part of the demolition work to a subcontractor and paid above board. The subcontractor was checked and approved by both the union, the construction federation and the tax office.'

'This is all a matter of presentation,' Patrik said.

Berit put her notepad on her lap. 'No, Patrik,' she said. 'This is nonsense.'

'But mediatime.se have interviewed a man who says he was paid cash in hand for working on the minister's luxury flat!'

Schyman slapped his forehead. 'Mediatime.se! Patrik, we've already talked about these gossip sites.'

'*If* the source mentioned by mediatime.se is telling the truth, there's a story,' Berit said. 'How come people are being forced to work outside a regulated industry even though all the companies involved are above board? Who stands to gain from it? And who are these black-market workers? Are they Swedish, and, if they are, are they claiming unemployment benefit at the same time? Or are they illegal immigrants living in basements and working for peanuts?'

Patrik was chewing a biro intently. 'How can he be running a consultancy business at the same time as being a minister?' he said. 'How does that work? There must be no end of conflicts of interest. We could check to see if he's awarded contracts from his department to his own company.

There's a scandal here, if we can just dig deep enough.'

'The renovation was carried out seven years ago,' Berit said, 'three years before Jansson was appointed minister. He sold his share in the company as soon as he became a member of the cabinet.'

'Maybe he still gives them favourable treatment. Jobs for the boys?'

Schyman raised his hand. 'Patrik,' he said. 'We're going to have to drop this. There is no story about Jansson's luxury renovation. But, on the other hand, a series of articles about dodgy business practices in the construction industry isn't a bad idea. How much fraud is there with building grants, for instance?'

Patrik threw his pen on to Schyman's desk and stood up. His chair hit the wall behind him. He left the glass box without a word.

'Sometimes it isn't possible to fit reality into a tabloid frame,' Berit said. 'Were you serious about the construction industry?'

Schyman rubbed his face. 'About it being a good idea, sure,' he said. 'But we haven't got the resources to do something like that.'

Berit stood up. 'I'll go and see if I can find someone who's suffering from alien hand syndrome,' she said, and left the office.

Schyman sat there and watched them both go.

If his wife died before him, would he lie dead in his bathroom for three years before anyone found him? Would anyone miss him? Some former work colleague, maybe?

Annika put the tripod down and tossed the bag containing the video-camera on to the sofa. It was a bit brighter outside – the sun was trying to break through the cloud. She padded silently into the bedroom.

Halenius had fallen asleep on her bed, lying on his side with one knee pulled up, his hands under a cushion. He was breathing quietly and rhythmically.

Then he opened his eyes. 'Already?' he said, sitting up. One of his shirt buttons had come off.

'There's only one way to get the money there,' Annika said. 'A foreign payment to an account in Nairobi. All the other options are crap.'

Halenius stood up, swaying slightly. 'Good,' he said, walking out of the room. 'We'll get it sorted.'

She heard him go into the bathroom and lift the toilet seat. There was a pile of newspapers on the floor next to the bed – he must have been lying there reading them when he fell asleep.

His hair had settled down when he got back – he had tried to flatten it in front of the mirror. There was a gap in his shirt where the button was missing.

'How's that going to work?' Annika said. 'I haven't got a Kenyan bank account.'

He sat down beside her on the bed rather

than on the office chair. 'Either you fly down and open one, or we find someone we can send the money to.'

Annika studied his face. His blue, blue eyes were fringed with red. 'You know someone,' she said. 'You've got him or her in mind.'

'Frida Arokodare,' he said. 'She was Angie's roommate at university. Nigerian, works for the UN in Nairobi.'

He had the bluest eyes she'd ever seen, almost luminous. Why were they so red round the edges? Had he been crying? Or perhaps he had an allergy. To what, though? She reached out her hand and touched his cheek. He stiffened, a response that transmitted itself to the mattress beneath her. She took her hand away. 'Can we really do it?' she said.

'What?' he said in a low voice.

She opened her mouth but nothing came out. Oh, no, she thought. Is this how it is now?

He got up and went over to the computer. His hand hid his groin.

'Grégoire Makuza wrote an article in the *Daily Nation* five years ago. At the time he was still at the university. It was extremely critical of Frontex, the way the various countries shifted the blame elsewhere and pretended their closed borders were some sort of all-encompassing decree from above, and the hypocrisy of that at a time when Western Europe was exploiting illegal immigrants more than ever before . . .'

'The *Daily Nation*?'

'The biggest newspaper in East Africa. To be honest, the article makes some good points. His argument is shared by plenty of critics today, even within Europe. He could have had a career as a political commentator if he'd chosen that path.' Halenius sat down in the office chair, then pushed it backwards so he ended up near the door.

'Instead he chose to become the new bin Laden,' Annika said, reaching for the pile of papers on the floor and holding up the copy of the other evening paper. The front page was dominated by a freeze-frame image from one of the videos, with the turbaned man staring intently into the camera.

'There's a number of flaws in that comparison,' Halenius said. 'Bin Laden came from a very wealthy family. Grégoire Makuza may have been a Tutsi, but his family doesn't seem to have had much status. His father was a teacher in the village school, his mother looked after the house. He was the youngest of four children, and both parents and two of his brothers disappeared in the genocide. Presumably they're in a mass grave somewhere.'

'So I should feel sorry for him?' Annika said.

Halenius's eyes looked slightly less red now. 'It's no justification, but possibly an explanation. He's completely mad, but not stupid.'

He handed her the printouts, and she took them hesitantly, as if they were hot.

'That's him. You have to take the conversation

for what it is. I've spoken to him several times now, and this is what it's like. We've been through this dialogue a couple of times.'

She glanced at the document. 'What do "N" and "K" mean?'

'Negotiator and Kidnapper. Remember, my aim has been to reduce the amount they want in ransom, and to reach agreement as soon as possible. At the end he finally gives in. You can read from here.' He pointed some way into the text.

K: Have you been to the bank?

N: First we want proof of life.

K: Don't try my patience. What does the bank say?

N: Annika, Thomas's wife, is there now. But how are we to know that Thomas is alive?

K: You'll just have to trust me. What does the bank say?

N: She isn't back yet. It's still early in the morning here in Sweden. But if we don't have proof of life, we can't pay anything at all, as I'm sure you understand.

K (*screaming*): Forty million dollars, or we'll cut the infidel's head off!

N (*loud sigh*): You know it isn't possible for her to get hold of that much money. It's completely unrealistic. She has an ordinary job, two small children and lives in a rented apartment.

K (*calmer*): She has the insurance money from a fire.

N: Yes, that's right. But that's nowhere near enough. How is she going to get hold of the rest?

K: She'll have to put a bit of effort into it.

N: What do you mean?

K: She's got a cunt like all the others, hasn't she? She'll just have to go out and use it. How much does she want her husband back?

N (*loud sigh*): She's thirty-eight years old. Have you seen what she looks like?

K (*chuckling*): You're right, my friend, she wouldn't bring in much money that way. It's lucky she has a job, or the children would starve . . .

She looked up from the text. "'*Have you seen what she looks like?*'"

'I think you're beautiful,' he said. 'I've always thought so.'

She was having trouble breathing, and returned to the text.

N: She wants him back badly. She's sad and upset because he's gone. And the children are missing their father. In my opinion, she is absolutely prepared to pay a ransom, as much as she can, but she has very limited resources.

K (*snorting*): That's not my problem. Have you spoken to the police?

N: No. You know we're not talking to them. I understand your dilemma, but perhaps you can understand hers as well. She doesn't have forty million dollars. There's no way she could get hold of that sort of money.

K (*agitated*): Either she gets hold of the money or the infidel dies. Her choice.

N: You know better than that. If you don't lower the ransom, you won't get any money at all. We want to come to an agreement. We want to resolve this. We're prepared to do as you ask, but you have to drop the demand for forty million dollars.

(*Silence.*)

K (*very calm*): How much is she prepared to pay?

N: Like I said, she's a woman with an ordinary job, without any assets . . .

K: How much has she got in the bank?

N: Not that much, but she's prepared to give you all she's got. She hasn't been very successful, if I can put it like that.

K: Can't she borrow more?

N: With what security? You know how the capitalist banking system works. She has no house, no shares, no nice car. She's an ordinary Swedish woman who goes out to work. She's working class – they both are.

K: Can't the Swedish government pay? He works for the Swedish government.

N (*derisive snort*): Yes, as a committee secretary. You should know that the Swedish government doesn't care about its citizens, whether they work for it or vote for it. The men in power care only about themselves, their own power and their own money.

K: It's the same everywhere. Those bastards rape their people the whole time.

N: Governments don't care if people die.

K: Piss on their graves.

N: True.

(*Silence.*)

K: How much has she got? A couple of million?

N: Dollars? Dear God, no, much less.

K: The infidel says she's got a couple of million.

N: Swedish kronor, yes. That's completely different. It's more than Kenyan shillings, but it's not dollars.

(*Short silence.*)

K: What sort of fire was it?

N: That she got the money for? They had a small house and she got the money from the insurance when it burned down. It's

not much, but it's all she's got. And, like
I say, it's really not much . . .
(*Silence.*)
K: We'll be in touch.
(*Call ends.*)

She lowered the printout to her lap, feeling sick. She didn't know where to look. She felt as if he'd sold her out, humiliated and belittled her, like he'd betrayed his boss and his government, actually the whole of Sweden. He had lined up alongside the bastards and made her out to be old and ugly with no assets and no way of getting any, a real loser who could do nothing but sit and whine and hope the bastards would show a bit of human mercy, which wasn't particularly likely.

'Remember the purpose of the conversation,' Halenius said. 'You know what we're trying to do.'

She couldn't look up, and felt her hands start to shake. The printout slipped on to the pile of newspapers. He got up from his chair and sat beside her on the bed, put his arm round her and pulled her to him. Her body became a coiled spring and she hit him in the side, hard. 'How the hell could you?' she said, in a thin voice, and felt the dam burst. Tears fell and she tried to push him away. He held her tight.

'Annika,' he said. 'Annika, listen to me, listen . . .'

She sniffed into his shoulder.

'It's all lies,' he said. 'I didn't mean a word of it, you know that. Annika, look at me . . .'

307

She burrowed her face into his armpit. He smelt of washing powder and deodorant.

'It's all just strategy,' he said. 'I'd say whatever it took to help you.'

She took several breaths through her mouth. 'Why did you show me the transcript?' she asked, the words muffled by his shirt.

'I'm here on your behalf,' he said. 'It's important that you know what I'm doing, what I'm saying. This is what it sounds like. Annika . . .'

He pulled back and she peered up at him. He brushed a strand of hair from her face and smiled. 'Hello,' he said.

She shut her eyes and couldn't help laughing. He let go of her shoulders and moved away. Everything became bright and cold around her.

'I hate this,' she said.

He moved to the computer, sat down at the screen and read. The silence in the room grew, eventually becoming too much for her. She picked up the bundle of papers from the floor and got up. 'I'm going to catch up on what's been happening in the world,' she said, and left the room.

CHAPTER 15

The murdered women in the Stockholm suburbs filled the daily papers, and now the violence was important, down to the smallest detail. Linnea Sendman's killer had been lying in wait for her behind a fir next to the path at the back of the nursery school, she read. The victim had probably been chased up the slope and stabbed in the neck with excessive force. Her spinal column had been severed at the second vertebra.

Annika tried to envisage the scene, but failed: her own memories kept taking over – the boot sticking into the air.

Sandra Eriksson, fifty-four, from Nacka, was running away across a car park when she had been stabbed from behind, the knife going straight into her heart. She was dead in a matter of seconds. She had four children, the youngest a daughter of thirteen.

Eva Nilsson Bredberg, thirty-seven, from Hässelby, had been stabbed fourteen times, most of the blows going all the way through her body. The murder weapon was described as long and powerful. The victim had probably tried to run into her house, but fell and was stabbed from behind on the street outside.

Just to be on the safe side, the similarities were listed in the articles and fact-boxes: murder weapons, modus operandi, the proximity to children and playgrounds, and the fact that there were no witnesses in any of the cases. It wasn't stated in so many words, but intelligent readers would understand that the police were hunting a particularly cunning and emotionless perpetrator.

Annika got her mobile phone and went into the children's room, closing the door behind her. She dialled Berit's direct line at work.

'You don't want to know,' Berit said, in reply to Annika's question about what was going on in the world. 'I've spent half the day on a ridiculous story from mediatime.se, claiming that the minister of finance had a luxury renovation done on a luxury flat, using black-market labour.'

'Sounds like a brilliant story,' Annika said.

'In an ideal world,' Berit said. 'Now they've put me back on your serial killer.'

'Sorry,' Annika said. 'That's why I'm calling. You don't happen to have the official addresses of the five murdered women?'

'Why?'

'It's the scenes of the murders that are the problem,' Annika said.

'How do you mean?'

'The women in Sätra, Hässelby and Axelsberg

were killed outside their homes. But what about Nacka and Täby? Did those murders take place close to the victims' homes?'

Berit rustled some papers.

'In the Nacka case, she died pretty much outside her front door. But it doesn't work with the girl in Täby.'

Annika took a deep breath. The safest place for a man to murder his partner was indoors. It was easier to get at her, and there was less chance of being seen. But if the man no longer had access to the woman inside the home, he might have to do it outside.

That was what Sven, Annika's ex, had tried to do all those years ago. Annika was no longer letting him into her flat, so he had waited for her in the woods. He had chased her all the way to the old works in Hälleforsnäs, into the blast furnace where he had caught up with her – and her cat, poor little Whiskas, had got in the way . . . She remembered his sandy fur, his little miaow and his soft purr.

'The further away from her home she dies,' Annika said, 'the further away she seems to be, in terms of their relationship, from the perpetrator . . .'

'I know,' Berit said. 'I've looked at the statistics. There are, admittedly, a few factors which, in purely scientific terms, support the theory that we're dealing with a crazy serial killer. But, as you say, the overwhelming weight of evidence on the subject suggests that these are instances of violence within relationships.'

'Mikael Rying's report?'

'*The Development of Fatal Attacks Against Women Within Close Relationships*,' Berit confirmed. 'The statistics are a few years old now, but they're beyond dispute. From 1990 onwards, female victims knew their killer in ninety-four per cent of all solved cases.'

Annika's mobile bleeped: a text. She ignored it and leaned back on Ellen's bed, tucking her feet beneath her. She knew those statistics by heart. In almost half of the cases, the murderer was the victim's former husband or partner. She had spent years covering this sort of issue, often to the groans and rolled eyes of the newspaper's management. Knives were used as the murder weapon in 38 per cent of cases, followed by strangulation, firearms, axes and other bludgeoning instruments, violent abuse, such as kicks or punches, and finally more obscure methods such as electric shocks and bolt-guns.

'The victims of crazy killers fall into three categories,' Berit said. 'Mass murder, sexual killings, and murder as a consequence of another type of crime, most commonly robbery.'

'Which doesn't fit these cases,' Annika said.

She picked up a copy of the prestigious morning paper and studied the photographs of the five murdered women: Sandra, Nalina, Eva, Linnea and Lena, ordinary women wearing makeup with their hair in a variety of styles; they had probably battled with different diets to keep their weight down, and stressed about children or relationships spinning out of control.

Could they have been the victims of a crazed killer? What if she'd actually got it right with her teasing comment to Patrik?

'What are you going to write?' Annika asked.

Berit sighed. 'I've been ordered to interview the women's former husbands, apart from the one in custody, with the angle that at last the police are focusing on the real killer.'

'Shouldn't be too hard,' Annika said.

'Not at all. So far I've spoken to Nacka and Hässelby, and they were both remarkably talkative.'

'Why aren't I surprised?' Annika said.

'They don't mince their words about what whores their wives were. Obviously, they're both distraught about what's happened, but considering the way their women behaved, it really isn't surprising.'

'And all that stuff about their wives being beaten and threatened before was lies,' Annika said.

'Exactly. The husband who was convicted of abuse was entirely innocent, and if he did happen to hit her a few times, it really wasn't as bad as she made out.'

'In fact it was probably her fault,' Annika said.

Her mobile bleeped again: another text. The light was fading outside, either because the clouds were getting thicker or because the day was drawing to a close. She wasn't sure which.

'The question is, what can I write? I can't just let these men make speeches about how innocent they are. I'd have to go into all the background, and there isn't space for that.'

'The biggest problem in any murder case,' Annika said, 'is that we only have access to one side of the story.'

'I'll have to trust the readers to draw their own conclusions,' Berit said.

'Most will believe the men,' Annika said, opening the paper. 'How many of them have been charged with anything, did you say?'

'Only Barham Sayfour, Nalina Barzani's cousin. If he's released he'll be deported, because now his reason to stay has vanished.'

'Oops,' Annika said. 'Didn't think of that.'

Annika's mobile buzzed: call waiting.

'Someone's trying to ring me,' Annika said. 'I'd better answer.'

'And I need to do some writing,' Berit said. 'Get back up on the tightrope.'

She clicked to get rid of Berit, then took the other call. It was Anne Snapphane.

'I'm standing outside your building. Can I come up?'

Anne sparkled and twinkled as she stepped into the hall, with her glittery top, fake diamond bracelet and loads of shiny hairspray. 'It worked!' she said triumphantly, giving Annika a hug. 'At last, it worked!'

Annika hugged her back and smiled. 'Congratulations. What worked?'

'I could really do with a stiff drink now, but I'll have a cup of coffee.' She had been a recovering alcoholic for years.

Annika went into the kitchen and put the kettle on.

'I've just sent in the first invoice for my new interview series, so I'll be able to buy you a proper coffee-machine,' Anne said, as she sat down at the kitchen table.

Annika looked at her in surprise.

'They accepted my pitch.'

Annika searched her memory frantically. Had Anne mentioned this before?

Her friend threw her arms out. 'You've got a memory like a sieve. Media Time! You promised you'd help me. Don't tell me you've forgotten?'

'Of course not,' Annika said, spooning instant coffee into the mugs.

Anne picked up her handbag, a multi-coloured affair with gold studs and an expensive-looking logo, then fished out a mirror and her lip-gloss. Annika poured boiling water into the mugs and put them on the table.

'The bosses at Media Time were really keen. They want me to get going straight away. Is that okay with you?'

Annika smiled at her and got the milk out of the fridge. 'Sounds great. What sort of company is it?'

'A modern media stable. They've got a digital television channel that broadcasts on the internet, a digital radio station for music and news, and an online news agency.'

Annika stopped in the middle of the floor with the milk in her hand. 'Mediatime.se?'

'They really have been a breath of fresh air for journalism. They dare to publish things that no one else will touch.'

'Have they published information about the minister of finance doing a luxury renovation of his apartment with black-market labour?'

Anne threw out her hands again. 'It's just like I've always said – all these Social Democratic ministers do is fiddle things to feather their own nests.'

Annika sat down on a stool at the kitchen table. All of a sudden she was aware that there was an elephant in the room, something large and grey, and it was using up all the oxygen. 'Anne,' she said, 'what's the pitch you managed to sell to them?'

'The interview series,' she said. 'Serious programmes with interesting people. It's going to be called *Anne Investigates*. Isn't that a great title? Me interviewing and investigating. You're my first guest.'

Annika put her hands round the mug, which stung her palms. 'What do you mean?' she asked, although she already knew.

'You can talk about the kidnapping,' she said. 'We'll have plenty of time, twenty-five minutes.

316

You can just say the things you want to say. I'm not going to push you.' She leaned over the table and put her hands round Annika's. 'It'll be entirely on your terms,' she said. 'I'll adapt to whatever you want. We don't have to do it in an anonymous television studio, we could be here, in your home. At the kitchen table, like this, or in the children's room . . .'

Annika pulled her hands away. The elephant was filling the entire room now, threatening to crush her against the wall and break the window overlooking Bergsgatan. 'Anne,' she said, 'you can't be serious.'

The elephant stopped breathing. You could have cut the silence with a knife.

'This will be really good for you as well,' Anne said breezily, but her voice sounded tight and forced. 'You couldn't get better terms. You can see the end result and have editorial approval. I'll cut out any sensitive questions or any answers that you regret.'

Annika put her hand to her forehead. 'I can't believe you've done this.'

Anne's eyes opened wide. 'An interview isn't that terrible. It's recognition. Think of all the countries and cultures where you're not allowed to say what you think and how you feel. You ought to be grateful that people are interested. Imagine if no one gave a damn about you and Thomas and your problems.'

Your problems?

All of a sudden Annika was back in Anne's stair-well in Östermalm, with her soot-stained children beside her, asking to be let in because her house had burned down and she had no money and nowhere else to go. She'd had to lower her children out of the upstairs window, away from the flames, and then she'd had to jump. The taxi had been waiting outside, and Anne had said no. Anne had met a new man; Anne couldn't believe Annika could be so thoughtless that she was demanding to be let in under such delicate circumstances – didn't she want Anne to have a future?

'You really are crazy,' Annika said. 'You sold me out so you can be a TV celebrity.'

Anne jerked as if she'd been slapped. Her eyes darkened and the hand beside the mug was shaking. 'Are you going to let me down now?' she whispered. 'Now that I've finally got a chance?'

'I take everything away from you, don't I?' Annika said, with a rising sense of disbelief. 'Your men and your success, maybe your daughter as well. The fact that Miranda lives with Mehmet, is that my fault too?'

Anne was breathless with shock. 'There really are no limits to your selfishness,' she said. 'But you're not going to get away with it this time. You promised to help me. I'm going to do this, with or without you.'

Annika pushed her coffee aside. 'You can do exactly as you please,' she said. 'I'm all for democracy and freedom of expression.'

Anne stood up, spilling her coffee and scraping her chair on the wooden floor. She hurried out into the hall and put on her outdoor clothes. Her eyes didn't leave Annika for a moment. 'The way I've supported you,' she said. 'The way I've listened and helped and comforted you. If I hadn't been so busy helping you, I'd be in a far better position myself. I held back to support you, and this is the thanks I get?'

Annika gulped. 'You've said all that before, so presumably you really do believe it. It's almost sad.'

'You'll regret this,' Anne said, and left the flat.

Annika stayed in her chair at the kitchen table, listening to the lift descending in the stairwell. A nagging anxiety began to grow in her. Her hands and feet felt numb. Was Anne serious? Was she really going to hurt her deliberately?

She closed her eyes, forced herself to think rational thoughts.

Anne had no power. No one was interested in her. She was clinging to the outside of the media world but had never managed to gain any influence. She wasn't a threat.

Annika breathed out and let her shoulders relax, then shook some life into her hands.

Then she heard the lift rising again, and her shoulders tensed. Had Anne forgotten something?

It was Kalle and Ellen coming home from their afterschool club.

'Mummy, I passed the swimming test! Can we buy the badge? Please?'

She took them into her arms and held them tight. 'How was today, then?'

'Good,' both children replied mechanically.

'Did anyone ask about Daddy?'

Ellen shook her head. 'Can we buy the swimming badge? It's on the internet.'

'Only that man,' Kalle said, pulling off his hat and throwing it on the hall floor.

Her anxiety woke up again. 'What man?'

'From a newspaper. He had a massive camera.'

Halenius appeared in the living-room doorway and Kalle's jaw clenched. 'Hello,' he said to the children, then to Annika, 'Can you come?'

She couldn't move. 'Tell me,' she said. 'Tell me now.'

Halenius glanced at the children. 'It's the Spaniard,' he said. 'He's been released.'

Schyman was clicking frantically between various translation programmes. For the first time ever he regretted not going with his wife to those never-ending Spanish classes: he had always blamed work, saying he didn't have time, and now he was trying to read *El País* with the help of Babel Fish. It wasn't going very well. He tried Google Translate instead, and that was slightly better: 'man the Spaniard is to be found in the city Kismayo this afternoon'.

Things were obviously going to hell for the hostages down there. The Frenchman had been dismembered, and now the British woman had been found dead. The Spaniard's release was the first bit of good news in the whole wretched business.

He was keeping an eye on the news agencies as he wrestled with the translation programmes, and when 'Urgent – Hostage Free in Kismayo' appeared from Reuters, he gave up the translation and clicked to open the report.

He scanned it quickly.

Alvaro Ribeiro, thirty-three, had been found dehydrated and exhausted outside the university in the Somali harbour city of Kismayo on Monday afternoon. He had two broken ribs, and showed signs of malnourishment, but was otherwise in reasonably good health. A student lent him a mobile phone and he was able to phone both his family and a friend who was a reporter at *El País*. The Reuters report seemed to be a direct translation of the Spanish article. After a short summary of what had happened (delegation from the Frontex conference in Nairobi stopped at roadblock near the Somali border), the Spaniard's story was related in its entirety. It described how they were stopped and taken away, how they were driven around, forced to march through the night, then held prisoner in a shed made of cow shit and denied food, water and toilet facilities.

Schyman squirmed: he wasn't good with excrement and things of that nature.

Captivity in the hut was described as unbearable, the hostages were starving and soaked in sweat, and they were forced to watch as the French delegate was killed and dismembered.

Grotesque, Schyman thought, skimming the misery in the hut.

The Spaniard had been moved to another hut, and after that he hadn't seen the Dane or the German delegate, Helga Wolff, again. But he did see the other hostages on the morning of Sunday, 27 November, when they were taken out into the open area between the huts. The British woman, Catherine Wilson, was lying naked on the ground outside one of the mud huts. They had driven large spikes through her hands and feet, crucifying her on the ground. First she was raped by three of the guards, but not by the leader. Then the male hostages were dragged forward, one by one, and encouraged to rape her. When they refused the kidnappers threatened to cut off their hands. All the male hostages then chose to violate the British woman, but he hadn't been able to: he lived with another man and had never felt any attraction to either women or sadism, but out of fear for his life he had pretended to rape her. Then the leader had killed the woman by raping her with his machete.

There followed an account of the Spaniard's release, how he had been driven around in a large vehicle and eventually thrown out.

Schyman pushed the screen away and peered towards the newsdesk.

The details about the British woman were so hideous that they felt unreal. Could he publish that sort of information? It turned Swedish dad Thomas into a rapist. But the story was already out, spread round the world by Reuters. And surely forcing someone to commit rape also counted as abuse.

He fingered his beard. It wasn't clear if a ransom had been paid, but he presumed it had been. The British woman's death was nothing short of bestial.

All the evil of the world wasn't his fault, or his problem. On the contrary, he had a duty to describe things as they really were, how the world worked.

He looked through the report again. It was strangely lacking in tastes and smells, mechanical, almost sterile. In this state it wasn't fit for publication in the *Evening Post*. They'd just have to follow old Stig-Björn Ljunggren's theory and dramatize it to liven things up.

He heard Patrik cry out, and realized that he had found the report as well.

He clenched his teeth.

At least tomorrow's front page and fly-sheets were sorted.

Thomas always made love so carefully. To start with, Annika had thought that was wonderful, that he was so gentle and sensitive, perhaps mainly because it was so far removed from Sven and his roughness. But over the years she had become indifferent to his feather-light touch, and found herself wishing he would take hold of her properly, hold her tight, hard, really want her.

323

She took a deep breath and pressed 'call' on her mobile. She imagined the phone ringing at the villa in Vaxholm, echoing across parquet floors, and making the prisms in the crystal chandeliers dance.

'Doris Samuelsson,' Thomas's mother answered. She sounded weaker than usual, slightly more hesitant, as if the obvious superiority of being Doris Samuelsson was no longer beyond question.

'Hello, it's Annika,' Annika said. 'Am I disturbing you?'

Doris cleared her throat. 'Hello, Annika. No, you're not disturbing me. We've just finished dinner, so it's fine. Have you heard anything from Thomas?'

'Not since the video I told you about on Saturday,' Annika said. 'But we've had some news concerning him. One of the other hostages, the Spaniard, Alvaro Ribeiro, has been released by the kidnappers, safe and sound.'

Doris breathed out. 'It's about time these people came to their senses. You can't keep people prisoner like that. Well, at least they've realized . . .'

Annika pressed a hand to her forehead. 'Doris,' she said, 'Alvaro Ribeiro's description of what the hostages have been going through is extremely difficult to hear. They've been subjected to violence and starvation and abuse. Thomas . . . has also been threatened and forced to do terrible things.'

Doris was silent for several seconds. 'Tell me,' she said.

Soundless breathing.

'They threatened to cut off his hands unless he did as they said.'

A gasp on the line. 'Have they? Have they maimed him?'

'No,' Annika said. 'Not as far as we know. The Spaniard didn't say anything about that. I don't know how many of the details the papers are going to publish tomorrow, but . . .'

She fell silent, unable to go on. *Your son raped a woman who'd been crucified. She was the woman he went to Liboi to seduce.* 'They've been forced to commit sexual assault,' she said at last. 'They've been badly beaten. The Spaniard had two broken ribs as a result of being kicked. They've been forced to eat food full of maggots . . .'

'That's enough,' Doris said quietly. 'I understand. If you'll excuse me, I must—'

'One more thing,' Annika said. 'I can't have the children with me in the city. They keep being pestered by journalists, and I don't want them at school when the Spaniard's story goes public.'

'Hmm,' Doris said, in her inimitable, unhappy way.

'And we're hoping to reach agreement about the ransom soon,' Annika said, 'and that will mean going to Kenya . . .'

'A ransom? Are you serious? You're going to give money to these murderers?'

Annika swallowed. 'The Spaniard's partner is in Kenya at the moment. He left a million dollars in a rubbish bin on the outskirts of Nairobi

325

yesterday evening. That's why the Spaniard was released. We're probably going to have to fly down there, with a bit of luck maybe this week . . .'

'There's so much going on here,' Doris said. 'We've got people coming for lunch on Wednesday and Friday, and I have to clean the house. I hope you understand.'

You'd have been only too happy to look after Eleonor's children, she thought, but Eleonor hadn't wanted kids. Eleonor hadn't wanted to spoil her figure and her career, but she never told you that, did she? Thomas's ex-wife just smiled rather sadly when you asked about children, and whether she and Thomas had talked about having any, and then you thought she couldn't have any, and you felt so sympathetic, didn't you? And that was why you said what you did to Thomas: 'Having children, even a dog can manage that, but looking after them, that's another matter.' That's how you see me, isn't it, as a bitch? And your own grandchildren aren't important enough to play on your Persian rugs . . . 'Of course,' Annika said. 'I understand perfectly. I'll be in touch if anything new happens.'

She pressed to end the call, shaking with anger.

'No luck with Doris?' Halenius asked from the bedroom.

Someone had been eavesdropping.

'And guess how surprised we are,' Annika said, dialling her mother's number.

Barbro sounded sober but tired. 'I'm slaving away all week,' she said, 'nine to six.'

Slaving away? Ordinary full-time hours? She let the exaggeration pass. 'Mum, can I ask a favour?'

'It's not that I'm complaining. You always need a bit of money before Christmas.'

'We've had some news about Thomas,' she said. 'The hostages are being treated very badly down there. We need to try to get him home as soon as possible, so I was wondering if you'd be able to look after Kalle and Ellen for a few days.'

'I'm babysitting Destiny in the evenings because Birgitta's got some extra shifts at Right Price.'

She hit her forehead on the coffee-table three times. What had she expected? 'Okay,' Annika said. 'Have you got Birgitta's number?'

'Are you going to apologize at long last?'

She sat up on the sofa and took a silent breath. 'Yes,' she said.

Her mother gave her the number, and they ended the call.

She shivered. The chill in the room had eaten its way into her. Her fingers and feet felt icy. Halenius came into the living room. 'Is it really cold in here?' she asked.

'We might have to fly down tomorrow or on Wednesday,' he said.

'I know,' she said. 'I'm trying. I'm prepared to humiliate myself as much as necessary if it means I can get someone to look after the children. Okay?'

He went back into the bedroom.

She dialled her sister's mobile number. Birgitta answered at once.

'First and foremost,' Annika said, looking into the video-camera that was set up next to the television, recording everything she said and did, 'I want to apologize for not coming to your wedding. It was wrong of me to put my job first. People are always more important than articles. I know that now.'

And as she said it she realized it was true.

'Wow,' Birgitta said. 'Little Miss Perfect has come to her senses. What are you after?'

There was no point skirting the issue. 'I need help,' Annika said. 'I need someone to look after the children while I go to East Africa and try to get my husband back. Can you help?'

'Like you helped me on Saturday, you mean?'

'Birgitta,' she said, 'we've got a kidnap-control centre in my flat. I've got people here from the Ministry of Justice trying to negotiate with the kidnappers to get Thomas released. We've got computers and recording equipment and God knows what else, and we're trying to stay in touch with the other negotiators and their respective governments.'

'Is this where I'm supposed to be impressed by how smart and special you are?'

That shut Annika up. Birgitta had a point. Annika had spent the last thirty years trying to beat her by being smarter and more special, and she'd succeeded, by God she'd succeeded, first with Sven, then the College of Journalism, then all her lovely jobs, crowned by her time as correspondent in the USA, and a husband who worked in Rosenbad, and two children at an international private school. She'd won the status race, no doubt about that.

But Birgitta still had her friends. It was Birgitta who went round to Mum's to watch the Eurovision Song Contest, she was the one who'd bought the old cottage next to Lyckebo and had managed to grow her own apple trees.

'Sorry,' Annika said. 'Sorry I called. I shouldn't have. I don't deserve any help, not from you.'

'Psh,' Birgitta said. 'I'm at work from noon until we close all this week and next, otherwise they could have stayed here.'

The room got slightly less cold. Her shoulders relaxed. 'Christmas rush?' Annika said.

'And all the extra money I'm earning will go on presents, so the whole thing just goes round and round.'

Annika laughed. It really was that simple.

'Mind you, they could be with Steven, but he's not that great with children . . .'

Annika looked down at the covering of the sofa and heard Birgitta's voice get small and lost when Steven wouldn't get up from the sofa on Saturday night. *Don't pull him like that. He might get angry . . . Don't talk to Steven like that.*

No, it was probably just as well for the children to be somewhere else.

'It's okay,' Annika said. 'I'll find someone. But thanks anyway.'

'What are you doing for Christmas? Are you coming down to Hälleforsnäs?'

Birgitta sounded happy, keen.

'I'm not sure,' Annika said. 'We'll have to see if Thomas . . .'

'But you have to meet Destiny. She's the cutest baby in the world.'

They hung up, and Annika lowered her mobile to her lap. She couldn't ask Berit again. Both she and Thord worked full-time and commuted to Stockholm.

Halenius popped his head into the living room again. 'Is it safe?' he said.

She didn't answer.

'Can you switch the camera off?' he asked, as he sat down next to her on the sofa.

'What for? I'm supposed to be recording what happens behind the scenes.'

'Please,' he said.

She got up and pressed pause.

'I think the kidnappers will be in touch this evening,' Halenius said. 'They want to get this over and done with now. How are you doing?'

'Haven't found anyone yet,' she said.

'This is important,' Halenius said. 'You need to leave your comfort zone. A teacher at school, a neighbour, someone at the afterschool club?'

'So there are universities in Somalia,' she said.

He sat silent for a few seconds.

'Apparently it's a small private university that trains medical staff and nurses. I've no idea how well it works.'

'Do you think that's where Thomas is? In Kismayo?'

Halenius leaned back and closed his eyes. 'It's nowhere near certain. Kismayo is two hundred, two hundred and fifty kilometres from Liboi. The Spaniard thinks he was lying in a vehicle for at least eight hours, so he must have been driven a fair distance. And we're not talking motorways here.'

'Where is he now?'

'The Spaniard? The Yanks' base in the south of Kenya. They went in and picked him up with a Black Hawk.'

She didn't bother asking how the American military had got permission to fly an attack helicopter through Somali airspace to pick up a foreign citizen. Presumably they hadn't. She cleared her throat. 'I'm going to make another call,' she said.

Halenius got up from the sofa and went back into the bedroom.

She took several deep breaths. She knew the number by heart, but her fingers burned as she pressed the buttons.

It rang three times, four, five.

Then there was an answer.

'Hello, this is Annika. Annika Bengtzon.'

When I was little I used to fly a kite behind Söderby farm, on the meadow where the cows

331

grazed in the autumn. It had an eagle painted on the stiff plastic, wings and head and beak, all yellow-brown. It used to frighten the birds in the meadow: they'd leave their nests and do all they could to protect their young because they thought that my kite was a real eagle.

It was a brilliant kite. It flew high, high up among the clouds, sometimes just a little dot in the blue sky, and I was good: I could make it dive towards the ground, then pull it up at the last moment. It had the strength and tension of a large, powerful animal, but it always obeyed my slightest command.

Holger was always nagging and wanting to borrow it, but I'd asked for it for my birthday and I took really good care of it. I looked after the lines, and always wiped any dirt off it afterwards.

Once, when I was ill with measles, Holger took my kite anyway. He went to the forest behind the youth hostel because there he couldn't be seen from our house. The kite got caught in the top of a pine tree, the plastic tore and the line broke.

I've never forgiven Holger for taking my kite.

I've never felt as free as I did when I was flying it. Space was bright and white and stretched all the way to eternity, I can see it now – I can see my kite among the clouds, flitting and dancing, coming closer and closer. The Earth is dark, but all around the kite the stars are shining, crackling and sparkling. It opens a door to the truth, and soon it will be here.

DAY 7

TUESDAY, 29 NOVEMBER

CHAPTER 16

HELL
ON EARTH
'An inferno of brutality, starvation and sexual abuse – sensitive readers should look away'

Anders Schyman nodded to himself. The calculation had paid off. Sjölander and young Michnik had managed to include every grotesque detail of the Spaniard's story without seeming to wallow in the misery (or, at least, not in such a way as to be obvious). 'Alvaro Ribeiro, 33, has come back to life. He has been on a journey to hell and back. Together with the other hostages in East Africa, among them Swedish father-of-two Thomas Samuelsson, he has had to endure unimaginable cruelty . . .'

It might not win a Pulitzer Prize, but it worked. The idea of warning sensitive readers about the content of the article was a stroke of genius: it aroused interest and instilled trust. The group rape and murder of the British woman was described as 'a sadistic assault, calculated in its raw

335

brutality'. Even the pictures were good: there was a technically inadequate photograph of the Spaniard's filthy and mosquito-bitten face, presumably taken with a mobile phone (they had bought the Swedish rights from *El País*), and an agency picture of a dusty street in Kismayo (which in contrast had cost almost nothing).

The article covered four pages: six and seven, eight and nine.

Ten and eleven were dominated by a freeze-frame video-still of the kidnapper, Grégoire Makuza. The headline was:

THE BUTCHER
OF KIGALI

The article included few facts about the man. It reported that he came from a suburb of the Rwandan capital and focused mainly on the genocide in the central African state almost twenty years ago. It meant that the horror carried on building across those two pages as well, but that was unavoidable. They had reasoned that, for readers to have any chance of understanding how the man had become such a monster, his life had to be seen in its social and historical context.

Schyman read the text once again. It made him feel as dizzy as he had when he had first read it in outline (on the printout of the final layout) the previous evening.

Nine hundred and thirty-seven thousand people,

most of them Tutsis, had been murdered by the Hutu militia between 6 April and early July in 1994. Most had been killed with machetes. Rape was the rule rather than the exception. Up to half a million women and girls (some extremely young) were violated during the conflict, and not just by the militia. Forcing family members to rape each other was part of the militia's campaign of terror. For this reason, neighbours would often swap places with each other at night so that the girls would at least escape being raped by their own fathers and brothers (a Google search for *rwanda forced incest* produced over 5.6 million results). Family members were also compelled to eat each other (so-called *forced cannibalism*, which, with the additional search-word *rwanda*, produced 2.7 million hits). Amputations were common, not just hands, feet, arms and legs: breasts and penises were sliced off, the walls of vaginas cut out, pregnant women split open. Raped women were impaled on spikes until they bled to death.

He pushed the newspaper away. He'd had enough horror. He reached instead for the first edition of the rival evening paper and leafed through it quickly.

They had pretty much the same layout, with similar headlines (they called Grégoire Makuza the 'Rwandan Executioner'), but towards the end of their coverage they had one story all of their own. A picture of Annika's children in a school playground (the lack of definition revealed that it had

337

been taken with a long telephoto lens), accompanied by a text about how sad they were that their daddy was gone. According to the article, Kalle had said, 'I hope he'll be home for Christmas', which also gave them their headline. (Clearly the boy had said nothing of the sort: the reporter would have asked, 'Do you hope Daddy will be home for Christmas?' and the child would have replied, 'Mm.')

There'd be a fuss about this. The fact that African women had been impaled on machetes in their thousands usually passed without comment in the Swedish debate, but the fact that a secretly taken picture of two (Swedish) children had been published would make the acolytes of the Journalism God furious. Okay, so the editor hadn't done anything wrong, but plenty of commentators and ordinary readers had trouble telling the difference between the two big tabloids. In a few weeks' time half of the readers would swear the picture had been published in the *Evening Post*. That was why there was never any point in criticizing the other paper. It was like shooting yourself in the foot, which he usually tried to avoid.

The one thing that might deflect attention from the snatched photograph was that the boy had evidently said that 'Jimmy from Daddy's work' was in their flat helping to get Daddy released. The reporter went on to explain that there was only one Jimmy in the whole Department of Justice, and that was Under-secretary of State Jimmy Halenius, the minister's right-hand man, and the question was whether the Social Democrat justice minister wasn't guilty of exceeding his authority by allowing a senior official to negotiate with terrorists . . .

Schyman leaned back in his chair.

In all likelihood, some right-wing MP would report the minister to the Parliamentary Committee on the Constitution before the afternoon was out, and the right-wing members of the committee would make a lot of noise before it was agreed that a group of terrorists could not be regarded as an official body and that there was therefore no question that the minister had exceeded his authority.

And at that moment, just as he was imagining the flushed, indignant faces of the committee members, the back-rest of his office chair broke and he tumbled backwards into the bookcase.

The lift glided soundlessly up the marble stairwell and stopped with a little jolt at the top floor, the 'penthouse', as the building's owner liked to call her home.

Annika had never imagined she would ever again set foot in the place or be about to ring at that door. Everything was so familiar in its chilly elegance, even though she hadn't been there in more than three years: the white stone floor, wooden doors, thick carpet.

'Mummy,' Ellen said, clutching her hand. 'Why do we have to stay with Sophia?'

GRENBORG, Annika read, on the brass sign

on the door. She could still see the mark left by the removal of the sign bearing the name SAMUELSSON.

She stroked her daughter's hair. 'Sophia's asked about you lots of times,' she said. 'She missed you while you were in Washington, and wanted you to come and visit.'

'I call her Sofa,' Kalle said.

Annika opened the folding gate of the lift and pulled the children and their little suitcases on to the landing. The cases were the ones they had used during the year they had spent shuttling between her and Thomas, and the sight of them made her stomach clench.

'How long do we have to stay?' Ellen asked.

'Why can't we go to school?' Kalle said.

She rang the bell. They heard quick footsteps and the door opened.

Sophia Grenborg had cut her hair. Her blonde bob was shorter, almost boyish. She was dressed in black and wasn't wearing any makeup. Her hand was trembling as she brushed her fringe from her forehead. 'Welcome,' she said, taking a step back into the flat (the penthouse apartment) to let them in.

The children huddled behind Annika's legs and she had to nudge them inside. Sophia Grenborg sank to her knees in front of them, and Annika saw tears in her eyes. 'So big,' she said in amazement, raising a hand towards Ellen without touching her. 'You're so big now.'

Then Kalle walked straight into her arms and held her tight, and Ellen dropped her rucksack on the floor and went to Sophia for a hug too. The three of them stayed there rocking each other, and Annika could hear Sophia sobbing.

'I've missed you so much,' Sophia Grenborg said, into the children's chests.

Annika was breathing quietly through her mouth, and could feel her hands and feet growing, becoming heavy and clumsy, in danger of banging into the walls or telephone table.

Thomas had abandoned her and the children in a burning house and come here, to this ice-palace. He had lived here with an open view across the rooftops while she had been living in an old office that was never touched by the sun. She knew it wasn't his fault alone.

'I really am very grateful,' Annika said.

Sophia looked up with tears in her eyelashes and snot under her nose. 'I'm the one . . .' she said. 'I'm the one who should be thanking you.'

There was a pale sun somewhere behind the white clouds. Annika was walking slowly through Stockholm back to her flat on Agnegatan, heading up Kungsgatan towards Hötorget from Östermalm. Hadn't Abba recorded one of their videos on this street, 'I Am The Tiger'? With Agneta driving around in an open-top American car with Anni-Frid sitting next to her, a handkerchief round her head? She had loved that song as a child: it reeked of the big city, danger, tarmac and adventure. Maybe that was why it wasn't included in the musical *Mamma Mia!* – it didn't suit the idyllic Greek setting.

She stepped into the road to cross it. A bus braked sharply and the driver blew his horn. She jerked and leaped back on to the pavement, where she knocked into a pram, causing the mother to shout something incomprehensible at her.

She waited for the bus to pass, then crossed to the other side, as carefully as if the road were made of glass. It was a road she walked down fairly often, even if it was a bit out of her way. She usually avoided going past the NK department store on Hamngatan because the ground always lurched there. It was where she had seen Thomas kiss Sophia Grenborg for the first time. The Christmas lights had been up, as they were now, red Father Christmases and flashing LED lights spreading fake cheer over the windswept streets.

She walked quickly and jerkily the rest of the way, cruising between the yummy mummies, the homeless people and the businessmen.

Halenius was waiting for her in the hall when she got back to her flat. He held out a printout to her. She saw the Ks and Ns and shook her head. 'Just tell me what it says,' she said, going into the living room. She didn't want to hear the kidnapper's squeaky voice, not even in written and translated form.

'We're almost there,' Halenius said. 'I think he's going to agree to a million dollars today.'

She sat on the sofa, leaned back and shut her eyes.

'I've spoken to Frida,' he said. 'We can use her account. You can transfer the money whenever you like.'

She pressed the palms of her hands to her eyelids. 'One million dollars, to a Nigerian woman living in Kenya. And you think we'll ever see the money again?'

She heard him sit down on the sofa.

'Her uncle is an oil tycoon in Abuja. The family isn't short of money, to put it mildly. If I hadn't told her the money was on its way, she'd never have noticed. Probably best to transfer a bit more than a million, just to be on the safe side.'

She raised her head from the sofa and gave Halenius a quizzical glance. He handed a different printout to her. 'A lot of Africans live in huts, but not all of them. Here's her account number, the bank's IBAN number and Swift address.'

She took the sheet of paper, picked up her laptop and went into the children's room. It was possible to send money abroad using the bank's online service. She transferred everything that was in the account, 9,452,890 Swedish kronor, to the Kenya Commercial Bank, account holder Frida Arokodare. She filled in all the numbers, addresses and codes, chose 452 ('other services') for the tax office, accepted the transaction fee and pressed 'send'.

The money vanished instantly from her savings account.

The balance glowed out at her in red: 0.00 kronor.

She blinked at the screen, trying to imagine her burned house swirling around in cyberspace, floating as a series of figures through the electronic smog. She looked inside herself in an attempt to find any emotional response to the empty account: nothing.

'How did you get on?' Halenius asked from the doorway.

'Fine,' Annika said.

The entire procedure had taken less than ten minutes.

She slept for a while on Ellen's bed, haunted by dreams. When she woke she was anxious and sweaty, and spent a long time standing under a cool shower. She prepared lunch for herself and Halenius (vegetarian pasta sauce, made with fresh tomatoes, peppers, onion, garlic, pesto and honey, and fettuccine).

After that she shut herself into the children's room and spent several hours working on her freelance article and filming herself (on Kalle's bed this time), then went into the living room and sank down on the sofa.

It was already dark outside. The streetlamps were casting shadows across the ceiling.

Halenius was sitting in the armchair with a bundle of newspapers and journals in his lap. He waved the top one. 'There's a good article here about Kibera,' he said. 'A district in central

Nairobi, often described as the biggest slum in the world, although that opinion's been revised now.'

'Can I ask you something?' she said, studying him through the gloom.

He raised his eyebrows.

'It's a bit personal,' she said.

He put the journal down. It was an African business magazine.

'If you had the choice, would you have chosen to be born?'

He was silent for a while. 'Difficult to say,' he said eventually. 'There's no obvious answer. Probably.'

'Do you think it's an odd question?'

He looked at her thoughtfully. 'Why do you ask?'

She clasped her hands. 'I've come to the conclusion that I'd rather not have been born. But saying so tends to be very provocative. Mum was furious, told me I was spoiled and ungrateful. Thomas was furious and accused me of not loving him and the children, but it's not about that – of course I love them. It's about whether you think life is worth the bother . . .'

'I think I understand what you mean.'

She shifted position on the sofa. 'I know there's no point in wondering why we're here. If we were supposed to know, we'd have all the answers by now, wouldn't we? So there's no sense in worrying about it. We aren't meant to know.'

'But?' he said.

'It just doesn't feel like much of a reward,' she said. 'More like a trial. You have to get through it and try to do your best along the way, and of course there are things that are great, the children and work and a few summer days, but if I'd had the choice . . .'

She brushed the hair from her face. 'Do you think I'm spoiled?'

He shook his head.

'I understand that it might look like it. Especially when you're aware of how much other people have to put up with.' She pointed at one of the papers on the coffee-table – she presumed it was the *Evening Post*, but it might just as well have been the competition. The headline was 'The Butcher of Kigali', above a photograph of Thomas's kidnapper, Grégoire Makuza.

Halenius reached for the paper. 'The Brits have dug up more detail about his background,' he said.

She looked out of the window. The sky was grey and dark red.

'There were a number of testimonies at the International Criminal Tribunal for Rwanda, held in Arusha, Tanzania, describing a massacre in Makuza's suburb in May 1994.'

She sank deeper into the sofa.

'Several thousand people were killed, women and young girls raped, teenage boys forced to eat their own testicles . . .'

She put a hand to her mouth and turned to face the wall.

'That would explain his unnaturally high voice,' Halenius said quietly.

'I don't want to know,' Annika said.

'He had a sister in France. She was the eldest of the children, had left Kigali in the autumn of 1992 and was working illegally in a textile factory outside Lyon. She must have earned a bit of money because she paid for his education at university in Nairobi, until the penultimate term.'

'Shame she didn't carry on,' Annika muttered.

Halenius's face was no longer visible in the darkness. 'The factory caught fire and she died in the blaze. The fire escapes were blocked and there were no extinguishers. Makuza had to give up his education. Instead of returning to Rwanda he made his way to Somalia.'

Annika got up and switched on the main light, then the lamps in the windows.

'When did the fire happen?' she asked, getting her laptop from the children's room. The internet cable flowed behind her, like a snake.

'It must be almost exactly five years ago now,' Halenius said.

She Googled *factory fire lyon*. It took a while to find the right result. It hadn't been a particularly well-publicized event. A short article from the BBC World Service said that six seamstresses had died, and twenty-eight had survived. The factory made designer handbags, which cost tens of thousands of kronor in luxury boutiques, under the label Made in France. All of the dead were illegal immigrants, six of the hundreds of thousands in Western Europe who lived in conditions not far

347

from slavery, people who had fled to get a better life but found themselves trapped in a cycle of debt to pay off their journey to the old, free world.

There were no pictures to illustrate the article.

'Not an excuse,' Halenius said, 'but an explanation.'

His mobile phone rang and Annika shivered, as if she feared the worst. He disappeared into the bedroom, connected the phone to the recording equipment and spoke quietly, as he always did when he took important calls from the JIT in Brussels, the security services that were involved, the other negotiators, or the liaison officers from National Crime. He was speaking Swedish, which suggested that it was the latter who had called.

Unless it was someone from the department. That lunchtime, a right-wing MP (a woman, to be specific) had reported the minister of justice to the Parliamentary Committee on the Constitution for exceeding his authority, so perhaps that was what they were discussing. Unless it was the embassy in Nairobi wanting to find something out. It could be any one of a number of interested parties.

She made two mugs of coffee.

When she returned to the living room, Halenius was standing there, white as a sheet.

She put the mugs on the coffee-table.

'Annika . . .'

'Is he dead?'

He walked over to her and took hold of her

shoulders. 'A box has been found outside the police station in Liboi,' he said. 'It contained a severed left hand.'

Her legs gave way and she slumped on to the sofa.

Halenius sat beside her and fixed his eyes on hers. 'Annika, are you listening? I have to tell you this.'

She was clinging to the arm of the sofa.

'It's a white man's hand,' he said. 'It still has a plain gold ring on it.'

The whole room began to spin, and she could feel herself starting to hyperventilate. They had really been too late to get the rings engraved – it was just before Christmas and all the goldsmiths were busy – but they had found a large man in a leather apron on Hantverkargatan who did it while they waited. It had added something extra to their engagement, the fact that they had found each other so late.

'The inscription on the inside of the ring says *Annika*, and a date, thirty-one/twelve . . .'

She pushed him away, stumbled through the hall to the bathroom and threw up. The vomit splattered across the porcelain sides of the toilet and hit her cheeks. She howled, the flush swirled. Her hands were tingling and her ears singing.

She came to her senses, gasping into the toilet, and felt Halenius's hands on her shoulders.

'Can I do anything?'

She shook her head.

'The date, New Year's Eve?'

'The day we got engaged,' she whispered.

He sat on the bathroom floor and pulled her to him. Her teeth were chattering, and she cried silently until the fabric on the shoulder of his shirt was dark and wet. He rocked her gently and she clung to his shoulders. When she had calmed down and was breathing in little gasps against his neck he helped her to her feet.

'Is he dead? Is he going to die?' she asked, her voice hoarse.

'Let's go and sit on the sofa,' Halenius said.

She pulled off some toilet paper, blew her nose and dried her face.

Astonishingly, the living room looked the same as before. The main light and the lamps were all lit, and the papers were in a pile on the coffee-table. Their mugs were still there, the coffee with skin on it now.

They sat down beside each other on the sofa.

'It's not entirely certain that this is Thomas's hand,' Halenius said. 'The ring is his, but that doesn't necessarily mean that the hand is. It was the guys from National Crime who called. They're waiting for the analysis of the fingerprints. Then we'll know for sure.'

She took some deep, silent breaths. 'Analysis?'

'Everyone entering Kenya has their fingerprints taken by Customs.'

She shut her eyes.

'But even if it is Thomas's hand, it isn't necessarily an absolute disaster,' Halenius said. 'Is he right-handed?'

Annika nodded.

He stroked her hair. 'Thomas will be okay,' he said. 'Having a hand amputated doesn't kill you.'

She cleared her throat. 'But it must bleed really badly. Maybe he's bleeding to death.'

'It would bleed a lot. Apparently there are two arteries that run into the hand, but they contract out of some sort of reflex. If you help them by holding your arm up and applying a tourniquet, the bleeding stops after ten, fifteen minutes. The biggest danger is infection.'

'It must hurt?' she whispered.

'The pain can make you pass out, and it aches really badly for two or three days.'

She blinked at him. 'The liaison officers knew all this? About arteries and reflexes?'

'I called a doctor friend at Södermalm Hospital.'

He really did think of everything. Now his eyes were edged with red again, as if he, too, had been crying. She stroked a lock of hair from his forehead, and he smiled at her. She pulled her legs up and curled into a ball with her head on Halenius's lap. The glow from the lamps was reflecting off the glass in the windows, red and green against the winter sky, as the tassels on the shades swayed in an imperceptible draught. Soon she fell asleep.

★   ★   ★

The quality of our office furnishings matches our journalism and ability to hit deadlines, Anders Schyman thought, as he gingerly felt the bandage round his head.

The six o'clock meeting was gradually slipping to half past six, sometimes even later, but it was still called the six o'clock meeting. It was already a quarter to seven. Schyman felt as if he'd been sitting at his desk for several centuries, while Entertainment and Features and Comment and Sport and Online and Pictures and the newsdesk made their way noisily into the room, slopping their coffee on the way to their time-honoured places.

Schyman let out a deep sigh. 'Shut the door and sit down so we can finally make a start.'

The editors fell silent and looked at him expectantly, as if he was about to pull a rabbit from a hat, as if he set the agenda for the world.

He nodded to Patrik. News was the most important department, he was always careful to emphasize that. Patrik was wriggling with excitement on his chair.

'The police have a suspect for the suburb murders,' he said triumphantly. 'We haven't had formal confirmation yet, but Michnik and Sjölander will be working on it during the evening.'

Schyman nodded thoughtfully to himself. 'The Suburb Murders' wasn't a bad name: they could use it as the overarching tagline. 'Do we know any details?' he asked, clicking his ballpoint pen.

'There are witnesses who can link him to at least one of the murders, and his mobile phone left an electronic trace at another. So we've got our front page and fly-sheet for tomorrow.' Patrik exchanged a high five with his deputy.

Schyman touched his bandage. He'd had to have four stitches at the back of his head, and had managed to get blood on the latest set of annual accounts. 'Well,' he said, 'let's wait and see what we've got. We need to maintain interest in the kidnap story as well. Things are going to be happening there.'

Jimmy Halenius had called him just before the meeting and told him that Thomas Samuelsson had probably had his left hand cut off, but the editor-in-chief had no intention of mentioning that now.

'The Spaniard yesterday was good,' Patrik said, 'but now we're running on empty again.'

'We've got pictures of him being reunited with his partner and mother,' Picture-Pelle said.

'Has he said anything else? Anything about Thomas Samuelsson?' the girl from the online edition asked.

Schyman closed his eyes in despair, and Patrik groaned. 'Not a word. He's put out a statement through some press spokesman that he wants to be left in peace. Have we got any more about the guy in the turban?'

Schyman blinked uncomprehendingly.

'The Butcher of Cairo,' Patrik added.

Anders Schyman could see Thomas Samuelsson's elegant figure in front of him, wearing a suit but no tie, and tried to imagine him without his left hand.

Halenius hadn't been able to judge if the mutilation was a way to exert more pressure about the ransom, or the usual sadistic cruelty. They had agreed that it was probably a mixture of the two.

'I want a double-page spread on the kidnapping,' Schyman said. 'Pictures of the victims, maybe, with heavy captions along the bottom: MURDERED, CAPTIVE, FREED. Run the basic facts again, who the hostages are, how they died, all that.'

He wasn't about to let it go: it could well prove to be the lead story over the weekend. The hand-over of the money and release of the hostages constituted the most critical phase of the entire kidnap story, according to Jimmy Halenius. Once the money had been delivered, the victim became a dead weight and no longer served any purpose. The majority of deaths among hostages occurred after the ransom had been paid. Either they never turned up or were found dead.

Patrik wasn't impressed. 'We need something to have happened. That's just heating up leftovers.'

'Get your saucepans out then,' Schyman said. 'What else?'

Patrik looked down at his notes unhappily. 'It's time we did dieting again,' he said. 'I've put one of the temps on to it.'

Schyman made a note and nodded, good idea.

In the past articles had been published because people had contacted the newsroom and tipped them off about different events or stories, such as the fact that they had lost weight on some fantastic new diet. But that was a long time ago. These days, the newspaper's front pages and fly-sheets were planned to fit a predetermined timetable based upon sales figures (unless something exceptional happened, like Swedish fathers-of-two being kidnapped or serial killers stalking Stockholm's suburbs). When it was time for a new diet story, they had always started,

LOSE WEIGHT
WITH NEW
MIRACLE
DIET!

They had gone out and found the diet. There were always plenty to choose from. Then they found a professor who could verify the miraculous nature of this particular diet. All that was left was to get hold of a really good case-study with before and after pictures, preferably a decent-looking young woman who'd gone from size twenty-four to twelve in three months.

'Anything else?' Schyman asked.

'It's the anniversary of Karl the Twelfth's death tomorrow, so the baby Nazis will probably be out waving their swastikas. We've got people on it. It's also twenty-five years since reactor number one at Chernobyl was shut down. It's Winston Churchill and Billy Idol's birthday, and it's your name-day.'

Schyman suppressed a yawn. 'Shall we move on?'

'Media Time called,' Patrik said. 'They were asking if you wanted to comment on your concussion.'

Anders Schyman leaned back carefully in the conference-room chair and felt with every fibre of his being that it was time for him to do something else.

'We've been to Skansen!' Ellen said. 'And do you know what, Mummy? We saw an elk! A great big brown one! It had really big horns and a little calf with it – the baby was super cute.'

Annika swallowed a sigh. Maybe it wasn't such a good idea that the children were at an American school.

'Was it really the elk with the horns that had the calf with it?' she said, into the phone (she had read somewhere that you shouldn't point out when a child made a mistake, just repeat the words in the right way). 'It's usually bull elks that have horns, and the calves normally go with the cow elks . . .'

'And Sophia bought fizzy drinks for us. Kalle had Coke and I had a lemon Fanta.'

'I'm glad you're having fun.'

'And tonight we're going to watch a film, *Ice Age 2 – The Meltdown*. Have you seen it, Mummy?'

'No, I don't think so.'

'Here's Kalle.' She passed the receiver to her brother.

'Hello, darling, are you having a nice time?'

'I miss you, Mummy.'

She smiled and felt tears welling up. He was so incredibly loyal. He probably hadn't thought about her all day, but he wanted to reassure her that she was the most important person to him. 'I miss you too,' she said, 'but I'm really happy that you can spend a few days with Sophia while we try to get Daddy home.'

'Have you talked to the kidnappers?'

Where had he learned all the phrases?

'Jimmy has. We hope they're going to let him go soon.'

'They killed that woman,' he said.

She shut her eyes. 'Yes,' she said, 'they did. We don't know why. But they let a man go yesterday, a Spanish man called Alvaro, and the last time he saw Daddy he . . . was all right.' She couldn't bring herself to say, 'He was alive.'

Kalle sniffed. 'I miss Daddy too,' he whispered.

'So do I,' Annika said. 'I hope he'll soon be coming home.'

'But what if he doesn't? What if they kill him too?'

Annika gulped. Even at the post-natal clinic they had said you should never tell children something didn't hurt if it did. 'Darling, sometimes people get kidnapped, but they usually get back home to their families. We just have to hope that happens with Daddy.'

'But *if*?'

She dried her eyes. 'In that case we'll have each other. You and me and Ellen, Sophia too.'

'I like Sophia,' Kalle said.

'Me too,' Annika said, and it might well have been true.

She let herself slowly sink back to earth. She had made a meal that she hadn't been able to eat. She had written some more of her article, trying to capture the feeling of receiving incomprehensible news. She had watched the news and *Antiques Roadshow* without understanding what they were talking about.

Halenius was talking English in the bedroom, she didn't know who to.

She could just give in to this. She could stay on the sofa and sink down to the basement, then through the rock, past the underground tunnels and sewage pipes. Stockholm's underworld was like Swiss cheese, full of passageways and cubbyholes. She didn't have any sense of direction and could wander around down there for all eternity, hopelessly lost among the drains and water-damaged electricity cables.

She took a deep breath, got to her feet and went into the children's room. She ran her hand over their toys and duvets, picked up Kalle's pyjamas from the floor. The aftermath of her attempt to clear their wardrobes was piled against the wall.

She paused, absorbing the children's presence from the walls and bedclothes, feeling their breath as a pulse in her stomach.

It was going on, and on, and on.

Human beings were not their disabilities. They were not defined by them. A disability was a circumstance, a condition, not a characteristic.

'Annika? Can you come?'

She dropped the pyjamas and went to Halenius in the other bedroom. He had put his mobile down and was sitting with headphones on, typing something on his computer.

'I heard you mention the German woman's name,' she said, sitting on the bed.

He switched off the audio file, pulled off the headphones and turned towards her. 'She's been released,' he said. 'At the roadblock where they were kidnapped. She followed the road back towards Liboi and was found by a military patrol just outside the town.'

Annika tucked her hands under her thighs and tried to work out what she was feeling. Relief? Injustice? Ambivalence? She couldn't tell.

'She was subjected to some of the same treatment as the British woman. The guards raped her and the remaining male hostages were forced to . . . but Thomas refused. The leader chopped his left hand off with his machete.'

Annika was staring at the window. All she could see was her own reflection.

'This morning she was taken to a car, driven around for several hours, then thrown out by the roadblock.'

'When did it happen?'

'The rape? Yesterday morning.'

Thomas had been without his left hand for a day and a half.

Annika went into the living room for the video-camera. 'Can you say that again, please?' She raised the camera, located Halenius in the fold-out screen, and gave him a thumbs-up to begin.

'My name is Jimmy Halenius,' he said, looking into the lens. 'I'm sitting in Annika Bengtzon's bedroom, where we're trying to get her husband back home.'

'I was thinking more the bit about the German woman,' Annika said.

'I've often imagined myself here,' he said, 'in her bedroom, but not under these circumstances.'

She kept the camera where it was, wary now.

He looked away for a moment, then back, and their eyes met through the screen.

'Helga Wolff has been found outside Liboi this evening, exhausted and dehydrated, but without any other physical injuries. It isn't clear whether or not any ransom was paid to secure her release, but it seems likely.'

'You sound like a block of wood,' Annika said, lowering the camera.

Halenius switched off his computer. 'I think I'll go home and get some sleep,' he said.

She kept hold of the camera, but lowered it to her side. 'But what if they call?'

'I can forward calls on your landline to my mobile.' He started to gather his things.

She went into the living room, switching off the camera and putting it on the coffee-table. 'Have you talked to your children today?' she asked.

He came into the room, pulling his jacket on. 'Twice. They've been swimming out at Camps Bay.'

'Your girlfriend,' Annika said. 'Who is she?'

He stopped in front of her. 'Tanya? She's an analyst at the Institute of International Affairs. Why?'

'Do you live together?'

His face was in shadow so she couldn't see his eyes. 'She hasn't let go of her flat.'

He radiated warmth, like a stove. She stood where she was, even though she was getting burned. 'Do you love her?'

He stepped aside to get past her, but she followed him and put a hand on his chest. 'Don't go,' she said. 'I'd like you to stay.' She put her other hand against his cheek, feeling the roughness of his stubble, then took a step closer and kissed him. He was standing completely still, but she could feel how fast his heart was beating. She moved closer to him, laid her cheek against his neck and put her arms round his shoulders.

If he pushed her away now she'd die.

But his hands found the base of her spine and

he pulled her towards him with one hand, letting the other slide up under her hair and stop at her neck. His arm was broad and hard across her back. She ran her fingers through his hair and kissed him again. This time he responded. He tasted of salt and resin and his teeth were sharp. She caught her breath and met his gaze through the shadows, heavy and dark. He brushed her hair from her face. His fingers were dry and warm. She undid the buttons of his shirt and pulled his jacket off. It landed on top of the video-camera.

'We shouldn't,' he said quietly.

'Yes, we should,' she said.

If there was one thing she was sure of, it was this. She pulled her top off, undid her bra and let them fall to the floor, then put one hand against his cheek as the other caressed the base of his spine. She felt his hand cup one of her breasts. He squeezed her nipple and her vision went black. Jimmy Jimmy Jimmy from Himmelstalundsvägen in Norrköping, the cousin of Roland who always had a picture of her in his wallet. He pulled her jeans off, laid her on the sofa and caressed her thighs and stomach with hard, warm hands, and when he pushed into her she forced herself to relax and breathe through her mouth to stop herself going to pieces. She let herself be rocked by his rhythm until she couldn't float any longer and she came, she came and came, until her head was singing and the darkness dissolved and disappeared.

DAY 8

WEDNESDAY, 30 NOVEMBER

CHAPTER 17

The man was arrested in his home on Byälvsvägen in Bagarmossen at six thirty-two a.m. He had just made himself some porridge, with lingonberry jam and semi-skimmed milk, two open sandwiches, with smoked German salami, and a cup of proper coffee with three sugar-lumps when the police rang the doorbell. The arrest was entirely without drama. The man's only objection to going with them was that his breakfast would be cold by the time he got back.

It'll have had time to get more than just cold, Anders Schyman thought, as he put down the printout of the article. The *Evening Post* had done a thorough and systematic job, both with the creation of the serial killer and its coverage of his capture. Schyman had already ordered a new edition of the paper's print version for the city and surrounding area, but the rest of the country would have to enjoy the details about the sandwiches and sugar-lumps online.

He picked up the printout of the picture on the front page: Gustaf Holmerud, forty-eight, being led away by six uniformed and heavily armed police officers. The expression on the serial killer's face could almost be described as one of surprise. The police officers' clenched jaws were more likely their response to the *Evening Post*'s photographer than any danger posed by the arrested suspect.

Schyman hadn't hesitated. They had printed the man's name, age, where he lived, and complete details about his insignificant life and career (abandoned secondary-school education, back problems, incapacity benefit). Obviously there would be a debate about that as well, that they were identifying someone who hadn't been convicted, but he could give the counter-argument in his sleep.

If they weren't allowed to name criminals until they had been found definitively guilty in the eyes of the law, then to this day no one would know the name of the man who had been found guilty in the district court of the murder of Prime Minister Olof Palme. Anders Schyman could see Christer Pettersson's furrowed face before him: the old alcoholic was later released by the Court of Appeal and never served his sentence.

Besides, technological developments had outstripped the established and more responsible media: accusations, rumours and bare-faced lies spread like wildfire across the internet just minutes after people were arrested and taken into custody. At least the *Evening Post* checked its sources before going to print, and there was a publisher who could be held legally accountable for any errors – himself. And the newspaper had been careful to point out several times that the man was still only a suspect.

He examined the (suspected) serial killer's face and remembered his conversation with the mother of the murdered Lena. *It was Gustaf . . . He's been stalking her ever since she finished with him . . .*

He leaned back cautiously in his new office chair. The company nurse had said he could remove the big bandage that afternoon and replace it with a compress. His head still hurt, and he didn't usually suffer from headaches. He put his hand to the wound and thought he could feel the knots of the stitches beneath the bandage.

His eyes fell on the description of the man who had been seen walking away from the edge of the forest in Sätra: about 1.75 metres tall, average build, dark blond hair, clean-shaven, dark jacket and trousers. If he was honest, that description could apply to something like 80 per cent of all middle-aged men in Sweden. The notion that the paper might be heading into choppy waters drifted into his aching head, stayed long enough for him to dismiss it, then swirled away. The police investigated. The media observed and dramatized.

And while he waited for something to happen in the kidnap story in East Africa he picked up the letter he had written to the board and read the opening once more: 'I hereby tender my resignation from my position as editor-in-chief of the *Evening Post* newspaper.'

★　★　★

367

She was woken by the pale light of dawn and knew at once that they had overslept. Kenya was two hours ahead of Sweden, and anything could have happened during the morning.

It was definitely too late for something, but she didn't know what.

Her body was still heavy and warm under the duvet. She turned her head and found herself staring at the shock of brown hair on the pillow beside her. She reached out her hand and ran her fingers through it, strangely soft, like a small child's.

Too late, or possibly far too early. She didn't know.

She curled up next to him, twining her legs round his and stroking his shoulder. He woke up and kissed her. They lay there quite still, just looking at each other.

'It's eight o'clock,' she whispered.

He pulled her to him, tight, and with a gasp she felt him slip inside her again. She came almost immediately, but it took longer for him – she felt him grow and met his movements until his shoulders tensed and he gasped.

'Bloody hell,' he said. 'I'm desperate for a piss.'

She laughed, perhaps out of embarrassment.

They had breakfast together at the kitchen table, yoghurt with walnuts, and fruit-bread with liver pâté, coffee and blood-orange juice. He'd put his jeans and shirt on, but hadn't buttoned it, and was reading *Dagens Nyheter* as he fumbled for his mug of coffee and dropped crumbs on the floor.

She looked down at her yoghurt. It all felt so fragile, like glass: she didn't dare touch it because it might break – his hair in the morning light, the hardness of his chest, his total concentration on the editorial, the fact that he was there, that he had held her so close.

He folded the paper and put it on the window-sill. 'I'd better start things up.'

He stood up and walked past her without touching her.

She took a long shower. Her body felt bigger than before, slower somehow. The drops of water hit her skin like pins.

She took the opportunity to clean the bath-room, scrubbing the vomit stains from the toilet, polishing the mirror, wiping the basin and tiled floor. She could hear Halenius talking English on his mobile.

She got dressed, a clean pair of pale blue jeans and a silk blouse. Halenius ended one call and made another. She went into the children's room and carried on clearing out their wardrobes.

At ten past nine the landline rang and her heart stopped.

She flew into the bedroom, slipping past Halenius to the unmade bed. His movements were focused and jerky, starting the recording equipment, checking keywords, notes and pens, shutting his eyes and taking a couple of deep breaths. Then he picked up the phone.

'Hello? Yes, this is Jimmy.'

His lips were bloodless, and his eyes haunted.

'Yes, we received the message about the hand.'

He fell silent. His shoulders were so tense they seemed to be made of wood.

'Yes, I know we have to pay, that's—'

He was interrupted and sat in silence for a few moments. She could hear the kidnapper's squeaky voice rattling from the receiver.

'She's managed to get a ransom together, but it isn't—'

Another silence.

'I understand what you're saying,' Halenius said, 'but you have to try to see it from her perspective. She's scraped together every penny of the insurance money, and borrowed all she can from her family and friends, and now there isn't any more.'

Silence again, chatter.

'First we want proof of life . . . Yes, that's an absolute condition.'

She noticed that sweat had broken out on his forehead. She hadn't grasped until now how demanding and unpleasant he found these conversations. She felt a huge, uncontrollable wave of tenderness: he didn't have to do this but he was doing it anyway. How could she ever repay him?

'You've chopped his hand off. How do I know you haven't chopped his head off as well?'

Halenius's voice was neutral, but his fingers were shaking. She heard the kidnapper laugh loudly, then say something in reply.

Halenius looked up at her. 'Her email? Now?'

He nodded to her, then to his computer. She slid across the mattress towards the desk, turned his computer towards her and logged into the newspaper's email server, then pressed 'send/collect'.

Four messages landed in her inbox. The one at the top said *sender unknown*. She felt her pulse quicken as she clicked to open it.

'It's empty,' she whispered.

'Empty? But . . .'

'Hang on, there's an attachment.'

'Download it,' he said quietly.

It was a picture, dark and out of focus. Thomas was lying on his back on something dark, his head was turned to one side showing his chiselled profile, his eyes were closed as if he were asleep. Annika was filled with relief and warmth, and a pang of guilt drifted through her. Then she saw the stump. Where his left hand should have been, his lower arm now seemed to merge with the floor. She pulled back instinctively from the computer.

'That's not proof of life,' Halenius said into the phone. 'He looks stone-dead.'

The kidnapper laughed, loud and long. His high-pitched twittering seeped into her bedroom. She got up and opened the window to get rid of it.

It was cold outside, but not freezing. Hesitant

371

snowflakes hung on the air, unsure whether to fall or fly. It was darker now than when she had woken up. She turned round, and the cold embraced her from behind.

Halenius was listening intently, leaning forward. 'She's managed to scrape together one million, one hundred thousand dollars. That's right, one point one million.'

Silence. Even the kidnapper seemed to be waiting at the other end.

Then he said something, a light crackle.

Halenius was waiting with his mouth open. 'That's not possible,' he said. 'Stockholm is close to the North Pole and Nairobi is right on the equator . . . No, we can't hand over the money today. We . . . No, we . . . Yes, we can fly to Nairobi as soon as possible, perhaps this evening . . . My mobile number?'

He read it out, the kidnapper said something, and the conversation ended. Annika heard the click as he hung up.

'We've got twenty-four hours,' Halenius said, putting the phone down.

He led her to the sofa, then sat on the armchair facing her and took her hands in his. 'This is going to be a trial,' he said.

She nodded, as if she understood.

'He accepted my offer of one point one million dollars. He wanted the money in Nairobi in two hours, which he knew we wouldn't be able to do.'

'Why one point one?' she asked.

'It shows that you've really tried, that there's no more to be had. He's going to be in touch during the day, I don't know how, with instructions on how to hand over the money.'

She pulled her hands back, but he caught them. 'We have to fly to Nairobi, this evening at the latest. Can you sort out tickets?'

She nodded again. 'Sit down next to me,' she said.

He sat beside her on the sofa, but didn't touch her.

'Do you think he's alive?'

Halenius scratched his head. 'According to the handbook, he ought to be, because otherwise the kidnappers wouldn't have sent that picture. But with this man I just don't know. The Frenchman's wife paid up even though her husband was dead, so they managed to deceive her.'

'What happens now?'

He thought for a few moments. 'According to the rulebook? Commercial kidnappings usually have one of six distinct outcomes. The first is that the hostage dies before the money is paid.'

'That sounds like poor business,' Annika said.

'True. The hostage might have died trying to escape, or in a rescue attempt, or from a heart attack or some other illness. Sometimes kidnap victims have starved to death. The second scenario is that the ransom gets paid but the hostage is still killed.'

'Like the Frenchman,' Annika said.

'Exactly. It might be that the kidnappers think they could be identified, or that the leader of the group is a complete psychopath. That fits fairly well with our man. Scenario three: the ransom is paid but the hostage isn't released. Instead the kidnappers come back and demand more money, and negotiations begin again. That usually happens when the ransom demand is high and the money is paid too quickly, because they conclude that there's more where that came from.'

'Could that happen to us?'

'I don't think so. We've been through the whole routine. Four: the ransom is paid, the hostage is released, but kidnapped again at a later date. That isn't likely to happen. Five: the ransom is paid and the hostage is released. Six: the hostage escapes or is freed without any money being handed over.'

She sat there without saying anything for a long time. He waited.

'It's impossible to say which one it's going to be, isn't it?' she said quietly.

'He said he'd contact us again early tomorrow morning. Maybe he will, but it could just as well be late in the afternoon. We have to be prepared. We need to have the money, a car with a full tank and a driver, fully charged mobiles, water and food all ready, because it could be that the actual delivery will take time.'

She cleared her throat. 'What are the police doing?'

'The JIT in Brussels are reading my texts and keeping everyone informed, but right now it's vital the kidnappers see that we're on our own. They've no intention of getting caught. I'll demand to be allowed to hand over the ransom face to face, but there's no way they'll agree to that.'

'And the location where we'll hand over the money, that'll be somewhere in Nairobi?'

He went into the bedroom and emerged with a notepad. 'The Spaniard's partner left the money in a container in the Somali district in the south of the city,' he read. 'The German woman's son left it in a ditch at the foot of Mount Kenya, about a hundred kilometres to the north. The Romanian's wife is going to deliver eight hundred thousand dollars some time today in Mombasa, out on the coast. The Frenchman's wife also left her money somewhere in Nairobi, but she wasn't able to say where afterwards.'

'So they don't put all their eggs in the same basket,' Annika said.

He sat down beside her again and leafed through his notes. 'Usually the ransom is handed over somewhere fairly close to the site of the kidnapping, up to a couple of hundred kilometres away, maximum. But that doesn't seem to be the case here.'

'Then what?' Annika said.

'It can take up to forty-eight hours before the hostage shows up,' Halenius said.

She put her hand on his thigh. 'Then what?' she said quietly, looking at him. He turned away and she removed her hand. 'I don't regret it,' she said.

He went back into the bedroom without looking at her. She remained where she was, mute and leaden, as a vast emptiness filled her, making it hard to breathe. With an effort she got to her feet and went to the bedroom. He was writing something on his computer.

All of a sudden she felt utterly ridiculous. 'I'll sort the flights,' she said. 'Any particular preferences?'

'Not Air Europa,' he said. 'And not via Charles de Gaulle.' He smiled forlornly at her.

She managed to smile back, then went into the children's room.

The only flight with any seats left to Nairobi that night was with Air France, via Paris.

'And it's Air France all the way?' Annika asked. 'Not Air Europa?'

The woman in the *Evening Post*'s travel office tapped at her computer. 'Ah,' she said. 'The flight to Paris, Charles de Gaulle airport, is operated by Air Europa.'

'Isn't there anything else?'

'Yes, via Brussels, but that leaves in twenty minutes, from Bromma.'

She booked them on to the 16:05 flight from

Arlanda to Paris, then with Air France (operated by Kenya Airways) at 20:10. The plane was due to land in Nairobi at 06:20 the following morning, East African time. She left the returns open.

The tickets would be delivered by email for her to print out.

She hung up. It was the middle of the day but dusk already, and she was in a weightless vacuum between now and later.

Halenius went home to pick up some clothes, a toothbrush and his razor. Annika spent forty minutes working frantically on her article, then packed her laptop, a few clothes and the video-camera, but there wasn't room for the tripod because they were only taking hand-luggage. She went through the fridge and threw out anything that was about to go out of date, emptied the bins and switched off the lights. She stood in the darkness of the hall for a while, just listening to the sounds of the building.

Something was definitely too late, or far too early.

She walked on to the landing, locked the flat securely and went down to the entrance to wait for Halenius, who was going to pick her up in a taxi.

She called Sophia Grenborg while she waited. 'We're leaving now,' she said. 'We've agreed a ransom. The plane takes off in a couple of hours.'

'Do you want to talk to the children?'

A shiny black Volvo with tinted windows pulled

up through the swirling snow and stopped outside her door. One of the back doors opened and Halenius stuck his head out.

'I'll call again from Arlanda,' she said, and ended the call.

She stepped out into the wind and smiled at his messy hair. From the corner of her eye she saw a photographer raise a camera with a long telephoto lens and point it in her direction. The driver got out, wearing a thick grey coat. She recognized him: he was one of the men called Hans. He took her bag and put it into the boot, and she got in beside Halenius as the photographer followed her through his lens.

The under-secretary of state held up his mobile. 'The money is to be paid in American dollars, twenty-dollar bills, wrapped in thick plastic and tied with duct tape,' he said.

'Why have we got a Hans?' Annika asked.

The Volvo pulled way with a soft purr. 'Government car,' Halenius said. 'I need to make a load of calls. It wouldn't be that great to read about them on mediatime.se tomorrow.'

She remembered the banker in glasses at Handelsbanken. 'Twenty-dollar bills? That's going to weigh at least fifty kilos.'

'I've told Frida to buy two big sports bags.'

He took her hand. 'He wants you to deliver the money,' he said, letting go of it again.

The stone façades of the city slid past behind the falling snow.

He picked up his mobile and dialled a really long number, and she laid her head against the soft leather seat and let the city disappear behind her.

The departure hall at Arlanda airport was seething with people.

'I can't check you in all the way through,' the woman at the desk said, tapping at her computer. 'Air Europa's IT system isn't compatible with everyone else's, so you'll have to go to the transfer desk in Paris and get your boarding cards there for the flight to Nairobi.'

Halenius leaned over the desk. 'There isn't a transfer desk at Charles de Gaulle,' he said. 'And we don't have time to stand in a check-in queue.'

The woman tapped some more. 'Yes, you do,' she said. 'You've got an hour in Paris.'

Halenius's brow was damp with sweat. 'Have you ever been to Charles de Gaulle?' he asked quietly. 'The planes are parked over by the runways and you have to get a bus to the terminal. The terminals are several kilometres apart and there are no trains or buses between them. We have to get from Two B to Two F. It isn't going to work.'

'Yes, it will,' the woman said. 'You walk to Terminal F and—'

'We won't get in there. Not without boarding cards.'

Annika swallowed. She had had to ignore both of his preferences.

'This is a guaranteed booking, though,' the check-in woman said. 'If you miss the plane you'll be allocated seats on a later flight.'

'We have to catch this one,' Halenius said. 'It's extremely important.'

The woman tilted her head and smiled. 'Everyone says that.'

Annika, who had been standing half a step behind Halenius, pushed forward and leaned across the desk, standing on tiptoe. 'I was the one who made the booking,' she said. 'The travel agent guaranteed that we'd be able to check in the whole way through. Otherwise we wouldn't be standing here.'

The woman was no longer smiling. 'I'm terribly sorry,' she said, 'but I'm afraid—'

'I spoke to airport management at Charles de Gaulle and to Air Europa's head office in Amsterdam. Everyone gave me guarantees that this would work.'

The woman's lips had narrowed to a thin line. 'I can't see how—'

'I suggest you pick up the phone and call someone, or find someone who knows how to do this,' Annika said, pulling out a notepad and pen. 'Can I have your full name, please?'

The woman's neck was flushing red. She stood up and disappeared through a door to the left.

Halenius looked at Annika in surprise. 'I thought Air Europa's head office was in Mallorca.'

'I don't know where the fuck it is.'

She watched the clanking conveyor-belt carrying luggage that disappeared through an opening to the right. Golf bags and Samsonite cases and pushchairs in plastic bags, all swallowed by the dark hole in an unrelenting stream. The ceiling arched above their heads. The passengers behind them were starting to shuffle and look at their watches. Thomas was lying on a bare floor somewhere, bleeding to death, and she was in charge of logistics. This was her responsibility.

The woman came back with an older woman.

'So, what seems to be the problem here, then?' the older woman said.

'We've been guaranteed that we could check in all the way to Nairobi,' Annika said, 'but clearly there's been some sort of misunderstanding somewhere. It would be great if we could get it sorted out.'

The older woman smiled. 'Unfortunately, I'm afraid—'

Thomas's swollen face was talking to her in a monotone from the computer screen. The kidnapper's shrill voice seeped out from the baggage conveyor-belt. Halenius's guttural groan rose up and got stuck beneath the ceiling.

She leaned across the desk. 'Now,' she said. 'This instant.'

The older woman bent over the computer terminal and typed a few commands, reached towards a printer, then put two provisional boarding cards on the check-in counter. 'There,' she said. 'All sorted.'

★ ★ ★

Anders Schyman felt the shock run through his body as he read the messages from the TT news agency: we were actually right.

The custody proceedings against Gustaf Holmerud had obviously taken place behind closed doors, so the precise reasons as to why he had been remanded in custody hadn't been made public, but the district court's decision to hold him spoke for itself: the man was being remanded for having been the 'probable cause' of two deaths. And 'probable cause' was the highest level of suspicion.

Must be Lena Andersson and Nalina Barzani, Schyman thought, reaching for the intercom. 'Patrik? Can you come and see me for a moment?'

The head of news came bouncing across the newsroom with his ever-present biro. 'Probable cause!' he said, and landed in the visitor's chair. 'Now we're talking!'

'What is it we don't know?' Schyman said.

A vague description and some information from a mobile-phone operator would be enough to hold someone on the grounds of reasonable suspicion, but not probable cause.

Patrik chewed his pen. 'Q's in charge of the investigation, so Berit's on the case.'

Everyone knew that Berit Hamrin and Superintendent Q at National Crime had a good, close relationship, but no one, except Schyman and possibly Annika Bengtzon, knew *how* good and *how* close it was or, rather, had been. Berit had had an affair with the detective that lasted several years. Clearly she had managed to stay on good terms with her former lover because he had gone on giving her information that he shared with very few others.

The reason Schyman knew about it was because he had asked her how she came to have such brilliant sources inside the police, and she had replied without a trace of hesitation or embarrassment: she slept with the superintendent in a police-force flat at five o'clock every Tuesday afternoon. Schyman didn't know for certain if she'd stopped.

'It must be something really significant,' Schyman said. 'Forensic evidence, witnesses, murder weapon, even a confession. I want to know what it is.'

Patrik Nilsson looked out at the newsroom. 'Feels damn good,' he said, 'that we were on the ball.' He glanced at the editor-in-chief, and a little shiver ran down Schyman's spine.

'How do you mean?' he asked.

Patrik clicked his pen a few times. 'It was actually Annika Bengtzon,' he said. 'She only said it to wind me up, I know. I didn't think the body in Skärholmen was much of a story but she listed them for me, all those dead women, said maybe we were missing out on a serial killer, so I put Berit and Michnik on to it.'

Schyman leaned over his desk. The fact that even Patrik Nilsson occasionally worried about media ethics was an unexpected but welcome sign.

'We don't set the framework,' he said. 'Society is in a state of constant flux, and we change with it. We describe and we observe, but we don't represent any ultimate truth. Circumstances can change from one day to the next, and when they do, we reflect that.'

Patrik stood up, relieved.

'Find out why he's being held,' Schyman said.

When Patrik had shut the door behind him, he pulled out the envelope, addressed it to the chairman of the board, Herman Wennergren, took two deep breaths, then called Reception. 'I need to get something to the board. Is someone available to take it?'

He looked at his calendar and drew a circle around that day's date, 30 November. According to the terms of his contract, he had to give six months' notice, timed from the date when he informed the board of his resignation, which meant that he would leave on the last day of May the following year.

He watched the new caretaker heading across the newsroom and weighed the envelope in his hand. Would they accept his resignation? Or would they persuade him to stay, increase his salary and pension, drown him in flattery and pleas?

He handed the envelope to the young man. 'There's no panic,' he said, 'but it needs to arrive today.'

'I'll take it at once,' the caretaker said.

★　★　★

Sure enough, the plane parked a long way out on the airfield. First they had to wait for a bus to take them to the terminal, then another because the first was full, and then they spent fifteen minutes bouncing and rattling towards the airport building.

When they finally got inside Terminal 2B, Annika had tunnel-vision: she couldn't see people or walls or the cafés, just the big departures board where their flight to Nairobi was flashing *Final Call*. Halenius set off at a sprint, his bag bouncing on his back, Annika racing after him. They flew along corridors and moving walkways, past departure halls with combinations of letters and numbers that lacked any apparent logic, and by the time they reached 2F it said *Gate Closed* for the Kenya Airways night flight to Nairobi. There was a very long queue for the security check, so they rushed past, their feet barely touching the ground. Security staff asked to check Annika's bag and took her toothpaste. They arrived at the gate and caught a female ground crew member who unlocked the glass doors and let them board the plane, even though they were actually far too late.

'It's always like this,' Halenius said as he sank into his seat, 36L. 'It's always like this at this fucking airport.'

Annika didn't answer. Her knees were pressed against the seat in front. He was sitting very close to her and she thought she could smell his scent. On the screen before her a message read:

KARIBU!
Welcome onboard!

Beside it there were three lions, a male and two females, and the logo of Kenya Airways with the slogan 'The pride of Africa'.

The image changed. Text filled the screen: UMBALI WA MWISHO WA SAFARI 4039 MAILI. A map of the world, with a plane the size of Western Europe, appeared. The plane's projected journey was plotted in a gentle curve leading to a small square on one side of Africa. The flight would take eight hours and ten minutes.

Out of the window, she saw a man in ear-defenders and a padded jacket tugging at a pipe on the ground immediately below them.

The plane was full, the air in the cabin already thick.

The engines started and the plane taxied on to the runway. She felt the vibration of the metal transfer to her body.

His knee hit hers.

Twelve hours before she had been lying with him in her bed in Agnegatan, feeling that everything was too early or far too late.

She still didn't know which.

DAY 9

THURSDAY, 1 DECEMBER

CHAPTER 18

She woke at irregular intervals, with a stiff neck and saliva in the corner of her mouth. Each time she looked at Halenius beside her. Sometimes he was asleep with his mouth half open; at others he was staring at the film on the little screen.

At twenty past four in the morning (Kenyan time) she set about exploring the plane's entertainment system. She clicked until she found a film featuring a young Julia Roberts as a law student. Every fifteen seconds the picture flickered, the sound dropped out and the screen turned to static. Each time it happened she lost the plot: Julia came back as a new Julia, talking about things she didn't understand. After ten minutes she gave up and tried a film starring an ageing Adam Sandler. Same thing. She switched it off.

Outside, space was large and black. There were no stars visible, just the flashing light at the far end of the plane's wing. Inside the cabin the lighting was subdued; most people were asleep, a few were reading or doing sudokus in the light of the reading lamp set into the base of the overhead lockers.

She leaned down towards her bag and fished out the information she had printed out about Kenya from the Institute of International Affairs' website. It was twenty-nine pages long, and covered everything from geography and climate to ancient history, foreign policy and tourism. Perhaps it had been written by Jimmy's Tanya. Perhaps she'd helped analyse the content and provided expert advice about contemporary politics. She was bound to be well read and talented.

The cradle of humanity was in East Africa, Annika read. Several million years ago there were already human beings living around Lake Turkana in north-west Kenya. The 2010 census had found that the population was 39 million, an increase of a third in ten years. About half of the population lived in poverty, and that proportion was growing. Women were responsible for doing most of the work. In the year 2005, 1.3 million Kenyans were living with HIV; 140,000 died of Aids that year, and even more from malaria. At times a tenth of the population was dependent upon food aid from the United Nations.

After the presidential election in December 2007 violent disturbances had broken out in several parts of the country, including Nairobi's slums, but also in cities like Eldoret and Kisumu; 1,100 people were killed, and up to 600,000 fled their homes. The killing was in part racially motivated.

The worst afflicted were the Kikuyu, the tribe that had previously held political power.

She lowered the printout. That sounded like the start of the Rwandan genocide, with machetes slashing and maiming, but with one vital difference: this time the international community had intervened. Kofi Annan had acted as mediator, and a total bloodbath was avoided.

She shut her eyes and tried to locate Thomas. Where was he in all this? His hands and face, his blond hair and broad shoulders . . . He was somewhere out there but the images kept slipping away as the plane forged its way through the air currents.

She must have fallen asleep again, because when she jerked awake the pilot was saying over the speakers that they were beginning their descent into Nairobi. The screen had come to life, and the map with the enormous plane was back. Outside it was still pitch-black. According to the map, they were passing over a place called Nouakchott.

She rubbed her eyes and looked out of the window. She couldn't see any lights, but she knew there were people down there, in the city of Nouakchott, living in a moonless darkness.

'You missed breakfast,' Halenius said. 'You were fast asleep and I didn't want to wake you.'

She wiped the corners of her eyes. 'Quails' eggs and chilled champagne, I suppose?' she said, getting up and stepping over Halenius's knees.

'They've just turned on the seatbelt sign.'

'I don't think they'd like it if I peed all over the seat,' she said, and headed towards the toilet.

It smelt of disinfectant and urine. She sat there until the stewardess knocked on the door and asked her to go back to her seat and fasten her belt: they were about to land.

She stumbled back as the plane jolted and shook, feeling thirsty and sick.

'Okay?' Halenius asked, as she scrambled over him.

She didn't answer.

'How are you? Are you feeling sick?'

'I don't know if I can do this,' she said, so quietly that he might not have heard her over the roar of the plane.

The terminal at Jomo Kenyatta International Airport consisted of a badly lit passageway with a very low ceiling. The air was thick with sweat and stale breath. The floor was covered with grey plastic tiles that became red, then yellow. The ceiling was pushing against the back of her head, the walls against her sides. She was swept forward in a sea of people. Thomas was with her, right behind or just in front of her. Halenius was walking beside her.

She completed the yellow and blue visa forms, but was told she should have filled in the white one.

She had her fingerprints taken as she went through Customs.

Outside the building the air was surprisingly clear and cool. A vague smell of burned spices hung over the road. It had rained overnight and water hissed under the vehicles' tyres. Dawn was growing as a pink shimmer to the east.

'Are we going to rent a car?'

Halenius shook his head. 'We've been given very definite instructions about the sort of vehicle we have to use. I think Frida's managed to get hold of one. Wait here with the bags.'

She was left standing on the pavement outside the terminal building. There were people everywhere and she lost sight of Halenius at once. She could make out low buildings on the other side of the road. There were cafés on both sides of the terminal entrance.

'Taxi, madam, you want taxi?'

She shook her head and stared into the darkness, trying to see the buildings on the other side. White, yellow and blue cars swept past to her left, more people, faces with white eyes—

'Okay,' Halenius said beside her. 'The silver car over there.'

In the chaos she caught sight of a woman with long hair and black clothes standing next to a large silver car. Annika picked up her bag and headed towards it.

As she got closer she could see that the woman's hair was arranged in tiny plaits that stretched a long way down her back; about half of them were purple. In spite of the gloom she was wearing a pair of gold sunglasses, and the smart designer label sparkled on the glass. She wasn't smiling. 'I'm Frida. Nice to meet you.'

So this was Angela Sisulu's roommate, the wealthy Nigerian Frida Arokodare, who worked for the UN. She was tall and very thin, taller than Halenius. She was wearing a studded belt, lots of bangles and a nose-stud. Annika held out her hand and remembered in passing that she hadn't washed them after using the toilet on the plane. She felt short, pale and dirty. 'I appreciate your help so much,' she said, and was horribly aware of how clumsy and Swedish she sounded.

'Glad to contribute,' Frida said, then got in behind the wheel. She moved efficiently, with measured gestures. Annika opened the back door. The vehicle could seat eight, a bus-like shoebox: she had to sit bolt upright, as if she'd swallowed a poker.

Halenius jumped into the passenger seat.

'What sort of car is this?' she asked.

'Toyota Noah, normally sold only in Asia. Frida was lucky – she borrowed it from a colleague. I can see why the kidnappers picked it. It sticks out in a crowd and is easy to spot.'

He turned to Frida. 'All sorted?'

'My mechanic changed the brake-pads yesterday,' she replied, 'so it ought to be in perfect shape.' She ran a hand nervously through her plaits. 'I've done as you asked,' she said, pointing towards the luggage compartment. 'A full tank and two extra cans of petrol at the back.' She gestured to a cool-box and two boxes on the seat behind Annika. 'Food and water, a first-aid kit, toilet paper, two extra mobile phones and a satellite phone. I've had a vehicle tracking device fitted so the trip can be downloaded and studied by your police after-wards, but I haven't had a chance to try it so I don't know if it works. What do you want to do first?'

'Have you withdrawn the money?'

Frida started the engine. 'The bank opens at eight thirty,' she said, pulling out into the traffic. 'Have you had breakfast? My bank is on Moi Avenue, so we can wait at the Hilton until it opens.'

Halenius shifted position in his seat. Annika thought he seemed nervous.

They emerged on to a four-lane motorway, and a large sign announced that it had been built by the Chinese.

'China's busy buying up the whole of Africa,' Frida said. 'Land, forest, minerals, oil, all sorts of natural resources . . . So, tell me, are you still with that minister? How long are you going to slave away there?'

Halenius let out a short laugh.

'Power corrupts,' she said. 'And the children are with Angie?'

'They left on Sunday. Tanya took them. They've been having terrible weather in Cape Town, but it seems to have calmed down now.'

'How is Tanya? Is she still at the Institute?'

'Yep. But she's applied for a new job with the UN in New York.'

Frida nodded enthusiastically. 'Excellent! They could do with her there.'

Annika let the conversation in the important and highly educated front seat flow over her and took out the video-camera. She pointed it at the side window and experienced the city through the screen, a petrol station called Kenol, huge billboards advertising products she hadn't known existed (*Buy Mouida pineapple cola! Mobile provider Airtel! Chandarana supermarket! Tusker beer!*), five-storey buildings under construction, surrounded by bamboo scaffolding, water trucks, a petrol station called Total, another called OiLibya, 'Read the *Star* newspaper!' (*Fresh! Independent! Different!*), low-slung Citi Hoppers rolling over the road, piles of earth, a smell of burned spices. The Chinese motorway had come to an end and been replaced by a narrow asphalt road, still dark from the night's rain. No pavements, no hard shoulder, just long lines of people on foot heading somewhere or nowhere, in flip-flops, trainers, espadrilles, pumps and polished leather shoes. Women with brightly coloured hair in badly fitting outfits, with children on their backs, young men in T-shirts advertising exotic travel destinations and American liquor.

Daylight came quickly, but the sun hung back behind heavy clouds.

The amount of vegetation was immense, over-whelming.

The Hilton Hotel in Nairobi was a tall, round building in the heart of the city centre. Frida parked in the underground garage. There were security guards at the entrance, exit, and down in the car park itself.

The lobby was huge, with a crystal chandelier that looked like a spaceship, and they floated over a mirror-smooth marble floor towards its Traveller's Restaurant. They sat in a corner and Halenius ordered a croissant and coffee for her. To her surprise, she found she was able to eat.

'What happens now?' Frida asked, idly fingering her coffee cup.

Halenius finished his mouthful before he replied. 'The kidnapper is going to get in touch at nine o'clock,' he said. 'Presumably we'll be given instructions about where the ransom money is to be delivered, and I'm going to have to tell him you're driving the car. That could be a problem.'

Frida let go of the cup and leaned back in her chair. 'Why?'

Halenius took a large sip of coffee. 'Kidnappers always want the person delivering the ransom to be alone in the vehicle. If there are two people, they automatically assume that the second is a police officer. He knows both Annika and I are coming . . . It might be tricky to get him to accept you as our driver, but it has to work. We can't do this without you.'

Annika looked down at her coffee cup, and Frida stretched her back.

'He's already dictated the make of car, but if we're unlucky he might demand other ways of recognizing it or us – specific clothes, or stickers in the windows.'

Annika looked across the restaurant. Above the bar there were stacks of leather cases. They seemed to be aiming for the ambience of an old train. She remembered something Halenius had said – was it yesterday or last year? 'If the kidnappers say they want your head shaved, you just get your razor out.'

Would she shave off her hair to get Thomas back? Would she sacrifice her left hand? Would she have sex with the negotiator?

Frida was toying with her gold bracelet. 'You know what the Somali pirates use the ransom money for?' she said to Halenius.

'If they don't drown with their share of the loot, you mean?'

'They provide for entire villages, whole regions of the country,' Frida said.

'Well,' Halenius said, 'not all of them.'

'More than you think. They're keeping the economy going along the entire coastal area.'

Annika sat up straighter and Halenius finished his coffee. 'True,' he said. 'Prices have more than doubled since the pirates started their kidnapping racket. Everything from land to men's shoes, and it's created a whole load of social problems on top of everything else the population has to deal with, such as famine, civil war . . .'

Frida waved towards the coast. 'Oil tankers worth hundreds of millions of dollars float past the coast of Somalia every day, and starving people can do nothing but stand on the beach and watch them.'

'That doesn't give them the right to kidnap people and take hostages,' Halenius said.

Annika put her cup down, and noticed her hand was shaking. 'I understand the Robin Hood thinking,' she said, 'but my husband isn't an oil tanker, he's just being tortured. Do you defend that as well?'

Frida took off her sunglasses. Her eyes were pale, almost grey. 'How come,' she said, 'that violence is so much worse when it starts to affect white people?' She said it in a calm, neutral voice, without a trace of emotion.

Annika thought about Rwanda and had no answer.

'You're so particular about your employment laws and trade-union agreements and wage negotiations in the developed world, but only in so far as they affect you. You don't care about the working conditions of those in the textile factories in Asia who stitch your clothes, or the oil workers in Sudan who make sure you can drive your cars. You always talk about democracy and human rights, but you're referring to your own comforts.'

She put her sunglasses back on and smiled very briefly. 'Don't take it the wrong way,' she said to Annika. 'I just want to turn the argument round. Not everything in the world is always black and white.'

She looked at the time. 'If you've finished, we should go to the bank. Shall we get the case now or when we come back?'

Halenius turned to Annika and waited until she had put her bag over her shoulder. 'This was where Thomas was staying during the conference,' he said. 'They've packed his things and cleared his room, but they know you're coming and—'

She stopped abruptly. 'His things are here?'

Suddenly the smell of his aftershave filled the Traveller's Restaurant.

'We can ask them to send the case home to Agnegatan if you'd rather not take it with you,' Halenius said.

She was standing in the middle of the floor, unable to move. His things didn't matter, his razor and ties and jackets. 'I'll take it with me,' she heard herself say, she didn't know why.

Frida glided across the marble floor towards the concierge, who disappeared into some inner room and returned with Thomas's aluminium Rimowa case. Annika signed a receipt, then stood in Reception holding the bulky suitcase. She remembered him packing it. She had noted that he was taking his pink shirt with him. It wasn't there now, she knew. He was wearing it, and the left sleeve was dark with blood.

She trailed after Frida and Halenius, pulling the case behind her, towards the lifts and the garage.

It was only half a block from the Hilton and the large branch of the Kenya Commercial Bank on Moi Avenue. Frida drove out of the hotel's garage and straight into the bank's.

'This shouldn't take too long,' she said. 'I warned them I was coming. The plastic, duct tape and bags you wanted are all in the boot.'

Halenius nodded. Frida jumped out of the car, gave a security guard a little wave as she went past and vanished into a lift.

The silence was thick. The yellow lighting of the garage was casting brown shadows inside the car. Halenius was sitting with his head turned away, staring out of the side window; she could see his spiky hair silhouetted in the semi-darkness.

'The other night—' she began.

'We can talk about that later.'

She gasped as if she'd been slapped, and her cheeks burned red.

Suddenly the Rimowa case in the boot seemed to fill the whole car.

'Frida,' Annika said, with a dry mouth, 'she's not like I expected.'

Halenius glanced at her in the rear-view mirror.

'She's unusual,' he said. 'There was no need for her to get an education or a job but that was what she chose to do.'

'Purple hair,' Annika said.

'She does a brilliant job for the UNHCR, the United Nations' refugee agency. She's not afraid to get her hands dirty.'

Am I supposed to cheer? Annika thought, but said nothing.

Frida came back with two security guards, each carrying a box. She opened the door where Annika was sitting. The boxes of money (her money) were loaded on to the seats and the security guards went back to the lifts. Two of their colleagues, one by the lift and one by the exit, remained, watching them.

'What do we do now?' Frida said.

'Can we trust them?' Halenius asked, nodding towards the guards.

The Nigerian woman tugged nervously at her hair. 'I don't think it's a very good idea to repack the money now, not in the middle of a garage.'

'Can we go back to yours?' Halenius asked.

'To Muthaiga? It would take hours to drive there through this traffic.'

His forehead was wet with sweat, in spite of the damp cool of the garage. 'Well, we can't do it out on the street.'

'Shall we get a room at the Hilton?'

Halenius looked at his watch. 'He's going to call

in fifteen minutes, and we need to be ready to roll then.'

Annika got out of the car and opened the rear door. She grabbed the plastic, the bags, the duct tape and two large pairs of scissors. 'The contents of one box in each bag,' she said, taking a pair of scissors.

Halenius clenched his jaw and pulled out the first box of money. Annika stared at it: she'd never seen notes packed like that except in films.

Her house in Vinterviksgatan: there it was, packed into bundles of notes, five thousand dollars in each one.

Halenius put the box on the floor and opened one of the newly bought bags. It still had the price-tag on it, 3,900 shillings. It was a sports bag, black, with a red logo on one side, about half a metre long and thirty centimetres in width and height.

Annika tore her eyes away from the money and rolled the plastic out on the floor, it was two metres long, thick and unyielding, the sort you use to damp-proof buildings. With the scissors in her hand, she measured out a long strip by eye as Halenius began to unload the money.

'That's going to be too big,' he said, nodding at the plastic.

'I'll cut the end off,' she said.

Halenius passed the bundles of notes to her, grey-green bricks with straps round their middles, tightly packed, nine at a time.

'One hundred and ten bundles in each bag,' Halenius said.

'I know,' Annika said. She piled the bundles on top of each other, over and over, until the stack was forty-five centimetres long, twenty across and about thirty high. She wrapped the plastic round it, long sides first, tore off a piece of duct tape with her teeth and fastened it along the top, then folded the ends in the way she wrapped the children's Christmas presents.

It was 1 December, and in three and a half weeks it would be Christmas. Would she be home then? Would Thomas?

'Can you help me with the tape?' she asked Halenius, and he put the second box of money down, picked up the duct tape, then began to wrap it round the whole parcel. It ended up being surprisingly heavy and they worked together to get it into the sports bag. There was only just room for it.

Annika gazed at the bag. 'What does Kenyan law have to say about bringing large amounts of cash into the country?' she said.

Frida and Halenius looked up at her.

'Those Brits who were caught this summer with a load of money in Somalia,' Annika said, 'they got ten years in prison. Does the same rule apply here?'

'Fifteen years, actually,' Frida said. 'And they weren't just British. Two of them were Kenyans.'

'So could that happen here?' Annika asked.

Frida and Halenius exchanged a glance and Annika felt the hair on her neck stand up. She couldn't get stuck here, not her as well, not for fifteen years, in a Kenyan prison: what would happen to the children? Why hadn't she left any instructions about what she wanted to happen if she didn't get back? Who would look after them? Not Doris: she was far too precious about her own lifestyle, and her mum couldn't afford to. Anne Snapphane? Hardly.

With some difficulty Frida picked up the packed bag and put it on the floor by the seat where Annika had been sitting. The logo glowed in the gloom.

Annika unrolled another length of plastic and started to cut it.

Frida looked up at the concrete roof. 'Is there any reception down here?' she asked.

Halenius pulled out his mobile phone and swore through his teeth. 'I've got to get up to street level,' he said, and ran towards the exit.

Frida opened the driver's door and got in. She clearly had no intention of packing any money.

Annika finished cutting the second length of builders' plastic, trimmed the side, laid it out on the floor and began to shift the bundles. She filled her arms with green bricks of cash and tipped them on to the plastic, one of the bands came loose and the notes spilled out across the concrete. The guard by the exit was shuffling nervously. How much had he seen? With her fingers shaking, she packed the bundles in the same way as before, layer upon layer, nine bundles each time. Then she sealed the plastic. Finally she repeated what Halenius had done, and wrapped the whole package in several loops of tape. She shifted the parcel into the second bag, pulled the sides up and fastened the zip. It was heavy and she had to use both hands to lift it into the car.

The best solution would probably be for the children to stay with Sophia Grenborg.

Out of the corner of her eye she saw Halenius running back from the exit with his mobile in his hand.

'Langata Cemetery,' he said. 'We have to leave the money in Langata Cemetery, the entrance from Kungu Karumba Road.'

They tore out of the garage with the bags of money bouncing on the floor next to Annika's feet.

'And he was okay with me driving?' Frida asked, forcing her way out into the almost static traffic.

'He didn't have much choice. I said we couldn't do it ourselves, that we couldn't find the way.'

'Did you tell him my name?'

'First name, not surname.'

Frida let out a small yelp. 'For God's sake, Jimmy, you weren't supposed to tell him my name! You promised!'

Halenius looked out of the window – Annika saw that his lips had turned white.

'The kidnapper went mad. He refused to give us proof of life.'

Annika stared at the back of his head. 'But you said . . . we wouldn't pay unless . . .'

'I know.'

Frida muttered something in a strange language as she forced her way aggressively through the sluggish traffic. She braked at an almost rusted-through stop sign, then turned into Ngong Road. Electricity cables hung across the street like spiders' webs, and there were no white lines, just dust and tarmac.

Annika shut her eyes against the faces streaming past. What would she do if Thomas was dead?

And what would she do if he survived?

If he came back, mutilated and traumatized?

They had no money to buy a new apartment, and he hated her rented flat. Would he be able to go back to work? Were there prosthetic hands that worked like real ones?

What would it feel like to make love to him?

She took a deep breath. 'Where do I have to leave the money?' she asked.

'We're going to get the final instructions once we're there,' Halenius said, through gritted teeth.

It started to rain again. Frida switched on the windscreen-wipers. One squeaked. Langata Road swept, like a frayed cord, up slopes and down hillsides. Corrugated metal bus-stops, concrete walls topped with barbed wire. Trees whose trunks split at ground level, then grew up like roofs against the sky. There was a smell of exhaust fumes and brown coal.

Frida turned off to the right and the car lurched and shook. She slowed to a halt.

'Is this it?' Halenius asked. Annika followed his gaze to a rusting sign:

City Council of Nairobi
Area Councillor Ward manager
Mugumoini Ward
Welcome

The rain was falling silently on the windscreen. Frida pushed her sunglasses up into her hair and switched off the engine. They were parked next to a fence made of chicken-mesh, topped with barbed wire. There were several cars nearby, indistinguishable vehicles in various states of decay, but there was also a large, shiny black Mercedes.

'What happens now?' Annika asked.

'We wait,' Halenius said.

'Does he know we're here?' she asked.

'He's bound to,' Halenius said.

Annika swung round, as if the kidnappers' observer was hiding behind her back. Two men went past the rear of the car, a woman with a child, a boy on a bike. Which one, which one, which one? The oxygen in the car ran out and she put her hand instinctively to her neck. 'Can I get out?'

'No.'

She sat there with her hand on the door handle.

Seconds ticked past. Minutes. No one said anything.

Soon she would be getting out with a bag in each hand, assuming she could actually lift them. They weighed almost thirty kilos each. Soon she would be walking through the valley of the shadow of death, fearing all evil.

'How long have we been here?' Frida asked.

Halenius looked at his watch. 'Almost a quarter of an hour.'

Annika couldn't breathe. 'I have to get out,' she said.

'You have to—'

She slid the door open and stepped out on to the muddy ground. 'I won't go far.'

CHAPTER 19

The gates were made of chicken-mesh and held together by a rope.

Stepping round the puddles, she ducked under the rope and made her way into the cemetery. The silence felt more dense immediately. The noise of Langata Road faded away. A plane flew past at low altitude.

You could fly dead bodies home, she knew that. Did you have to call your travel agent, or did the body count as cargo? Maybe the embassy would know, or a funeral director.

It had almost stopped raining.

Where would she have to leave the money? Behind a wooden cross? In an open grave?

To her left, behind a barbed-wire fence, there was a field of fresh graves, the earth still brown and the crosses white. Further on there were more graves, covered with grass; some of the crosses had fallen over.

She couldn't see any natural place to leave two black sports bags with red logos. They would stand out too much – people would be curious and would investigate. She looked around carefully.

To her right was an official building, a little grey concrete house with a rusty metal roof and wrought-iron bars over the windows, with the words 'Mugumoini Ward' above the door. There was something familiar about it. The door in the middle of the longest wall had a window on each side, symmetrically arranged. Two chimneys emerged through the tin roof.

Lyckebo, she thought. Her grandmother's house, near Hosjön. A classic Swedish two-room cottage.

The door opened and three women stepped out, staring at her. They might have walked out of one of the building-blocks of Swedish construction history, but they couldn't see anything familiar in her: they just saw someone who didn't belong and was staring far too hard.

A funeral was taking place in the middle of the green part of the cemetery. A group of people were gathered round a grave she couldn't see. A man was talking through a crackling loudspeaker. He sounded devout.

She stood still and listened. The man's voice rose and sank. Several of the mourners were carrying large umbrellas.

She looked back towards the gate and saw the silhouettes of Frida and Halenius in the car. They were sitting still; neither seemed to be speaking.

Further away in the cemetery were some larger graves, little mausoleums made of tin or bricks. Maybe it would be possible to hide the sports bags there.

She walked up to the first. Red-tiled roof, ornate, perforated wrought-iron sides, painted turquoise, a white-tiled grave.

Blessed are the pure in heart for they shall see God. The man had been born in 1933, and died in 2005. There was a faded photograph of him. Annika thought he was smiling. Red earth had blown in across the white tiles. He had lived to seventy-two. He must have been much loved, and well-off, to have warranted such an elaborate resting-place.

When she turned to move on she saw that she was standing on an empty plastic bottle. It was embedded in the ground, half covered by earth, and made a clicking sound as she lifted her right foot. Next to the grave were signs of a large fire, charred wood and bits of rubbish, pink plastic, checked fabric and an old tyre.

Halenius hadn't moved.

She quite liked cemeteries. She ought to visit Grandma more often.

She crouched between two graves. Charles had died at twelve years old. There was a photograph of Lucy on her memorial cross, but the picture had faded so badly that only the outline of her hair was visible. Faceless Lucy, the weeds growing tall on her grave.

She turned her face to the wind. Would Charles and Lucy have chosen to be born, if they had had the choice? She wished she could have asked them because they'd done the whole journey now and returned. They knew the answer.

Grandma would undoubtedly have said yes. She had enjoyed life. She found joy in little things, picking mushrooms, lighting candles and watching variety shows on television.

And what about her?

She took a deep breath as images swirled past. Grandma pulling her out of the water after she had gone through the ice on Hultsjön when she was seven (she was only checking if it was safe). Grandma fetching a ladder when she had climbed to the top of the larch at the corner of the cottage and didn't dare climb down. Grandma encouraging her to apply to the College of Journalism, even though no one in the family had ever been to university: 'How do you know you can't do it, if you don't even try?'

Annika gulped. So if she was standing by the door leading to this earthly life and was asked if she wanted to give it a try, what would she say? 'No, I think it looks a bit too hard'? Would she, for the first and only time, refrain from doing something unfamiliar and possibly difficult just because it seemed a bit uncomfortable?

She let her head fall back and gazed up at the rainclouds.

So, she had made her decision.

She had chosen to come. Perhaps that was what made the difference. Perhaps you didn't come if you didn't sign up voluntarily. Charles and Lucy had also wanted to come.

She peered towards Langata Road, and her eyes

fell on a grave that was still brown, a beloved wife, mother and grandmother. 'Sunrise: 1960. Sunset: 2011. *May the Lord rest her in peace.*'

Sunrise. Sunset. So beautiful.

Her photograph was still very clear. She had curly hair and was wearing a big white hat.

'Annika!'

She froze to ice and looked back towards the gate. Halenius had got out of the car and was waving at her.

The funeral was still going on, but the crackling loudspeaker had fallen silent.

Another plane flew past at low altitude.

She ran towards the gate. 'What?' she said breathlessly.

'Not here,' Halenius said. 'We need to get going.'

She was gasping for breath as adrenalin surged inside her. 'What's happened?'

'New orders, by text. We have to go past the Life Spring Chapel and leave the money on the plateau above Kibera. Jump in.'

The atmosphere in the car was electric. Frida was chewing her bottom lip, and her eyes were darting about behind her sunglasses. She was talking about places and possible roads as she fiddled with the gear-stick: 'There's a Life Spring Chapel by the airport, but that's on the other side of the city. They might mean the turning circle above Mashimoni, behind the Ngong Forest road, right by the river . . .'

Annika turned to look back towards the cemetery. The vegetation had taken over the fence next to where they were parked, wrapping the rust and barbed wire with green leaves and tendrils, but through the foliage she could see the mourners closing their umbrellas and moving towards the far exit.

Why had they got new orders? Had she done something wrong? Did the kidnapper have an observer among the mourners?

Frida put the car in gear and it shot forward. The people in the cemetery disappeared behind the greenery.

They turned into a smaller road and the tarmac came to an end. Frida slowed down. Soon they were rattling forward at five kilometres an hour, moving at the same speed as donkey-carts and men on heavily laden bicycles.

Annika was sitting in the middle of the seat, as far away from the doors as possible.

Buildings close to the car, cracked clay and tin, rubbish trampled into the ground alongside the unpaved road, a goat eating on top of a mountain of garbage.

They had one point one million dollars in the car, on the floor by her feet: was it obvious from the outside? What would happen if the people on the other side of the windows knew?

A man selling waxed cloths slid past, women with children on their backs. Eyes following them along the pitted mud road.

Then the car was shaken by a sudden bang. Annika jerked, grabbed the seat and Frida braked.

'What happened?' Annika said. 'What was that?'

Frida pulled the handbrake on, took off her sunglasses and looked at Halenius, wide-eyed.

'Do exactly what you would have done if we weren't in the car,' he said quietly.

Frida took a few quick breaths, opened the door, got out and shouted, '*Acha! Msipige mawe!*'

Faces moved in the dust and Annika leaned instinctively towards Halenius. 'What's she doing?'

'Telling them not to throw stones at the car.'

Frida got back in, took the handbrake off and put the car in gear. Her top lip was glowing with sweat. Annika checked that the back doors were locked.

To their left a valley opened up and she followed the greenery with her eyes. On the horizon she could see how it changed and turned brown: a stone landscape? A moon crater? An endless plain of mud?

She heard herself gasp. Kibera, one of the most densely populated places on the planet, one of the continent's largest slums, shacks made of tin and mud as far as she could see, open sewers and garbage, a carpet of different shades of brown from here to eternity. She tried to say something but found no words.

'Mashimoni is down there,' Frida said, driving into a turning circle a couple of dozen metres above a dried-up riverbed. She stopped, switched off the engine and pulled the handbrake on again.

They sat in silence for a minute or so.

'Did they say where I had to leave the money?'

Halenius shook his head.

The monotonous landscape stretched as far as she could see on both sides. Washing hanging on lines. Smoke rising between the roofs. There were people everywhere. On the other side of the valley, mobile-phone masts reached towards the clouds.

'I'm not going to have to go down there, am I?' she said, nodding towards the warren of tin shacks.

'I don't know,' Halenius said.

Minutes passed.

She picked up the video-camera and filmed through the window. People walked past them on their way down to the slum.

'Can I open my window?'

'I think we can probably get out now,' Halenius said, opening his door and stepping out.

Annika and Frida followed suit.

They were standing on something resembling the Lion King's cliff, a plateau high above the savannah. They could hear voices as a faint rumble.

'There aren't as many people living here as everyone used to think,' Halenius said. 'They used to say two million, but now they think it's more like a few hundred thousand.'

She'd read about it and seen it on television and in films. *The Constant Gardener* had been set here, although she hadn't known it at the time.

Halenius's mobile buzzed.

He read the text with bloodshot eyes, and Annika stopped breathing.

It didn't matter where, as long as it was over soon. She could carry the bags over the riverbed and among the shacks, passing women in colourful clothes and boys in grey school uniforms. She could throw them into a container full of rubbish or leave them in a grocery shop. She was ready.

'The ransom is to be dropped at the entrance to Langata Women's Prison.'

Annika blinked. She didn't understand.

'That's not far from the cemetery,' Frida said.

'So we're heading back the way we came?' Halenius said.

They got back into the car and Frida started the engine. Annika hardly managed to get the door shut before Frida reversed and hit a pothole. Annika's head hit the roof.

'Sorry,' Frida said, glancing back.

She doesn't like me, Annika found herself thinking. She doesn't want me here. She'd rather be alone with Halenius.

Could that be right? Was that why she had agreed to help with this crazy task? If it was true, how long had she felt like that? Since she used to share a room with Angela Sisulu? Had she lain awake in the next bed, listening?

And what about now? Did she understand? Did she know? Could she see through them?

They were driving down dusty streets with shops the size of cupboards. A glazier's, a mosque, a slaughterhouse. The car bounced and lurched. Annika used her hands to keep herself upright and protect her head from the worst of it.

Frida slowed when they reached an area of gravel at the end of the road in front of something that looked a bit like a carport, and an iron gate painted in the gaudy colours of Kenya, green, black, yellow and red, with a sign above it. *Langata Women's Maximum Security Prison*. The sun was reluctant to show itself. It was very quiet.

Annika glanced around her. Was she really supposed to leave the money here? Or was this just another false lead?

She wound the window down. The complex didn't seem terrifying, just tragic. Barbed wire to the right, a residential area of new four-storey blocks to the left.

Frida nodded towards the visitors' entrance. 'I've got a friend in there,' she said. 'She had a good job, flight assistant, but a dodgy way of earning a bit extra, smuggling heroin. She had half a kilo on her when they caught her. She's served ten years of a fourteen-year sentence.'

Halenius was staring at his mobile.

'Do you think this is the place?' Annika asked.

Frida got out of the car and went to the security booth to say hello.

'Are you going to stay here?' Halenius asked.

Annika nodded.

He got out of the car and shut the door. A young woman with two small children was sitting beside a tin shack with three walls. A hand-painted sign saying *Visitors' Waiting Lodge* revealed that they were there to see someone. Annika raised the camera and filmed them. They were dressed in colourful clothes – how did they manage to look so neatly pressed? A woman in red jeans and a white top walked over the gravel and in through the entrance, pulling a large suitcase behind her. Was she moving in? What had she done? Annika followed her through the lens.

A gust of wind blew into the car, bringing with it a smell of rubber and sour milk. She lowered the camera and shut her eyes against the wind. A man was talking through a loudspeaker somewhere, but she couldn't make out the words or even the language. A car went past. The sun came out and hit her eyelids, and her vision became warm and red.

Thomas had been staying in that hotel. He had eaten breakfast in the Traveller's Restaurant, flirted with the British woman in the bar, she was sure. He had been on a bus tour of Nairobi, he'd told her, when he called the evening after the second day of the conference, but she doubted he would have seen either Kibera or Langata Women's Maximum Security Prison. Thomas inhabited a world where getting red wine on your tie was a disaster. Women in red jeans and white tops were regarded in terms of cost and integration issues. In the USA Annika had seen injustice and exclusion on grounds of race and class; Thomas had seen individual freedom and economic opportunity. She knew perfectly well that neither of them was right, or perhaps that they were both right. But Thomas was in no doubt. A person who was strong and free and shouldered their responsibilities always managed okay. If he came back, would his worldview remain the same?

She opened her eyes. Several people had sat down on the gravel around the car. She raised the camera and filmed them eating bread they had brought with them, rocking children in their arms. A man and a woman were sitting on a tree stump a bit further away. She was wearing a lilac turban, he had a mobile in his hand. Annika zoomed in on the man through the camera. Was he one of them? Was he sending Halenius a text, specifying where the money was to be left?

The man with the loudspeaker started to sing.

Frida yanked her door open.

'Put the camera down,' she hissed. 'This is a state institution. They'll arrest us if they see you filming.'

Halenius opened his door and held up his mobile, his mouth a thin line. 'It's not here either,' he said. 'They're sending us to Eastleigh.'

The sudden draught made her eyes water. Frida

slammed the door and Annika closed her window. She felt like bursting into tears.

'This time it's probably right,' Halenius said. 'Eastleigh is known as Little Mogadishu. That's where most of the Somalis live.'

Frida started the car.

The woman in the lilac turban had vanished.

The man with the mobile was still there. He didn't look at them as they drove away.

'Three million? *Three million!*'

Chairman of the board Herman Wennergren's cheeks were flushed with anger.

'The decision wasn't only based upon sales figures,' Anders Schyman said. 'In this instance it was also about saving lives, taking humanitarian responsibility.'

'But three million? Out of the newspaper's profits? For that unstable individual?'

Herman Wennergren was (with good reason) no great supporter of Annika Bengtzon. Schyman wouldn't have described her in that way. He was just grateful that his chairman hadn't picked up the most controversial argument, that the *Evening Post* was sponsoring international terrorism.

'She's in Nairobi now to hand over the ransom,' Schyman said. 'It's actually far more than three million, and she's put up most of the total herself. I think this money will turn out to be a profitable investment.'

Herman Wennergren muttered something

inaudible. 'Have you rearranged everything down here again?' he asked, sitting down on the visitor's chair in Schyman's glass box. He put his briefcase beside it, and draped his coat over the arm.

There hadn't been any budget for rebuilding or renovating the newsroom for years, which the chairman was well aware of. 'How do you mean?' Schyman said, leaning back in his new chair.

'Your office feels . . . smaller.'

'It's always been this size,' Schyman said. There's something seriously wrong with his sense of perspective, he thought. Wennergren was like a grown man returning to a place where he had played as a child and feeling that everything had shrunk. His way of thinking about all the companies he ran (four in total, plus a number of external committee responsibilities) was much the same, far more grandiose than the size of the companies warranted. In Wennergren's world, any expenses were always bad. He had once said, admittedly after a committee dinner with plenty of vintage wine, that 'The *Evening Post* would have been a well-run little business, if it weren't for its editors.'

The chairman of the board cleared his throat. 'Your resignation didn't exactly come as a surprise,' he said. 'We realized some time ago that you were on your way out of here.'

Anders Schyman studied him and concentrated on maintaining a strictly neutral expression. The statement surprised him immensely. The board hadn't had any idea that he was about to leave the paper: he hadn't breathed a word of it. On the contrary, there had been whispers from various board members about giving him greater responsibility within the empire of the family that owned the paper, hints that he had humbly acknowledged and graciously pretended to appreciate. 'That's good to hear,' he said. 'It ought to make the process of finding my successor easier.'

Wennergren raised an eyebrow.

'If you already have a list, I mean,' Schyman said, touching the compress taped to the back of his head.

'We were thinking you might be able to help us with that,' Wennergren said. 'One last task before you disappear.'

Anders Schyman folded his hands on his desk, making sure they weren't shaking. He hadn't been expecting this. Not this utter disregard for all the work he had put in over the years, or the man's failure to make any attempt to persuade him to stay. He couldn't think of anything to say.

Herman Wennergren ran a hand over his bald head. 'You're good at this sort of thing,' he said, with a degree of embarrassment. 'Your position here at the paper has given you an extensive network of contacts and a degree of insight into the industry.'

Really? Schyman thought. And I'd thought my position was the result of my own efforts and hard work. 'So what criteria should I be looking for in my successor?' he asked mildly.

The chairman made a sweeping gesture with his hand. 'You probably know that.'

The outgoing (dismissed?) editor-in-chief leaned back in his chair and noted that the back creaked in an entirely new, unthreatening way. 'Give me a few pointers,' he said.

Wennergren shuffled in his chair. 'He needs to be credible, obviously. Representative. Able to defend the paper in television debates. Financially responsible. Innovative and loyal, which go without saying. A good negotiator, with the ability to find new distribution and sales partners. And someone who can identify and kick-start complementary new projects.'

Kick-start. What a horrible expression. But presumably the Swedish Academy would soon give it its blessing, if it hadn't already done so. And the fact that his successor would be a man was obviously taken as read.

They don't deserve me, he thought. 'And in terms of journalism?' Schyman said. 'What sort of publisher should I be looking for?'

The chairman leaned across the desk. 'Someone like you,' he said. 'Someone who knows all the buzz words about democracy and freedom of expression, but is basically prepared to publish anything—' He broke off, possibly aware that he had gone too far.

Schyman put his hands into his lap, unable to hold them still any longer. He wondered if the old bastard was consciously trying to antagonize him,

or if he thought it was perfectly normal and unre-
markable to humiliate him in this way. Not a word
about his successes, the sacrifices he had made
for the paper, his indisputable competence with
regard to steering a ship of this magnitude.

Ever since Schyman had been appointed editor-
in-chief fourteen years ago, Wennergren had
been the proprietors' right-hand man on the
board of the paper, the paper that made the most
profit for its owners but which was always treated
with the least respect. The *Evening Post* was
something the cat had dragged in, but it managed
to keep all the rats fed.

But the board clearly thought he was a puppet
who could talk about responsibilities and freedom
of the press while at the same time printing crap
in the paper and, as a parting shot, he was being
made to find his own successor. That would save
the board a job, but leave them to bask in the glory.

'I'd suggest promoting someone internally,' he
said. 'There aren't many outsiders who combine
the necessary competence in tabloid thinking with
presenting a credible attitude about the press to
the outside world.'

'We'd rather bring in someone external,'
Wennergren said.

'From television, like me?'

'Perhaps someone from the competition.'

Of course. Buy the other team's best player.
Classic tactic in sport.

He studied the chairman's face. A stealthy,

destructive thought began to form in his mind. 'There are some good candidates here in the news-room that the board might not be aware of,' he said.

'Do you mean Sjölander?' Wennergren said. 'He doesn't come across well on television.'

Schyman looked out at the newsdesk. He had nothing to lose, and everything to gain. 'We have a new boss on the desk who's shown a lot of potential,' the editor-in-chief said. 'He's extremely loyal, very creative when it comes to publicity, and has a burning passion when it comes to tabloid thinking. His name is Patrik Nilsson.'

Herman Wennergren's face lit up. 'The one who wrote the articles about the serial killer?'

Schyman raised his eyebrows. So Wennergren did read the paper. And thoroughly, at that: Patrik had had a byline on only one of many articles.

'Gustaf Holmerud,' Schyman confirmed. 'We've just had confirmation of the grounds for his arrest, and they're sensational. So far Holmerud has confessed to five murders, and he's going to be questioned about all the unsolved murders in Scandinavia over the past twenty-five years.'

'Really?'

Schyman nodded towards the newsdesk. 'It was Patrik who first spotted the connection between the cases and put the police on the right track.'

'Patrik Nilsson,' Herman Wennergren said, as if he were tasting the name. 'That's an extremely good idea. I'll suggest it.' He pushed back his chair and stood up. 'When are you thinking of leaving?' he asked.

Anders Schyman stayed in his seat. 'As soon as the official figures say we've overtaken the competition.'

The chairman nodded. 'We must arrange a proper leaving ceremony here in the newsroom,' he said. 'And I very much hope that those three million turn out to be a profitable investment. Has the husband been released yet?'

'Not as far as I know.'

Wennergren grunted something and slid the glass door open, stepped cautiously into the newsroom and walked off, without bothering to close the door behind him. Schyman watched him walk towards the exit with his briefcase and coat.

There was nothing so vital for an evening paper as its credibility, its journalistic capital. With Patrik Nilsson as its editor-in-chief, it would be a matter of months, possibly weeks, before disaster was an inescapable fact. Herman Wennergren, as the man who had appointed him, would be forced to resign, and the newspaper would be seriously damaged for years to come.

But first he had to overtake the other evening paper. He would leave behind him the biggest newspaper in Scandinavia, in excellent financial condition and with a reasonable reputation for journalism.

He reached for his phone and rang Annika Bengtzon's private mobile.

CHAPTER 20

They were stuck in a queue of traffic, between a donkey-cart and a Bentley, when her phone rang. 'How are you getting on?' Anders Schyman asked.

'Things are moving, I think,' Annika said. 'Unlike the traffic.' She was thirsty, and needed the toilet.

'Have you delivered the ransom?'

'Not yet.'

'How do things look?'

No pavements, brownish-red soil, patched-up tarmac. Rubbish piled beside the roads, crumpled plastic and broken glass, paper and cardboard. Electricity cables strung between the trees, like lianas. But that probably wasn't what he meant. 'We've been sent to the wrong place a few times,' she said. 'But now we're on our way to a fourth location. We think this may be the one where we hand over the money.'

'I've just had Wennergren here. He's worried about the newspaper's investment.'

Annika shut her eyes tight. 'And what am I supposed to say to that?'

'I have to report back to the board, tell them how it's going.'

'The old bastard could always have a chat with the kidnapper once Thomas is free, maybe ask for a refund.'

Silence on the line.

'Did you want anything in particular?' Annika asked. She thought she heard Schyman sigh.

'No,' he said. 'No, not at all. I just wanted to hear how it was going.'

'Things are moving,' she repeated.

Halenius glanced at her. 'Schyman,' she mimed.

'Have you heard that the serial killer has confessed?' the editor-in-chief said in her ear.

A man cycled past her window with a dozen hens in a crate on the handlebars.

'Who?'

'Gustaf Holmerud. He's confessed to all five suburban murders. Patrik said it was your idea. Congratulations. You were right.'

The killings had been turned into 'suburban murders', nice and manageable. 'Schyman,' she said. 'That's ridiculous. All those women were murdered by their partners. You know that as well as I do.'

There was a crackle on the line and she missed a few words.

'. . . very interested in how things are going for you,' Schyman was saying. 'Are you doing any filming?'

She looked down at the video-camera on the seat beside her. 'Some.'

'We're on our way to becoming the largest online news site as well. A really good film from you could be what it takes to give us the final push.'

The traffic in front of them moved and Frida put the car back in gear. Annika looked out through the windscreen: girls in school uniform, men in dusty caps and jackets too big for them, schoolboys in grey shirts. 'Hmm,' she said.

'We'll be in touch,' the editor-in-chief said.

Halenius looked at her inquisitively.

'Sometimes I think there's something wrong with Anders Schyman,' Annika said, putting her mobile down.

'We need to eat,' Frida said. 'With this traffic it's going to take hours to get to Eastleigh. Do you want the sandwiches from the cool-box?'

'Maybe we should save those,' Halenius said. 'God knows how long this is going to take. Can we stop and get something on the way?'

Annika sat up straight in the back seat. 'I'm in charge of logistics,' she said. 'I can run out and get something.'

They drove for another ten minutes through the sluggish traffic, then Frida indicated right and turned into a car park at a large shopping centre. Nakumatt, Annika read, under a logo of an elephant.

Frida took a ticket from the security guard and parked between two Range Rovers. She pointed left, towards a row of pizza parlours and shiny chrome coffee bars, Tex-Mex joints and sushi restaurants.

'What would you like?' Annika asked.

'Something that won't get cold. Salad,' Frida said.

Annika walked over to the terrace of one of the trendy coffee bars, laid-back funk music from the speakers, red sunshades, brown metal furniture. As she waited for a member of staff, she consulted the menu: a salad cost 520 shillings. They also served French onion soup. This wasn't Africa, it was Marbella. How many people here were dependent on UN food aid?

A waitress appeared, half Annika's age and twice as beautiful. Annika ordered three Caesar salads with chicken and six mineral waters to go. The waitress disappeared towards the kitchen and Annika shuffled her feet restlessly.

Four young white men in their mid-twenties were sitting at the table next to her, eating hamburgers with ketchup and fries. Her stomach turned and she hurried to the Ladies.

The toilet had a changing mat and a black granite floor. She hadn't expected that. The water in the toilet was blue. Thomas might have remarked that the paper dispenser was loose, but the décor and cleanliness would have met with his approval. 'If the toilets are dirty, what do you think the kitchen looks like?' he usually said.

Once she had replied: 'Like parents who hit their children in public. What happens at home when no one's watching?'

Thomas had looked at her blankly. 'What have toilets got to do with child abuse?'

She flushed, washed her hands and went back out into the sunshine.

The salads were ready. She paid and went back to the car.

Frida pulled out on to Ngong Road, towards the city centre.

It made Annika think of *Out of Africa*.

She could see the famous mountains through the back window and picked up the video-camera to film them. It didn't work very well. They looked like the wooded hills they were.

It was hot and extremely muggy.

The roads got worse but the traffic improved. The sun disappeared. The car was moving at a decent speed. Out of restlessness, Annika was filming things at random, a young girl grilling corncobs at the side of the road, men pulling carts. She could feel the bags of money by her feet. Soon she would have to deliver them, pick them up with both hands and heave them into a container full of rubbish or a hole in the ground or maybe a ditch, because why else was the heavy-duty plastic so important?

The barbed wire gleamed, the oil-drums sang.

'Whereabouts in Eastleigh?' Frida asked.

'Al-Habib Shopping Mall, Sixth Street, First Avenue. Does that mean anything to you?'

'They make it sound so lovely,' Frida said.

'Streets, avenues, shopping centres . . . Little Mogadishu got its name for a reason.'

'What do you mean?' Halenius said.

'You'll see.'

The traces of tarmac on the road vanished altogether. Large water-filled puddles covered the carriageway. The wheels threw up mud. Annika filmed carts, mattresses, carpets, plastic tubs full of spices, rubbish, paper, plastic, women wearing the hijab – vast, organized chaos. This wasn't Kibera but the level of decay was the same. People brushed past close to the car windows, Annika caught their eyes through the windscreen.

There was a heavy blow on the window beside her, then another on the car roof, and suddenly the car was surrounded by men with their faces pressed against the windows, shouting and waving their fists.

Frida turned round. 'Are you filming? Here? Are you mad? These people are Muslims! They can't be filmed.'

Annika dropped the camera as if she'd been burned. The noise got louder as the blows continued to rain down.

'Oh, dear Lord,' Frida said. 'As long as they don't roll the car over . . .'

The car was shaking, and Annika was clinging to the seat with both hands. The video-camera hit the floor as someone pulled at the car door and the wheels slid sideways through the mud.

'Put it in first gear,' Halenius said. 'Drive forward very slowly.'

'I can't,' Frida cried. 'I'll run them over!'

'They'll get out of the way,' Halenius said. 'Just take it slowly.'

The street was blocked by donkeys, men and carts, but Frida did as she was told and rolled forwards slowly, blowing the horn and revving the engine. The men followed them, tugging at the doors and shouting, but Frida drove on.

'Al-Habib is up ahead on the right,' she said. 'That's where we're supposed to go.'

'Keep driving,' Halenius said.

Annika hid her face in her hands. This was her fault.

Suddenly the noise stopped. The men had been left behind and there was tarmac beneath them again. Frida put the car in second gear. Annika could see her hands shaking and tears in her eyelashes.

'What do we do now?' Frida said quietly.

Halenius scratched his head. 'I don't know,' he said. 'I really don't know.'

'Where should I be heading?'

'I don't know. I've only been on a course. This wasn't in the manual.'

Suddenly the rubbish around them disappeared and was replaced by tropical vegetation. The road was faultless; trees stretched up to the sky. High walls surrounded large villas.

'Has the kidnapper got an ordinary mobile phone?' Annika asked.

'How do you mean?' Halenius said.

'Can you reply to his text?'

He looked at her in surprise. 'I haven't actually tried.'

'Try to explain the situation,' she said. 'Tell him it went to hell, and blame me.'

'I'll pull into Muthaiga Golf Club,' Frida said, turning left past a pair of tall gates with armed guards on either side.

Halenius took out his mobile and wrote a long text message. Frida parked next to a wall of bougainvillaea and switched the engine off. Halenius pressed 'send', then waited intently. The mobile bleeped plaintively.

'Shit,' he said.

'Maybe you wrote too much,' Annika said. 'If a text is too long it gets turned into a multimedia message. Try shortening it.'

Halenius groaned and deleted the message. The car was heating up. Frida wound down her window. A cascade of birdsong rolled in.

'What is this place?' Annika asked.

'My golf club,' Frida said.

'Do you live near here?' Annika asked.

'Most diplomats and United Nations staff live in Muthaiga,' she said.

Annika could just make out a bright green golf course through the palm trees. They were less than a couple of kilometres from Eastleigh, but the contrast couldn't have been greater.

The mobile bleeped again. 'No good,' Halenius said.

'Try calling,' Annika said.

Halenius pressed a button and put the mobile to his ear, then lowered it again. 'The number you are calling cannot be reached,' he said.

Annika bit her lip. It wasn't her fault. Taking responsibility for the situation was a way of diminishing it and making herself more important than she was.

Frida opened the car door. 'We may as well go inside,' she said, gesturing to the club-house, which was also a bar and restaurant.

'I've still got some salad left,' Annika said quickly.

Frida didn't look at her. 'There's air-conditioning.'

The sun was going down. The air was heavy with thunder. Annika was sitting on the steps outside the smart golf club, which just happened to be the one to which Karen Blixen had been denied entry because she was a woman (if the film *Out of Africa*, starring Meryl Streep, was to be believed).

She looked out across the car park, and watched as several women went past carrying heavy bags of rubbish while a number of male guards relaxed in the shade.

'Woman Is The Nigger Of The World', she thought. Schyman and his serial killer were just one example. She recalled sitting in one of the paper's cars early one Saturday morning in June, on her way to cover a mass murder in Dalarna, and how the photographer, Bertil Strand, had described the situation: 'A sub-lieutenant who went mad, and shot and killed seven people. One of them was his girlfriend, but the others were innocent.'

The air really was very humid.

How guilty was a lover? How guilty was she?

Halenius came out on to the steps. His lips had that bloodless look again, and his eyes were sharp. She stood up instinctively.

'Have they texted?'

'Called. He was furious.'

'Because I was filming?'

'Because we didn't stop outside al-Habib as we were told. He said we'd broken the terms of the deal and wanted to start negotiations all over again. I told him his Somali brothers had tried to tip the car over, and that we'd had to drive off to save his money. That calmed him down a bit.'

He was sweaty and edgy. She hadn't seen him like that before.

'Sorry,' she said.

He threw out his hands. 'What the fuck were you filming for?' he yelled. 'Have you no sense at all? Don't you understand what could have happened?'

She swallowed hard. She wasn't going to cry. 'I didn't mean it.'

'You've dumped us right in the shit. Now we have to head north.'

He made for the car. Frida came out, holding

438

a copy of the bill. 'The traffic's terrible,' she said. 'This is going to take a while.'

'Where are we going?' Annika said.

'Wilson airport,' Frida said, behind her.

Halenius turned towards Annika. The sun made his face glow. 'We're going to Liboi,' he said. 'The kidnapper demanded that we fly there tonight, but I managed to get him to see sense. We need to arrange a flight for tomorrow morning.'

'Liboi?' Annika whispered. She saw Google Earth in front of her, that vast barren area, the scorched soil.

'There are no scheduled flights up there,' Frida said. 'You'll have to hire a private plane.'

'But I haven't any money left,' Annika said.

'You've still got some in my account,' Frida said, getting into the car.

The traffic was completely stationary. There were lines of people in the gloom along the sides of the road, quivering shadows flitting past in the headlights. Annika tried to fix them with her eyes, hold on to them for more than a fleeting moment.

Darkness settled round the car, like a blanket. Occasionally a light would shine somewhere in the distance. Warm air rushed in through the open side-window.

She curled up in the seat and fell asleep.

She opened her eyes and found herself staring at a leopard. It was several seconds before she realized it was a sculpture.

'Hello,' Halenius said, stroking her sweaty hair. 'We're here.'

She sat up and looked around in the darkness. Lights were shining through tropical plants. Warm light was streaming from an old house with a glazed veranda.

'Sorry,' he said. 'It was wrong of me to take it out on you.'

'Where are we?'

'The Karen Blixen Coffee Garden. Her old farm – it's a hotel now. I know Bonnie, the owner. Can you carry my bag, and I'll take those?' He pointed at the bags of dollars.

'Where's Frida?'

'She's sorting out rooms for us, then going home.'

Annika got out of the car. 'The airport!' she said. 'We need to hire a plane!'

'All done,' Halenius said, putting the bags on the ground. The handles creaked. 'We've made arrangements with someone Frida knows.'

She picked up Halenius's bag. It weighed practically nothing.

They stepped inside the old house, which could have been in Södermanland or Skåne: dark fishbone parquet floors, white wooden panels on the walls, a glazed veranda with stained glass.

'And Karen Blixen lived here?' Annika murmured.

'This is really the foreman's house, but she lived here for long periods as well,' Halenius said, then disappeared to the left.

The darkness outside the windows was damp and solid. She remained where she was, in the middle of the floor, and found herself staring at an old harmonium standing against one wall. The keys were brown with age and she reached out a hand to hear what it sounded like, but stopped with her fingers just centimetres from the instrument. Did she really want to know? Could she even imagine what tunes were hiding behind those bellows, those keys? Or was there nothing but screaming and poverty?

Halenius appeared from the innards of the house with an old-fashioned key in his hand. 'It doesn't work,' he said, nodding towards the organ. 'And it wasn't Karen's. It was given to Bonnie.'

He picked up the bags of money – their weight made him sway – then set off out into the night. She bent down, picked up their bags and followed him through the darkness. Low lanterns lit some of the winding slate path with circles of fire-coloured light. They were surrounded by nocturnal noises she'd only ever heard in films: croaking, rustling, scratching, singing sounds that she could neither identify nor locate. The darkness pressed around them.

'Where's the hotel?' she asked, into the shadows.

Halenius pointed to the left. She could just make out white stone walls behind a jungle of tropical plants.

'Our own house? Each room is a separate building?'

She stepped inside a room with white walls and black roof-beams that hung high above under the ridge of the roof. White linen curtains on black metal poles, a crackling fire in an open hearth, to the right a living room. She looked at the four-poster bed that stood like a galleon in the middle of the floor, with a wrought-iron hull and sails made of mosquito nets. Carefully she walked across the highly polished floor.

She put their bags on the floor and opened a door. The bathroom, brown slate from floor to ceiling, bigger than the living room at home.

'Will there be anything left of the ransom after we've paid for this?' she asked Halenius, when she came out.

'Costs the same as a shabby single room in New York,' he said. 'But there's only one bed. I'll go back to Reception and say we want separate rooms.'

She put her hand against his chest. He stopped and looked towards the fireplace. 'What I did was unforgivable.'

'To whom?'

He looked at the floor. 'Thomas is my responsibility. I'm his boss. If he can't trust me . . .'

'Thomas is responsible for his own actions, just as you and I are for what we do.'

'I exploited the situation,' he said. 'That was indefensible. You're in a position of total dependence on me, and I've broken every code of honour there is.'

442

She stepped closer to him and let her hands slip round his back.

'And when you see him again,' Halenius said quietly, 'how are you going to feel?'

'We don't have to decide anything tonight,' she whispered, nibbling his earlobe gently.

He breathed heavily against her shoulder for a few seconds before pulling her to him.

DAY 10

FRIDAY, 2 DECEMBER

CHAPTER 21

nnika woke up to the sound of a waterfall. She was lying tangled in the sheet,
close to Halenius, and didn't know where
she was.

'It's rain on the roof,' Halenius whispered in the
darkness. 'Isn't it wonderful?'

She lay there, just breathing, glimpsing the four-
poster bed's mosquito nets through the shadows.
The noise rose and fell with the squalls. There
was a faint rumble of thunder in the distance from
the Ngong Hills.

Dawn was breaking when she woke again. The
rain had stopped. Just a few drops from the trees
were hitting the roof, like little gunshots. Halenius
was pulling on his jeans on the other side of the
mosquito net.

She pushed the sheet aside and got out on to
the wooden floor. The room felt cool and damp.
She went to stand close to him, and ran her fingers
down his bare arm. She saw his jaw tense. 'We're
the ones who decide,' she said quietly. 'We're the
only ones who know.'

447

'Frida booked the room,' Halenius said. 'She doesn't know for sure, but she suspects.'

She wrapped her arms round his neck and kissed him gently. He put his hands round her and kissed her back, then let go of her abruptly and went to get the shirt he had tossed over the back of a chair. He put it on, did up two buttons, picked up the bags of money and headed for the door.

'Frida will be here in fifteen minutes,' he said, and left the room.

She stepped on to the veranda and found herself in Jacques Cousteau's underwater world. Cool moisture swept round her like a wave, as the light filtered through huge, swaying leaves, as tall as a man. She took several deep breaths.

She stepped cautiously into the garden. Pots, hanging plants, palms, trees with red leaves and orange flowers, wooden fences smothered with more plants. The air smelt of soil and rain.

A sandy-coloured cat jumped on to the path in front of her and trotted up it, tail in the air, miaowing inquisitively. A gardener, a huge man in wellington boots and dark blue overalls, dropped his spade and bent down to the animal. He tickled it under the chin, stroked its head. The cat lapped up the attention, purring and rolling over on to its back. It was clearly used to this treatment and was making the most of it.

She stopped on the path. For some reason she was finding it hard to breathe.

Frida was wearing boots and lilac clothes that matched her hair. 'Sleep well?' she asked.

Annika tried to smile and got into the back, where the bags containing the money were already installed.

Halenius came jogging out from Reception and got into the passenger seat.

Frida started the car and turned right on to Karen Road. Annika looked back and saw the leopard sculpture disappear behind the trees. They passed the Karen Blixen Museum and something called the Kazuri Beads and Pottery Centre, weaving between the puddles on the road. The traffic hadn't had time to build up yet and they cruised past furniture stores with canvas roofs, rows of shacks selling everything from second-hand cars and tin giraffes to ornate four-poster beds and firewood.

Red earth, overwhelming vegetation and endless lines of people. Where were they all going? Did their trek never end?

Wilson airport was surrounded by barriers and yellow gates. Frida paid something at a security booth and they were let through. Low cement terminal buildings, with signs that didn't mean anything to Annika, *Departments Wanausafari, Delta Connection, Safarilink*, then a runway behind some gates, and the smell of aviation fuel in the air.

Annika stared at the guards beside the gates, their guns slung across their chests.

Had she ever had an answer to her question of whether ransoms were legal in Kenya? The British (and Kenyans) who had been imprisoned in Somalia had been arrested at an airport.

Her palms started to sweat.

Halenius got out of the car, yanked the back door open and pulled out the bags of money. Annika climbed out on shaky legs.

'Do we have to go through some sort of security check?' she said.

Halenius didn't seem to hear her. He went up to Frida with a bag in each hand, put them down and gave her a hug. She was a head taller than him in her boots, but he rocked her in his arms and muttered something in her ear that Annika couldn't hear.

She looked towards the gates. Two men in yellow vests were weighing bags on a large set of scales. From beyond them she could hear the roar of aircraft engines. The terminal buildings had tin roofs.

Were they going to check the bags? What would happen if they found the money?

Frida walked over to Annika and hugged her tightly. 'Take good care of him,' she whispered, and Annika couldn't tell whom she was referring to.

★　　★　　★

The pilot, William Grey, stepped into the sunshine from one of the terminal buildings. He was wearing a dazzling white shirt and pale beige linen trousers. He had grey-blond hair and a sparkling smile. 'So you're heading up to Liboi?' he said, greeting them with a hearty handshake. 'A bit off the normal tourist track, you could say. We're going in that one over there.'

He pointed towards a row of small planes at the end of the runway. Annika had no idea which he meant.

'Are you ready? You've got everything?' He looked at their bags.

Halenius nodded.

William Grey strode off towards the yellow gates and they marched after him. Halenius was carrying a bag in each hand, Annika could see his fingers turning white from the weight. Would the guards notice?

The pilot showed the guards a little bundle of papers. One leafed through them, then called his colleague over. They read and discussed them in a language she didn't understand, Swahili, perhaps. She could feel the sweat running down her back and was concentrating on not fainting.

The guard folded the papers and opened the gate.

The pilot stepped on to the runway, followed by Halenius, then Annika. The guards looked at the bags but said nothing.

William Grey went up to a little single-engined

aeroplane, painted yellow with black lettering. It looked like a wasp. He nodded towards the bags in Halenius's hands. 'So, what's in them?'

Annika held her breath.

'Money,' Halenius said.

Shit, shit, shit.

'Ah,' the pilot said. 'Are we dealing with a hostage situation here?'

'Correct,' Halenius said.

'Frida didn't mention that,' William Grey said, still smiling. 'A special rate applies in this sort of situation. In and out, no complications, five thousand dollars. Cash.'

Annika stared at the man. Was he serious?

He gave her a rather apologetic look and shrugged. 'You never know if you're going to make it back from an expedition like this. Has the army been informed?'

This last was addressed to Halenius.

'I assume so. Interpol in Brussels is in charge of communications.'

'Hmm. Do you have any co-ordinates for the site of the handover?'

'Only that it's somewhere near Liboi. We're going to receive the co-ordinates during the flight. Are there plenty of landing strips up there?'

The pilot put on a pair of sunglasses. 'No,' he said, 'but it's semi-desert. It only takes a day or two at the most to clear a landing strip for a plane like this, fifteen metres by six hundred, that's all

452

you need. Clear a few bushes, keep the animals away, and you're basically all set.'

Annika followed his gaze. 'Do you do this a lot?'

'A couple of times a month, usually at the request of the British Army. I'll go and tell them we're ready to roll.'

'Can I use my mobile in the plane?' Halenius asked.

'Of course,' William Grey said, then disappeared into one of the low terminal buildings. The sun had come out and it was going to be a clear, hot day. Steam was rising from the runway.

Annika gestured towards the plane. 'Isn't it rather small?'

It was smaller than her Jeep.

'Any bigger and it probably wouldn't be able to land,' Halenius said.

'Let's go!' the pilot called, pointing at the wasp.

William Grey sat in the pilot's seat while Annika and Halenius squeezed into the two seats behind him. It was extremely cramped. The noise when the engine started up was utterly deafening. The pilot put on a pair of headphones with an external microphone, pointed at the headphones hanging next to their seats and signalled to them to put them on. Annika did so and found herself listening to a cacophony of voices. She assumed the tower was communicating with all of the planes that were ready to take off.

'Requesting permission for Liboi, one eighteen

north-east. We are ready for take-off,' the pilot said.

A woman said something in reply that sounded like static. The noise of the engine changed and the plane began to move jerkily past rows of hangars. William pointed towards a large logo on one. 'Those boys fly ransoms to the Somali pirates,' he said in her headphones. 'They put the money in watertight orange cylinders, then drop them into the sea. They look like fire-extinguishers, but with little parachutes.'

Annika watched the planes glide past, sparkling white in the sunlight. They were the largest, smartest ones in the whole of Wilson airport.

The plane left the ground with a gentle lurch and climbed upwards. Through the window on Halenius's side she could see the slums of Kibera disappearing behind them. Behind the shacks the buildings of Nairobi city centre rose, the round bulk of the Hilton Hotel, the Kenyatta Conference Centre next to it, the four-lane Chinese motorway.

The plane shuddered. She clung to her seat and looked out of her window. The landscape was flat. William Grey pointed out various places and land-marks, the Nairobi river foaming with pollution, the snow-capped Mount Kenya to the north-west. The rectangular mirrors of water to their right were a sewage works. The video-camera was by her feet and it occurred to her that she should probably be filming, but she couldn't bring herself to do it.

'It takes two hours and twenty minutes to get to Liboi,' the pilot said, through the headphones. 'Are you hungry? There are sandwiches in the bag behind your seats.'

They got some out, and passed one to the pilot. Annika felt the bread swelling in her mouth until it almost choked her. She drank a little water and studied the door that separated her from the emptiness outside. It was thin and there was no lock, just a little chrome handle and a sticker saying 'CLOSE'. Compulsive thoughts popped into her head and danced about. What if I didn't close the door properly? What if I nudge the handle and it flies open? What if the glass breaks? If I fall out of the plane I won't be able to deliver the ransom, Thomas won't be released and the children will have to stay with Sophia.

'You see that green area down there?' the pilot said. 'Del Monte's pineapple plantation. And the slightly darker green? Coffee trees.'

A chirruping sound in her headphones told her when their mobile phones were picking up a signal from the various ground stations.

'That's the road to Garissa. We're heading over the area occupied by the Wakamba tribe. They're skilful farmers.'

The countryside below them turned into a surrealist painting, with broad, sweeping strokes of soft colours, overlapping and circling each other. A river wound through the landscape, which was cut across by straight, light brown roads.

'That's the reservoir that supplies Nairobi.'

A lake spread out to their left.

Is he down there? Are we flying over him right now? Can he see the plane? Does he know I'm on my way?

Tanzania disappeared to the south; Uganda came closer to the north-west.

They passed Garissa.

'There aren't any more landmarks now until we reach the refugee camps in Dadaab. All the way to the border there's flat bushland. I'm going to climb to four thousand metres. It might get a bit cold. There are blankets on the floor.'

The chill came creeping up her shins, damp and sharp. She pulled up one of the blankets, a dark blue one, a Polarvide fleece from Ikea. 'How often do you fly ransom payments?' Annika asked.

'Mostly I fly tourists from Kenyatta who want to get straight to the safari lodges, and I do quite a bit of crop-spraying. But I know other pilots who've stopped carrying tourists and only fly ransoms now.'

His words felt almost like an insult. Was this just an ordinary working day, one of many? Was she just this week's desperate wife? 'What do you tell the authorities? Do they know you fly ransom payments?'

He smiled at her. 'Not exactly,' he said, handing

her a document stamped with *Office of the President* and *Police Headquarters*.

Clearance Certificate is hereby granted . . .

She skimmed through the text. Under the heading *Purpose*, the reason for the flight was explained: '*To carry out EU conservation and community development project.*' For Kenyan Customs officials, this flight was registered as a charitable project, an attempt to support development and improve the lot of people living in the Garissa district of north-east Kenya, along the border with Somalia. The document was signed *Commissioner of Police*. She handed the sheet of paper back to the pilot and wiped her hand, as if it had left her dirty.

'How often do you take hostages back with you?' Halenius asked.

'That's what usually happens,' William Grey said. 'The kidnappers are mostly fairly civilized. They look upon this as nothing but business, so it doesn't make sense to kill too many hostages. Bad for business.'

Annika swallowed the barbs in her throat.

The ground beneath them was dusty with drought. Sometimes there was a flash among the bushes far below, a sunbeam hitting a tin roof, a car, a water tank. On a few occasions they saw groups of buildings inside grey rings.

'When are we getting the co-ordinates?' the pilot asked.

'During the flight. The kidnappers didn't specify

a time. I've told them when we set off, and gave them a description of your plane, so they know we're on our way.'

Halenius took out his mobile. 'There's no reception here. Where's the next mast?'

'Dadaab.'

A red lamp had started to flash insistently on the instrument panel. William Grey tapped it gently. 'The radar's getting stronger the closer we get to the border. They know we're on our way.'

'Who?' Annika asked.

'The Yanks. They've got an unofficial base down by the coast. They're keeping an eye on us.'

That must be the base Halenius had mentioned, the one that had sent the helicopter into Somalia to pick up the Spaniard.

'We mustn't be visible on radar,' Halenius said. 'The kidnappers were very clear about that. How are we supposed to deliver the ransom without anyone seeing?'

'We head down towards Liboi but we don't land. Instead we fly under the radar at a height of about thirty metres until we reach the designated site. Then we head back the same way, climb when we reach Liboi and switch the radar back on.'

Thirty metres sounded very low.

William Grey laughed. 'It's not dangerous. When I'm spraying crops I fly six metres above the ground. If you look down to the right you can see the road between Garissa and Liboi. Only passable with four-wheel drive. And this is Dadaab.'

A sea of roofs spread out on either side of the plane in absolutely straight lines that showed this was a UN-sanctioned slum, not some improvised, chaotic version like Kibera.

'Holy Moses,' the pilot said, over the headphones. 'It's grown a hell of a lot since last time.'

The roofs stretched towards the horizon.

'Drought, famine and civil war,' Halenius said. 'Médecins sans Frontières estimate that there'll be almost half a million people here by the end of the year.'

At that moment his mobile buzzed. He picked it up and his lips turned white again. Annika's heart began to race.

'Fly to -0.00824, 40.968018,' he read, slowly and clearly.

'What else?' Annika said.

'Wife Annika to put money in driver's seat.'

She pressed the headphones to her ears. 'Say again.'

'You're to put the money on the driver's seat.'

'Driver's seat?'

'It doesn't say anything else.'

Here it was then, the handover location. On the driver's seat. She couldn't breathe.

William Grey was tapping at an instrument on the panel, and scratching his head.

'Problems?' Halenius asked.

'They've chosen a nasty spot,' he said. 'Just a

couple of hundred metres from the Somali border, right on the equator. Look, latitude 0.00, longitude 40.9.'

'South of Liboi?'

'About forty kilometres south, out in the semi-desert. Do you want to know exactly?'

Halenius shook his head and leaned back in his seat.

The pilot reached for his radio. 'This is Y-AYH, starting our descent to Liboi,' he said, to an air-traffic-control tower somewhere.

The sound of the engine changed, the ground came closer, the plane lurched and dropped in the air pockets. A column of camels heading south put their ears back in alarm, Annika saw a tent with a canvas marked 'UNHCR'. Maybe Frida had decided to put it there.

Liboi appeared below, a street lined with shacks and a few concrete buildings. The plane glided over a bumpy landing strip and carried on south, just above the ground.

Annika put the Ikea blanket back on the floor – it had quickly become too hot.

'It's going to hit forty-two degrees this afternoon,' William Grey said. Liboi disappeared behind them. The savannah rushed past some ten metres below; the plane shuddered in the heat. Annika gripped her seat and stared at the back of William Grey's head.

'How much further is it?' Halenius asked.

The pilot was gripping the control column hard,

and didn't look away from the direction of flight. 'Half an hour,' he said. 'At most.'

Forty kilometres in less than half an hour, so they were flying at something like a hundred kilometres an hour. Annika glanced down: the ground was a brownish-grey blur, without shape or content. Her headphones were silent, no crackle of radio or radar. She could feel the rumbling of the plane's engine as a vibration in her abdomen. Through the thin seat she could feel the bulk of the tightly packed dollars.

She had been so happy that she had that money in her account. It had given her a sort of freedom, illusory, perhaps, but the simple awareness that it was there meant she could go to work each day of her own free will and know she could stop whenever she wanted.

Her stomach was churning.

Thomas would be desperately disappointed the money was gone. It had been his ticket to a better life, proof that he was worth more, that he could live in a villa by the sea in Vaxholm if he wanted to. Would he be angry? She looked out across the landscape. Just scorched earth and thorny bushes.

'It ought to be up ahead,' William Grey said, sounding stressed now.

Halenius squinted at the horizon. His leg pressed against Annika's. She was staring intently out of her side window.

'There it is,' the pilot said.

Annika turned her head and squinted forward.

'Where?' Halenius said, craning his neck.

The pilot pointed, and Annika followed his outstretched fingers with her eyes.

He must have been flying a couple of kilometres from the Somali border because now he was banking left, heading directly east.

'I just need to see the state of the landing strip before I land,' he said.

Now Annika could see it as well, a narrow line on the ground in front of them. Her pulse started to race and she was having trouble breathing. She felt for Halenius's hand, found it and squeezed. 'I can't do this,' she said.

'Yes, you can,' Halenius said. 'I'll help you.'

William Grey flew in over the provisional landing strip, a few metres above the ground. After a couple of hundred metres he pulled a lever and the plane rose again.

'What?' Annika said. 'What's happening?'

'The strip's been used before,' he said. 'It's not exactly Heathrow airport, but it'll be okay to land on. There were a few warthogs halfway along, but they're gone now.'

He flew over the area in a fairly broad arc, and as he approached the landing strip from the south Annika caught sight of something to the right ahead of them.

The skeleton of a bus. It was so rusty that it was now the same colour as the soil. Plants stuck out through the windows.

She tapped Halenius on the shoulder and pointed. 'The driver's seat,' she said.

William Grey banked sharply and the plane dropped rapidly. Annika's stomach lurched and she thought she was going to be sick.

'Hold tight,' Grey said.

The wheels hit the ground hard. The plane hopped and bounced. Annika's head hit the ceiling and she ended up half on the floor.

'Sorry,' the pilot said.

They rattled over the uneven ground, the engine roaring. It was incredibly hot.

'You saw the bus?' Halenius said, through the headphones, and the pilot nodded.

The wrecked vehicle was standing at the southern end of the landing strip. The plane bounced slowly closer, and Annika forced herself to take slow, regular breaths. Fifty metres from the bus the pilot slowed and turned so that the plane was pointing north with the whole of the landing strip stretched in front of it, then switched off the engine.

The silence that followed felt deafening.

Grey took off his headphones. Halenius and Annika followed suit.

'Well, here we are,' he said, opening the door and climbing down to the ground.

Halenius helped Annika open her door – it was nowhere near as easy as she had thought when they were in the air. Together the men got the sports bags out. The wind was hot and dry, and her mouth filled with dust.

The bus had once been blue and white – she could just make out the colours through the rust. All of the windows were missing, although the windscreen had a few fragments of glass. One of the rear tyres was still there, but the front wheel was resting on its rim. A dead bush was sticking out of the radiator.

'I think I saw a door on the other side,' Halenius said.

Annika had seen it too. She screwed up her eyes and looked around. Why was it so important that she carry the bags over? Were they being watched?

The heat was making the air around them vibrate. She couldn't see anything but quivering air and scorched brown thorn bushes.

'It's probably best to make two trips,' Halenius said, but Annika shook her head.

She'd rather break her back than have to do this more than once.

She grabbed hold of the bags. Her knees almost buckled, but she forced them to obey her. She felt her spine contract as the handles cut into her palms. An insect caught in her hair.

She took one step, two, three, and when she was moving, she began almost to jog towards the wrecked bus, the bags hitting her calves. She stumbled but carried on, got caught on a bush and nearly fell.

Four metres from the bus she had to stop and put the bags down while she caught her breath.

It was an old Tata. The headlights had been removed and the holes were like empty eye-sockets.

She took hold of the bags again, barely able to lift them. She walked round the bus, past the dead bush sticking out of the front, and went to the door, where she dropped the bags on the ground.

She took a couple of deep breaths.

The door was still there. It was open, folded back, the glass long since gone. Inside the wreck she could see the rusty skeleton of two double seats.

She climbed cautiously into the vehicle.

The rear was empty, nothing but rust and dust and rubbish, and the remnants of a green vinyl seat. Towards the front the engine compartment formed a raised area, with the driver's seat along-side it.

She breathed out. 'Wife Annika to put money in driver's seat,' she said aloud.

She got out, grabbed the first bag with both hands and carried it into the bus. The chair cushion was missing, so she put the bag on the floor below the steering wheel. She took a breath, then went and got the second bag and put it on top of the first. Then she stood for a few moments, looking at her money and feeling nothing.

She turned away, jumped out of the wreck and ran back towards the plane. Halenius was holding the video-camera, filming her.

William Grey got back into the pilot's seat. 'Let's go!' he yelled, and started the engine again.

Halenius tossed the video-camera on to her seat and caught her in his arms. 'I don't regret it either,' he whispered, in her ear, above the noise of the engine.

She wriggled out of his arms, got into the plane and pulled the door closed.

Halenius had barely time to sit down before they started to move.

William Grey revved the engine as hard as he could. The plane groaned and bounced. Annika put on her headphones, looked out through the side window and saw a black vehicle driving across the savannah, a big black Jeep heading straight towards them.

'Look!' she yelled into her microphone, and pointed.

'The Toyota Land Cruiser,' Halenius shouted. 'Faster, for fuck's sake!'

The plane shuddered and left the ground. The engine shrieked as they climbed into the sky, sharply and steeply. Annika was pressed back in her seat, now there was no solid bag of money behind it. The pilot banked hard to the west, away from Somalia and into Kenya, and on the ground Annika saw the black vehicle stop at the southern end of the landing strip. A man dressed in khaki got out of the driver's door and ran to the wreckage of the bus. She saw him disappear round the other side, and a moment later the ground exploded beneath them. The air turned brilliant white. Halenius let out a shout and the plane was hit by the pressure-wave. A huge pillar of smoke was rising from where the bus had been standing. The Land Cruiser was ablaze and the ground was shaking. She fumbled for something to cling to.

'What the hell was that?' William Grey yelled.

The plane was lurching and shrieking as if it were caught in a storm. Halenius's face was shiny with sweat. 'Someone had had enough of Grégoire Makuza,' he said tightly.

The sound of the engine changed, becoming shrill and restless.

'Good Lord!' William Grey said, wrestling with the controls. 'I hope we can make it back to Liboi.'

'The ransom money,' Annika whispered. 'Now they'll never let him go.'

CHAPTER 22

She was in the sky, which was white. She was floating high up, nestled in cloud. Everything around her was silent. She took off the headphones but couldn't hear the engine, just the faint whistle of a distant wind, a winter's day through an ill-fitting window. She was bathed in light: everything had dissolved. High up a bird was drifting – it looked like an eagle. No, it wasn't an eagle, it was a kite! It was a kite shaped like an eagle, a brown sea-eagle, and it was flying high among the clouds, so light it might have been made of air. A little boy was standing on the ground far below, holding it. He was so careful with the lines, and he was moving his arms to make the kite dance, and the birds swirled around the boy, calling and chirruping. Annika smiled at him – he was so sweet.

She hit the seat with a thud and slid on to the floor of the plane. Halenius landed on top of her, the engine howled and the wheels slid as they careered across the ground. She put her hands over her head and forgot to breathe.

Finally they stopped. The engine died.

'Holy macaroni,' William Grey said. 'That was close.'

Halenius sat up, then helped Annika up from the floor. Her back hurt.

'Where are we?' she asked.

'Liboi,' Halenius said. 'William has to check if the plane's been damaged.'

'They blew up the bus,' she said. 'The money's gone. Who did it? Who blew up the bus?'

William Grey was looking at Halenius. 'Good question,' he said. 'Who did?'

'A qualified guess? The Americans.'

'How did they know where we were going?'

'My text messages were all forwarded to Interpol in Brussels, so they must have known. But that doesn't really explain things. They must have had their eye on that landing strip already. The whole bus must have been primed to explode. That's not the sort of thing you can do in a hurry.'

'They knew,' Annika said. 'They knew the ransom money was there.'

'The USA is at war against terrorism,' Halenius said. 'And they weren't the ones who started it.'

William Grey got out of the plane and went to talk to a soldier with a large automatic rifle on his back. A sea of people was approaching from the town, men and children of all ages, women in hijabs and burkas. They circled the plane and soon filled the runway.

The pilot opened the door on Annika's side of

the plane. She looked at him through a veil of tears. 'Now he's never coming back,' she said.

'There's a man here who wants to talk to you,' he said.

The soldier with the automatic rifle walked over. People crowded behind him, wide-eyed and open-mouthed.

'Who are you?' the soldier asked in perfect English. 'What is the purpose of your visit?'

Annika opened her mouth to speak, but could only sob.

He was gone. If he was still alive the kidnappers would torture him to death. They'd want revenge for the explosion and their dead leader – oh, God, she hoped he was already dead. She covered her face with her hands.

Halenius stepped up beside her. 'We're here for an aid project,' he said. 'The Swedish International Development Agency.'

People were shouting and waving – Annika could see them through a haze. It was incredibly hot. The sun was at its zenith, the light corrosive and white. She was crying helplessly, unable to stop.

'Your papers?' the soldier said to William Grey, who handed him the flight permits.

The soldier read intently for several minutes.

He would never be coming back to her, and not just because of the explosion. He would never have been the same as he was: the man she had married was long gone, even before the ransom money had disappeared.

Through her tears she looked towards the horizon, towards the south, into the caustic light. She thought she could make out the pillar of smoke, could smell burning.

'Come with me,' the soldier eventually said.

'Can I stay?' William Grey said. 'I don't really want to leave the plane.'

Halenius put his arm round her shoulders but she shrugged him off.

The whole crowd, several hundred people, followed them across the runway towards a group of cracked concrete buildings.

'What a fuss,' Halenius said. 'You'd think they'd never seen a plane before.'

The man stopped and turned towards Halenius. 'Only military planes,' he said. 'You're the first private plane to land in Liboi.'

Halenius looked away.

The ground was covered with stones and rubbish, torn-off branches and car tyres. Annika stumbled several times. She could see houses in the distance, low and white, a goat, people resting in the shade, trees with leathery leaves, fences of chicken-mesh and barbed wire.

The sky was so high, endless.

The soldier led them to a fenced-off yard with a large, round bamboo hut at its centre. She staggered inside, the darkness intense after the sunlight outside. The walls were lined with battered, flowery chintz sofas, she sank on to the nearest one and put her hands over her face. She felt her body shake as tears trickled through her fingers. The air was completely still. It was a hundred degrees outside. An insect was buzzing somewhere.

Thomas was sitting in his office in the council building in Vaxholm, the sun shining on his face and broad chest. He was so young, thinner back then. She was interviewing him, and he was speaking in stuffy, bureaucratic Swedish. She interrupted and asked, 'Do you always talk like that?'

And he replied, 'It took me a bloody long time to learn how to do it.'

Three men in military uniforms were standing in front of her in the hut, heavy guns strapped to their waists.

'So, you are from Sweden?' the officer in the middle said. 'For an aid project?'

They stood there, feet wide apart, with all the power bestowed by firearms.

'We're here to evaluate the collaboration between the UN and the World Food Programme,' Halenius said, shaking hands with all three.

'Really?' the soldier said. 'How?'

Annika got to her feet and walked up to him, her eyes stinging. 'We're here to look for my husband,' she said, 'and it's your fault he's gone.'

All eyes turned towards her. Halenius took hold of her upper arm but she pulled free.

'And the aid project?' the soldier said. He was wary, his tone suspicious.

'He was kidnapped here ten days ago,' Annika said. 'He landed at this airstrip, just like we did, and

he was promised protection and security from *you!*'
She pointed at the man in front of her and felt
herself turning into an angry little animal, a vicious
creature with sharp teeth. '*You* promised to protect
him and the others, but what have you done? You
found his amputated left hand, that's what!'

She was practically screaming, and the soldiers
pulled back.

'Madam, we aren't—'

'He was here to help Kenya secure its borders,
and what thanks did he get for it? Well? What sort
of men are you?'

'Annika . . .' Halenius said.

She screamed up at the roof. There were bats
up there – she couldn't see them but she could
smell them.

The ground was stony. She passed homes made
of tin and branches, blankets and mattresses. The
road was covered with rubbish. No cars, just
donkeys and carts.

She cried against the light.

They were taking her to the police station, one
of the low white buildings she had seen in the
distance. The door was painted blue, and through
the window she could see a tangle of electricity
cables.

A man (the chief of police?) received them in his
office, the size of the lift back home in Agnegatan.
A fan squeaked rhythmically on the ceiling, without
actually creating any draught. Several other
policemen crowded in and stood round the walls.

'You're here for an aid project?' the man (the police chief?) asked, gesturing towards some chairs crammed next to his desk.

Halenius sat down, but Annika remained standing. She noticed that she had stopped crying. She felt empty inside, hollow. 'No,' she said. 'My husband, Thomas Samuelsson, was kidnapped near here ten days ago. The Kenyan authorities were supposed to guarantee his safety, but you failed. I wonder what you, as chief of police, have to say about that?'

The police chief stared at her. 'You're the wife of one of the hostages?'

'The Swedish man, Thomas Samuelsson,' she said. 'It was his hand you found in a box outside here a few days ago.'

She started to feel dizzy, and grabbed the edge of the desk with both hands. The police chief wrote something on a piece of paper.

'Can you give me a description of your husband?'

'A description? What for?'

'Hair colour, height, distinguishing features?'

She was panting. 'Blond,' she said. 'One metre, eighty-eight centimetres tall. Blue eyes. He was wearing a pink shirt when he went missing.'

The police chief stood up and left the room, then came back with a file. 'This arrived from Dadaab yesterday evening,' he said. 'A shepherd found a white man outside his *manyatta* south of Dadaab yesterday morning. He was lying on the ground and the shepherd thought he was dead.

But he was alive, and the shepherd got a team from UNHCR to collect him. The man is at the medical centre in Camp Three.'

Annika's knees gave way and she sat down beside Halenius. 'Do you know who he is?'

'He hasn't been identified. The information must have been passed to UNHCR headquarters, and the Red Cross, but the refugee situation in Dadaab is chaotic and things like this take time.'

Annika closed her eyes for several seconds. 'Why are you telling me this?'

The police chief closed the file and looked at her intently. 'The man had been maimed – his left hand was missing. And he was wearing a pink shirt.'

EPILOGUE

ELEVEN DAYS LATER

DAY 0

TUESDAY, 13 DECEMBER

Anders Schyman looked at the picture covering the centrefold with an ambiguous mixture of loss and euphoria. It showed endless rows of hospital beds and tents in the background, everything brown and grey, a visual depiction of the refugee camp's hopelessness. The bed containing the blond man was in the middle, a woman leaning over him, putting her hand to his scorched cheek. At the bottom of the picture you could just make out the bandaged stump where the man's left hand had been.

It was so beautiful it almost brought tears to his eyes.

In purely technical terms the picture was worthless (it was actually a still from a video recording), but it had struck home. The global rights to Bengtzon's diary of the kidnapping had been sold to Reuters, and twenty seconds of her film had been shown on CNN.

He scratched his beard. It really was a hell of a story, the way Thomas had been left to die in a tin shack but managed to get out, then how Annika had found him, and their journey back to Sweden.

481

They had sold a ridiculous number of papers, enough to overtake the competition. The next time the circulation figures were published, they would show that the *Evening Post* was biggest, which in turn meant that he could leave.

But this achievement wasn't down to Annika Bengtzon alone, he reminded himself.

He closed the paper and looked at the front page:

**SWEDEN'S
WORST
SERIAL
KILLER**

ran the headline, next to a photograph of a smiling Gustaf Holmerud dressed up for a crayfish party.

The headline wasn't actually true (as usual, he was on the point of thinking) because Sweden's worst serial killer was an eighteen-year-old national service nurse from Malmö, who had killed twenty-seven old people in a hospital by feeding them corrosive disinfectant. Gustaf Holmerud had confessed to only five murders so far, but because the investigation was ongoing there was still hope of more.

He leafed through the paper.

Pages six and seven, always reserved for the biggest news stories, consisted of portrait photographs of five men and the headline: 'CLEARED!' The five were the husbands and boyfriends of the

482

murdered women, and even this headline was misleading, at least in part. Oscar Andersson, one of the supposedly cleared men, had never been a suspect. The real news was that the prosecutor had initiated proceedings against Gustaf Holmerud on five counts of murder, which meant that suspicion against anyone else had been dropped.

He pushed away the paper and looked at the time.

Annika Bengtzon was late, which wasn't like her. Schyman had always regarded her as a bit of a Fascist when it came to punctuality, which was an excellent quality in a news reporter. It didn't matter how well you could write or what stories you managed to dig up if you couldn't stick to a deadline.

'Sorry,' Annika said breathlessly, as she tumbled into his glass box. 'The underground isn't working, and I—'

He stopped her with a raised hand. She closed the door, dropped her bag and jacket on the floor and sank on to the visitor's chair. Her cheeks were flushed with cold and her nose looked sore.

'How's Thomas?' Schyman asked.

She caught her breath. 'The infection has eased and the malaria's almost gone,' she said, putting the newspaper's video-camera on his desk. 'Do I need to sign anything when I hand this back?'

Schyman shook his head. 'How's he taking everything?'

'Which bit? Losing his left hand? He hasn't said

anything about that yet – it probably feels fairly insignificant under the circumstances.'

He looked at Annika, her restless movements. She wasn't remotely sentimental, which was another quality he appreciated. 'Have you got a cold?' he asked.

She looked surprised. 'Why?'

'Would you consider writing a chronicle about it?'

'About having a cold?'

'About Thomas, the whole situation, your lives now?'

She smiled faintly. 'Sure,' she said. 'For three million.'

He smiled back.

'I saw they'd managed to locate where Thomas and the others were held captive,' he said.

Annika nodded. 'An abandoned *manyatta* twenty-three kilometres south of Dadaab,' she said. 'Thomas says they must have been driving round in circles, maybe because they didn't know what to do with them. We'll never know for sure.'

The Americans had announced triumphantly that they had blown up Grégoire Makuza on the day Thomas was found in the camp in Dadaab. The president had even made a short but forceful speech to the nation on the subject, but of course there was a presidential election next year.

Schyman hesitated for a few seconds, then took a deep breath. 'Have you looked at mediatime.se recently?'

'*The Black Widow*? Oh, yes.'

'I don't think you should worry about it,' Schyman said.

She shrugged. 'The article was written by Anne Snapphane. We're old friends, and everything in it is true. I did kill my boyfriend, and my husband has been maimed by terrorists. One of my sources was murdered and my house was burned down by a professional assassin. But to compare me to a spider that kills everyone close to it strikes me as something of an exaggeration.'

'I thought Media Time were going to tidy up their act, or so they claimed when they launched their new television programme, *Ronja Investigates*.'

'Was she the one who worked here as a temp a few years back?' Annika asked.

'How many journalists do you know called Ronja?' Schyman asked.

'Too many,' Annika said, leaning over his desk and turning the paper round, still open at 'CLEARED!' and the five photographs. 'This is really nasty,' she said.

Schyman sighed. 'Annika . . .'

'I've started looking into it,' she said. 'I've already spoken to Viveca Hernandez. Linnea's abuse started when she got pregnant. All the classic signs were there. She got hit if she looked at him the wrong way, hit if she said the wrong thing. He threw her out into the stairwell naked once – that was when Viveca found out what was going on.'

'Annika . . .'

Her hand paused on the newspaper, but she didn't look up at him. 'I need to work,' she said. 'Otherwise there's no point in it all. Not for me, and not for those women. They deserve it.'

'Annika, I've handed in my notice.'

Now she looked at him. 'What? When are you leaving?'

'In May,' he said.

She sat back in her chair. 'I wondered how long you'd be able to bear it,' she said. 'Patrik and all his crappy made-up reporting. You look like a worm on a hook every time you have to keep a straight face when he comes up with another of his ideas. I know you say it sells, but I think those successes are fleeting, and very short-term. People aren't that stupid. They can see through this.'

He regarded her in silence for a few moments. 'You're wrong,' he said, 'on all counts. People are pretty thick. They believe everything they read – just look at all the crap online. Half of Media Time's readers now think you eat little children.' He stood up. 'And as far as Patrik is concerned,' he went on, 'I've suggested to the board that he should be my successor.'

She sat where she was, gazing up at him with those big green eyes. 'That's never going to work,' she said quietly.

He stood there in silence, feeling unease creep down his spine.

'You won't be declared a hero just because the newspaper collapses without you,' she said. 'Quite

486

the reverse. You'll be the scapegoat. The board aren't going to take any responsibility. They'll blame everything on you. Surely you can see that.'

She got to her feet, then picked up her bag and coat. Schyman could feel his heart pounding, and puffed out his chest to hide it. 'Think about my offer,' he said. 'A column about you and Thomas and your new life together now that he's home. You won't get three million for it, but maybe enough for you and the family to get away for a break in the new year.'

She pulled on her coat and put her bag on her shoulder. 'That would be a bit tricky,' she said. 'I'm not going to be living with Thomas from now on.'

He stood there with his mouth half open, unable to find any words.

'Thomas doesn't know yet. I'm going to tell him today – I'm on my way to the Karolinska now.'

She slid the door open, closed it behind her, and was gone.

The sky fills my whole window. It's low, solid as concrete, cool and grey.

Sometimes I see a bird fly past, like a black silhouette against the light, but apart from that the view is empty. I might have wished for a tree, or just a few bare branches.

It's deathly dull here.

My hand has started to ache, the hand that is no longer there. Sometimes it itches between the fingers, sometimes the palm. That's normal, they say.

I'm going to get a prosthesis.

They say they're very good, these days. Some are controlled by Bluetooth: they react to muscle contractions and respond to pressure and movement. Soon there might even be one that can feel things. That's a Swedish invention.

Annika's been so fantastic. She's listened and listened.

I'll never be able to forget.

It got so quiet outside my shack. They brought me no water, no food. In the end I kicked the sheet of tin away from the doorway.

All the men were gone, the cars and guns. My memories stop out in the savannah. I don't remember anything about the refugee camp, only Annika's face above me in the plane on the way home to Sweden.

They haven't found the Dane. His daughter thinks he's alive, even though I've explained that he's dead. She thinks I made a mistake.

Annika saved me. She took all the money she had and tried to free me, but by then it was already too late.

Kalle didn't dare look at my hand to start with, but Ellen wanted to take the bandage off at once and investigate. She's inherited Holger's doctor genes.

I miss Annika so much. She's been here as often as she can, but there's so much to do, what with the children and Christmas and everything. She'll be here soon – she's bringing mulled wine and gingersnaps.

They say I'll be able to go back to work, but I don't know if I want to. My boss, Jimmy Halenius, has been an incredible source of support. He's come in several times to see me. The prime minister and the minister of justice have sent their best wishes.

She'll be here soon. I asked her to bring some Lucia buns as well, fresh ones, with raisins and lots of saffron.

I want us to celebrate Christmas in Vaxholm. If we're lucky we'll get snow this year again, a white Christmas.

It isn't over, it's only just beginning.

They say I'm going to be fine. Completely fine. Just with a prosthetic hand.

You can even learn to tie shoelaces, they say.

She's here now. I can hear her coming – I recognize her footsteps in the corridor, her heels on the cork floor.

She'll soon be here with me.

THE END